VORTEX OF CRIMSON

LISE MACTAGUE

BELLA
BOOKS

2016

Bella Books, Inc.
P.O. Box 10543
Tallahassee, FL 32302

Printed in the United States of America on acid-free paper.

First Bella Books Edition 2016

Editor: Medora MacDougall
Cover Designer: Sandy Knowles

ISBN: 978-1-59493-515-2

Other Bella Books by Lise MacTague

Heights of Green
Depths of Blue

Acknowledgments

My deepest gratitude to my alpha and beta readers: Lynn, Christina, Fern, Shari, and my mother Penny. It is only with your able assistance that Jak and Torrin's story could be brought to such a fitting end. Thank you also to my writing partner, Mary Lou, who sat across the table from me once a week and put up with my bellyaching when the book wasn't doing what I wanted. Of course, a big thanks must go to Medora MacDougall, my editor. I'm still working on those crutch words, but I think there's been some progress! Many thanks for helping me tighten up the manuscript into something we can truly be proud of. Finally, I cannot thank Linda Hill and Karin Kallmaker enough for taking the chance on *Depths of Blue*, the first step on this adventure. To my cover artist Sandy Knowles and everybody else at Bella Books who helps us make these books by lesbians, for lesbians, my deepest gratitude.

About the Author

Lise is the author of *Depths of Blue* and *Heights of Green*. She left Winnipeg, Canada for warmer climes. She flitted around the US, living in Ohio, New Jersey and Wisconsin, before most recently settling in North Carolina. Lise crams writing in and around work, family, and hockey—definitely not in that order.

Dedication

For Lynn, Whit and CeCe. Thank you for welcoming me into your family. I love you all. While this wasn't the path I thought my life would take, I can't imagine it any other way.

PROLOGUE

There wasn't much left of the bread loaf in her hands, little more than the heel. Nat considered it carefully before breaking off a small chunk. She didn't know how much longer she'd have to make the bread stretch. Her captor had taken off three days ago, leaving her a loaf of already-stale bread, some fruit and a couple of slices of meat.

"Make it last," he'd advised her. "I don't know when I'll be back."

Nat shivered. He gave her the creeps. When he looked at her, she was pretty sure he didn't see a person. All he saw was a pawn in whatever game it was he was playing. She was unaccustomed to being at somebody else's mercy and she didn't like it at all. The first couple of days she'd spent in the tiny shack, she'd gone over every inch, looking for a way out.

The shack was a piece of crap. It was maybe three meters on a side and made of wood. There were gaps between many of the boards. She could tell that it had been painted at one time, but most of the paint had long since worn away. The gaps had given her a sense of hope that was quickly dashed. It might be a piece of crap now, but whoever had built the shack had known what they were doing. Maybe if she'd had a tool, something she could have used as a lever, but she had nothing.

The dirt floor was hard-packed and all Nat had accomplished when she tried to dig her way out was to bloody the tips of her fingers and to tear out three nails. He'd noticed, but hadn't said anything. Somehow, that had been scarier than if he'd screamed at her. His blue eyes had simply traveled over her still-bleeding fingertips. A slight jump in his jaw muscles was the only indication she'd had that he'd taken note. That night she hadn't gotten any food.

With trembling fingers, she popped the piece of bread under her tongue and sucked on it. Her mouth was immediately awash with saliva. The bread was hard as rock but tasted so good and she moaned slightly. The fruit was long gone. She'd learned after his first multiday absence to eat the fruit and meat first. They didn't keep very long. The bread was hard to start out with and once it had gone stale, it would cut the inside of her mouth to shreds if she wasn't careful. After the scant mouthful of bread had softened, she chewed it slowly, trying to make it last.

Wherever he was holding her was usually pretty quiet, but she would occasionally hear vehicles in the distance. She'd tried to get a glimpse of them from between the wooden slats of her prison but had yet to actually see anything. It wasn't much of a surprise to her; the engine noises were usually very faint. If she could only see that there was some way of getting out, Nat could start planning her escape.

Her enforced idleness was as big a torture as the lack of food. At least she didn't lack for water. When it rained, which was almost every night, the bucket by the door was filled through a short spout in the wall. That looked newer, and Nat suspected it had been added to the shack for her benefit. She wondered how long he'd been planning her abduction. A bitter laugh forced itself up from her chest, the sound surprising her.

He'd killed her partner before nabbing her. Nat rubbed her forearms, trying to warm the chill that moved through her. As long as she lived, she didn't think she'd be able to forget Rudrani trying to keep the blood from spilling from her neck, then collapsing when her hands proved inadequate to the task. Nat's hands hadn't been any more successful. She'd had no chance to mourn before her captor had tranquilized her. She'd done little else since waking up in the shitty little shack. That and try to figure out why he had kidnapped her. She had the feeling that she wasn't specifically necessary to his plan. That either one of them would have done. It had seemed to her at first that she was the lucky one, but from her current perspective it was starting to look like Rudrani was. At least her suffering was over.

One more shard of bread. She could afford that, at least. Her stomach ached, but she paid it little mind. It ached constantly. Even when he fed her daily, there still wasn't enough. She placed the piece under her tongue, then pulled a couple of rags up around her. Dusk was falling. At least the gaps in the boards let her know what time of day it was, though they did very little to stop the wind or rain. Her first night, she'd learned to move the pile of rags that was her bedding into the middle of the floor and as far from the leaky walls as possible. Her shipsuit kept her warm enough during the day, but at night she got chilly and the rags helped insulate her a little bit.

As she moved the rags around in a vain effort to find a configuration that would both keep her warm and offer some comfort, the door opened. She scuttled back on all fours and looked up.

It was him, but her captor looked different; gone was the usual mask of indifference. For the first time, she could see real emotion on his face. He was excited, almost giddy, and his eyes gleamed in the dim interior.

"She's here," he said, smiling. "It won't be long now." He rubbed his hands together.

Nat stared at him. When she didn't share his glee, his face lost some of its excitement.

"What do you want from me?" Nat asked, as she had every time she'd seen him since her abduction.

"Keep doing what you're doing," he answered. "It's perfect."

With that unenlightening answer he left the shack, closing the door securely behind him. Nat stared at the door. In another first, he'd come in armed with more than a knife. Slung across his back was a familiar weapon. It was configured a little differently than the ones she'd seen Jak use, but there was no mistaking it. It was a sniper rifle.

CHAPTER ONE

"Did it work?" Torrin's voice was tense. Jak placed one hand over hers, trying to calm her edgy girlfriend.

Kiera stood and walked over to the wall. With a sweeping hand motion, she transferred the image from the tablet in her hand to the wall. A graph with peaks and valleys appeared from floor to ceiling. She stood in front of it and moved her hands in opposite directions, zooming in on one of the graph's peaks.

"You see this peak?"

Jak nodded.

"This represents higher brain activity. We see this kind of activity when you're actively thinking about something."

"That second wave is still there," Torrin said. She sounded vaguely accusing, and Jak tightened her hand warningly.

"That's the problem," Kiera said. "The treatment isn't helping much. The additional brain activity comes and goes, but we can't eradicate it completely."

Jak nodded. "That makes sense. The information from that last data dump is degrading and...migrating, for lack of a better word. They usually keep a sharp lookout for soldiers who haven't had their last memory dump purged, but with my situation, I fell through the cracks. The symptoms are pretty obvious after it gets to a certain stage. Soldiers get treated once someone notices they're having problems."

Her hopes had plummeted during Kiera's explanation. While it wasn't the first time Jak was seeing the results of a data dump degrading in someone's memory, it was the first time she'd experienced it herself. She'd hoped the doctors in Nadierzda could treat at least the symptoms of her condition, but the continued disorientation she was feeling told her that her hopes were in vain. The treatment had cleared up some of the mental echoes she was experiencing, but the maps of Sector 27 still lurked, trying to superimpose themselves again and again upon her thoughts. They'd been downloaded into her brain via the port in her hand for the mission that had led her to Torrin. Unfortunately, those same maps were now leading to irreversible brain damage. They should have been removed months ago, but with everything that had happened, Jak had missed her chance. Thankfully, they'd lost less than a day with this procedure. She was all right for now, but no one knew when the corruption would overwhelm her. Jak thought they had some time, but she couldn't say how much.

"So how do they treat the condition on your planet?" Kiera asked.

"Since your treatment didn't work, there's only one way that I know of." Jak looked over at Torrin. She wasn't going to like the answer. "I need to get the data dump removed, and you don't have the technology. If you weren't able to fix things when you were tinkering around inside my brain this time, then the data dump needs to be completely erased."

"Oh no," Torrin said, voice heated. "You are not going back. There has to be another way."

"I don't think there is." Jak looked over at her lover. Two spots of color bloomed high on Torrin's cheeks, evidence of how upset she was about Jak's revelation.

"Can't you go back in for another try?" Torrin asked Kiera. "Surely there's something you can do here."

"I'm sorry, Torrin." Kiera's face was grave. "I think Jak has the right of it. There's simply no way we can treat her here. The last procedure had its own risks and I won't do it again. Besides, to go further I would need to bring in a neurologist *and* a cybernetics engineer. We have a neurologist, but the only cybernetics engineer that I know of is on Castor III, getting your factory set up."

"Then we go to Castor III."

"Torrin, it's not going to get any better." Jak hated to see her worked up like this, but she had to make Torrin understand there was no other way. She wasn't exactly ecstatic about going back to Haefen. While she had unfinished business there, she'd gotten used to the freedom of being herself. Going back to her home planet would mean putting the mask back on, and so soon after she had gotten a taste of what it was like to bare her real face to the world. "If I wait too long, they won't be able to reverse the information transfer. I'll end up as a vegetable."

"Even if we go to Castor III with the right personnel, there's no guarantee that we'll be able to fix the problem," Kiera chimed in, to Torrin's visible irritation. "In my professional opinion, it's time to talk to the experts."

Frustrated, Torrin tried to glare at both of them at the same time. It was no mean feat as Jak and Kiera were on opposite sides of the room. "Are you ready for this? It's not going to be easy."

Jak grimaced. "I don't know. I don't really think I have much choice." She squeezed Torrin's hand again. "If you'll go with me, I know I'll be able to handle anything."

"If you're sure it's the only way, then I guess you're right." Torrin didn't look happy but seemed resigned to reality. Jak was a little surprised. She thought for sure Torrin would put up a big enough fuss that she would need to get firm with her. Maybe this was a sign that Torrin wasn't going to go back to her old ways of trying to keep Jak swaddled away from all harm.

"Thanks baby," Jak said. "I'm going to need your help. I really don't know how I should present myself when we get back there."

Torrin cupped the side of Jak's face with her hand. "I think you should go as yourself. You're amazing and they should know exactly how amazing you are."

"I'm glad you feel that way, but you don't know how it is there." She closed eyes and turned her face into Torrin's hand. "If they find out I'm a woman, they'll discount everything I have to say." Her people were remarkably hostile to women, though not as hostile as their enemies. The Orthodoxans made the Devonites look like the most enlightened bunch in the galaxy, and since her time on Nadierzda, Jak knew they were anything but. She'd worn the breastbinder for years and putting that thing back on was the last thing she wanted to do. Stomach acid tried to churn its way up her esophagus. Jak swallowed hard to force it back down.

"I can see you have things to discuss." Kiera smiled at the two of them. She was a lot less tense around Torrin than she had been the last time Jak had been at the clinic. "I'm going to continue on my rounds. Jak, I want you to stick around for a day so we can make sure that you won't have any complications from your treatment. I'm pretty sure we'll be able to release you tomorrow."

"Thanks for everything, Kiera."

"You're welcome. Don't take this the wrong way, but I don't want to see you any time soon after you're released."

Jak nodded vigorously.

"We'll have you over for dinner once this is all over," Torrin said. She turned to Jak. "It will be good for you to get to know her out of the clinic. She's pretty great."

Kiera smiled at them again and left the room, doors hissing open to let her pass. Torrin looked into Jak's eyes and grasped her hands tightly. "If you want to go as Jak Stowell, the mighty sniper that the Devonites knew, I'll support you. But I think you're doing your people a disservice. Most of them treated me pretty well. Your General Callahan especially. And they all knew I'm female."

"How could they miss it?" Jak raked her eyes lasciviously over Torrin's frame. "You're gloriously female."

"Stop that." Torrin swatted Jak lightly on the chest. "You're in no condition for that kind of activity right now."

Ruefully, Jak had to concede that Torrin was right. Her head still pounded, most likely from the aftereffects of day-long brain surgery. Thankfully, the doctors had taken care of the worst of the problems she'd been suffering from days of exposure and dehydration. Kiera hadn't offered any painkillers. She should have asked. "I don't suppose you can ask the nurse for something for my head?"

"Sure I can." Torrin gave her a look, her heart in her eyes. Jak wondered if she was going to say the three words she longed to hear. For a moment, she was almost certain that Torrin would say them, but she stood up and headed out of the room after a long silence.

Torrin does love me right? Jak knew she loved Torrin. She'd loved her since their trek across the Haefonian wilderness. Even when she thought Torrin had cheated on her and Jak's heart had been rent in two, a part of her had been unable to let go.

Torrin had first told her she loved her when Jak was in the hospital recovering after everything had gone south with Tanith and she'd ended up wandering the countryside for days. Why hadn't she said it again? Had she only said it because she thought Jak was about to die?

Not that she'd said anything to Torrin either. But…what if she was misreading the signals and Torrin didn't really love her? Jak didn't think she could be reading them wrong, not by that much. Still, something held her back. It wasn't the right time, she finally decided. After all, it was barely a day since they'd been reunited and Jak had spent much of that time in the care of her doctor.

Torrin returned a few moments later followed by the stout nurse that Jak remembered. "We talked to the doctor and she's prescribed a pain blocker." Torrin resumed her place at Jak's bedside.

"I guess they can't give you the strongest medication, not with the treatment we put you through, but it should take the edge off." The nurse smiled at her encouragingly as she pushed a medication into Jak's IV drip. It didn't take long before Jak felt some of her pain recede.

True to the nurse's word, the pain wasn't completely gone, but it was at a much more manageable level. Jak received a pat on the leg from the nurse before she left.

"That was weird," Jak said.

"What do you mean?"

"The nurse. She was being all nice to me. Last time I was here, she was all business."

Torrin laughed. "Everyone's concerned about you. You've become a minor hero. The local news keeps hounding me for updates on your condition. Even the Ruling Council wants to know when you'll be well enough that they can talk to you."

They do? Jak was confused and her consternation must have been visible on her face.

"It was terribly brave, what you did. Not only did you kill a vicious animal that was terrorizing the countryside, but you unmasked and escaped from a traitor in our midst. You have to understand, this planet is more like a small village. It's a safe place and not much really goes on here, so when something out of the ordinary happens, everyone wants to know about it."

Jak pushed herself up into a sitting position, her back against the headboard. Everyone knew about her? Her skin crawled and her face heated. She worked best flying just under the radar. Sure, in the Devonite forces, a lot of people had known about her, but they hadn't known who she was. Not really. No one had. No one except Bron. The idea that all of these women not only knew who she was but were also following reports of her exploits made her feel incredibly vulnerable. Exposed, even.

"There isn't anything that interesting about me." She stared at Torrin, horrified. "All I did was what I had to at the time."

Torrin grinned. "There's plenty interesting about you. And the best part is, you're all mine." Now it was her turn to look concerned. "You are, aren't you? We haven't talked about it, not really. We're back together right?"

"If that's what you want." Jak watched Torrin, making sure she was answering correctly. "I mean, I only broke up with you because I thought you were cheating on me. And then I find out that Tanith set the whole thing up, and all to get back at you. There's something really wrong with that one. She hates you."

Torrin wore a rueful grimace. "We hadn't gotten along for years. Growing up, we were best friends. Somewhere along the way, she turned our friendship into a competition. I didn't even know we were competing, but I guess I was winning, at least in her mind.

"At least we don't have to worry about her again. Her ultralight was found in the sands not far from the cliff where you shot the tiger. There was plasma damage to the fuselage, and it looks like she crashed."

"Did you find her body?"

Torrin looked pained at the question. "No, we didn't. That's not unusual though. The sands are brutal and they'll swallow up a body in no time, dragging it down. The ultralight was already half-buried when the Banshees found it."

"I don't know." Jak hoped Tanith was dead. The lunatic was in a unique position to do a lot of damage if she was alive and had found a way to make it off the planet undetected. She shook her head and grimaced slightly at the resulting pain. "I'll believe she's dead when I see her body." The feral grin on her face was ugly, she knew. "Am I wrong to hope that she's alive somewhere so I can have the pleasure of taking her out?"

"I know what you mean." Torrin nodded somberly. "I found out she was the one behind my trip to your home world. The Orthodoxans were supposed to kill me or at least get me out of her hair. I bet she was royally pissed when I came back, better than ever and with you."

"I guess I should thank her then. If it weren't for her, I'd never have met you. I'd still be moping around on Haefen, trying to avenge my brother and hiding in plain sight."

"I bet it drove her nuts knowing that without her interference, we wouldn't be together." Torrin stood up and squeezed herself onto the bed with Jak. There wasn't a whole lot of room, but they'd gotten the maneuver down the first time Jak was here after her disastrous thawing from cryostasis. Jak slid over to give her as much room as possible and Torrin lay on her side, an arm wrapped around Jak's waist. She leaned her head on Jak's shoulder. They lay together for a few minutes in companionable silence.

"Why does the Ruling Council want to see me, do you think?" Jak asked after the silence stretched a little too long. Torrin shrugged, the motion carried through her shoulder to Jak's torso. It was nice to have Torrin's lanky body pressed against her again. For so long, she'd felt that she was immune to the need for companionship. Jak had scoffed internally at the men in her unit who mooned over one woman or another. She finally understood. It was something she hadn't known was missing from her life until she'd found it. The weeks Torrin had been gone after she thought she'd walked in on her with her ex had been so long and empty. It wasn't companionship in general that she craved, it was Torrin's company in particular. She smiled and snuggled in to Torrin's warm body.

"I don't know. Maybe to congratulate you for finding out about Tanith."

"Hmmm." Jak snuggled tighter up against Torrin.

"So when do we leave?" Torrin asked.

"Soon, I guess." Jak closed her eyes. Now that the pain in her head was back to a reasonable level and the warmth of Torrin's body wrapped around her, she was getting tired. "I should talk to the council first."

"Your health is more important than talking to a bunch of old biddies who only want their curiosity satisfied." Torrin's voice was indignant and she squeezed Jak around the waist again. "You can talk to them when we get back."

"It's all right. I'll let them know I can see them tomorrow, before we head to Haefen. We can leave the day after that. It won't really add any extra time." Jak smiled; Torrin would appreciate where she was going with this. "If they can't make time in their busy schedule tomorrow to see me, than I can stop in on them when we get back."

"Excellent plan," Torrin said. Jak kept smiling, content in the knowledge that she had somebody who cared for her. The thought made her warm inside as well as out. Knowing Torrin would be there when she woke up, she closed her eyes and allowed sleep to take her away.

CHAPTER TWO

Torrin waited until Jak's breathing slowed. She stayed, wrapped around Jak, for longer than she should have. There were arrangements to make, but she was enjoying simply being with Jak, even if she wasn't awake. She'd missed her so much. Her body craved Jak's touch and now that she had it again, she was loath to let it go. It still didn't seem quite real. After the heartache and depression of the past weeks, her heart felt so light and free that Torrin was surprised it didn't float out of her chest. It was a feeling she never thought she would experience. It seemed her footloose days were over. Far from mourning the loss as she once thought she would, she was glad. Happy. Giddy, even. A grin unfurled, unbidden on her face. They'd talked and were back together and she was never letting Jak go.

Torrin's arm tightened across Jak's abdomen, pulling a quiet moan from her sleeping lover. She let go in a hurry and checked to see if she'd woken her. Jak resumed the deep rhythms of sleep when she could breathe again.

It was time to go, Torrin decided. She stayed snuggled against Jak's too-thin rib cage for a few more precious moments. Finally, steeling herself, she unwrapped herself from Jak with delicate precision. She stood by the side of the bed and watched her sleep. *A little longer, that's all*, she told herself.

Finally, when she couldn't put off leaving any longer, she reached over and gave Jak's hand a quick squeeze goodbye and left the room. The duty nurse waved at her as she passed by the nurses' station. Kiera was nowhere to be seen, so she didn't stop. The clinic doors hissed open and Torrin stepped into Nadierzda's hazy sunlight to be greeted by a group of waiting reporters. When they saw her, they rushed over. It wasn't a large group, but Torrin quickly realized there were representatives from all the planet's news organizations. There were reporters from news organizations who didn't even distribute in the Landing crater. They talked over each other, trying to get her attention.

"Torrin!"

"Over here, Torrin!" A woman waved a tablet over her head, trying to snap a holopic.

"What is Captain Stowell's condition?"

A third woman shoved a small holorecorder in her face.

Torrin knew Jak's story had gained a lot of media attention. Or at least, a lot for the small planet. She'd been teasing Jak about it, but she hadn't realized quite how badly word of Jak's condition was desired.

"Um, no comment," she choked out into the recorder. She wasn't about to violate Jak's privacy without checking with her. Torrin knew that Jak wasn't fond of the limelight. If their positions had been reversed, Torrin would have eaten up the attention. She felt ill at ease basking in Jak's reflected glory and tried to push her way through the small crowd. It wasn't that she begrudged Jak the attention. As far as she was concerned, everyone should know exactly how amazing she was, but not at the price of Jak's discomfort. She in no way wanted Jak to feel that she was using her.

"Is it true that Captain Stowell is suffering brain damage as a result of Major Merriam's assault?" The woman with the holorecorder wouldn't give up. She followed along at Torrin's side. Torrin shoved women out of her way, trying to rid herself of the persistent newswomen.

"What?" The question was close enough to the truth that Torrin came to a sudden stop in the crowd. "Who told you that?"

"So it's true?" The crowd tightened around her as the reporters scented blood in the water. Torrin was hemmed in on all sides. She'd made a tactical error, she realized. Now that she'd stopped moving, it was harder to get going again. The noise level in the crowd rose as the women yelled competing questions to her.

"Ladies!" A strong voice cut through the din and they all looked to the source. A small group of Banshees stood at the crowd's edge. Captain Axe Yozhin stood at the head of the group and raised her hands. "I need you to hand over Miss Ivanov. She's been summoned before the Ruling Council."

Good deal, Torrin thought. *For me and for the reporters*. Things had been about to get hairy. She'd been about to start swinging to get them to move. Grudgingly, the small mob parted. She strode through their ranks and nodded gratefully to Axe.

"Thanks for the assist," she muttered. "That wasn't going to end well."

"No problem," Axe said, as quietly. "Let's get this over with." She took Torrin by the elbow to escort her away from the disappointed reporters. She glanced back over her shoulder at the reporters and raised her voice a bit. "You might want to stop by the Ruling Council chambers in two hours. They will have a statement to make on the situation."

Torrin lengthened her stride to keep up with the blocky captain. She was actually taller than Axe by about ten centimeters, but Axe set a grueling pace. She was also built like a fireplug. Torrin had no doubts that if she'd wanted to, Axe could have tossed her over a shoulder and carried her wherever she wanted to.

"I'll head over to the office," Torrin said when they'd gotten out of view of the reporters.

"No, you won't," Axe replied evenly. "I have orders to convey you before the Ruling Council. They've set up an emergency meeting to talk to you about Jak."

"That wasn't just a line of bull that you made up for the reporters?" Torrin grimaced. She was on a deadline. She had to make sure everything was set in motion to get Jak back to Haefen as quickly as possible. Going before the Ruling Council would only delay her. She had planned to comm the council from her office and tell them that they could meet with Jak the next day, right before the two of them left.

"Afraid not. We've brought a vehicle for you."

"I can get there on my bike."

"My orders are very clear on this. We're to escort you in front of the council. Apparently you've made a habit of ignoring their directives."

Torrin shrugged. "They have a habit of letting me know they want to see me after I've already left the surface." She didn't like feeling as if the Ruling Council had her at their beck and call. It was true that on some previous occasions, she'd ignored their summons and left the planet instead. It wasn't like she had that option now, not with Jak under observation at the clinic. They had her cornered. She sighed. "All right, let's get this over with."

She was escorted over to the first of two large antigrav sleds modified to carry personnel. Banshees milled around the two vehicles and the open back already held half of the Spec Ops women. Axe jumped into the passenger seat at the front and gestured her to take a place in the back.

"Is this really necessary?" Torrin asked. She didn't need a full squad of commandos to drag her in front of the council. Three would have sufficed. She was a little pleased though. Clearly the council understood that the only way she would be muscled into something against her will was with the application of a whole lot of brute force.

"The council told me to make sure you couldn't resist their request."

"A brace of Banshees makes it a command."

The other Banshees took up places in the second sled. Olesya waved at her from the passenger seat and grinned broadly when Torrin glared at her. Let them think that she was displeased with her treatment.

Women watched them curiously as they wended their way through surface streets to Assembly Hall. Military activity outside of the base was limited to training exercises that were conducted far from human habitation. So many of Nadierzda's women were the products of oppressive societies. The Ruling Council was well aware of that fact and did its best not to remind them of their past, and so the militia was kept as divorced from the citizens' daily life as possible. Sometimes, however, it couldn't be helped.

Torrin noticed more than one couple, arms around each other, some clutching children to them, as the small convoy drove past. Jak's words rang in her mind, cautioning her about the security breach that Tanith represented. Even with the bitch dead, they didn't know what information she'd passed on and to whom. She hoped a more pronounced military presence didn't become these women's new reality. Never for a minute did she believe that the local militia would become the oppressive force that some of these women remembered and feared. Instead, she worried that they would realize that the increased presence was there for a reason and start wondering what that reason could be.

Instead of pulling up to the wide steps in front of the hall's main entrance, the two sleds pulled up to a side entrance. Axe and Olesya hopped out of their sleds and Torrin followed, but more slowly. It wouldn't do to seem overeager. She'd considered what the council could possibly want from her and the possibilities were sobering. Torrin never approached negotiation from a position of weakness if she could help it, and now wasn't the time to start. She needed to keep everyone off balance until she knew exactly what was going on. A few half-formed guesses weren't enough.

Axe preceded her through the nondescript door and into the somewhat dingy hallways behind it. Olesya took up the rear—making sure she didn't make a break for it, Torrin guessed. They negotiated their way through the maze of hallways and offices until the captain and lieutenant stopped in front of a door as featureless as the rest. The halls were narrow enough that they had to stand aside when a bureaucrat or minor functionary came scurrying down the hall toward them.

It had been a long time since Torrin had been in the government offices that took up the back half of Assembly Hall. It never ceased to amaze her how different the offices were from the impressive and elegant gathering hall. It was as if the architects had decided they needed to balance the grandeur of the hall with the insignificance of the offices. Not for the first time, she wondered if it was a tactic to keep the members of Nadierzda's governing body from feeling too self-important. The crappy, windowless offices would kill the ego of most women she knew.

In response to Axe's peremptory knock, the door slid open, revealing a small conference room. The seven councilors, one from each of Nadierzda's districts, looked over at the open doorway. They were grouped at one end of a long table. It was clear they'd been interrupted mid argument.

Councilor Yozhin motioned them to take their seats. As the eldest councilor, she was considered first among equals, and the others acquiesced to her leadership, though some more grudgingly than others. She nodded to Axe, and as always when Torrin saw them together, she was struck by the family resemblance. Both of them had the classic Yozhin hatchet face. Prominent, beak-like noses framed by eyes hard enough to strike sparks off steel made Axe's nickname no mystery. Torrin hadn't been able to find anyone who remembered what her given name was; everyone simply referred to her as Axe.

"Captain Yozhin, that will be all. Thank you for the prompt execution of your order." So today was not the day that Torrin would find out Axe's real name. She'd half-hoped the councilor would let it slip, but no such luck. She did wince slightly at Yozhin's use of the word "execute." No one had been officially executed on Nadierzda's surface, at least not in the official histories she'd read. With the planet's pirate background, she suspected that their early history had included more than one state-sanctioned death. These days, however, the only executions that happened were carried out by the Banshees during their rescue operations.

Tanith might have actually been the most recent exception. To be honest, Torrin wasn't even sure if the Nadierzdan penal code included capital punishment. She would be surprised if it did. It did include exile. Tanith would likely have been banished from the crater system with little to no supplies. Not an official death sentence, but for all practical purposes the result would have been the same. With what the psychopath had done to her first girlfriend and what she'd almost done to Jak, Torrin wouldn't have shed a tear, even though they'd once been the closest of friends. Those days were long gone. If she'd caught up with Tanith before she was pulled down by the treacherous sands, Torrin would have pulled the trigger herself.

"Have a seat, Torrin." Councilor Yozhin waved her to the only empty chair at the table. "We have some questions for you."

"About what?" Torrin eyed them suspiciously as she sat down.

"First things first. How's Captain Stowell doing?"

"She's doing well. She said she can see you tomorrow for a little bit, right before we leave for her home planet. The doctor is keeping her overnight for observation."

Yozhin sat back in her chair and folded her hands beneath her breasts. "That's excellent news."

"You will postpone your trip." Councilor Tachay leaned forward and drove a finger into the table's surface for emphasis. "We will block your clearance to leave the surface if we need to."

"That won't be possible. Jak needs medical treatment that only her people can provide." Torrin glared at Tachay. They hadn't gotten along since Torrin had dallied with her daughter. Lynnie hadn't really minded when they'd broken up. Torrin had seen her socially a few times since then but had never rekindled their brief romance. It seemed her mother resented Torrin's actions more than her daughter had and continued to hold them against her.

"Nevertheless Torrin," Yozhin said. She added her glare to Torrin's and Tachay sat back in her chair, disgruntled. "Surely delaying your trip by a day or so won't hurt. We need to discuss important issues with her."

Torrin was unwilling to give in without a fight. "You'll have to run that by Kiera. If she says it's all right to delay, then we will. But not without the doctor's say-so."

"That's a reasonable request." She raised her hand when Tachay looked ready to interrupt. "It's not why we wanted you here though."

"What is then?" Torrin was already wearied by the council and she'd only been there a few minutes. Bunch of busybodies, trying to tell her what she could or couldn't do. Her relationship with the Ruling Council was sometimes contentious. She didn't appreciate when they tried to exercise control over her business. Sure, there were times when it was prudent for her to keep them apprised of what she was up to and they had a duty to keep the planet safe and hidden. More often, their interference felt like meddling, like they had some power and thought they had the right to exercise it over all aspects of her life. No one had that right, and she wasn't shy about telling them when she thought they'd overstepped.

"You were close with Major Tanith Merriam?" Councilor Mashir asked. She was the youngest of the group, a few years younger than Torrin's chronological age. She represented the smallest crater group, one that was almost exclusively agricultural. Her election to the council had been a bit of a surprise; she was the youngest member they'd had in years. Torrin actually liked her, in no small part because she imagined the councilwoman's relative youth irked the other council members to no end.

"I haven't been close with Tanith for years. Decades almost." They'd been extremely close, almost sisters. "She got…competitive. Couldn't stand losing. Apparently, she killed my first lover when she wouldn't leave me for her." Jak hadn't been very lucid when she'd related that part of the story, but Torrin had understood well enough.

Back then it had never even occurred to her that Tanith would kill Galya, but now it made only too much sense. She had tried to track Galya down, she'd been that head over heels in love with her. She'd been so hurt when there was no trace of her and she'd assumed that Galya had disappeared on purpose.

"So you don't know who she was involved with?" Mashir probed further.

"Romantically?" When the council didn't crack even one smile, Torrin continued quickly. "I do know that my ex, Breena, was involved in a plot to set me up and wreck my relationship with Jak. There was also that gangster on Tyndall. Beyond that Monton knew her, I don't know how closely they worked together."

"Major Merriam often left on trips, ostensibly to procure weapons for the militia. She may be dead, but we don't know who her contacts were. We've been unable to locate Breena. It looks like she left when the truth about Merriam came to light. Her ship left the surface without clearance. It may be that she is on her way to them." Mashir looked her in the eye. "Are you sure you can't think of anyone else who might be close to her?"

Torrin shook her head. "I'm sorry, I don't. Like I said, I haven't had anything to do with her for years. Some of the Banshees might know or other members of the militia maybe."

"This is a waste of time," Tachay said, glaring at Torrin like it was her fault she hadn't kept up with Tanith. "We need to be doing something about this, not wasting time talking about it."

"And we will," Yozhin said. "But we need to find out as much as we can, to minimize the damage." She turned to Torrin. "Tell Captain Stowell that she is to report to the council tomorrow immediately following the noon hour. We will clear it with her doctors. This is important, Torrin. Try to understand that this is bigger than any one person. We know Jak understands."

Torrin stood up so quickly that her chair shot back across the smooth floor. "I'll tell her, but it's up to her if she comes. Her and the doctor."

"It's not up to her, Torrin." Yozhin stood and the other councilors followed her lead, rising to their feet as one. "As the heads of Nadierzdan government, we are summoning Captain Stowell to a war council to prepare the planet for possible attack or invasion."

CHAPTER THREE

Jak stood at rigid attention before the table of councilors. Torrin was probably still peeved that she'd agreed to this meeting. Kiera had seen no reason they couldn't postpone their departure by a few days, though, so who was she to ignore a summons by the Nadierzdan government?

She was in a curious position and was of two minds about it. She still thought of herself as Haefonian, yet for the most part, the women of Nadierzda had accepted her without reservation and with open arms. None of them had questioned who she was or whether she was fit for the position in which she'd found herself. Many women could have objected to her instantaneous attainment of the rank when she became a captain in their militia, but if they had, none had done so where she could hear. Instead, she'd gotten the feeling that most of them had sat back to see what it was she brought to the table. They'd given her an opportunity to prove herself, and she felt a debt to them. Jak would do what she could to discharge that debt.

She understood, better than most, exactly how serious a threat Tanith was to the continued existence of this strange society on the edges of colonized space. Beyond some shady characters Tanith had been in contact with on Tyndall, no one knew who else she'd talked to. She could easily have sold her knowledge of the planet. Apparently, the equipment Jak had seen in Tanith's home had been communications equipment. There was no reason that Tanith would have needed it, not unless she was communicating with people off the planet.

Jak was certain that there were many potential markets for the information. A handful of the women she'd trained had told her stories about their backgrounds and the abuses they'd suffered as a result of direct and indirect slavery. She understood the horror of their situations only too well. That could so easily have been her. Other women were the daughters of those who had been rescued from similar circumstances. She felt a responsibility toward them, and so she stood, waiting, for what it was the Ruling Council wanted to discuss with her.

"At ease, Captain Stowell," the bluff-faced Councilor Yozhin said to her. "Take a seat. This will take a while."

Jak snapped off a salute and dropped into parade rest before depositing herself stiffly in the indicated chair. She sat up straight, hands folded on the table in front of her. Seven female faces stared at her from around the table. Sometimes, it was still a shock to see so many women in one place.

Yozhin turned her attention to the tablet in front of her. She swiped her finger across the screen, nodding as she perused the contents. "We've read your debrief."

"I'm afraid it's incomplete, ma'am," Jak said, chagrined. "I'm still experiencing issues with my memory. It's better than it had been, but I know there are still things I can't access. The doctor hopes I'll recover all my memories when the corrupted data in my head is removed."

A young councilor, only a little older than she was, leaned forward. Jak thought her name was Mashir. In truth, the problems with her memory were affecting more than her most recent memories. Everything from before her last data dump was intact, but the memories she'd created after receiving the information were more tenuous. Some she couldn't access at all, others she questioned. The biggest memory hiccups clustered around the trauma she'd received at Tanith's hands.

"Can you tell us anything else that isn't in the report?" the woman she thought was Mashir asked.

"Not much, ma'am." Jak closed her eyes in concentration. Tanith's face swam behind her eyelids, first as the happy, laughing woman she'd initially been around Jak. Her face blurred and was replaced by the ugly, bitter mask her face had transformed into when Jak had rebuffed her advances. "She really hates Torrin."

"You made that clear in the report," another councilor snapped.

"Tachay," Yozhin said too mildly. "We've been over this."

Though Tachay subsided at Yozhin's words, an undercurrent of mutiny still flickered in her eyes.

"I think it's important, ma'am." Jak made sure to address Tachay directly. "She really hated Torrin. Her bitterness led her to kill one of her...lovers." Jak wasn't sure what she thought of Galya. She hadn't discussed her with Torrin, but Jak got the feeling that Torrin had been very close to her, in contrast to the way she talked about her other former lovers. "She almost killed me. I think you have to admit that her level of obsession brings up a lot of worrisome possibilities. You need to consider what she might have done to punish her."

"An excellent point and one that I agree with," maybe-Mashir said, "which is why we've asked you here."

"For the record, I object to the pursuit of this line of inquiry," Tachay said, almost on top of the other woman. "We have no reason to assume that Major Tanith Merriam did anything that would result in an invasion on Nadierzda." She waved a hand dismissively at Jak. "We don't even know for sure that she attacked Stowell. All we have is her word."

A slender woman with close-cropped brown hair stood up and pointed a finger at Tachay. "All we have is her word and the physical evidence that was recovered from where Merriam attacked Captain Stowell, did you forget that? And then there's the evidence that Torrin Ivanov discovered on Tyndall."

Tachay lumbered to her feet, face marred by an ugly scowl. She'd been a powerful woman once, but the muscle hadn't held up well to the encroachment of her middle years. She placed both hands on the table and leaned menacingly across the table toward the slender woman. "She's practically a stranger!" Tachay roared, flinging her own finger in Jak's direction. "Why should we trust her over one of the true daughters of our planet? Major Merriam's family has been here since the founding! We don't know where this one's loyalties lie!"

The slender woman didn't back down, even though by the end of her tirade, Tachay was screaming in her face. She drew a deep breath to respond to Tachay in kind.

Yozhin jumped to her feet and brought both palms down onto the tabletop with a thunderous crack. "Tachay and Jakande, enough!" A glass of water by her hand rattled from the power of her blow. "Sit down, both of you. We've had this to a vote, and the majority consensus will rule, as our laws state."

The two councilors continued to glare at each other, but each sat, if grudgingly.

"If I may say something, ma'am?" Jak was quiet and she could feel the heat of her cheeks. She didn't often allow people to know what she was feeling, but Tachay's accusations had cut a little too close to the bone. "The fact that I'm here, with all of you, instead of on my way back to my home planet for medical treatment should demonstrate my commitment. Maybe I wasn't born here, but I feel a bond to many of these women and a responsibility to do what I can to protect them. Ma'am." She ground the last out, not because of any respect she felt for Tachay, but because she knew she needed to avoid any appearance of insubordination.

"Well said," Jakande murmured, barely loud enough for Jak to make out. Of course, if Jak could hear her, then it was likely that the other women at the table could as well.

Tachay stared at her. Jak wasn't sure what she'd done to make an enemy of the woman. She was going to have to watch her back with Tachay.

"Very well, Captain Stowell." Yozhin cleared her throat, bringing all eyes at the table back to her. She appeared irked that control of the situation had slipped from her grasp, and she looked each of them in the eye before she proceeded. "We've brought you here today not only to get your feelings on the former Major Merriam, but to offer you her position."

"Ma'am?" Jak sat up straight in her chair. She'd expected a more extensive debrief, not to be offered command of Nadierzdan ground forces.

"We've discussed it, and we believe that you are the most qualified woman to take over her position. You'll be getting a promotion to major. Your first order of business is to prepare the military forces for the possibility of invasion."

"I see, ma'am." Jak plucked at her lower lip before she could stop herself. "This is a lot to ask."

"Indeed it is," maybe-Mashir said. "But we think you're up to it. As the only woman in the militia who has recently served in an extended conflict, we believe your experience is invaluable."

"You will report directly to General Lethe," Yozhin continued. "You will work closely with Major Lutnova, who commands our space defenses."

"I appreciate the offer, ma'am. Ma'ams." She aimed a nod around the table to include all of the Ruling Council. "But I can't accept without a few conditions. You may rethink your plans when you hear what they are."

"I knew it," Tachay said, her eyes flashing. "Conditions. Now that she knows we need her, she'll hold us hostage."

"It's a big deal. We're asking a great deal. Let's hear what she has to say," maybe-Mashir said.

"Figures Mashir." Tachay sneered at the young councilwoman. "You've been in her camp this whole time. You're the one who suggested her."

Yozhin shook her head fiercely and pushed herself back in her chair. "Tachay, if you don't calm yourself down, I'm going to call for a vote on your fitness to remain on council."

Tachay stared at Yozhin, her mouth agape. Finally, she folded both arms beneath her breasts and sank down in her chair, pinning Jak with an aggressive stare.

"Let's hear your conditions, Captain Stowell," Mashir said.

"I have two of them, ma'am. The first is to change the militia's status. Militia implies a part-time organization that needn't be taken seriously. We need to create a viable armed military service. To do that, the women who are serving need to be taken, and to take themselves, seriously. Frankly, I've been unimpressed at the quality of the armed forces here. The only real professionals I've met among these women are the Banshees. If I take over the ground forces, I expect that we'll be taken seriously and I'll be working to impart a sense of professionalism to these women. I can't do that without your support."

"I think that's reasonable," Yozhin said. She looked around the table, and when no one disagreed she nodded. "We can do that. It will take some legislative maneuvering to make sure that our laws will support a full-time military service, but we can make this happen. What's your second condition?"

Jak swallowed hard. This one was going to be the real kicker. "My second condition, ma'am." She paused for a deep breath. "My second condition is that you take in the Orthodoxan female population at the end of the Haefonian civil war."

The women stared at her. For a moment everyone was so still that it seemed as though they'd quit breathing. Predictably, Tachay was the one to break the silence.

"You see?" She leaped to her feet, pounding a fist on the table. "You see! This is what comes of embracing outsiders. And now she wants us to bring on a whole population of them?"

"Ma'am," Jak tried to break in.

"They'll come in, take what viable land we have left and consume our dwindling resources." Tachay continued to rave, giving no indication that she'd noticed Jak's interruption. The councilors stared at her, a few with looks of disgust, though a couple were nodding slightly as if they might actually agree with her.

Jak stood and waited for the councilor to finish shouting. No one else made any attempt to stop Tachay's tirade. Eventually, she wound down and collapsed back into her chair, short of breath. The other women noticed Jak and turned their attention to her. Six sets of eyes bored into her; Tachay had her gaze focused on the table between her hands.

"It's the right thing to do," Jak said quietly. "These women have been treated as reproductive machines for generations. This is part of what you do. I've met many women here who were rescued from similar situations or who are the daughters or descendants of women who were rescued."

Yozhin rested her chin heavily on her hand. "Captain Stowell, as much as we'd like to, we simply do not have the resources to undertake any rescue actions on such a large scale."

"I'm not asking that you do it now." Jak looked around the table, catching each councilor's eyes with her own. She had to make them understand. "The civil war is years away from any conclusion, even with Torrin supplying the Devonites with weapons. But these women have no chance if we don't do something for them. And their children will have no chance. We have time to plan for it."

One of the councilors, a woman with a multitude of braids like Kiera's who had been silent until this point, nodded. "Are you so certain that these women will be mistreated, even after the war is over?"

"Of course they will be. Devonite attitudes toward women are more enlightened than the Orthodoxans, but only by comparison. They don't have the resources or a reason to do anything about it. Oh, they'll probably set the women free of the breeding pens, but they'll be set free into the society that caged them in the first place."

"Breeding pens?" The councilor was taken aback by her phraseology.

"Breeding pens, Ararat," Yozhin answered. "I've heard of them. The Orthodoxans keep women only for breeding purposes, isn't that right, Captain?"

"That's right, ma'am. Women who aren't lucky enough to be purchased by a man as a 'wife' are condemned to a life in the breeding pens where men who can't afford a woman of their own still get the 'opportunity' to procreate. It's how they have a steady stream of soldiers for the front. Boys born to the breeding pens end up as enlisted soldiers. Girls end up in the same pens unless they get chosen as wives."

Ararat looked like she was trying not to be physically ill. Many of the other councilors had similar expressions. Tachay still stared at the table, ignoring Jak and the conversation.

"How can we not try to help these women?" Ararat asked, pinning Yozhin with a hard stare.

"We don't have the resources." Yozhin wrung her hands, unsure what to do. "How are we going to handle all those women? How many women are we talking?"

"Probably about three hundred thousand or so, ma'am. It's impossible to get an accurate count, but based on what we know of their male population, it's a reasonable estimate."

"Three hundred thousand?" Ararat's eyebrows traveled halfway up her forehead. "That's more than the population of Landing. More than the population of the whole crater chain even."

"They won't all want to stay, I'm sure, ma'am." Jak hastened to reassure her. "It's likely a lot of them will want to return to Haefen eventually. But we can teach them how to take care of themselves, that they aren't useless things meant only to bear sons who will turn around and treat them like crap."

"What if we didn't bring all of them here?" Mashir added her voice to the conversation. "We bring in the most damaged ones, the ones from the breeding pens. Let's leave the ones who've married on

Haefen. We can send some of our women to open schools and the wives can be reeducated on the planet."

It wasn't exactly what she'd wanted, but Jak could see the wisdom of the strategy. "I can live with that, ma'am. That would leave maybe two hundred thousand to be moved to Nadierzda. How many would stay and for how long, I'm not sure."

Yozhin leaned forward and captured Jak's eyes with her own. "You need to remember, Captain Stowell. Our first priority is to complete the terraforming of Nadierzda. Without that, we won't have a planet ourselves within three generations. Planning will start for the women from your planet, but it will not happen at the expense of that goal."

Jak nodded. "I understand, ma'am. With your guarantees on these issues, within the strictures you've placed, I will take on the position of command of Nadi's ground forces."

There was a collective sigh of relief from around the table. Tachay stared out the room's window.

"Excellent," Yozhin said. "We've discussed the matter with your doctor. She doesn't want us to delay your trip by more than a week."

"Then I will do what I can do to get matters arranged before I leave."

"You'll want to head back to the base. Your officers are waiting for you, as are General Lethe and Major Shanya Lutnova."

Jak recognized a dismissal when she heard one. She snapped a hand to her lips in salute and left the room. Torrin sat on a hard bench across from the door and stood as Jak emerged.

"How did things go? I heard shouting. A lot of it. I almost came in at one point."

"Some differences of opinion, is all." Jak smiled and stretched up to press a kiss into the side of Torrin's neck. "They asked me to take over Tanith's old position. I'm the new head of the planet's ground forces."

"You are? You said yes?" Torrin's voice rose in surprise.

"Of course I did." Jak drew back from her. Torrin's surprise offended her. Did Torrin really think that she could abandon the planet? Well, she wouldn't, not when it needed her so badly.

Quickly Torrin reached out and took Jak's hands. "Jak, baby, it's not like that. I'm only surprised because we need to get you back to Haefen."

"And I'll go, but I need to get things on the right track here."

"But not at the cost of your health."

"You know as well as I do that if Tanith decided to sell out the planet, my health will be the least of everybody's problems." She looked up at Torrin and took pity on the concern she saw on her face. "Besides, I thought you'd be happy about my decision."

"Why's that?" She could tell Torrin was trying not to sound sulky, but a little of her dissatisfaction bled through in her tone.

"Because it gives me one more reason to stick around. Not that you're not more than enough, but it binds me even closer to the planet."

"That's right." Torrin nodded for emphasis. "It also means that you can't go galloping off by yourself on dangerous assignments when we get back to Haefen. You have *responsibilities* now." She brandished the word like a threat.

"That's true." Jak hadn't thought of that. Truly, she hadn't even considered going after her brother's killer when she got back. The reminder rekindled some of the old anger and grief, but it wasn't the same. It was removed, not as immediate as it had been for the past two years. Torrin had a point. If she got herself killed going after the sniper, who would take her place on Nadierzda?

"So what's the plan?" Torrin asked.

"I need to head to the base. We have a lot of planning to do before I can go. Apparently Kiera has cleared me staying a week."

"She has, has she?" Torrin looked irritated. "Not that I don't trust them, but I don't trust them. I'm going to follow up with her, make sure that's what she really said."

"Whatever you want, honey."

Torrin grinned down at her teasing tone and pulled Jak against her, wrapping her up in a strong hug and lowered her head, taking Jak's lips with hers. Jak melted against Torrin as their mouths moved against each other. Torrin nibbled gently at her lower lip, sucking it in before sliding a tongue in to taste Jak's sweetness.

The sounds of a throat clearing sent Jak trying to scramble away from Torrin, her face hot with embarrassment. Torrin felt no such compunction. She broke off their kiss but refused to relinquish her grip.

Councilor Mashir grinned at the two of them. "You two might want to find a better venue for that. Council's broken for the time being. Last thing you need is Tachay getting on your case for dereliction of duty."

Torrin returned her grin lazily and tightened her arms around Jak before reluctantly letting her go.

"Understood ma'am," Jak said, her voice breathy. She was so turned on by the passion of Torrin's kiss that what she really wanted to do was find a secluded spot so they could finish what Torrin had started. Her sense of duty asserted itself and she pulled down the hem of her shirt. "Let's head out, Torrin. I need to change into my uniform and I don't want to keep everyone waiting any longer than I need to."

CHAPTER FOUR

The outside of her glass was slick; condensation rolled slowly down the side and pooled at the base, leaving a wet ring on the table. Torrin scooted the glass out of the way and idly dragged her fingertip through the small puddle. Three days had passed since Jak had decided not to leave Nadierzda to seek immediate treatment. She still struggled with Jak's decision. Surely her love's own welfare should have come first. If Jak ended up with permanent brain damage, how was she going to help the women of Haefen? And where had that argument been when Torrin had been trying to convince her to leave early?

There was a fine line, she thought. Jak didn't want Torrin to tell her what to do, but her behavior was dangerous. The last time she'd tried to push it, Jak had drawn herself up to her full height and simply looked at her, never saying a word. If only Jak had screamed at her. It would have been so much easier to deal with than the quiet dignity Jak presented. She was getting pretty good at reading Jak's moods and there was no point trying to shift her when Jak got that look in her eye. So she sat alone at the bar and waited for Jak to get done with the day's work.

"Is this seat taken?"

Torrin looked up into Lieutenant Olesya Krikorian's smiling eyes. She returned the grin and kicked out a stool. "Hop on."

"Thanks." Olesya took a seat with an economy of movement that revealed her training. There were no wasted motions in the way she moved. Torrin had lost the hallmarks of that training years ago, though she was no slouch when it came to hand-to-hand combat. Olesya would probably dismantle her if they faced off, though Torrin was confident she'd still be able to make the lieutenant work for it. She wasn't above giving Olesya crap, but she would make sure it never came to the point where she had to put her money where her mouth was. Above all else, Torrin hated to lose.

"What do you know?" Torrin asked without much enthusiasm. She asked more to make conversation than because she was really interested. She quite liked Olesya, but she was a little put out with Nadi's military at the moment and Olesya was the nearest available target.

A waitress came by and deposited a drink in front of the lieutenant.

"Why the attitude?" The question was direct, but Olesya's tone was mild. She watched Torrin over the rim of her stein before taking a deep pull of the dark beer within.

"Attitude? No attitude here. Tired."

"Bullshit." Olesya put down the glass and cocked her head. "You should be proud of Jak, you know."

"Why's that? Because she's risking becoming a vegetable?"

"That is awfully noble, but not what I'm talking about. She's damn good. I don't agree with everything the Ruling Council does, but putting her in charge was a great move."

"I thought they put her in charge of the ground forces only." Torrin went back to tracing random designs on the wooden tabletop.

"They did, but even Lutnova is taking her lead." Olesya laughed loudly, her merriment exploding from her somber mien. "I think she might have a bit of a crush on your woman."

"She what?" Torrin's head snapped up and she glared at Olesya. "You've got to be kidding me. Shady Shanya's putting the moves on my girlfriend?"

"Cool your engines there, tiger." Blue eyes pierced Torrin where she sat. "Jak hasn't even noticed. You don't have anything to worry about with her. She only has eyes for you, crazy girl that she is."

"Oh." Torrin settled back into her chair. That was good news, at least. Not that she worried about Jak's commitment to her. Jak had proven that the night after she'd been released from the clinic. Multiple times. And the night after that. And last night too. Torrin looked forward to another energetic session of lovemaking tonight.

The fact remained, however, that Jak wasn't exactly experienced. Oh, she had the moves down now. She and Torrin were in perfect synch when it came to making love, but Torrin was the only person Jak had ever slept with. For a while, she'd worried that Jak might have succumbed to Tanith's undeniable charms. As much as Torrin loathed the woman, she couldn't deny that Tanith could be very charming when she had wanted to be. Fortunately, there was nothing to worry about on that front anymore.

Olesya realized that Torrin wasn't going to elaborate further. "It must be a bit of a shock. After all, you aren't the one who's ever had to worry about her partner. Your partners always worried about you, wondering when you were going to move on."

Torrin grunted and stared down at the bottom of her glass. The ice cubes were almost completely melted into the whiskey. She'd wanted cold whiskey, but she hated when it was watered down.

"It's all right though." Olesya continued her prattling. "Jak seems confident in a way I've never seen from her before. She has purpose and she's going after it. If that's what she's like when she's on a stalk, I'm not surprised she's such a good sniper."

"That's good, I'm glad to hear it." What was wrong with her? Torrin wondered. Olesya kept going, chattering about Jak's wonderful qualities. It was driving her nuts. "So what's it to you? You have a crush on her too?" She thrust her jaw out and stared aggressively at the lieutenant.

After taking another long pull from her beer, Olesya stared back at Torrin. "I'm glad she's happy, but I bet you have no idea why it's now that she's finally in a good place, emotionally. I know you've known her longer than me, but have you ever seen her this happy?"

"Well, no." Torrin scowled. She wished Olesya would get to the point already.

"Look, she's not that hard to figure out. She has a job that she enjoys and she's good at, she has a woman who loves her and who isn't unattractive. I don't know all of her hang-ups, but she's told me a little bit. What do you want to bet she's finally moving beyond losing her brother?" Olesya watched Torrin expectantly. When she didn't say anything she let out an exasperated sigh. "She's happy and she's crazy about you, so why are you moping around in this bar, getting hammered?"

"It's not that," Torrin protested, stung by the lieutenant's critique. "She won't let me take care of her. How can I be there for her when she keeps pushing me away?"

"That's what this is about? Why should she let you take care of her? I haven't met many women who're more capable than Jak Stowell. She's only being who she is. She needs a partner, not a nursemaid."

"I know that. I really do. But I'm worried about her."

"She knows her limits, better than you do, probably. Trust her, she'll let you know when it's time." Olesya stood up and drained the rest of her beer. She clapped Torrin on the shoulder. "I like you, Torrin, we go way back. I like her too, so it's only fair of me to warn you. You fuck this up by doing something stupid because you're hammered and I will hurt you. Very badly."

Instead of making her feel better, Olesya's words had only served to make her feel like so much useless crap. She couldn't help but think of the moment of hesitation that had occurred after she'd poured her heart out to Jak. She'd said she loved her and Jak had paused. In that moment, Torrin felt her heart stutter and falter. Sure, Jak had stopped her from leaving and had shown her how much she cared every night since, but the pause still hurt. Her eyes prickled and she blinked fiercely. She would not cry, not in front of Olesya.

"What's the matter?" Olesya stared at her, concerned at first. The concern was replaced by anger as she leaped feetfirst into the wrong conclusion. "What did you do?"

"Me?" Torrin was aghast. She wiped her eyes angrily on the back of her wrist. She stood up. There was no way she was going to sit around and listen to the lieutenant.

"You." Olesya put her hand on Torrin's shoulder, stopping her from storming out of the bar.

"I didn't do a fucking thing, except tell her that I love her. You know what she did? She hesitated!"

The lieutenant sat back on her stool. "Really?"

"You heard me. What, you think I'd lie about this?"

"Lie about it? Not with those waterworks. I don't think I've ever seen you cry before. You're tough as old leather, Torrin, though a good deal more attractive." Olesya shook her head. "Did she say anything else?"

Torrin laughed wetly and scrubbed her palms over her still-tearing eyes. "She said she loved me too. Eventually."

"Then why are you worried?"

"If she really loves me, then why did she have to think about it?"

"I don't know. Have you talked to her about it?"

"Of course not!"

Olesya rolled her eyes. "Then talk to her, for crying out loud. You'll never get anywhere by keeping this crap inside."

"No way. She has enough stress right now without me emoting all over her. I'm sure you're right. I'm being completely crazy about it. I'm not used to being the one with all the feelings."

Olesya shrugged. "Suit yourself. I think you should ask her." She stared at Torrin. Torrin stared back. Neither of them spoke and the noise of the crowded bar washed over them. Women's voices raised in excited chatter that was threaded through by loud laughter. The bars that Torrin frequented on the various Fringe planets were almost always dominated by men. If they were loud, it was usually from fighting, not from hilarity. Normally she enjoyed being surrounded by women's laughter. Not tonight. All it did was remind her that she wasn't at home with Jak.

"I need to go. Jak gets off work soon and she'll need a ride home."

"Is she still having issues?"

Torrin nodded, her lips twisting in a sour grimace at the reminder of Jak's condition. The one that she wasn't getting treated. "I have to drive her home. She gets lost if she tries to make it back on her own. She has an assistant to help her get around on base."

"She'll be getting medical help soon enough." The sympathy on Olesya's face irritated Torrin further. "It's hard loving someone who's found something bigger than herself."

"Sure." Torrin pushed herself away from the table and stalked away, throwing a wave over her shoulder without looking back at Olesya. The last thing she needed was her platitudes. It had all been so much simpler on Haefen. All they'd had to do there was stay alive.

She wove her way through the press of bodies. When she'd entered the bar in late afternoon, there hadn't been many patrons. Now that night had fallen and more people had gotten off work, the bar was filling up. A number of the women nodded at her or sent a smile her way. She knew most of them, some intimately. Some of them she didn't know at all and suspected that they'd heard her reputation as a bit of a player. *Shows what they know*, she thought sourly. She was taken, well and truly, by Jak.

The alcohol she'd consumed over the past couple of hours had her head buzzing. After a quick stop at the bar where she downed a shot of sobrahol to straighten her out, she headed to her bike. She'd been an ass to Olesya, she realized. She would have to apologize the next time she saw the Banshee. It was hard though. She wanted to know that she was first in Jak's heart, just as Jak was in hers. How could she compete against the welfare of the women of Nadierzda? She felt like an asshole for even wanting to, but she couldn't help it.

The full-throated roar of the bike's engine between her thighs cheered her up a little bit. Things would have to be very dour indeed if the feeling of all that power couldn't make her grin at least a little bit. All that power and it bowed to her every whim. She opened the throttle again to ramp up the vibration and peeled out, tires squealing, the end fishtailing slightly. She rode out the slight wobble and blasted down the side street until she hit the main drag. It was risky to open up all the way while still in the city. The local police force took a dim view of citizens attempting to double the speed limit. She glanced down at her speedometer and backed off the throttle. Make that triple the speed limit. Torrin settled on a more sedate pace and chafed at the delay until she cleared the Landing city limits.

Once on the rural road, she opened it up. The road to the base was mostly a straight shot and she gunned it. Her lips stretched into a wide grin. There wasn't a problem so big that a little power and a lot of speed couldn't make it pale into insignificance. Every ounce of power gave her that much more speed, which got her that much closer to Jak. Her heart tripped in her chest and sped up. Butterflies curled in anticipation at the pit of her stomach.

Torrin felt like she had when she'd first courted Galya. The girl's smiling bright blue eyes floated in her mind's eye for a second before being replaced by the serious blue-gray of Jak's. Deep sorrow choked her for a moment. She very much regretted the fate Galya had suffered at Tanith's hands. She didn't regret the time they'd spent together. She missed Galya, but with the dim ache of a hurt long healed, one she'd gotten over, only to have the news of her death tear off the emotional scab. She had no doubt that Jak was the one for her. Her life would have been very different if Galya hadn't disappeared.

Jak was her future now. Unsure where the maudlin streak had come from, Torrin put electric blue eyes from her mind and looked forward to seeing Jak, taking her home and making thorough love to her until she begged for mercy. The power between her legs whetted her appetite and she forced the throttle open to its widest point.

Torrin had been awfully quiet and Jak wondered what her problem was. Preparations had been proceeding rapidly. It was unlikely they'd be needed soon, but it didn't hurt to be ready. She'd already set in motion pretty much everything she could for now. With only a few more points to wrap up, she would be ready to leave Nadierzda in the next day or so.

The scenery whipped into and out of the headlights and Jak was glad for the helmet. Torrin's driving bordered on reckless on the best of days; tonight it had jumped the edge and plunged right into suicidal. She tried not to watch as Torrin weaved through obstacles and tore around corners at speeds that defied understanding.

The ride was mercifully brief. At the speeds Torrin had been driving, the ride couldn't have been anything else. To her relief, her legs were steady when she dismounted from the bike.

Torrin hopped down and swept the helmet off of her head, shaking her hair out. It lacked a little something without the locks that had been shorn from her head those months ago on Haefen. The hair had grown out and curled around her ears, halfway to her chin. It had more curl than Jak recalled. She would probably lose that when the hair grew out, the weight pulling the strands straight.

"What is it?" Torrin asked.

Jak blushed, embarrassed to be caught staring, then was chagrined at her embarrassment. Torrin was her girlfriend, she had carte blanche to stare if she wanted to. She pulled her helmet off, minus the dramatic flourish. "Watching you, is all." Jak's face still flamed hotly and even in the dim light, Torrin didn't miss her discomfiture.

"Is that right?" Torrin grinned lazily. She licked her lower lip in a casually provocative display that Jak was almost certain was deliberate. Her groin tightened and she stepped forward. Torrin took Jak into her arms as soon as she was within reach and brought her mouth down hungrily, crushing Jak's lips against her teeth. Taken aback at the ferocity of Torrin's desire, Jak parted her lips. Torrin's tongue marauded through her mouth as it swirled over her tongue and swept deep inside. For breathless moments, Torrin took what she wanted from Jak and then, gradually, her fervor lessened. The kiss deepened in sweetness, more than making up for the loss of intensity and Jak found herself moaning. Hands loosened on her upper arms and glided up the back of her shirt, skimming lightly over skin that heated to Torrin's touch.

Torrin gently drew back on the kiss, nibbling on Jak's lower lip for a moment before relinquishing her mouth with a gasp. She rested her forehead against Jak's and closed her eyes, gulping in air. Jak panted along with her.

"Maybe we should go inside," Jak said when she'd gathered herself enough to talk. Torrin's hands tightened against the muscles of her back before reluctantly letting her go.

"Maybe we should." Her eyes met Jak's and she inhaled sharply. In them, she saw a frightening intensity of emotion. Torrin was holding nothing back. Love shone at her—along with something else. Something darker, something Jak couldn't quite make out. Possessiveness, maybe. Or was it something worse? Jak shivered and looked away, disturbed by the fierce implacability of Torrin's feelings.

Torrin grinned, misinterpreting the shiver for desire and when Jak looked back into her eyes, the shadow was gone. All she saw was love with a healthy serving of lust. She shivered again, this time as overwhelming ardor swept through her body. Putting her reservations aside, she reached out for Torrin's hands and pulled them to her.

"Let's go inside before I take you out here." Hunger flitted across Torrin's face and for a moment Jak thought she was going to do exactly that. Instead, she pulled Jak along after her on the way over to the entrance of her building. Jak had to trot along in her wake, her speed no match for Torrin's long legs.

They kissed again in the elevator. Hungrily, each devoured the mouth of the other. Torrin barely had the presence of mind to swipe her arm over the chip reader that unlocked the door. The door whooshed out from under Jak's back and she half-stepped, half-fell backward into the darkened apartment. Only Torrin's grip on her waistband saved her tumbling ass over teakettle to the floor.

Loud meows greeted them. Nat's cats cried for attention or, more likely, for food. Torrin seemed content to ignore them, and as soon as the door closed in their wake she focused on tearing open the fasteners of Jak's coat. The cats redoubled their demands, and Jak tore her mouth away from Torrin.

"We need to feed the cats," she breathed.

"They can wait." Torrin recaptured her mouth and walked Jak backward until her back hit the wall. She pushed Jak against the wall as her fingers attacked the fasteners again. Jak's jacket conquered, Torrin parted the coat's sides and for a moment Jak was transported back to their first time in the Devonite sniper barracks. Her breasts heaved with emotion and arousal when Torrin brushed the pads of her thumbs over hard, erect nipples.

A low growl rumbled from Torrin's throat and she reached down to Jak's hips, skimming over them to her rump. She grabbed handfuls of Jak's ass, kneading. Jak moaned again, then gasped in surprise when she was hoisted off the ground and against Torrin.

Reflexively, she wrapped her legs around Torrin's waist. With a triumphant grin, Torrin captured a nipple between her teeth and bit down on it, drawing a groan of ecstasy from Jak's throat and drowning out the indignant cats. Torrin hoisted her up and carried her to the bedroom, dropping her on her back on the bed. Torrin frantically yanked at the closures on Jak's pants while she lifted her hips and kicked off her boots, allowing Torrin to slide the pants and underwear off her.

Pleasure rocketed through Jak's body as Torrin opened her to the air. A cool breeze caressed her labia before being replaced by the scalding heat of Torrin's mouth. She grabbed the hair on the back of Torrin's head and held her in place.

"Oh baby. That's so good."

As Torrin lipped her way along the edge of her labia, Jak couldn't keep from moaning aloud. The sounds that Torrin could wring out of her were no longer a surprise. They were so breathy, so feminine that it was hard to countenance that they came from her throat. The tip of Torrin's tongue swirled around her erect clit, sending waves of pleasure careening through her body with each lick. Helplessly, Jak lifted her hips, desperate for more sensation.

"Give it to me," she moaned. "Baby, I need you. Take me, oh god, baby..." Her voice trailed off into more groans and whimpers. Her toes curled at the sensation. Torrin latched onto her throbbing clit and sucked Jak into her mouth hard. Without relinquishing her hold, she slid two fingers into Jak's opening and slid them home in her pussy. The sense of being filled so suddenly was more than Jak could bear and she grabbed Torrin's head with both hands, clasping her to her moist pussy as she quaked. Her passion given full voice, she screamed her release, back bowing before collapsing back to the bed. Her limbs weighed her down and she whimpered when Torrin slowly withdrew her fingers, running them along the inside of her canal as her muscles continued to quiver.

"Give me a second," Jak panted.

"Take all the time you need," Torrin replied, her voice satisfied and a smug grin plastered on her face. She licked her lips and closed her eyes as she savored Jak's juices where they painted her lips. "We've got all night."

Jak grinned over at her. It wasn't going to take long at all. Already her arousal ramped back up as she watched Torrin's performance. They did have all night, and Jak intended to take full advantage of the time and of Torrin.

CHAPTER FIVE

The short hairs on Jak's head tickled the outside of Torrin's nose, and she rubbed her nose slowly to get rid of the tingling before she worked up to a sneeze. Jak had fallen asleep, completely wrung out from their exertions. Torrin was feeling close to sleep herself. She drifted in a pleasant haze, right on the edge of dozing off but she held onto the edge of wakefulness. She wanted to savor the feeling of Jak in her arms a little longer. When they were like this, she had no worries. Everything was as it should be and seemed so simple. It was only when they were apart that doubts crept in.

I wonder what Nat would think of all this? Probably smack me on the arm and ask what took so long. Torrin trailed her fingers up and down Jak's upper arm. *I can't say she'd be wrong.* A slow smile took over her face. It was just as well Nat wasn't around; she would give Torrin so much crap if she ever saw her with that goofy grin on her face.

As much as she'd fought Nat on coming to work for her, it had been a good idea. She did a good job and she had enough self-confidence that she wouldn't let the assholes among the Devonites keep her from the job. About the only good thing Torrin could think of about going back to that place was the opportunity to see her sister again. Better that than Nat getting back to Nadi while she was gone and getting the story from everyone here. Who knew how garbled that would be? No, better if she could fill Nat in on what had really happened.

The light around the room was already starting to lighten, matching the false dawn that would be breaking outside. Torrin didn't want the night to end. When the sun came up, Jak would head back to the base. At least she could be satisfied knowing that the sniper would go to work still feeling what she and Torrin had done the night before. Their lovemaking had been enthusiastic. Torrin knew she was going to have some soreness and suspected that Jak would as well. It was worth it. Every twinge would remind her of what they'd done together.

Jak sighed in her arms and shifted. Her eyes fluttered open and automatically sought out Torrin's. The smile that curled her lips pulled an answering grin from Torrin. When Jak was around, very little could keep her from smiling.

"Hey there, sexy," Torrin rumbled quietly. "You should go back to sleep. You have to get up in an hour and head to work."

The kiss that Jak planted on her lips quickened her breathing. Jak continued to kiss Torrin until she was truly breathless and her heart hammered in her ears. She pulled back with a wicked smile at Torrin's little whimper of protest. "No, I don't. I told them I won't be in until noon today. After all, we do need some time to prepare."

Torrin leaned forward to recapture Jak's lips then paused. "What do you mean prepare?"

"I thought we could leave tonight."

"Didn't the council want you to stay for a week?" Torrin sat straight up in bed, steadying Jak even as she dislodged her. "Are you feeling okay? Are the symptoms getting that much worse?"

"The council wanted me to stay as long as it took to get affairs in order. I've set enough in motion. I'm going to have to trust that my assistants can get the job done without me watching over their shoulders the whole time."

There was no sign Jak was glossing over the truth. She'd learned that Jak couldn't lie to save her life. It was a bit funny. On Haefen, her life had literally hinged on an enormous falsehood. Somehow, she'd managed to pull it off for years and yet trying to get her to be dishonest about anything else was almost impossible. Her face was too open, her emotions too close to the surface. It made her easy to read and Torrin saw no sign of dissembling. Still, she was suspicious.

"You didn't really answer my question?" Torrin accused. "You're not worse, are you?"

"No more than is to be expected." Jak held a finger over Torrin's lips when she opened her mouth to protest. "We know I'm not going to get better on my own. Yes, it's bad, and yes, the symptoms are a bit worse, but I should be fine. I don't think I've passed the point of no return. I still know my own name, after all."

The explanation wasn't as reassuring as Jak probably thought it was. "I'm so glad we're going to get you back there so you can get the help you need. I'll start getting things together." She moved to throw the covers back, but Jak snagged the edge and wouldn't allow her to remove the sheets from their bodies.

"I want to spend the time here, with you." She smiled, sadness playing around the corners of her eyes. "We probably won't get many chances to when we're back home."

Home. Jak still thought of that backwater planet as home. Torrin had hoped she would start to think of Nadierzda that way. They simply hadn't spent enough time together on Nadi yet. And they couldn't. They had to head back to Jak's home planet so she could receive treatment. The thoughts chased themselves around her brain until she wanted to scream.

"Sure. Let's spend time together while we can."

"Hey." Jak pulled Torrin's head around to look her in the eyes. "I'm not going to stay there. I want to store up cuddling with you while I can." She smiled and Torrin found herself smiling back.

How had she ever thought that Jak was a man? She trailed the backs of her fingers down pale cheeks. Her skin was so smooth, her jawline so delicate. High cheekbones framed large gray-blue eyes. Torrin could only suppose that she'd been temporarily insane to think that this beautiful, sensual woman was anything but gorgeously female. Not always feminine, but female, absolutely.

"I love you so much, you know that?"

Jak beamed at her and rewarded the statement with a sizzling kiss. "I love you too," she whispered when they parted. She tucked her head under Torrin's chin and tightened her hold on Torrin's rib cage.

They lay there, entwined, enjoying each other's presence until Jak drifted off again. Fatigue saturated her limbs and Torrin allowed herself to drift. She would need to let her business partners know that she would be out for a while again, but that could wait until she woke.

* * *

The interior of the car was quiet. Jak watched buildings speed by. They were traveling at a reasonable speed and she guessed that Torrin was over her pique from the previous night. She wondered what had set her off, but she couldn't figure out how to ask. They'd made love for hours and she hadn't wanted to spoil their time together. There were other issues that would spoil things, one that she needed to talk to Torrin about before they could leave. Jak suspected that Torrin wasn't going to like her idea, which was why she'd been putting it off, but if they were going to leave by that evening, she had to address it now.

"So, the women who work for your company offworld, what type of training do they get?"

Torrin spared her a quick glance before returning her attention to the road. "How so? I mean, they get trained in the areas they need to know to work for the company. Inventory, sales, management, negotiation. That kind of thing."

"What about self-defense?"

"Well, no." Torrin looked surprised at the idea. "Some of them served in the militia before coming to work for me, but there's been no reason to get them any formal training. Why?"

"It's something I've been kicking around is all." Jak felt hopeful. Torrin didn't seem immediately resistant to the line of questioning. Maybe this would be easier than she'd thought. "I think we need to get all of your women enrolled into some basic close-combat training before they're allowed to leave Nadi."

"It really hasn't been an issue." Pursed lips and furrowed brows told Jak that Torrin wasn't being entirely forthcoming.

"You've never had something come up where one of your women could have used a little extra training?"

"Well, there was the issue Laiya and I had on Tyndall. But Laiya used to be militia. She's handy with a weapon and handled herself pretty well."

"And what would've happened if she hadn't had that training?"

"Yeah, but it's come up about once since we started opening satellite offices."

Jak sighed. Torrin was digging in her heels. The way her jaw was clenched told Jak that she needed to close this soon before Torrin could get further entrenched in her argument. "What about Tanith,

Torrin? She knew about your satellite offices. They're a point of weakness. If I'd wanted to make a little money on the side, exploiting that point would be a nice, quick way to do that, especially if I knew who was ex-militia and who wasn't. Don't you want to make sure that your employees have the best shot possible?"

"Of course I do," Torrin said hotly. "But I don't want the Ruling Council in my business any more than I have to. I open this up and they start trying to regulate everything about the satellite offices. I've managed to keep them out of that part of the business for this long. I'm not opening the door to them now."

"Torrin, this isn't the Ruling Council asking, it's me." The buildings were whizzing past them faster and faster. Torrin's agitation was coming out as breakneck speed. "All I want is to make sure that our women are taken care of and safe, on Nadierzda and off!"

"My employees aren't the only women who leave Nadierzda. What about them?"

About to shoot back a heated response, Jak paused. What about those women? They were another point that could be compromised, one that Tanith would have been able to exploit. She'd been told that the women were reintroduced onto Fringe planets without anyone being the wiser. Tanith had likely been aware of the reintroductions and could have taken advantage of them. It was hard to believe that anyone from Nadierzda could be that heartless, but Jak couldn't afford to have any blind spots. Tanith had proven herself willing to do all sorts of unsavory activities, and her motives were still unclear. So far, they had all assumed that Tanith had been looking to turn a quick credit, but there was no telling if those assumptions were correct. They were also assuming Tanith was the only traitor. If Tanith could have betrayed them, anybody could.

"You're right," Jak finally said.

"And another thing–" Torrin had worked herself into a full head of plasma and broke off when she realized that Jak had actually agreed with her. "I am? I am!"

"I hadn't considered them. Do they receive any self-defense training before they leave Nadierzda?"

Torrin shook her head. "I don't think so. A few of them seek out training on their own, but not all of them."

"If I push for requiring all women who leave the planet to have some proficiency in hand-to-hand combat and some basic weapons training, will you be okay with that? It doesn't put the council right in your company. All of these women should know how to defend themselves."

"I'd be all right with that, *if* it's run through the militia and the women are not subject to council approval before being able to leave. You, I trust. I don't quite trust them."

"It's a deal. This is long overdue. I can't believe it's taken a crisis like Tanith to push us in this direction." Jak was appalled. Appalled that no one had thought of this and equally as stricken by the fact that she'd almost left out an entire group. She was supposed to know better. "Oh, and stop referring to them as the militia. It's the Nadierzdan Armed Forces. We're trying to get past militia."

A raised eyebrow signaled Torrin's amusement. "Armed Forces? That sounds a little too grand for them."

"It won't be, not for much longer. Militia makes these women sound like a bunch of amateurs. They won't start taking themselves seriously until you all do. You're a leader in the community, Torrin. If you refer to us as the Armed Forces, others will take note and follow your lead."

"Oh fine." Torrin still looked amused, but she seemed willing to go along with it. "If it'll make you happy."

"It will. And more importantly than that, it will make the women of the Armed Forces feel valued and will make them more effective soldiers, which will give Nadierzda more effective protection."

"You're really fired up about this, aren't you?" The amusement was wiped clean from Torrin's face and she watched Jak out of the corner of her eye.

"I really am," Jak said with quiet dignity. "It's important if we're to survive. The possibility that Tanith sold us out is only one way the planet could be discovered."

"You're right." Torrin's voice was uncharacteristically sober.

"There's one other favor I want to ask you."

"What's that?" Torrin was too much the negotiator to agree before hearing what she was in for. Jak wished that this one time, Torrin would stop being the savvy businesswoman.

"I'd like it if your offworld employees would keep an ear to the ground and let us know if they hear any rumblings about Tanith or other threats to Nadi."

"I'm not comfortable having my people report to yours, Jak. I'm sorry, but I'm going to have to draw the line on this one."

Frustration bubbled up inside of Jak's chest. "It's the same as when they report back on women who are in distress. I know that your employees are the ones who pass along most of the tips about the crap they see happening."

"They do, if they see something. But it's not like they're going out looking for the information. I won't put them in harm's way. Why can't you rely on whatever spies you already have?"

"I will be, but I know your employees can supplement their coverage in ways they can't. The women who are out gathering intel on the movements of the scum who profit from women's suffering aren't embedded in those communities. They come in as strangers while your employees are living there and are already trusted."

Torrin shook her head. The muscle in her jaw was flexing again. If Jak couldn't get her to move on this one now, it was never going to happen and they would have missed an important opportunity. "Torrin, you know I wouldn't ask if I thought it would put them in danger. All I'm asking is that they pass on their observations, if they have any."

"I don't know. The whole idea makes me nervous." Doubt had crept into Torrin's voice and Jak jumped on it.

"They won't have to do any more than they have been, just let us know what they hear. I'll assign an officer to liaise with Troika Corp and she'll be responsible for reporting back to us."

"You want me to take on a military minder? Jak, you're really pushing it here." Sparks practically flew from Torrin's eyes, and she seemed to be grinding her teeth.

"Not a minder, a point person to report the intel to. She won't even be stationed in your offices." Jak was getting exasperated. It made so much sense, but Torrin was only dragging her feet out of a misguided sense of independence. One of the traits she found so appealing about Torrin was her independence, but sometimes she felt like she was being independent for its own sake, not for any good reason. This was one of those times. If she couldn't be brought around to it, Jak knew she could always approach Audra and Mac, her partners. She hadn't tried it yet because she knew the tactic had some very real potential to damage her and Torrin's relationship.

"I really don't like the idea." Torrin's lips held a distasteful twist, like she'd bitten into a piece of rotten fruit.

"Why don't you bring it up to your partners? See what they say?" Jak wished she could have the suggestion back as soon as she made it. Now that she'd said it, there was no way she'd be able to approach them separately. Maybe it would be better this way. She didn't have to worry about going to them behind Torrin's back.

"I'm going to have to. I can see the wisdom of making sure that every woman who leaves the planet can protect herself, but I'm not prepared to let the armed forces into my business. I trust you, but you can't guarantee that you'll always be the one calling the shots." Torrin's eyes sought out hers, begging Jak to believe her. She could tell by the discomfort she saw in their depths that Torrin didn't enjoy turning her down, but she felt strongly enough on the subject to dig in her heels.

"I understand. And I'm not asking because I want to tie your company to the military. I hope you know that I'm only doing this because I believe it will help Nadierzda."

"Like I said, I trust you. I don't trust the Ruling Council, or at least not all of it."

"Please, can you bring it up to your partners and let me know what you all decide? Will you talk to them today?"

"I'll run it by them. I can't guarantee that we'll make a decision today, but I can get them thinking about it and we can address it again when we get back, if we need to."

"That's reasonable. All I ask is that you let me know what the verdict is as soon as you can."

"I can do that."

Jak became aware that they'd been sitting, idling in front of the walls, just out of sight of the entrance.

"I wanted to finish our conversation without getting interrupted," Torrin said.

"Thank you." Jak leaned over and pressed a kiss to one tanned cheek. The smile that the impulsive move brought out was worth it and she felt her lips curling in response.

"Let's get you dropped off." Torrin put the car back in gear and they approached the gate slowly. "You let me know as soon as you're ready to leave. I'll have everything ready to go when you are. I don't want to delay any more than we have already."

Jak nodded. Her thoughts were divided between concerns that she was missing an important point of preparation and a sudden burst of anxiety over going back to her home planet. She still hadn't decided how she was going to approach her countrymen about her identity. She barely noticed when the sentry at the gates glanced into the car then waved them forward.

* * *

The console hummed beneath Torrin's fingers. The engines had kicked into gear. To her practiced ear they sounded as good as ever. She'd been over the ship from stem to stern and had gone through the computer with a fine-tooth comb after she'd found out that Breena had left Nadierzda. Her ex had been one of the main computer techs to work on the *Calamity Jane*. She had no doubt that she was the one who was responsible for the information swap that had stranded Torrin with the Orthodoxans. There was no way that the population demographics for Tyndall had been accidentally switched with Haefen's.

The implications to that thought were grim. Breena and Tanith had been working together for a while, plotting Torrin's downfall. It was only through Jak's unwitting intervention that their plan had been foiled.

She glanced over at the neighboring chair. Jak looked around her with wide eyes. This wasn't her first ride on the *Jane*, but it was the first time she would be aware of her surroundings for the trip and be able to properly appreciate it. Torrin had forgotten how little experience Jak had with space travel. The way she'd rubbernecked when they came aboard had reminded Torrin of her inexperience. As with other areas in which Jak was inexperienced, she made up for her lack of knowledge with enthusiasm. Torrin grinned. Jak was a very quick study.

"Tien, let me know when our takeoff window opens," Torrin said, speaking to the empty air.

"Affirmative Torrin," the AI replied.

Jak looked around to see where the voice had come from. After a moment a hologram of a small Asian woman in traditional regalia shimmered to life on the console in front of her. Jak smiled and reached out hesitantly for the shimmering apparition. The hologram wavered where her finger passed through it, but Tien gave no indication of discomfort.

"Sorry," Jak said and withdrew her finger in a hurry.

"That is quite all right, Jak. Do you have any questions that I might answer?"

"If I'm talking to you, won't you miss the takeoff window?"

Tien's hologram smiled indulgently. "Jak, I am capable of monitoring tens of thousands of functions concurrently. Adding a discussion with you will not tax my processing functions."

"Tens of thousands?" Jak looked skeptical.

"Indeed Jak. Traveling through peripheral space requires a thorough knowledge of the space between jump points. Certain astronomical phenomena create so much disturbance in real space that they bleed into peripheral space. Jumping through those areas of distortion can rip a ship apart or throw it radically off course. And while I am calculating for those anomalies, I must keep the ship on course, make sure that the cryopods are functioning at full capacity and attend to potentially thousands of other minutiae."

"Wow." Jak's eyebrows had climbed up her forehead. "I didn't realize it was so complicated. Can humans pilot spaceships without help from you...people?"

"Of course we can." Torrin broke in. She wasn't going to let Tien fill Jak's head with glowing reports of the wonders of artificial intelligence. "We might not get there as quickly, but humans have been exploring space for hundreds, almost a thousand years. Most of that time, we've been without real AI technology. The first fully functional AIs were only developed a couple hundred years ago."

"This is true, Torrin," Tien said. "However, you must admit that the functions I attend to make the ride a lot smoother."

"It's true, you do help. A lot. But we could do without you, if we had to."

"Can you pilot the ship without Tien's assistance?" Jak glanced at Torrin with thinly veiled skepticism.

"You bet." She drew herself up proudly even as she continued to run through diagnostics on her console. "I've been trained to run the ship myself in the event that Tien is compromised or I need to disable her. She's right, it is harder, but that doesn't mean it's impossible. Anyone who is stupid enough to go into deep space without learning how to run a ship on their own deserves to have the worst happen to them."

"Torrin, our window is upon us." Tien's voice was as dry as usual. She displayed no discomfort about being discussed by the two of them.

"Thanks Tien." Torrin danced her fingers over the console. The engines throbbed in response and the *Calamity Jane* lifted smoothly. When they hovered a few meters above the ground, Torrin moved them away from the spaceport. She watched in amusement as Jak craned her neck to see out the bridge window. It seemed she was determined not to miss anything. Her enthusiasm was infectious, and Torrin told herself that one day soon she and Jak would take a trip together where one of them was not in the midst of a medical emergency.

Torrin throttled the engines smoothly open, and they took off, leaving the spaceport behind them. Within moments they'd broken free of the buffeting of the atmosphere. The sky turned from sandy blue to black, then Nadierzda, too, was left behind them, a dusty tan marble splattered through with blots of emerald green.

Jak stared, mouth agape out of the screen. "I'd seen some holos," she said. "They were from before the war. I think most of them were from when the first colonists landed on Haefen. There were a few from later on. Holos don't really do space justice, do they?"

"They never do," Torrin said. "It's one of the things I love about coming out here. There's so much to see. The universe goes on practically forever."

"It makes me feel more than a little small."

"That's not always a bad thing. Sometimes you feel so small that you lose all sense of yourself. All that's left is the glory of a long-dead star or a shifting nebula of infinite hues."

Where had that come from? Torrin didn't usually wax poetic, but speaking with Jak about her love of space was pulling out words and sentiments that she could hardly believe.

Her face thoughtful, Jak nodded, never taking her eyes off of the viewscreen. They passed Naiad, one of the Nadierzdan moons. It winked at them, a pale blue. Compared to the blue of Haefen, it looked anemic. Its surface was almost featureless, covered as it was in ice. Jak gaped at it also.

"If you like that, you'll get a kick out of the asteroid belt."

"Asteroid belt?"

"It's coming up." Torrin nudged up the sensors and zoomed in on the asteroids. She scanned the field for the buoys that would allow her to navigate it safely. "It keeps us hidden from the rest of the galaxy. Nadierzda tucks nicely into the shadow of the field."

As they got closer, the field started to break up, individual asteroids becoming visible instead of being lost in a featureless cloud of brown. By themselves, each asteroid wasn't much to look at, but the field itself was so vast it was almost overwhelming.

"We need to clear the field before we can slip into peripheral space." They'd entered the field and Torrin slowed the *Jane* to a much slower clip. She'd received the safest path from one of the nav-buoys and was broadcasting the latest clear passage signals to the defense-buoys. It was a good thing that Tanith had been in charge of the ground forces and not their space defenses. Torrin hoped she hadn't acquired the codes to get through the field at will. Only a few women had access to the level of clearance that would allow them to access the buoys at any time. Everyone else had to go through the spaceport and get the latest set of codes. If Tanith had managed to get her hands on the master codes, that, more than anything else, would spell disaster for Nadierzda and her inhabitants. A shiver crawled down her spine.

Torrin hoped that Jak's silence was a product of awe and not terror. She couldn't think of much that would terrify the sniper. From what she'd seen of Jak, the woman had ice water in her veins. She sneaked a quick look away from the field as she maneuvered them deftly through it. The move was safe enough. The *Calamity Jane's* proximity sensors would squawk if anything got too close. Jak looked entranced and Torrin breathed a mental sigh of relief. If Jak had turned out to have some sort of phobia about space travel, it would mean a lot of time apart for them. It wasn't unheard of, especially around those who hadn't experienced much space travel during their formative years.

It was a relief to be able to take the field at a reasonable pace. Torrin had been frantic to get through the asteroids the last time she'd navigated this area with Jak. She hadn't been able to entrust the navigation to Tien. The AI would never push the ship as far past the safety limits as Torrin had; her programming would have prevented it. While this wasn't a sightseeing trip, it was still nice to know that she could take her time and not fly by the seat of her pants. *Not too much time*, she reminded herself. Jak's condition would continue to deteriorate. They were on a mission, after all.

A mission to heal Jak, but who knew what would happen after that? Would her lover want to stay on Haefen, to go after her brother's killer again? Beyond the unknown way Jak's superiors would react when they found out she was a woman—if they found out she was a woman—the very real possibility existed that Jak would get dragged back into the endless war that gripped the planet. Surely her decision to help defend Nadierzda meant that Jak planned to come back with her. They'd declared their love for each other. That must count for something. And if Jak wanted to stay, what would she do? Torrin wasn't ready to be separated from her lover. She'd finally found her, had finally found the connection that made everything else seem like it no longer mattered. All that mattered was Jak and being with her as much as possible.

CHAPTER SIX

The last vestiges of Jak's postcryosleep headache stubbornly refused to dissipate. The thawing experience hadn't been as traumatic as the first time, though she certainly remembered more of this one. A little headache was nothing compared to the discomfort that Torrin seemed to be suffering. The skin around her eyes was drawn and pinched, and her hands shook with continual tremors. The slight shaking didn't slow her down as she danced her fingers over the console. Jak marveled at Torrin's confidence. She hoped that one day, she too could give off that aura of competence.

"Tien, make sure that our sensor footprint is as small as possible."

"Affirmative Torrin." Jak jumped a bit. She still wasn't used to the AI. None of their computer systems on Haefen were that advanced. Tien's voice sounded almost natural, which made her slight mechanical tone that much more unnerving. Torrin didn't seem to notice.

"Is there a problem?" Jak asked.

"Maybe, but I won't know how much until we're closer. If someone's out there, and they probably are, by the time we can pick them up on our sensors, they'll be able to do the same to us." Torrin furrowed her brow in concentration as she pored over one of the many small viewscreens on the bridge. "I know where to look for them, which is more than I can say for them. They don't know what direction we might be coming from or when."

"So it's the League of Solaran Planets that you're worried about?" Torrin spent a lot of time fixated on the League. The level of animosity she held for them seemed out of all proportion. But then Jak had a great appreciation for any group that could keep the peace. Torrin hadn't lived in the perpetual anarchy that warring states created.

"Yep. I was able to sneak by the picket pretty easily last time, but they had no reason to believe that Haefen was receiving any offworld visitors. I'm afraid I tipped my hand when we left. The League captain is good, probably good enough to pick up our first shipment too." A small smile cracked her face for a moment. "Still, Nat and Rudrani should have been able to get by without too much issue. They're only one ship and Rudrani is one of the best pilots we've got."

"I see." She didn't really. When they'd left her home planet, she'd been ensconced in the medical bay and had been barely conscious. Her memories of their hasty flight from the surface were spotty. She remembered flashes of Torrin looking over her with concern bordering on panic and the discomfort of her introduction to cryostasis. It hadn't been so bad this time around, but then, she'd had a better idea of what to expect.

The view out the main viewscreen was spectacular. The system's sun burned so brightly that Jak could barely make out the edge of a brilliant purple and pink blob. The color was arresting and she tried to make it out.

"Tien, what is that pink cloud thing?" Because Torrin was so engrossed in what she was doing, Jak thought it prudent to address the AI instead.

"That is a nebula, Jak." To her relief, Tien didn't seem to have any qualms about communicating with her. "It's a cloud of ionized dust and gases that has collected in a corner of the quadrant. This one is rather small."

"Shush, both of you," Torrin admonished. "I'm trying to concentrate."

Surprised by Torrin's uncharacteristic terseness, Jak subsided and went back to watching the viewscreen. They were passing a huge gas giant. If her memory served her right, it was the outer planet of the solar system. It had been a long time since her school days and she hadn't been all that interested in astronomy. She'd found most of her time in school to be incredibly boring and to be suffered only until she could escape from the stuffy confines of the schoolroom and get back into the woods with her father and brother. A couple of her classes had been all right and she'd shown an intuitive knack for mathematics that had infuriated Bron. He'd struggled with math and hadn't understood how she could pick it up so easily. She hadn't understood how he'd made friends so easily. Most days, she thought he'd gotten the best of that particular bargain.

A brilliant blue pebble winked at them on the screen before the body of the gas giant slid in front of it. Was that Haefen? It had to be. Jak felt her heart rate pick up, tripping in her chest. She still hadn't decided what she was going to do. Her mind screamed at her to hide, to assume her identity as a man. There was safety in concealment, but what was the cost? She knew the consequences of discovery, but what about the consequences of hiding? Oddly, her heart resisted the urge to stay concealed. Her time on Nadierzda hadn't been the easiest, but she'd felt an easing of her identity. She knew a little better who Jak Stowell was. Would she ever be Jakellyn again? She doubted it, but she was beginning to like Jak.

Even though the sight of her home planet sent her adrenaline spiking in nervous anticipation, mixed in was a pang of homesickness. It was altogether unexpected. Her time on Haefen had been full of struggles and hardship, both physical and emotional. But there she was, longing for another glimpse of home. She wished the gas giant, whose name escaped her, wasn't blocking her view. It was taking them a long time to move past it.

"Are you doing that on purpose?" Jak asked.

"Doing what on purpose?" Torrin didn't look up from the console.

"Putting this planet between us and Haefen?"

"I am. I've identified one ship and it's not the *Icarus*. There's a different ship on picket around your planet."

"That's good right? They won't know us."

"It's only good if they're the only ones out here. What if…" Torrin's voice trailed off and she leaned forward to stare more intently at the screen. "Mother of…the *Icarus* is also down there. There are two League ships in orbit around Haefen. Getting to the surface without being noticed or stopped is going to be a bit of a trick."

"So that's it then?"

Torrin looked up, confident smirk in place on her face. "Not even close. It's going to take a little bit more finesse. Fortunately, I'm very good at finessing things."

"I'll say." Jak blushed as the double entendre fell from her lips before she could censor herself. She blushed harder at Torrin's delighted chuckle.

"We're going to need to take our time getting into the system," Torrin said. Now that this new challenge had presented itself, Jak was amused to see that Torrin's symptoms were almost completely absent. She sat straight up in her chair and was much more alert. The slight tremor in her hands had ceased.

"What can I do to help?" Jak asked. Torrin chewed on her lower lip for a moment and fixed her gaze on the screen by her console. She seemed torn about letting Jak help. "I'm not completely helpless. And you know I'm good at following orders."

"You're not used to the equipment."

Jak sighed and gave Torrin a hard stare. "Do they know we're here?"

Still refusing to look at her, Torrin shook her head.

"Then show me what I need to know while we're hiding out behind this planet." When Torrin still didn't look convinced, Jak sighed. "You can set Tien to keep an eye on me, I don't care. I need to feel useful."

"Fine." Torrin looked up at her. Doubt lurked in her eyes, but she at least tried to keep it from showing too nakedly on her face. "We know there are at least two ships out here. I need you to keep an eye on the readouts and make sure there aren't any more ships hiding out there." She leaned over and pulled up a couple of screens on Jak's console. The screens were upside down to her, but Torrin was still able to navigate them with the ease of much practice. One screen was nothing but lines of numbers, all roughly the same. They scrolled by almost too quickly to read. The other screen looked like a chart of the solar system. Haefen was marked out in pulsating blue and two blinking icons circled it.

"What am I looking at?"

"Keep an eye on the numbers. They're a readout of ambient power signatures. If you see one that's anomalous with the others, tag it and ask Tien to look into it. It should be pretty easy to pick out if there's any fluctuation. The other is a system chart. If you see any blinking lights beyond what's already on there, you tell me."

"Seems simple enough."

"It is and it isn't. Keep your eyes peeled for anything out of the ordinary. If you question it at all, let me or Tien know."

Jak nodded, her eyes already flitting between the two screens.

"I mean it, Jak. Don't worry about being wrong or getting a false positive. We want false positives."

"I got it, Torrin." She'd discovered that the lines of numbers needed much more constant attention than the chart, but that she could flick her eyes over to peruse it and be back before the screen of numbers had completely changed. A new blip sprang to life on the monitor and she inhaled to say something before realizing that Torrin had put the *Calamity Jane* into motion. "I take it the new blip is us?"

"That's right. Good catch."

Torrin sounded a little distant and Jak spared her a quick glance. The smuggler had her attention split between multiple screens. Her motions were much more muted than they had been before and the *Jane* crept along in response to her tense commands. By watching the system chart, Jak could track their progress and still keep an eye on her readouts. She had to keep the chart-watching to a minimum however. When she watched for too long, the lines kept trying to writhe into the too-familiar lines of Orthodoxan topography. They went away with a blink, however, and with Jak's renewed focus on the numbers readout. Jak decided not to say anything to Torrin. She was already tense enough; there was no point in worrying her.

At first, their trajectory puzzled her. They were heading into the system, but away from Haefen. She smiled when she realized what was going on. That was clever. Torrin was maneuvering to keep Haefen and as many other planets between their ship and the League picket. Her slow pace mirrored their movement around the planet. They were on a slow trajectory to the next planet in the system, a smaller, brilliant yellow gas giant. From her dimly remembered school days, she thought it was called Cwikfyr. It had something to do with the color, though she couldn't recall exactly what the connection was.

As she followed their cautious course, she couldn't help but tense up through the shoulders. Jak flexed her muscles, trying to relax like she did when out on a run. It was different though. When she was stalking a target, she controlled the pace. Torrin was running things now. She knew better than to try to second-guess Torrin's actions. This was clearly her area of expertise. Jak still would have been happier if she'd been in charge.

They continued their steady progress into the system. The longer they were at it, the more Jak felt like she did when she was stalking a target. Torrin's tactics were very similar, not leaving herself exposed for any longer than she had to. During the short periods when they were exposed, Torrin piloted with deliberate care, doing everything in her power not to attract the attention of their targets.

As they hugged the far side of the fourth planet, Jak was tenser than ever. Recognizing Torrin's strategy was helping her trust the smuggler, but she still wasn't used to being in someone else's hands in this type of situation. The next planet was Haefen and she couldn't see how they were going to make it to the surface without being spotted.

"What now?" Jak asked.

"We wait." Tension sang in every line of Torrin's hunched form. "They'll make a mistake sooner or later. They're good and they know that someone's getting to the surface, but they can't keep this up forever."

"Got it." She was used to having to outwait her prey and settled into her seat, flexing her muscles to keep them limber. It was a little funny how she'd slipped into the state of hypervigilance she used to such good effect when sniping. The circumstances were so much different than the times she'd gone sneaking through the woods, but still so familiar. This time she was the spotter, more or less.

"Keep an eye on your screen and let me know if you see a point where both ships are obscured along this sight path." Torrin tapped some entries into her console and a blinking line appeared on the system chart. "We won't have much of an opportunity so we'll need to jump on it when it presents itself."

"I can do that." Jak stared at the console. She could approximate when the other ships would likely be obscured by Haefen's bulk. "Tien, can you show me the sensor envelope for the two ships?"

"Affirmative Jak." Lighted cones of bright yellow sprang up around the League ship icons on her console. At the moment at least one of the cones would intercept their ship if they ventured out from behind the planet. The color of the cone reminded her of the sun, which gave her an idea.

"Tien, can you maintain sort of a shadow on the screen?" There was no answer from the AI and Jak knew that she'd confused her. Hell, she was confusing herself. She knew what she wanted, but she wasn't sure how to articulate the question.

"What are you thinking, babe?" Jak looked up to see Torrin watching her from across the bridge.

"We've been hiding out behind planets because it's harder for their sensors to pick us up right?"

"Yep. It's not foolproof, but large masses in space disrupt sensor beams. We're a very small target by design, so hiding in the wake of the planets helps us to stay much less visible."

"So if we keep a planet or some other mass between us and them, it's harder for them to see us."

"Right." Torrin watched her, eyes intent. Jak inhaled, pleased to know that Torrin was letting her work through this. Torrin trusted her and valued her input and Jak loved her for that as much as anything else.

"And if we can get out from behind this planet and keep one or both of Haefen's moons between us and them, then we can avoid their sensors."

"Yes and no. Moons are smaller and if we're not hugging them then we'll be picked up eventually."

"But it will buy us some time right? Time we could use to get to the surface?"

Her question was met with a slow nod. "Tien, calculate the pattern of dispersal that both moons will cause within the League sensor envelopes."

"Affirmative Torrin." The yellow envelopes were abruptly bisected with areas of negative space. It looked like the moons were casting shadows, with the ships as the light sources.

"Good thinking, honey. You're going to be a natural at this smuggling business."

Jak grinned. "Thanks Torrin. It feels a lot like stalking a target."

"I'm glad you're on my side. If you were on the bridge of one of those League ships, I think I'd be in some trouble."

"The only side I'm on is yours, love." Jak still wasn't comfortable with Torrin's animosity toward the League, but she knew better than to confront her on it. The ships were blocking their access to the surface, and she didn't have time to consider the merits of each side's argument.

Jak settled back in her seat and kept her eye on the screen. Torrin worked away at her station, monitoring their power output and keeping them barely out of orbit, holding them steady in the safety of the planet's lee. Slowly, Jak felt herself slipping into the watchful, semimeditative state of her training. She let the quietness wash over her, content in the knowledge that Torrin was there, watching her back.

The League ships continued their orbit of Haefen. Torrin watched with growing frustration as they kept up their circuit. So far, they hadn't shown any sign of falling out of sync. They were burning precious time, trapped on the far side of the fourth planet. Jak sat behind the other console, watching the slow dance of the League ships as it played out on her monitor. She barely moved and Torrin kept glancing at her to make sure she was still breathing. The trance was familiar; she'd seen it when they'd been traveling through Haefen's wilderness. It had unnerved her then and apparently it still did.

All they needed was one break. Jak had rightly pointed out how they could use Haefen's moons as cover. Torrin spent her time watching for a break and calculating the best trajectory to the planet's surface. Using Haefen's moons was an excellent idea, and she had expanded the plan to include the fourth planet's moons. But the moons all orbited their respective planets at different rates and she kept continually revising their course. She wanted to be ready at the first sign of an opening and she wasn't going to waste precious moments keying in a new course.

It had been six hours and Torrin keyed in the latest course change. After a dozen changes, she'd lost track of how many courses she'd plotted. That had been a couple of hours before. Fortunately, plotting a course was second nature to her and she was able to work it out while keeping an eye on the nearest consoles.

"Hey." Jak sat forward and stared at her console. "Hey! Torrin, the numbers dropped way down. I think we're going to get a—yes, there it is!"

"I see it!" Torrin glanced over at the long-range sensors and watched them register a moderate drop. For a moment, both League ships had finally slipped behind the planet. Without pausing to think about it, Torrin activated her course in the computer and punched up the engines. They whined in protest at the sudden demand for output, but they complied. Torrin trusted Tien to take care of any proximity alerts. The AI would feed the information to Torrin's station and she would steer to compensate.

This latest course took them away from the fourth planet at an oblique angle and sent them spiraling toward Haefen. They had to match the orbit of the *Icarus* and the second League ship for as long as they could while staying on the far side of the planet. There was still the chance that a particularly alert sensor tech would catch the fluctuations in the ambient power levels of the system. Torrin suspected that at least one, if not both, of the ships was going through a shift change. It would account for the slipup in pacing. If that was the case, then they might get a little more of an opening. Torrin would exploit any weakness if it meant getting Jak to the surface that much faster.

The proximity alarm sounded and Torrin sent the *Calamity Jane* into a looping spiral to avoid a rogue asteroid passing through the system. There weren't many of them in this corner of the galaxy, which was good for Haefen and the other planets in the system. All the planets had many fewer impact craters than she was used to seeing on Nadierzda. Her home planet hadn't been hit by any significant meteors since it had been colonized by Zana Krikorian and her motley crew. That Nadierzda had been shifted away from the asteroid field at some point along the terraforming process also made her planet safer.

The two ships were still unaware of their presence, and she planned to keep it that way. It would be easier for them to leave if the League pickets didn't know they'd slipped in. *How did Nat and Rudrani manage to get by?* She'd scanned for debris that might belong to another ship as soon as she'd realized the picket had been doubled. To her relief, nothing had come up on her sensors.

As they got within a few kilometers of Haefen's atmosphere, Torrin cut the engines and trusted their momentum to slide them into orbit. The League ships had kept a constant speed, and she matched it, sitting right outside their sensor envelope. The atmosphere would obscure them from sensors. Not completely, and a sudden power surge would snag the attention of one—if not both—of the ships, especially if they happened to be orbiting close by. She and Jak had run into that misfortune when they'd left Haefen the first time.

As atmosphere buffeted the ship, Torrin powered the engines back up, but not to full capacity. It would take longer, but she could use a tiny fraction of their output to guide them down to the surface. She pored over a chart of the planet's surface. Tien had mapped the planet as best she could when they'd left. There were some major gaps; they'd only been able to grab images of one side of the planet. Fortunately, those images included Fort Marshall. The fort was in the opposite direction from their current trajectory, and Torrin settled in for the trip around the planet. Reversing direction would put them within sensor range of one of the orbiting ships. She didn't think it was the *Icarus*.

It was unlikely that the ship would pick up their presence, but she wasn't going to give them the chance. The comm crackled to life and Torrin swore.

"Unidentified vessel, disengage your engines, enter orbit and stand by to be boarded." The voice was familiar; apparently the same League officer was still in command of the *Icarus*. How had they even noticed the *Calamity Jane*? The closest ship of the two was the other ship and if either of them was going to notice them, it should have been that one.

"What are we going to do?" Jak's voice was tight with concern.

"We're not going to do what they say, that's for sure." Torrin wasn't even going to slow down. Far from it, she punched up the engines. "The ride's about to get rough. Make sure you're strapped in."

As she picked up speed, she noticed the *Icarus* come around the far moon. The damn League bastards had used their own trick against them. It was a good move, she admitted to herself. One of these days, she wanted to meet the captain of that ship.

"Unidentified vessel," the *Icarus*'s captain said, her voice frosty, "you have not complied with our directives. If you do not return to orbit and power down immediately, we will open fire."

"I'd like to see you try to hit us," Torrin muttered. "Tien, execute evasive maneuvers."

While the AI put the ship through a series of high-speed evasions, Torrin would be able to steer them closer to the surface. It was a pity that Haefen wasn't more densely populated. If they happened to be over a settlement, the *Icarus* would hesitate to fire. From the corner of her eye, she could see Jak's knuckles, white on the edge of her console. The buffeting of the atmosphere had increased when Torrin kicked up their speed, and Tien's maneuvers were tossing them around. They were close enough to the surface that shipboard gravity had been overwhelmed. Competing gravities could be extremely uncomfortable, not to mention lethal, and shipboard gravity had automatically deactivated when they entered Haefen's gravity well. Unfortunately, being subject to the planet's gravity meant that there was a definite up and down and it wasn't the ship's deck any longer. When Tien slammed them into a barrel roll, Torrin could hear Jak yelp.

"If you're going to lose it, try to miss the console," Torrin yelled, her attention still on the screen. "Tien, keep an eye out for that other ship. The *Icarus* will have notified them of our presence."

"Affirmative Torrin." The AI's dispassionate tone betrayed no evidence of the various tasks she was performing.

A bright light flashed past the *Jane's* stern and Torrin piloted them through the tail end of a plasma burst. That was their warning shot. The placement of the next one would be much more accurate. At least it wasn't a torpedo. Torrin had been right about the League's reluctance to wipe out a Haefonian farming village. She dropped the *Jane's* nose and screamed down through thickening layers of atmosphere. Dimly, she heard Jak retching as the buffeting increased. The sour smell of stomach acid and bile assaulted her nostrils, and she clenched her stomach to keep her own gorge from rising in response.

A series of plasma bursts streaked past the ship. They hadn't been expecting her to dive toward the planet and the shots went wide. It was a risky maneuver, one that could tear her ship to pieces. All she needed was to hit a particularly strong updraft and she would lose a wing.

"Torrin, the second League ship has joined the *Icarus*. Both vessels are now in pursuit."

"Good."

"How could that possibly be good?" Jak gasped. The occasional heave still wracked her frame, but she seemed to have thrown up everything in her stomach.

"At least it's not on an intercept course. The captain of the other ship isn't nearly as good as the *Icarus*." It wasn't a terrible maneuver, but on an intercept course the ship could have blown them out of existence with impunity.

Torrin glanced at the viewscreen. Haefen's swathes of blue had filled the screen, broken only by the white of snow-capped peaks. She couldn't get caught in those. Not only would the pursuing ships have an excellent idea of where she was headed, but the updrafts were too unpredictable.

"Jak, check the planet chart and tell me which direction to go so I'm over ocean."

"Got it." She paused for a moment as she glanced over the planet's topography. "Head north."

Torrin yanked hard on the *Jane's* yoke, skewing the ship to the left, turning her laboring ship to the north. The ship's entire frame groaned from the strain of her maneuvers. Dodging fire from two ships was much more difficult than dodging one. It was a good thing that the *Jane's* exterior was already black. They'd had enough close calls that plasma burns would have scorched off large chunks of any other paint job. After a couple of harrowing minutes and as many close calls, they were over the ocean. As soon as Torrin saw they were over the intense blue of Haefen's oceans, she threw the yoke forward, sending the ship into a steep dive. They needed to get within a few hundred meters of the planet's surface. Once there, the League ships should back off.

All they had to do was to hold it together. Torrin gave her ship a silent apology as the *Jane* shuddered and creaked around them. Her hull pinged and protested in response to the enormous pressures being exerted by Torrin's erratic course changes and Tien's continued maneuvers.

"Holy shit!" Jak was watching the water's surface come at them with incredible speed. She seemed to be trying to scramble behind her chair, but the safety harness held her firmly in place.

Torrin wanted to time it down to the last second before she straightened out. She prayed that the ship would hold together that long. Finally, when it seemed that they were about to impact the surface of the water, Torrin hauled back on the yoke and leveled the *Calamity Jane* back out. The noise and buffeting of the wind abruptly died out, leaving the tortured whine of the engines and Jak's panicked panting as the only sounds.

She couldn't rest on her laurels though. The gunners on the League ships would have no compunctions about taking potshots at her over open water. She needed to get them back over to land. They were out of their dive, so updrafts wouldn't cause them much trouble beyond the occasional bout of turbulence. Torrin pulled on the yoke and yawed the *Jane* over as plasma bursts rained down toward them. More close calls singed the outside of their hull, but beyond the heeling of the ship in response, no damage was done.

The coastline filled the viewscreen, and suddenly they were flying over tall trees. If someone had told Torrin how happy she'd be to see the Haefonian rainforest after her earlier ordeals there, she would have laughed in their face or slugged them in the jaw. Maybe both. But as the tops of the trees passed below them and the League ships peeled off, she heaved a sigh of relief.

"So, how does it feel to be home?" Torrin asked.

CHAPTER SEVEN

The first thing Jak noticed when she stepped out of the *Calamity Jane* was the smell. Jak hadn't realized how much she'd missed the scents of rich loam and dampness until they filled her nostrils again. She inhaled deeply and let the scents of home fill her nose. Homesickness flooded her. It was funny that she hadn't really felt any nostalgia until she was back on Haefen.

She was in the street clothes she'd gotten on Nadi. Her Devonite uniform had been trashed, and she wasn't comfortable wearing her militia uniform on Haefen. There was nothing about the cut of her clothing to betray her gender, and the breastbinder was back on. Torrin hadn't said anything when she'd put it on, but Jak couldn't see facing her people without it. She took a deep breath, but the binder still felt too tight. She hadn't gained any weight while on Nadi, quite the opposite in fact, but the binder made her felt heavier, confined.

Torrin proceeded down the cargo bay ramp and Jak hurried behind her. They'd finally set down in a small field a short way outside Fort Marshall. This was not the first time this patch of ground had been used by a spaceship; long burns marred the ground. Jak doubted, however, that the field had been there very long. It seemed likely that

Torrin's transport ships had also been using it. There was no sign of Nat's ship, which was disappointing. She wouldn't have minded getting to see Torrin's sister again.

"Ma'am," said a uniformed Devonite enlisted man. "We weren't told when to expect you." His hand twitched as if he wanted to salute. If Jak had to hazard a guess, she would have said that he was fresh out of basic training. She shifted herself so she stood a little behind Torrin, not hiding, exactly, merely being unobtrusive.

"Why would you be expecting us?" Torrin asked.

"Command said that another ship would be along, but that it might take a little time."

Torrin looked confused but didn't push the issue. "You might as well take us to Central Command. He'll want to see us." She raised her voice slightly when he looked ready to object. "Tell him Torrin Ivanov is here."

This time the young soldier did salute. "I'll pass the request along to my superior officer. You should wait here while I contact him."

"I don't think so," Torrin said. "We're going to head into the fort. I know the way."

"That's not a good idea, ma'am. Women shouldn't go about unaccompanied inside."

With that, Jak's sense of homesickness was snuffed out. Once again, she was forced to put on the charade. "I'll make sure no harm comes to her, soldier," she rasped, stepping out from behind Torrin.

"I'm sorry, sir, I didn't see you there." He paused and looked at her more closely. Jak was glad for the breastbinder; it hid her inconvenient breasts from his gaze. "Are you…They said you were dead. You're Sniper Sergeant Stowell, aren't you?"

Jak sighed. She'd been hoping to disguise her identity a little longer.

"Yes, he is," Torrin said. "You're not to reveal his identity to anybody however. His presence here is highly classified. General Callahan will not be pleased to hear that his identity has been compromised."

The young soldier swallowed hard. "Then I'll go let my commanding officer know that you're on your way to the fort. Ma'am. Sergeant." He saluted again and scurried off.

Torrin took the lead. Jak knew that she didn't really know the way. The last time they'd been there, Torrin hadn't been at the fort long enough to really get her bearings. Jak supposed it had been easier to tell the young Devonite that Torrin knew the way than it would have been to explain that she had an AI giving her step-by-step directions as they walked. Fort Marshall was well within the range of Torrin's subdermal transmitter.

The trek to the main gate took them about twenty minutes. Jak took in their surroundings. The trees were as she remembered, tall and majestic, their canopies stretching to block out the sun. A sense of calm seeped into her muscles and deeper into her bones. Everything was the right color, shades of blue that soothed her vision.

Torrin led them unerringly to the gate, for which Jak was grateful. Her condition had deteriorated to the point where she found it very difficult to stay on the right track, even when she could see where they were going. The urge to conform to the erroneous information her brain was feeding her was almost irresistible.

That she knew the information her brain was sending her down the wrong path only made it worse. One part of her mind tried to point her in the right direction, but the other part, the corrupted part, was growing steadily stronger. Jak only hoped the condition was still reversible. She hadn't mentioned the possibility to Torrin; she hadn't wanted to worry her. Torrin was twitchy enough about the whole business. Delaying probably hadn't been the best move, but she'd had responsibilities to fulfill on Nadierzda. If Torrin had known, she would have insisted that they leave before things were settled. In order to put Nadi's military affairs in some semblance of order, she'd had to downplay the seriousness of her condition. It was a choice she'd make again if she had to.

"Sergeant. Ma'am." A Devonite soldier came to attention in front of them. They were right outside the gates of the fort. The man didn't salute, but he nodded gravely to them. "General Callahan would like you to attend to him immediately."

"Of course," Torrin said.

Jak returned the soldier's nod. He was a sergeant, exactly like she was. Well, not quite like she was. From his collar insignia, he was in the artillery brigade. *No sense of finesse*, she thought a touch derisively. *Why use a scalpel when a sledgehammer will do the job?*

"Follow me." He stepped up to the gates and gestured to the sentries who stepped to either side. A small lorry idled inside the gate and he pointed them at it. "Hop in."

Jak easily climbed into the back of the small truck. Finding the right hand and footholds was only a matter of muscle memory. Torrin's climb into the truck was more of a scramble, and her face clouded in irritation as she struggled to find a graceful way in. She ignored Jak's outstretched hand and gave herself one final heave into the backseat. Torrin hated looking silly, Jak knew, but she hated being beholden to someone else even more. It was a little amusing, the way they settled so easily back into the patterns of their previous visit. Jak wondered if Torrin even realized that she was treating her the same way she had before she'd known Jak was a woman. She would have accepted Jak's help on Nadi, but she couldn't allow herself to be seen accepting a man's help on Haefen.

"You all right?" Jak muttered when Torrin settled herself.

She received a crooked smile for her concern. "I was going to ask you the same thing." Torrin's hand twitched toward hers before she moved it back to lie on her thigh. "I think you've got more to worry about than I do."

"I'm fine." It wasn't that big a lie, Jak told herself. She was happy to be back where everything looked like it ought to. Though, had everything been so blue before? Being back in the environment wasn't the problem, dealing with the people was.

"So am I."

The truck took off with a squeal. Jak rode the bounce easily, her body remembering the movement of trucks over roads and around tight turns. Torrin grabbed onto the side of the open back and her seat to keep from being bounced around.

"You should put on your harness," Jak yelled over the roar of the engine, taking care to roughen her voice. She'd been out of character as Sergeant Stowell for too long. The persona that had once been second nature was going to require her attention to keep up until she got used to it again.

"I don't see you putting one on," Torrin replied. She made no effort to be heard over the engine, but Jak could make out what she said anyway. Grudgingly, she did strap herself into the harness. She didn't think it was necessary, but with Torrin's glare, she gracefully bowed to the pressure and secured herself.

The ride through the fort's narrow streets was hurried, and soon Jak was glad for the additional support. She would easily have been thrown through the lorry's open back without it. The driver laid on the horn to hurry people out of his way. Their escort hung onto the roll bar in grim silence. He would sneak the occasional look back at them but made no move to engage them in further conversation. His interest was divided equally between the two of them. Which of them was more fascinating, Jak wondered, the exotic smuggler from another planet or the sniper returned from the dead? For one crazy moment, she had the urge to ask him but was able to clamp down on the insane impulse. A smirk crawled onto her face and a laugh bubbled within her. Try as she might, she couldn't wipe the small smile off her face. The best she could do was to throttle the urge to laugh. Torrin's elbow in her side didn't help. She had to bite her lip.

"What's wrong with you?" Torrin hissed.

"I'm not sure," Jak wheezed.

"Pull yourself together or you're going to blow our hand." She glared at Jak, who only found Torrin's ire more hilarious.

"I'm sorry, I'm sorry." In desperation Jak closed her eyes and tried to think about something else. Anything else. The northeast corner of Sector 27 had some broken ridges running through it. *Not that.* Her eyes popped open, the urge to laugh gone. The ridgelines swam before Jak's eyes and wouldn't go away until she blinked several times. That hadn't happened before. *Not good.* The harder it was to clear the erroneous information, the worse the condition was getting. It was a good thing they were here; Jak didn't think she had a lot of time left.

"What's wrong?" Concern shot through Torrin's voice.

"The data corruption is getting worse. Nothing we haven't expected."

As soothing as she tried to be, she could tell Torrin wasn't buying it. Torrin stared at her, dismayed. Once again her hand twitched over, but she stopped before taking Jak's hand. Being able to feel Torrin's touch would have helped her feel better, Jak admitted to herself. She was scared, and Torrin made her feel like they could take anything on together. The truck stopped in front of the nondescript building that Jak remembered from her last visit.

"Central Command is waiting for you," their escort said as he climbed out of the front passenger seat.

"Good," Torrin said, already moving to get out of the truck. "We can't afford to wait." She clambered out a good deal more gracefully than she had entered. Jak grabbed the roll bar and swung herself over to land on the ground.

The soldier held the side door open for them. Jak took the lead for a moment before realizing that she had no idea how to get them to the general's office. She stopped, confused. As had become normal, when she tried to orient herself, she found herself retracing the steps of their journey through the Haefonian wilderness.

With a strange look, the sergeant took the lead. Torrin gave Jak a tight smile of commiseration and strode after him. Jak lengthened her stride to keep up with them. The soldier was really taking Torrin's words to heart. He kept up a good clip to the point where Jak was on the edge of breaking into a jog to keep up with them.

They traversed the corridors in a hurry. The few men they came across wisely stayed out of the way of the strange little group. The office they ended up in wasn't familiar to Jak. The last time she'd been in this building, she'd met with the Intel and Ops colonels on another floor. A young lieutenant stood up from behind a small desk when they entered.

"I'll let General Callahan know you're here," he said. "Sergeant, thank you for bringing them so swiftly. You can go now."

The sergeant snapped off a sharp salute and slipped out the door.

"Miss Ivanov and Sniper Sergeant Stowell." The lieutenant paused to size Jak up. "Word was you died, Sergeant."

"Word was wrong, sir." Jak brought herself up to attention and snapped off her own salute. For all that she hadn't used that salute for months, the crispness of the salute shivered through her body.

"I see." He looked her up and down a final time. "Please wait here. Both of you."

Jak didn't relax until the lieutenant left the room and then it was only to drop into parade rest. The officer hadn't looked overly happy to see her. He hadn't seemed angry, not exactly. She supposed she qualified as a deserter, and fear quivered in the pit of her stomach. As a deserter, they weren't obligated to treat her. They could let the data corruption take its inevitable course.

"Are you all right?" Torrin asked her in a low voice. "You look like you're about to pass out."

"They think I'm a deserter," Jak said. Her voice didn't quiver, and for that she was thankful and amazed. She bit off a bitter laugh. "I guess they're right. At this point, they don't owe me anything."

"We'll just see about that. If they want to keep dealing with me, they need to keep me happy. I'll call the whole deal off if they won't treat you."

Call the whole deal off? Jak knew how much this deal meant to Torrin, to Nadierzda. Without the revenue the Haefonian implant technology could bring, Torrin's planet wouldn't be able to complete the terraforming process. Nadierzda would be choked with dust and silt in less than a generation. She shook her head mutely. Her well-being wasn't as important as the planet's. She opened her mouth to tell Torrin that in no uncertain terms, but her protest died in her throat when the door at the back of the office opened. Jak pulled herself back to attention and saluted again.

The lieutenant finally returned her salute and gestured them in. "He's waiting for you."

This is it. Jak took a deep breath and prepared herself for the worst.

"Thank you," Torrin said and brushed past the young officer. Jak followed on her heels. The lieutenant closed the door behind them.

Behind the desk, General Callahan stood. To one side of the room, Colonels Wolfe and Elsby stood as well. Jak saluted again and Torrin wondered if her arm was getting tired. General Callahan returned her salute and then waved at her with one hand.

"Sergeant Stowell," Colonel Wolfe said, "you're looking awfully good for someone who's supposed to have died behind enemy lines."

"I'm sorry, sir," Jak replied. She kept her gaze fixed on the far wall and didn't look him in the eye.

"You're sorry?" His eyebrows lowered dangerously as he glared at her.

"That's not important right now," Torrin interrupted Wolfe. She turned her attention to the general. "We need something from you, and I'm not going to take no for an answer."

"Miss Ivanov. Torrin. Of course we will do whatever we can–"

Torrin leaned forward, palms down on his desk, her face inches from his. "I mean it. You get in my way and our deal is done."

Something was wrong, Torrin could feel it. The men were too nervous. There was more going on than simply taking a deserter to task.

Jak must have felt it also. "Torrin…" she said in a quiet voice.

"Not now, Jak." Torrin held up a hand in her direction, silencing her. She wasn't going to be put off now, and if she had to steamroll them into agreeing, she would. The core of Jak's personality, and who knew what else, was at stake. No matter how brave a face her lover was putting on it, things were bad. Her lapse in the hall was one too many and too close to the last one. This *would* be resolved, and now.

"Sergeant Stowell needs medical treatment. She's suffering from data corruption and needs to be taken care of. Now."

"She?" The shocked exclamation came from three throats in ragged unison. Heat suffused Jak's face and she looked up at the ceiling. The muscle at the corner of her jaw jumped; Torrin could see it from where she stood.

As soon as the words left Torrin's mouth, she wished she had them back. She quickly recognized there was nothing else she could do. The tiger was well and truly out of the cage. It was time to keep going as if she'd meant to let the revelation drop. She continued on as the three officers gaped and stared, back and forth between her and Jak.

"Don't even think you can deny her treatment based on her gender either." Better to let the mess play out as if she'd intended it to go this way. Jak could hate her for this later; she certainly had every right to. This was not how Torrin had meant for the information to come out, not at all. She kept her focus on the Devonite officers in front of her. It was better than looking at Jak. "I'm serious. If you withhold treatment from Jak for any reason, I will take my goods elsewhere."

General Callahan recovered first while the colonels continued to stare. "Sergeant Stowell has been an excellent asset for us. Of course we'll take care of him. Uh her."

"We're going to do what?" Wolfe's face had grown ugly. It was redder than Jak's, but not from embarrassment. "Not only did this… whore desert, but she was serving under false pretenses in the first place." He sneered. "We should leave her be. Let her deal with the consequences of her actions."

"You call her a whore again, and I will kill you," Torrin said. She struggled to keep her voice level. Her hand twitched and she clenched it to keep from striking the colonel.

Elsby barked a short laugh. "Really Wolfe. You can't be mad at her both for enlisting when she shouldn't have and for deserting." Wolfe shot him a murderous look which he shrugged off. Elsby looked uncomfortable, but at least he didn't look ready to tear someone's head off.

Now that the initial shock had worn off, Callahan was dealing with the bombshell quite well.

"You already knew, didn't you?" Torrin accused.

He vacillated a bit, glancing over at the apoplectic Wolfe. "Not about her specifically. But I've known for decades that we've had women serving in the ranks."

"What?" Wolfe shot to his feet. "You've known we've had females in our ranks and you haven't done anything about it?"

"Calm down, Colonel," Callahan said. "It only makes sense. If you'd get past your wounded ego for not having picked the sergeant out, you'd see that. Our men are a finite resource and if our women want to go to all the trouble of enlisting, then why not? Obviously, the ones we've got are resourceful enough not to get caught. Sergeant Stowell is a prime example of the kind of person we want serving. After all, she still has more confirmed kills than any other sniper, and that's without counting most of her production over the past two years."

"Did you think we haven't used women in any other capacity over the past thirty years?" Elsby said, a shade scornfully. "I have a number of operatives and informants who are women. Orthodoxans don't pay any attention to women. They think they're too 'inferior' to be taken seriously."

Wolfe didn't say anything to either of them. He exhaled sharply through widely dilated nostrils and sat back down into his chair. Sitting didn't seem to do much for his blood pressure. He might not have been standing, but he certainly wasn't any calmer.

"Sergeant." Callahan paused before taking a deep breath and pulling himself together before continuing. Maybe he wasn't as resigned to all of this as he pretended. "We will do what we can to take care of your problem. Torrin said it was data corruption?"

"Yes sir." Jak had brought herself up to attention again. Her muscles seemed to tremble on the edge of movement, though she held herself rigidly still. It seemed to Torrin that Jak was purposefully avoiding looking at her.

Callahan gestured at the chairs in front of his desk. "Sit down, would you? I'm getting exhausted watching you salute all over the place. There's a time and a place, son." He looked embarrassed at his slip but said nothing further.

Jak looked him in the eye for the first time since Torrin's untimely revelation. Having apparently assured herself that he was serious, she gingerly took a seat. Perched on the edge, she looked ready to leap to her feet at the first sign of his disapproval. Torrin slid into the other chair.

When Callahan waved her on, Jak continued. "Sir, it's from the last data upload I had before I went out after...well, after Torrin, as it turned out."

"That was months ago," Elsby said, sounding horrified. "That upload should have been erased weeks ago."

"Yes sir. In all the excitement, I forgot. And then it was too late."

"Maybe the 'sergeant' would like to tell us more about her desertion." Wolfe's voice was heavy with sarcasm.

"I don't think—" Torrin started.

"It's okay, Torrin." Jak's voice was firm, and she received a pair of startled looks from Elsby and Callahan. "I'm not ashamed of my actions, sir," Jak said to Wolfe with quiet dignity. "I took almost two straight weeks of stims, sir. Sirs. When it was decided that Torrin needed to be returned to the ship, Captain McCullock sent me into the trenches to evaluate enemy defenses."

"Not the brightest move by the good captain," Elsby observed quietly.

"A brilliant move if you realize someone's immune system is severely compromised and you want to get rid of them without anyone being the wiser." Torrin couldn't let the colonel's comment go by. Let them know that McCullock had tried to kill Jak.

Jak sent Torrin a quelling look and she subsided. "I got sick, sir. Really sick. I knew we had to get Torrin to her ship so she could open lines of supply to us, but I couldn't go to the doctor. If I was found out…Well, I couldn't let that happen. So I got Torrin past the fence and she got me to her ship. Once we got past the fence, I knew there was no coming back for me."

"And yet, here you are, Stowell." Callahan's voice was quiet and sympathetic. "I have a couple of daughters, you know." Torrin looked at him, taken aback by the non sequitur. He smiled at her, amused at her reaction. "The older one is very traditional. She's been married for three years and has given me my first grandchild. The younger one has a wild streak. She's not interested in marriage. She's more like me than my son is and I don't know what we're going to do with her when she reaches majority."

"Sir." Jak was plainly at a loss for words. Torrin imagined she would have a hard time feeling up to advising a superior officer, let alone the head of their armed forces.

"It's nothing, really. But you've given me a lot to think about."

"General, this isn't the reason you wanted to see Miss Ivanov." Wolfe's interruption was smooth. He'd recovered his composure and smiled at her a little too widely.

"You're right, Wolfe, it isn't." Callahan stood up and walked around the front of his desk. "I thought you'd come in response to the message we sent your people, but you haven't mentioned it."

"What message?" Torrin was confused. She hadn't had any communication from Nat's ship. She also hadn't been expecting any contact from them until they got home. Because of the League's blockade of the planet, there were no working comm relays in the vicinity. Nobody in the system would have a legitimate reason to use them, so the League would have removed the relays as one of their first steps in setting up the picket on the planet. Unfortunately, it seems that Nat and Rudrani had left the planet while she and Jak were on their way here. It was likely their paths had crossed while each had been in cryostasis for the journey.

"One of your women has been killed and another one's disappeared."

Torrin jumped to her feet, then teetered there, uncertain what to do next. Her heart raced. It couldn't be. Not Nat. She tried to calm her rampaging thoughts, to focus them on the situation at hand. *Irenya is going to kill me! And I'd let her. How could I have been so stupid? Nat wasn't ready for this trip. She's so young. Too young to-* Torrin tore her mind away from the rest of the thought. It was too horrible to contemplate.

"What do you know, sir?" Jak's voice was strong—worried, but strong. She looked like she wanted to reach over and touch Torrin, to give her some comfort. The strength helped Torrin focus, and she plopped herself back into the chair. Her landing was less than graceful as she collapsed more than sat.

"My men have been out looking for your missing woman for two weeks, ever since she disappeared," Callahan hastened to assure Torrin.

"Who was killed?"

"Her name was Rudrani?" Callahan looked to Wolfe and Elsby for confirmation and they nodded.

Torrin sagged with relief. Not Nat then. But if Rudrani was the one who was killed, then that meant that… "Nat's the one who's missing." It wasn't a question, she didn't need to ask. Her voice was so flat, she barely recognized it. This time, Jak did reach out. She covered Torrin's hand with her own and gave her a quick squeeze which she barely felt.

"Is it Nat Ivanov, sir?" Jak asked.

"Yes."

Torrin's vision grayed out for a moment and her ears roared.

"Your woman, Rudrani, was shot through the throat."

Pain in her hand shocked Torrin back to reality. She looked down. Jak's hand was clamped around hers so hard the knuckles had gone white.

"Through the neck?" Jak's voice was hollow and distorted. All of the blood had drained from her face. It was completely gray. A muscle in Jak's jaw jumped and her eyes were flat. Dead. "Was the bullet red?"

"It was."

CHAPTER EIGHT

Jak paced the floor of the general's small office. The three officers watched her closely while Torrin stared at a spot on the floor. There were no tears from her, not yet. At the moment, she seemed numb, shocked beyond comprehension.

"I want to see the spot where Nat was kidnapped, sir," Jak said.

"Absolutely," General Callahan responded.

"We should leave immediately."

"No." Torrin's emphatic negative drew the eye of everyone in the office.

"Why not?" Jak was frustrated. They'd already lost so much time, almost two weeks it seemed, and they needed to gain it back somehow. The trail was cold and would only get colder.

"You need your treatment." Torrin brooked no argument, Jak could tell from her tone. She needed to be made to see.

"We need to get on Nat's trail as soon as possible."

"I know that." She looked up at Jak, anguish in her eyes. "But you can barely function right now. We need to give Nat the best chance, and to do that you need to be healthy."

"It's going to put me out of commission for at least a day. We don't have the time."

"Our men have been tracking your missing woman since she was taken," Callahan said.

"She's my sister," Torrin said.

"I see. I'd wondered."

"The problem was that we didn't find out that they were missing for at least twelve hours," Elsby chimed in. "By the time we could have watched the border crossings closely, Crimson was probably already back on the Orthodoxan side."

"Crimson?" Torrin sounded disgusted by the nickname.

"They call him that because of his signature ammunition," Jak explained to Torrin. She addressed the general. "He's always been able to slip back and forth across the fence without any problem, sir. Is there anything else that's being done?"

"Everything we can on this side of the fence," Wolfe responded for the general. "Our men have been checking every known sniper blind and Orthodoxan hidey-hole on our side." His eyes glinted maliciously at her frown. "Surely you're not suggesting we start incursions into Orthodoxan territory for the sake of one…woman." He'd been ready to use a different word than woman, Jak was sure of it. One look at Torrin and the violence she barely held in check had convinced him to use a more acceptable term. Torrin looked ready to destroy something. Or someone. Jak knew Torrin could have taken down any of the men in the room. Given enough focus and the proper impetus, she could have taken them all out, decapitating the command structure of the Devonite armed forces.

The dark road Jak's thoughts had taken surprised her. It also brought home exactly how much of an outsider she'd become. Already, she felt as if she was distancing herself mentally from her home planet. Their struggle didn't matter to her anymore. She needed to kill that sniper and to rescue Nat. She was the only one who could do it.

"You know, Sergeant Stowell," Wolfe said in a conversational tone, "you're probably our best bet for killing Crimson."

"Yes sir," Jak agreed. "I know him better than anyone."

"You certainly do, Sergeant." His voice was silky and Jak wondered what game he was playing. "In fact, he seems to have a special affinity for you or rather those around you. First he takes out your father, then your brother. Now he's taken the sister of your…friend."

"What are you suggesting?" How dare he bring her family into this?

"*Sir*. What are you suggesting, *sir*? The general may think your infractions don't merit any punishment, but until he says otherwise, you are still a part of these armed forces and you will observe the niceties. I can still have you flogged."

Jak exhaled heavily through her nose. As they dicked around, Nat could be Johvah-knows-where and he wanted to make sure she was observing proper military etiquette? "What are you suggesting, *sir*?" Jak asked, pushing the words through tightly gritted teeth. Her jaws ached.

Wolfe smiled, lips thin. "Why nothing, of course, Sergeant. You couldn't possibly be Crimson, this last attack happened while you were offworld." He paused, then started again as if something had only now occurred to him. "Of course, we only have your word, that of an admitted liar, and Miss Ivanov's, a smuggler. You'll forgive me if I don't take your word for it. How do we know you aren't the sniper? While we're at it, how do we know that your friend here isn't playing both sides of the fight?"

Jak took a step toward him and was pulled short by an iron grip on her wrist. She looked down in shock to see Torrin's hand clamped around her lower arm. Torrin shook her head once and pulled Jak down into her seat.

"Colonel!" Callahan's voice was a whipcrack. "Now is not the time!"

"What is he talking about, Callahan?" Torrin's voice was quiet, and she glared at Wolfe like she hoped his head might explode from the force of her stare. "Of course I'm not funding the Orthodoxans. They were going to kill me. Or worse."

Callahan sighed and reached into his desk. He withdrew a lumpy object wrapped in canvas and wordlessly pushed it across the table to her. Torrin picked it up and unwrapped it. She turned a pistol of a variety Jak had never seen before around in her hands.

"Where did you get this?"

"The Orthodoxans have started showing up with them," Callahan said.

"It's not one of mine."

"Of course you'd say that." Wolfe slapped his hand down on the desk with a sharp crack. "You don't want us to know that you're no better than a profiteer!"

Torrin looked at him, her eyes level. Jak knew her lover was doing her best not to lose her composure, though she doubted anyone who didn't know Torrin as well would realize exactly how close to the edge they were treading. "It's a League weapon. My merchandise comes only from sources on the Fringes."

"A likely story." Wolfe's lip curled back and he glared at her.

"A true story. The problem with League weapons is that they come equipped with transponders. You can bet this has one. It wouldn't take long for the League to track me down if I smuggled their weapons. The question is where these came from, and I'm betting the answer's circling right above our heads."

"That is such utter crap. I know your kind, the only thing you want is to make a buck."

Torrin's hand tightened around the barrel of the pistol in her hand until the knuckles pulled white against her skin. "If I'm working with the Orthodoxans, then why did they kill one of my people and kidnap the other?"

"That's what I told you," Elsby said. "Your theory doesn't hold water. Sorry Wolfe."

"You've said enough, Colonel." Callahan jumped in before Wolfe could open his mouth and snap back at Elsby. "You're dismissed."

"Yes sir." Wolfe saluted and stalked from the room, his back ramrod straight.

"Wolfe." Callahan's voice stopped him shy of the door. "Everything that's been said in here is classified. If I hear about any of this outside of this room, I'll have you busted down in rank, and that's for starters."

"Sir." Wolfe stormed through the open door and slammed it behind him.

"He didn't take that well," Callahan said to no one in particular.

"He's a little on the traditional side," Elsby said. "Finding out that one of the men he held in the highest esteem is actually a woman has rocked his neat and ordered world." He shook his head ruefully. "I have to admit, it's thrown me for a bit of a loop also. No disrespect meant, Sergeant."

"Sir." Jak nodded to him.

"He does have a point though," the general continued. "Not about the weapons and certainly not that you could be the sniper. That's ridiculous. But Crimson does have a strange number of intersections with you."

"I can't explain that, sir." It was true and Jak wondered how she could have missed that. He was practically all she'd thought about for two years, and it had never occurred to her to wonder why he'd taken so much from her family.

"Jak," Torrin spoke up for the first time in a while. Her voice was a thin mockery of her usual confident timbre. "You need to get your treatment. While you're doing that, I need all the data you have on Crimson, General." Her emphasis of the sniper's nickname was loaded with disgust. "My ship's AI can analyze the intelligence you've gathered on him and determine if there are any patterns. Maybe we can pin down the sites where he's most comfortable working."

"Sir, I don't think we should be putting this kind of sensitive information into the hands of a civilian." Elsby looked deeply troubled at the idea of Torrin looking through their files.

"Because you've been doing such a good job of finding my sister so far." Torrin stood, hands fisted at her sides. "You need to use all the resources you can marshal at your disposal, General. My ship is now one of those resources. Do you have anything with that kind of computing power?"

"I doubt that very much." Callahan raised his hands in a mollifying gesture to both Torrin and Elsby. "We'll make the information available to you, never fear, Torrin. However, Colonel Elbsy has a point. You are a civilian and you will have access to some very sensitive military information. I want you to have one of ours on hand while you're analyzing the data." When Torrin opened her mouth to protest, Callahan shook his head at her and continued without missing a beat. "It will only be to your advantage. I'll assign one of our intelligence analysts to you. He'll be able to help you interpret some of the data. I'm thinking maybe Lieutenant Smythe?" He cocked an eyebrow in the colonel's direction.

Elsby relaxed perceptibly. "Perfect choice, sir."

"As for you, Sergeant, we need to get you to the doctors as soon as possible."

"I'm afraid I need to respectfully decline, sir." Jak hated disagreeing with the general. Though she wasn't sure quite how far her loyalties extended anymore, she had a great deal of personal respect for the man.

Torrin turned toward her, face like a thundercloud. "I need you, Jak."

"I know you do. But you also need me to take a look at the kill site before it grows any colder. After that, I'll let everyone know what I've read from it. Only then will I go in to the doctors."

"I don't like it. You should get treatment first, then take a look at the site."

"You're not going to win this argument, Torrin." Jak spoke with quiet authority and Torrin glared back at her stubbornly. After a few tense moments, Torrin dropped her eyes in assent.

"If you ladies have worked out your problems…" Callahan watched them closely. Jak stared back at him, face impassive. *He knows about us, I'm sure of it.* The question was, what would he do with his suspicions? Officially, he could have them locked in the stockade and sent up on trial for their perversions. Unofficially, they could be taken out to the woods and shot, then buried in a shallow grave. Those were the best of a large handful of chilling options.

"Colonel, arrange an escort for these two to survey the site of the young Miss Ivanov's abduction. I think it's best if we keep Sergeant Stowell's true identity a secret for now. Is that acceptable, Sergeant?"

"Yes sir. I would prefer that." Jak knew she should feel grateful, but suddenly she didn't relish the idea of being alone in the woods with a squad of men. *He still needs Torrin*, she consoled herself. *Surely, he won't try anything.* The whole line of thinking was paranoid, and she knew it. But she hadn't stayed alive this long without reading all the possibilities and accounting for them.

Why had the sniper taken out Bron, not her, the little voice in the back of her head asked? She was only alive because the sniper had decided to kill someone else, even though he'd had her in his sights more than once. The anger that had been burning through her veins since she learned about the red bullet surged through her with renewed vigor. There was only one way to end this. Jak had to find and kill the bastard. For her father and her brother. For Nat. For herself. She wouldn't be free of him until he was dead at her feet. A little risk couldn't be allowed to get in her way. She would inform Torrin of the danger they were in, but they would have to deal with it and fulfill both their goals.

The top of Hill 372 looked innocuous but for the abandoned spaceship and the partially assembled equipment. Torrin watched as Jak crouched over a patch of ground. She ran her fingertips through the dirt and brought them up to her nose, sniffing at the loam that clung to her hand.

"Did you find something?"

Jak shook her head as she had the half dozen other times Torrin had asked the question. She betrayed no irritation, but Torrin couldn't help but feel that she was pissing off the sniper. She looked around the clearing for something to do and her eye fell on the communications arrays.

"You there." Torrin gestured to one of the groups of soldiers who were scattered through the clearing on the top of the hill. One of the men looked behind him as if wondering who she was referring to. He made a comment to his companions and they chuckled.

"Me miss?" He asked.

"I need all of you."

The man grinned. "She has a healthy appetite," he said to the man beside him, loud enough for Torrin to hear. His companions laughed again, louder this time. They froze at the audible click that echoed through the clearing. The men crouched into watchful positions, weapons out and at the ready. Their careful perusal of the clearing quickly fell upon Jak, who watched them through the scope of her rifle.

"A little respect for Miss Ivanov," was all Jak said in her gravelly voice before putting up her weapon.

The cheeky soldier blanched and nodded jerkily. "Got it, Sarge." Even after her unexplained reappearance, the men still had a healthy fear of Sniper Sergeant Stowell.

"How can we help, Miss Ivanov?" the man's companion asked. The group of six men crossed the clearing to stand before her. Jak's method of intimidation was certainly effective. Gone were the sidelong glances they'd given when they'd thought she wasn't looking. Torrin had actually been looking forward to disabusing them of the notion that she was a poor helpless female. Jak's act of chivalry had been expedient, but it did nothing to convince them she could handle herself.

"You're going to help me assemble this equipment." She gestured to the three arrays around the clearing's edges. "You're going to finish unpacking the crates while I get the specs and some tools."

"Yes, ma'am." They reacted to the command in her tone. She knew how to give orders. Running an intergalactic corporation had made her comfortable with command. It probably didn't hurt that being in charge came naturally.

With one last glance at Jak, Torrin wandered over to the ship. Much as she needed to get inside, she was a little hesitant. What would she find in there? The ship wasn't even completely locked down, though there was no evidence that anyone had entered it. Without prior knowledge of how to open the exterior hatches, it was unlikely the Devonites had been able to puzzle out the locking mechanism. Keeping it that way sounded like a good idea to Torrin, and she blocked the hatch's mechanism with her body while she opened it.

The ship's interior smelled musty. It had been closed up for weeks without the need to run life support. Haefen's dampness had seeped into the ship's cabin. The lights flickered on when she stepped through the hatch.

"Identify yourself," boomed a low female voice. It had a strange accent and Torrin groaned to herself. Not another AI.

"Torrin Ivanov." She turned in a slow circle so the ship's AI could scan her features. "Acknowledge command override alpha-sierra-niner-one." She and her partners had access to top level overrides for every ship in their fleet. Ultimately, the *Melisende* belonged to Troika Corp and the partners had insisted on having the overrides in place. For good reason, as it turned out.

"Override acknowledged," the AI said. "Welcome aboard, Torrin."

"Thank you." Torrin moved forward again, now that she knew the AI wouldn't engage her in hostile action for breaking onto the ship. She headed toward the bridge. The ship's design was similar to her own and she suspected the interior was laid out accordingly. "How may I address you?"

"You may call me Eowyn, Torrin." Eowyn's speech patterns were eerily similar to Tien's, though the voice and accent the AI had chosen were very different.

Torrin entered the bridge and a hologram of a warrior woman bowed formally to her from the main console. As she bowed, the huge sword strapped across her back was very much in evidence. A long braid came out from under the back of her helmet. Torrin nodded in acknowledgment.

"Eowyn, please bring up the schematics for the communications equipment."

The main viewscreen flickered to life and schematics spread out across half the room. Torrin wished she had her tablet, but she'd left it on the *Calamity Jane*, unable to foresee a need for it.

"Torrin, you are investigating the murder and kidnapping of Rudrani and Nat." It was a statement, not a question. Torrin nodded and before she had stopped moving her head, another screen came to life. A view of the clearing unfolded and she recognized Rudrani bent over one of the open boxes. There was no sound, but she could see that Rudrani was speaking to someone off the screen.

Her heart stuttered in her chest when Nat entered the screen. The two women exchanged words and Nat turned to leave at the same moment that Rudrani's neck exploded in a smear of crimson. Nat dropped to her knees to help her partner, then plucked something out of her neck and slumped over. They both lay there for long minutes. Torrin thought she could tell the exact moment when Rudrani bled out. It didn't take long.

A third figure entered the screen. He was tall and thin, almost painfully so. The profile of a familiar weapon rose over his shoulder. Torrin had seen so many sniper rifles in recent months that she thought she could have recognized one in the dark. The barrel on the weapon was definitely distinctive, rising high over his shoulder.

"Jak!" Torrin was pounding down the hallway to the open hatch, screaming for her lover. "Jak, we have the bastard on a holorecording!"

When she stuck her head out of the hatch, Jak stared up at her, a concerned look on her face. Realizing that no one had been able to tell what she was shrieking about, Torrin modulated her tone but couldn't control her excitement. "Get your ass up here, Jak. We've got a recording of the bastard."

The excitement on Jak's face must have mirrored her own. She leaped out of her crouch and sprinted over to the ship, climbing the ladder rungs on the ship's hull two at a time. Torrin waited at the top of the ladder, bouncing up and down from excitement. As soon as Jak got within arm's reach, Torrin reached down and hauled her the rest of the way up and into the ship, then dragged her down the hallway at a sprint.

"Eowyn, run the recording again!" she called out.

"Affirmative Torrin," boomed the AI.

As they entered the bridge, the recording started up from the beginning. Torrin found the recording more difficult to watch the second time around. She averted her eyes when Rudrani's throat disappeared in a spray of gore and watched Jak's reaction instead. When Crimson appeared on the screen, Jak's face creased with... something. Recognition wasn't the right term, but confusion was too strong. Torrin looked from the screen to Jak's face then back again.

"Do you know him?"

"I...don't think so. He reminds me of..." Her voice trailed off and she stared at the screen while the Orthodoxan hoisted Nat over his shoulder and carried her off. "Computer, rewind and freeze the recording on the best view of his face."

Her only response was a musical chime.

"Eowyn, do it. You may treat a request of Jak's the same as one coming from me."

"Affirmative Torrin." The viewscreen flickered and reversed before freezing on an image of the sniper. He appeared to be looking right into the camera.

"What do we have here?" Lieutenant Smythe entered the bridge. He looked around curiously, eyes wide, not missing a thing.

"We have an image of Crimson, sir," Jak said. She stared hard at the image, brow furrowed.

"Excellent!" Smythe walked up next to Jak and joined her in studying the man on the screen. "Can we get copies made?"

"I'm not sure," Torrin admitted. "I don't know if our systems are compatible."

"If you can get a portable copy of the image, we'll make something work. May I see the footage in its entirety?"

"Eowyn, once again from the beginning please."

As the clip was replayed, Torrin busied herself trying to find a tablet. She didn't need to watch the recording again. It was a scene she was sure she'd take to her grave. Watching a woman she knew and liked bleed out while she could do nothing to help was bad enough. Having to watch Nat be taken again was more than she could bear. She rummaged through the various cabinets and drawers on the bridge without finding a tablet.

"I'll be right back," she said on her way out the door. Two grunts were all the answer she got. Both Smythe and Jak were glued to the screen.

A little ways down the corridor, she stopped in the first cabin. It was a mess, clothes were strewn across half the floor and littered on the bed. Strangely, the bed didn't look slept in. Torrin recognized the clothing as belonging to her sister. She also recognized the mess. Nat was on the slovenly side of messy. There was no way she would have made her bed. A suspicion forming in the back of her mind, she rifled through the drawers looking for Nat's tablet. When she found nothing, she checked the other room.

"You've got to be kidding me!" The second cabin also had articles of Nat's clothing on the floor. Not as many as in the first cabin and they were strewn around the bed, as if they'd been taken off in a hurry. She'd warned Rudrani not to get involved with her little sister. At least now she didn't have to fire her.

The thought had barely crossed her mind before she felt an upwelling of remorse. Rudrani hadn't deserved to die. She felt awful and smacked her forehead with the heel of her palm. The bed was a mess. It had definitely been slept in, quite enthusiastically by the looks of things. A tablet sat on a stand next to the bed and she snagged it and opened it up.

The digital lock responded to the same override she'd given to Eowyn and before long she was downloading a copy of the recording to the tablet. While she was at it, she also snagged copies of the communications array schematics. With a final sad look around the room, she rejoined Jak and Smythe on the bridge.

"Are you all right?" Jak asked quietly.

"I'm fine," Torrin grumbled. "I just found out that Nat was sleeping with her partner, despite my specific instructions to Rudrani to keep her hands off."

Jak smiled. The expression warmed Torrin, though it barely touched Jak's eyes. "Don't be too hard on her. Rudrani may not have had much choice. Nat can be very…insistent."

Smythe cleared his throat and they turned to look at him. "Did either of you notice which direction Crimson came from?"

"Sure," said Jak. "He came from the west." Understanding dawned on her. "He came from the west!"

"What does that mean?" Torrin asked, not sure what they were getting at.

"He came from Devonite land." Excitement dawned on Jak's face and this time the expression made it to her eyes. "We're close to the border, but he came at them from within our lands."

"So?"

"He could have taken them out from across the border, we're close enough here, but he didn't. He probably has a blind or some kind of place where he goes to ground around here." Jak turned back to the viewscreen. "Computer, bring up a topographic map of the area."

Crimson's face was replaced by a chart and Jak ran her fingers over the console, manipulating the image until she could see the contour of the land. She blinked at the screen a few times. Torrin was sure she was seeing the other map, the one in her head that was causing all sorts of trouble.

"You're quite good at that," Smythe said.

"I've gotten good at a lot of things, sir," Jak replied absently. "There. That's where I would hide if I were on this stalk." She pointed to a hilltop a few kilometers away.

"That's too far for him to shoot them and then get here in the time shown in the recording," Torrin objected.

"Oh, he didn't shoot them from there. That's the most likely place for him to hide out. He could have observed them from there, then made the trek over. He shot them from relatively close range. I've already figured out where he most likely took the shot." She looked over at Smythe. "We need to get over there and see what we can find."

"You're not going anywhere." Torrin and Smythe looked at each other as they spoke in near unison.

"I have orders to get you back for treatment as soon as you've determined what you could, Sergeant. From where I'm standing, it looks like that time is now."

Torrin nodded emphatically, backing the lieutenant up.

Jak looked from one to the other. "But this is important."

"So are you, Jak." Torrin looked her in the eye and played the one card she knew Jak wouldn't be able to resist. "I can't do this on my own. Without you, we'll never find Nat." It was true. The gambit worked so well because she really believed it. Without Jak, there was no way she would get her sister back alive. Whatever this Crimson's connection was to her lover, it all hinged on Jak.

Helplessly, Jak stared back at her. Her shoulders slumped in defeat. "Fine, we'll leave in a second, right after I look around one last time."

CHAPTER NINE

"So tell me again why we're still out here?" Torrin asked. She watched the nearby men as they grunted and worked to assemble the rest of the communications arrays. "We have the footage of the attack and we know what he looks like."

Jak sighed and continued her search of the ground. "I want to know what he used to take down Nat. It wasn't a bullet or she wouldn't have survived."

"Why is that even important? We should be getting you back to Fort Marshall so you can be taken care of. Then you can find Nat."

Torrin was in rare form, Jak thought. She'd known from watching Torrin interact with others that the smuggler could be pushy, but it was something else to have the full force of her personality brought to bear on her alone. She was certainly used to getting her own way, but that didn't excuse the way she'd trotted out Jak's secret. *Why would she do that? I know she doesn't think it's a big deal, but it is to me.* Her lover hadn't even apologized. She seemed content to pretend it hadn't happened. This wasn't the time to bring it up, but she and Torrin were going to have a long conversation about this when they had Nat back.

Her fingertips moved through the dirt at the top of the hill. It was already dry, which made sense. The hilltop would drain quickly.

"Have there been any cloudbursts recently?" Jak asked the nearest man. She ignored the irritated burst of air that Torrin expelled in her direction at the brush off.

"It's Haefen, Sarge." The soldier shrugged. "There's always rain."

"I know that," Jak growled, irritation bleeding through. "I'm talking real torrential downpour. Since the offworlders were attacked."

"Could be." The soldier lifted his shoulder again and looked uncomfortable. She glared at him and he busied himself ratcheting together the equipment he was working on.

"Pay him no mind, Sarge." A stocky corporal approached her. He drew an arm across his forehead to sop up some of the sweat dotting his face. "He doesn't pay attention. It rained hard like you're talking about ten days ago."

"Then I'm looking in the wrong place." She looked over at Torrin, who stood to one side, arms crossed and annoyance written large across her face. "Can you check the recording, then go stand where Nat was lying?"

At the flicker of hurt that flashed across Torrin's features, Jak felt a tiny pang of remorse. This wasn't easy. She knew that better than anyone. She glanced over her shoulder to the place where Bron would have been and felt the emptiness open up inside her again, like a chasm filled with nothingness. Being back on Haefen and in the middle of a similar situation brought her loss screaming back to her psyche. There was no way she could let the same thing happen to Torrin. She added another promise, this one to Nat. She would find her, and if she was too late, she would add Nat's death to the tab she'd opened for Crimson.

Jak blinked and looked up. Torrin was already over to one side of the clearing, standing and waiting expectantly for her. Jak had expected more resistance or at least the need for an explanation. She walked over to join her, only to have her arm caught in Torrin's grip and drawn closer to her. Jak tensed, this was not the place, not in front of the men.

"Where did you go, right then?" Torrin demanded, voice quiet.

"I was thinking, that's all." Jak tried to get her arm back, but Torrin's hand didn't budge. Jak probably could have forced her to let go, but she didn't want to create a scene. The corporal was already watching them with an expression of bemusement. She didn't want to draw any more attention than they already had.

"I know what you're thinking of. I won't lose you, not to that bastard."

"And I won't lose my chance at him." Jak firmed up her jaw and glared into her lover's eyes. "We need to get Nat back. I won't lose her to him and I won't give up my chance to get some of my own back. For Bron," she added, unnecessarily.

"You need to know that I'm not going to trade one of you for the other. I plan to keep you and get my sister back."

"And if you have no other choice?"

"I refuse to believe that's an option."

Her grip slackened and Jak was finally able to reclaim her arm. It stung a bit from the force of Torrin's grip, but Jak refused to rub it. Who was Torrin to tell her how far she should be prepared to go to take down Crimson? She dropped into a crouch and ran a critical eye over the ground. There was a bit of a slope along which something small could have been washed away. It would have gone that way. Jak sidled along the ground toward the edge of the hilltop. The top of the hill was mostly dirt. All but the hardiest vegetation was routinely scrubbed away by hard downpours. Runnels carved out by thousands of years of runoff gouged long trenches into the hill's sides.

She continued her sideways shuffle until she caught sight of a strange puff of red against the exposed root system of a scraggly bush. She dialed in her ocular implant and brought the object into focus. It looked like feathers. Jak pushed herself up to take a closer look.

As she stood, a soldier on the opposite side of the clearing burst forth with an inarticulate scream. He clapped both hands to his neck, too late to staunch the explosion of blood. Stunned, he had enough time to look at his companion before toppling forward to lie motionless in the dirt.

"He's here!" Jak shouted. "Get to cover." She launched herself at Torrin, hitting her behind the knees and throwing her to the ground. They weren't far from one of the crates and she shoved Torrin toward it while she crawled behind her. Another cry caught her attention and she glanced to her right in time to see another soldier bleeding out into the dry dirt on the top of the hill.

"Where are the shots coming from?" Jak yelled at the nearest Devonite.

The man was down behind a different crate, and he pointed north as he unlimbered his assault rifle. Another soldier slid in to join Jak and Torrin behind their crate. There was barely enough room for the three of them back there. Jak glanced at him, then looked again.

"Collins?" In her surprise she forgot to roughen her tone. The last time she'd seen the private had been at Camp Abbott. "What the hell are you doing here?"

"Got a transfer, Sarge," Collins panted. His assault rifle was ready in his hands and he crouched with them, keeping his head down. "Lucky me right? Marshall's a much safer posting than Abbott." He gave her a crooked smile.

Jak surprised herself by chuckling in response. "Did you catch any sign of Crimson before going for cover?"

He shook his head, then peeked over the top edge of the crate. A bullet slammed into the crate, splintering the edge and Collins ducked back down.

"Give me a scope," Torrin said. "I can help you find the bastard."

"No way." Jak shook her head emphatically. "You keep your head down. This isn't your kind of fight at all." She could tell Torrin wanted to argue with her. Not wanting to get into a fight, Jak did the next best thing. She ignored her long enough to unsling her rifle. All her old instincts had come roaring back when she'd returned to Haefen. It had been a matter of course for her to grab her weapon when they left for the hill. She hadn't even thought about it.

On her belly, Jak slid over far enough to get her head and the rifle around the corner of the crate. She cleared her throat and made it a point to lower the register of her voice. "I need covering fire on that hill," she hollered, pointing. That was the best vantage point on their position from the north and it was where she would have set up. "Keep him busy while I get a bead on him."

"Got it, Sarge." Collins bobbed out from behind the crate long enough to squeeze a few rounds off at the far hill, then ducked back behind cover. Two more thuds shook the crate as more rounds slammed into it.

"And be careful," Jak yelled. She looked through the scope, checking the far hill for a likely blind. Of them all, she was the most exposed. Hopefully, Crimson's attention would be taken up by the Devonites who were shooting at him. Heat roared through her body and her heartbeat spiked with anticipation. Rage drove her now. Rage and the promise of vengeance.

"He's not far from the hill's crest," Collins said. He sat with his back against the crate and looked over at her. "I saw a muzzle flash about a quarter of the way from the top."

"Got it," Jak grunted, swinging the rifle to the area he'd indicated. Nothing jumped out at her so she kept watching the area with her naked eye, implant zoomed in, but not as far as she could manage with her scope.

Around her, the remaining soldiers were popping up and peppering the far hill with sporadic gunfire. She waited, patiently, for Crimson to tip his hand.

"Eowyn," Torrin's quiet voice reached her ears. "Do you read me?"

Torrin's quiet conversation with the *Melisende's* AI barely registered. Jak was completely focused on the far-off hill. When the ship's main cannon went off with a massive whoosh, Jak jumped and watched with chagrin as a large swath of the hill disappeared in a liquid gout of flame. Another plasma burst followed the first and another swath of the hillside went up in flames.

"Call off the ship," Jak hissed.

"Why?" Torrin sounded surly. "We have the chance to kill him right now."

"And how will you know if he's dead? We're going to send him to ground if we're not careful. He needs to be drawn out. That's what I was trying to do."

There was a long silence during which Jak didn't dare look in Torrin's direction. She watched the hillside, her implant dialed in to the highest magnification it offered. All she could hope now was that the plasma fire had landed close enough to his hiding spot that he chose to move.

"Stand down, Eowyn," Torrin finally said.

"Thank you," Jak said. She knew how much it had cost Torrin to call off the AI. She understood more than anyone how badly Torrin's heart was calling out for the bastard's death. If they killed him now, though, it would make finding Nat that much harder. She froze for a moment when she realized that her promises were at odds with each other. Given the opportunity, which one would she keep?

A flicker of movement drew Jak's eye, and she trained her rifle on the deep patch of shadow where the movement had originated. It should have been impossible for her to have seen anything where it was that dark. She hadn't engaged her implant's night-vision capabilities.

It was midday; there had been no reason for her to do so. Why then was she sure the motion had come from the deep shadows under the trees? Collins popped up again to squeeze off a few rounds at the hill. As he did, Jak saw movement again. She was looking in the right place after all. She dialed in the scope in time to see the muzzle flash and to hear Collins drop. He choked and coughed wetly, but Jak couldn't spare him a glance. She'd finally found Crimson where he lay under the trunk of a downed tree. It was a good spot, she thought. He was almost completely hidden there.

He smiled. Jak recoiled and cursed, throwing herself and the rifle back behind the crate. A split second later, a bullet slammed into the corner, right where she'd been lying. He'd known she was there. There was no reason why he couldn't have killed her, but he'd chosen not to.

She looked over toward Collins as Torrin pulled his slumped body upright. His head flopped back, exposing the ruined mess of his neck. Blood covered Torrin's hands and her front. She'd been unable to staunch the bleeding. Jak could have told her that it was useless. Bron had bled out in much the same way. As she watched Torrin, she was struck by the similarity in the bloodstains.

"What?" Torrin asked when she looked up and caught Jak watching.

"I had him," she said. "But I couldn't...I wasn't fast..." her voice trailed off. She'd broken her promise to Bron. She could have taken the shot, but she'd left him alive, stunned by the smile. Which promise held more weight? The one to her dead brother or the one to her lover's still living sister?

Torrin sat at the controls, guiding the *Melisende* through Haefen's atmosphere. They'd ended up staying on the hilltop for an extra couple of hours while she waited for the League blockade ships to complete their sweep. With Jak to watch over them, the Devonites had completed the installation of the remaining communications arrays. Torrin had stayed in the ship, watching the blips of the League ships on the viewscreen until they had enough separation to head back to Fort Marshall. Her contribution had been minimal and she was disgusted with herself.

This was why she'd left military service to begin with. The soldier Jak knew had bled out in her arms and there had been nothing she could do to stop it. She'd been helpless and he'd paid for her deficiency. The taste of blood filled her mouth and she unclamped her teeth from the inside of her lower lip. For a moment, the pain comforted her. She deserved to feel it.

The trip back to Marshall was uneventful. They were behind their own lines, so there was no artillery fire to contend with. If either League vessel noticed the ship, they chose not to accost them. She flew them in, straight as an arrow. The *Melisende* handled easily enough, though Torrin felt like it should have pulled to the left. Three bodies were stowed on that side of the cargo bay and their weight dragged at her soul.

It was late afternoon when they landed and the setting sun was being covered with the clouds of that evening's rain. Some things never changed, and on Haefen it was the weather.

"Marshall Control," Torrin opened up a channel on the Devonites' rudimentary communications center. "*Melisende* here, requesting clearance to land. Come in, please."

There was no response for a moment before the comm crackled to life. "This is Marshall Control." The voice at the other end sounded surprised but professional. "You have clearance to land. There's space in the clearing next to the *Calamity Jane*."

"Understood. We have casualties on board. Please meet the ship with transport for three bodies." Torrin could hear the emotion choking her own voice. She felt bad enough over the other two dead soldiers, but Collins's death still ate at her. She hadn't known the man much beyond having met him a couple of times at Camp Abbott while she had waited to make her way back to her ship. There was no telling if he'd even recognized her, but she'd known him even if it hadn't been well.

"Roger *Melisende*. Your casualties will be taken care of." The professional timbre sloughed off the voice a bit. "I'm sorry to hear it. I hope you gave the bastards hell."

"Thank you, Marshall Control. *Melisende* out." Torrin disconnected from the comm. The last thing she needed right now was sympathy. She needed a target for her anger, but everyone had been keeping to a wide berth around her. Everyone except Jak, but being angry at her was like raging at a cliff face. The bleakness was back. She'd been seeing glimpses of it since they landed, but since Crimson's attack on Hill 372, it was out in full force. There was no hiding it.

"We'll be landing soon," Torrin said to Smythe. He was ensconced in the bridge's other chair. It was Jak's chair and Torrin felt a certain amount of resentment over his presence. It wasn't his fault that Jak had decided she had better things to do. She had said something about examining the one piece of physical evidence she'd found and disappeared into the cargo hold. "Let everyone know that they need to secure themselves." The ship wasn't equipped to see to the safety needs of all the men they'd crammed into it. Securing themselves meant grabbing on to the nearest immovable object.

"Okay." He looked down at the console and reached toward it hesitantly. It lit up at his touch and all he could do was stare at it. "How do I do that?"

"Never mind," Torrin said. She should have thought. It wasn't that the Haefonians didn't have computer technology, but theirs was all controlled through direct mental interfaces. It had taken Jak weeks to become adept with the touch interfaces that most of the galaxy took for granted. She'd admitted to Torrin that she still felt uncomfortable with touch screens, but she had gotten used to them. Smythe didn't have a couple of weeks. "Eowyn, please alert everyone on board that we're about to land."

"Affirmative Torrin." Eowyn's low voice issued through the speakers on the bridge. A moment later a tone rang through the ship, followed by the AI's booming warning. "Landing is imminent. Please secure yourselves to the best of your ability."

As she gave her human cargo a few seconds to comply, Torrin engaged her safety harness and held still as it snaked past her rib cage, hooked together, then drew itself tight against her, pulling her snugly back into the chair.

"It's this button," she said, pointing at her chair. Seconds later, she heard the harness in Smythe's chair engage.

That was more than enough time, she decided. She swooped the *Melisende* in over the clearing where she'd landed the *Jane* only hours before and skewed the ship into place, maneuvering it so it could slot into the space that remained in the small clearing. The clearing had been made to accommodate two ships, but only barely. They hovered for a moment as she rotated the ship a little further, then lowered her gently to the ground.

Like a glove, she thought, pleased with herself. Piloting a spaceship afforded her pleasure she got in very few other areas in her life, though making love was one of them. The pleasure of bringing a woman to her peak and over gave her almost the same thrill as piloting a ship through an impossible situation.

Safely down, she disengaged the exterior hatches and released the cargo bay ramp.

"You're now clear to move about the ship," Torrin said over the loudspeakers.

"I'll get the men out of here," Smythe said as he waited for the safety harness to retract. "All of them." A shadow of sorrow passed over his face before he stood and left the bridge.

Torrin stayed behind a few more minutes, shutting down the ship's systems and running diagnostics. The *Melisende* had been sitting for weeks, and she wanted to be certain everything was all right with the ship. The AI would probably have noticed any serious errors, but Torrin's suspicious nature wouldn't let her cut corners when it came to double-checking. At least Eowyn wasn't a League AI, so she didn't have to worry about any of those sorts of biases.

There was no sign of Jak when she finished up, so Torrin went looking for her. Both cabins were empty. Nat's actually looked a little cleaner until Torrin realized that the men who had been crammed into the room for the return trip had shoved most of the strewn-about clothing under the room's small desk. She sighed. Nat was still out there. From what they'd learned on their trip to the hilltop, she didn't feel they were any closer to tracking down her abductor. And what had they learned on the hilltop? Jak had figured something out, but she hadn't been willing to share yet. Hopefully it would get them closer. It had to. She knew what the Orthodoxans were like. Goosebumps pebbled the skin on her arms and she resisted the urge to rub at them. Colonel Hutchinson was never as far from her thoughts as she would like him to be, and he'd only had her for three days. Nat had been with them for weeks now, and who knew what they would do to her. What they could be doing to her right now.

No. The fretting would do her no good. *Fretting?* she asked herself. *It's a little beyond that, don't you think?* There was no time for such thoughts. Terror would get in her way, would slow her down. Now wasn't the time to go rushing into things, no matter how much she wanted to. It was the smart thing to do, but why did she feel the need to go running full speed ahead when she didn't even know which direction "ahead" was?

She slid down the ladder between decks to the cargo bay. It echoed, empty of the pallets and crates of comm equipment. A light was on in the small work area and Torrin stuck her head in.

Jak knelt on the floor and scribbled with a china marker. The small flechette she'd found on top of the hill lay forgotten on the workbench.

"Did you find something?" Torrin asked, curious.

Jak was completely engrossed in what she was doing and didn't seem to hear her. The workbench was covered with curving black lines that continued down its front and sides and onto the floor.

"Jak baby?" Torrin raised her voice. "What are you doing–" She cut off as she came to a stop next to Jak's hunched form. She turned her head to take in the entire picture and the lines snapped together into a meaningful image. It was a topographical chart. *This must be Sector 27.*

She leaned over and hooked an arm under Jak's armpit. "Come on, Jak. You're done."

Jak pulled her arm back and went back to drawing. "I'm not finished yet," she said, her voice flat.

Torrin laughed, desperation sharpening it to a frightening edge. "That's enough. You need to see the doctors." *Is it too late?* Torrin needed Jak. Not only to get Nat back, but for herself. The void that Nat's abduction had opened in her chest cracked open further at the idea of losing Jak. Jak's bleakness was so much more understandable and Torrin pulled herself away from the seductive darkness of that chasm. While she saw and understood the emptiness, Torrin wanted nothing to do with it. She grabbed Jak's upper arms and snatched her up, distress giving her the strength to haul Jak's resisting body against her.

"I need to finish," Jak muttered, trying to get back to the floor.

"After you see the doctors, honey." Torrin let go long enough to stroke her fingers through the blonde hair that plastered Jak's forehead, which was beaded with sweat. She didn't feel feverish to Torrin's touch, but her eyes glittered alarmingly. Looking at her, it was entirely evident that something was very wrong.

Jak was smaller than Torrin, but her training gave her strength that was out of proportion for her small frame. Her struggles ceased with a startling abruptness when they left the caged-in area and she could no longer see what she'd been drawing out, and Torrin moved her more easily across the cargo bay and down the ramp.

Three bodies were laid out at the bottom of the ramp. Two of them had been enclosed in body bags and two soldiers were closing the third bag over Collins's face. A pang stabbed through Torrin's chest to see his face disappear behind the heavy plastic.

"Was that Collins?" Jak asked, her voice rough. "What happened?"

"Don't you remember?" Torrin was appalled. Barely two hours had passed since they'd been engaged by Crimson at the top of the hill. "He was shot through the throat. Crimson got him."

Shocked blue eyes met hers and Jak paled. "Wait, when did that happen?"

"Yes Jak. We just got back…"

"From Sector 27. I got you past the fence."

Torrin had seen this before, not too long ago. But there was no head injury this time to disorient Jak so badly. She waved at the two men at the bottom of the ramp.

"You guys have transport?"

One of the men nodded, straightening to greet them. "Yes ma'am."

"Good, we need to get Sergeant Stowell to the hospital right away. His data corruption condition has been exacerbated by the firefight." Torrin had no idea if that was true, but it sounded good and she didn't want to argue with the man. As it was he hesitated.

"Look, I'm only asking to be polite. You will take me to the hospital. There's no more help for these men, but Stowell needs help now."

He still hesitated before the other man stepped up and whispered in his ear. "Apparently the lieutenant said you were to be accommodated in any way you asked." His tone was grudging.

"Good." Torrin dragged an unresisting Jak over toward the small truck at the edge of the clearing. Jak still stared at Collins's body bag.

"I remember," she said, softly. Her voice was back in her normal register and Torrin glanced at the two men who trailed after them to see if they'd noticed. "A little bit, I think. I could have killed him, you know."

"Collins?"

"No, Crimson." Her brow creased in pain. "I decided not to. I broke my promise to Bron." Tears lurked in her eyes, unshed but threatening to spill over the dam of her lower eyelids. "I had to. I couldn't keep my promise to him and to Nat. If I killed him, how would we find her?"

"Oh honey." Torrin was overwhelmed by Jak's words. To think she'd been worried that Jak would choose revenge for Bron over rescue of Nat. Obviously, she'd thought about it but had come out on Nat's side. She hugged Jak to her, tightening her grip around Jak's shoulders and seeking out her lips for a desperate kiss, one that sought as much comfort as it gave.

* * *

Nat lay on her side, partially covered by the pile of rags in the corner of her small prison. Dawn was approaching; she could tell by the way the sky lightened steadily through the cracks between the wooden boards that made up the wall. She should have been sleeping. She wished she'd been sleeping, but the night had been cold enough that even with the rags for insulation, she'd been awake, huddled and shivering.

He was still around. He'd left on a couple of longer excursions since she'd been taken. While he creeped her out, at least when he was around she ate regularly. The food was nothing to write home about and her stomach growled as she thought of Raisa's cooking. Her mom made the best food, especially for the seventh-day meal. Even Torrin had been happy to visit on those days, though she didn't talk much to their mother. A roast of pork would really hit the spot, Nat thought.

Her stomach growled and a deluge of saliva rushed into her mouth. That line of thinking wasn't helping, and Nat sent her thoughts elsewhere. To that loose board near the roof of her small enclosure, perhaps. It wasn't big enough that she'd be able to get through, even if she did manage to pry it free from the wall. But it did bring up some interesting possibilities.

She definitely wasn't going to get any more sleep until the day got warmer. Though how warm it would get today, she wasn't sure. She could smell moisture in the air. That meant rain. How much rain, she never could tell. As long as it wasn't a torrent, she'd be able to stay pretty dry.

Carefully, she stood. Even with him there, she wasn't getting a lot of food and she already felt weaker for it. That was probably part of his plan; it certainly kept her more docile than she'd been when she'd first arrived. Let him think she was beaten then. It would only work to her advantage when she escaped.

She felt along the wall, wood rough under her fingertips. It was lighter outside, but still pretty dark inside the shack. The boards were silhouetted starkly against the gray light that filtered through them. She hissed as a splinter jabbed under her fingernail and pulled it back to suck on the abused digit. The splinter was a big one and she worried at it with her teeth until she could pull it out. Undeterred, she went back to feeling the board.

It was loose. Nat had a brief memory of wiggling a front tooth when she'd been six. The board felt like the tooth had when she'd first noticed some wiggle to it. It wasn't ready to fall out, but like the tooth, she could hurry it along with some prodding. Some prodding turned into wrenching, but to little avail. Was it looser than it had been when she started? She couldn't tell. The wood was so damned hard, some kind of oak, she figured.

Nat worked in silence, not daring to give way to the cursing as she wanted to. If he found out what she was up to, he would be angry. He'd already made it clear that he didn't need her in one piece for his plans, merely alive.

What those plans were, she still didn't know. Her captor kept referring to "her." That must mean Torrin because nobody on the planet knew that Jak was a woman. She had told Nat so herself. Jak's brother had been the last person on Haefen to know the truth of her gender. But what had Torrin done to piss this Orthodoxan off so badly? True, she did occasionally rub people the wrong way, but from the stories she'd heard of the two women's trip through the wilderness, they hadn't been with anyone long enough for Torrin to piss them off that much.

Crunching footsteps warned her of his approach. She abandoned the loose board and scooted quietly over to her pile of rags. He fiddled with the lock on the door and when he opened it, Nat blinked at him as if he'd awoken her.

He was grinning, the expression out of place on his lean face. As usual, he didn't look right at her. "She's here and she knows you're mine. We'll be together again, like we were meant to be. It won't be long now."

That was strange. Nat started to doubt her assumption that he was after Torrin. Her sister had most assuredly never belonged to this man.

"What are you going to do with me?" Her voice was creaky with disuse.

"Don't you worry," he said earnestly. "Your part in this is almost done." Done? She didn't like the sound of that. Her concern must have been visible to him because he hastened to reassure her. "You've been so good, following all my instructions. I won't hurt you unless I have to. Killing is so wasteful, and there's no sense wasting you."

She stared at him. She wanted to believe him, but he was so off. Unstable. It was hard to predict what he would do.

"Here's your food for the next few days," he said, putting down a bucket full to the brim. A hard roll fell out of the bucket and bounced when it hit the ground. "I'm going to be gone for a little bit, but when I come back, I should have some good news." He looked right at her for the first time in a while. "Behave."

He closed the door behind him and locked it. She waited until his footsteps had retreated down the path before grabbing the bucket. It was the usual fare. Bread, vegetables and some fruits; there was no meat this time. Greedily, she stuffed a roll in her mouth and grabbed a couple handfuls of vegetables. Carrots, by the look of them, though it was strange to see blue carrots. If he was going to be gone for a few days, she would have time to see what she could do about that loose board.

CHAPTER TEN

The hospital smelled like every other hospital Torrin had ever been in. The smell of antiseptic overwhelmed almost every other odor. A loudspeaker overhead crackled to life. It spewed forth a garbled announcement that Torrin didn't understand, but somebody did. A team of doctors sprinted down the hall, followed quickly by half a dozen nurses. The nurses were all female, of course. That was a respectably feminine job. Torrin wondered how the Haefonians would react when they found out that on most Fringe worlds, there were as many female doctors as there were male nurses.

She smirked a bit at the thought, but the amusement was short-lived as her worry came rushing back. Jak was in one of the operating rooms across the hall from the small waiting area where Torrin currently cooled her feet. She'd tried to force herself in with Jak when they'd taken her back, but she'd been politely but firmly rebuffed by the medical staff.

It had already been three hours and the longer she waited, the more her nerves frayed. So far, this trip had been all about waiting around while others did the work. What was it about Haefen that seemed to turn her into an onlooker?

Her hands twitched on her thighs and she gave in to the urge to drum her fingers. The movement helped a little bit. At least she could pretend she was doing something constructive. She licked her lips and looked at the ceiling. Her shirt felt too tight across her shoulders and she rolled them in an attempt to loosen the binding fabric. In truth, the fabric wasn't the problem, it was her skin. Waiting always made Torrin feel like her skin was too tight.

"Have you heard anything?" Smythe sat down in a chair across from her.

"Not a damn thing. They didn't tell me how long this was going to take."

"It could take half the day. It's unlikely that they had any nanomechs prepared for…the sergeant." His slight pause betrayed the strain of keeping Jak's gender under wraps.

"Does the team know about his situation?" Torrin glanced around casually to see if anyone was close enough to overhear their conversation. A gaggle of nurses were hanging out at a nearby station. They joked and laughed with a young doctor in military uniform. The openness of their conversation was a little surprising based on what Jak had told her and her own interaction with Devonite men.

"The doctor who programmed the nanomechs was apprised of the circumstances. The rest of the medical team has been apprised as well." Smythe smiled slightly at Torrin's pained expression. "Don't worry. They were all chosen to operate on the sergeant because of their discretion. The general has made it clear that there is to be no discussion of Stowell's situation. If anything gets back to Callahan, there will be grave consequences."

His reassurance helped a bit, but Torrin knew that Jak was probably freaking out, if she was even conscious. She wished they could be open about Jak's gender, but it was easy enough for her to say it. Torrin wasn't the one who had been hiding who she was for years. No, she was the one who'd opened her mouth and spewed out the truth of Jak's identity as soon as she stopped concentrating on keeping it a secret. If she was lucky, Jak would still be talking to her after they found Nat. It had been a stupid lapse, one she dearly wished she could take back. That revelation had been Jak's to make, but in her blind rush to make sure she was taken care of, Torrin had trampled all over it. She shook her head to clear it. The maudlin crap wasn't going to help anyone, not now.

"So where have you been? This is the first I've seen of you since we got back to Marshall." Torrin fixed the lieutenant with a curious gaze. The least he could do was distract her from her anxiety and guilt.

"I had to debrief my superiors on the outcome of our visit to Hill 372." Weariness pressed down heavily on Smythe's shoulders for a moment. "It was supposed to be a quick in and out with little chance of engaging with the Orthodoxans. Since it didn't turn out that way, they wanted to know why."

"That's an excellent question. How did things end up going so badly sideways?"

Smythe gave her a crooked grin. "I have the data you requested. Why don't we head to your ship to break it down?"

Torrin opened her mouth to object to the subject change and closed it with a snap. She thought she knew where he was going with this.

"You think they'll be working on Jak for hours yet?"

"I do. And it's unlikely that he'll regain consciousness for another thirteen to fourteen hours after the procedure is complete. His neural hardware will need a complete reboot and the doctors will probably keep him sedated to allow the synaptic connections they'll be rewiring to set." He'd slipped seamlessly back into referring to Jak as a man, even though nobody was within earshot. It was a habit that Torrin was trying to get back into as well, though it was harder for her when she knew without a doubt exactly how female Jak was.

The data called to her. It was a chance to do something about her sister's abduction. But the need to be there when Jak awoke was equally strong. Torrin hesitated.

"We'll station a runner to wait while Sergeant Stowell recovers from his operation. He will notify us when the doctors are ready to lift the sedation."

"All right." Torrin stood up from where she'd been slouching. "As long as I know Jak won't wake up without me there."

He nodded gravely and stood. He crossed the hallway between the nurses' station and the waiting area. After a few moments of quiet conversation, he rejoined Torrin.

"We're good?" At his nod, Torrin walked down the hall at a brisk pace. Despite his assurance that it would be many hours before Jak was conscious, she wanted to have the data analyzed and be back by her bedside long before she regained consciousness. They walked out of the building in companionable silence and into the street where Smythe waved to a waiting private. The soldier saluted and took off at a swift clip, disappearing around the corner. The sound of a combustion engine filled the air and the private pulled up in a small transport.

"Thank you, Gesher," Smythe said and returned the private's salute.

"Ma'am," Gesher said to Torrin as he exited the vehicle.

"Hop in," Smythe instructed while taking the private's place in the driver's seat. "We'll get to your ship much faster than walking."

"I was going to ask about that," Torrin said. "Hardly anyone drives while in the fort. It's certainly big enough that having a ride would be helpful."

"You'd think so, wouldn't you?" He shifted the truck into gear with a loud clash. "The problem is that we're running out of materials for all sorts of things, including the transports. They break down and both fuel and parts are scarce. We're making do with what we have and the occasional replacement, but they get damaged at a higher rate than we can fix them. So most people walk." He grinned. "Besides, they're soldiers. They're supposed to be in good shape."

"And what if you could get parts on a regular basis, would that help?"

"It would help extend the useful life of the vehicles we have. Are you thinking of another business opportunity for us?"

Torrin smirked in reply. He was beginning to know her too well.

"So I have a question for you." Smythe's voice was hesitant, and he kept his eyes glued to the road in front of them. Torrin was glad for his attention to the driving. There was no roof over the cab, simply rust-pitted roll bars. They'd seen better days and she had no confidence that they would hold the truck's weight if tested.

"Shoot."

The lieutenant cleared his throat roughly, loud enough that Torrin heard it clearly over the roar of the engine. "So Sergeant Stowell is… you know."

His discomfort was visible again and Torrin smiled to reassure him. She would have to point out to Jak that dealing with her gender deception was hard on others also. It might put some of her own struggle in perspective.

"She is, yes," Torrin answered, wondering where he was going with the line of questioning.

"You two seem very close." He flicked his gaze from the road and in her direction so quickly that she would have missed it if she hadn't been studying his face closely. When he saw her watching, he colored slightly and went back to studying the road.

"We are." Where was he going with this? Jak was dead set against anyone finding out about their relationship, especially those who knew her actual gender. So far Torrin hadn't admitted to anything the Devonites would consider unsavory. All she needed was some plausible deniability to cover her behind if need be.

He didn't say anything for a long time. Torrin could see him sorting through appropriate questions and failing to find one. That she could read his expression meant that he either really trusted her or was really rattled by the situation.

"Are you two lovers?" Smythe blurted the question out after half an eternity of facial gyrations.

"Would it bother you if we were?" Torrin still watched him, her face uncharacteristically serious.

He gave her a twisted smile, pain briefly flashing through his eyes. "Not for the reasons you think."

"Try me."

"I have your same…affliction. If you two are—lovers, that is." His face flushed a brilliant scarlet. So that was what was bothering him so much. No wonder he was upset.

"We are. We have been for a while."

"How do you do it? Knowing what you do?"

"What do you mean, knowing what I do?"

"That it's morally reprehensible."

"Your definition of morals and mine are probably very different." Torrin kept a lid on her anger. It wasn't directed at Smythe, but at the society that twisted good men and women into individuals terrified of their own sexuality. "I think Haefonian views on women are morally reprehensible, even the Devonites'. You're better than the Orthodoxans, but if it wasn't for them, I'd think you were one of the most backward societies I'd ever run across."

Smythe looked a little taken aback at her vehemence. "I'm not like that," he protested. "I respect women. I've used them in my work on more than one occasion."

"And you don't see anything wrong with that?" Torrin plowed on as the lieutenant gaped at her. "You're using them? They should be your partners. Equals. Not subordinates. Not objects."

"I get that. I do…" He trailed off, looking thoughtful.

"To answer your original question, I can deal with my preferences because I know they aren't morally reprehensible. On my home planet, same-sex unions are the norm, not the exception. On many Fringe planets, those who are attracted to their own gender are tolerated at the very least. On most planets they're completely accepted. It doesn't even occur to people that it's something to be concerned about."

Smythe shook his head slightly in disbelief.

"It's true," Torrin said. "Haefen could really benefit from more offworld influence. You've been too insular for too long. There's a galaxy of other perspectives. Most of them aren't right or wrong, they're different. That's it. Maybe if your people had been exposed to more perspectives than the two you hold so closely to, this asinine civil war might never have happened."

"It's funny, isn't it?" Smythe's voice was wry. "My ancestors left Earth to be free to worship how they wanted. They thought they were going to find freedom out here in the stars. Instead, they found enslavement to a set of ideals whose time had come and gone."

Now it was Torrin's turn to be surprised. She raised an eyebrow at him. These were sentiments she'd never thought to hear from a Haefonian, no matter how enlightened. Maybe there was hope for them after all.

"You're welcome to leave with us when this whole mess is wrapped up." The offer took them both aback when it came out of her mouth. "Not to my home planet," Torrin hastened to add. "Adult males aren't permitted on its surface. But there are plenty of Fringe planets where you would feel more at home."

"My people need me," the lieutenant said after a long pause while he contemplated her offer. "I won't abandon them."

"Even with the way they treat those like you? Like us?"

"I'm afraid so. I suspect Sergeant Stowell would have made the same decision if circumstances"—he shot her a smile—"if you hadn't intervened. Whatever else we are here, we have a strong sense of responsibility."

"Don't I know it."

They were waved through the main gates and Smythe bounced them over the dirt track that led up to the landing site. The track wasn't much more than flattened patches of grass and Torrin had to grab on to the roll cage to keep from being flung about. She sorely missed her antigrav sled when her teeth clashed together as they hurdled a particularly large bump. Thankfully, their cross-country trek was short and Smythe was slowing down next to the *Calamity Jane* in no time. Torrin leaped down from the truck. She swore she felt like she was still being jostled about.

"Tien, lower the ramp, please."

"Affirmative Torrin." The AI's answer rang through the transmitter implanted behind her ear and was followed in short order by the sound of the cargo ramp clamps unlocking. Smythe joined her as she waited impatiently for the ramp to lower. The end was still a few feet off the ground when Torrin hopped onto it and headed into the ship's bowels. Lights flickered on in the cargo bay as she strode through, Smythe hot on her heels.

She avoided the elevator that opened in front of her, preferring to take the ladder two rungs at a time up to the main deck.

"Where's the data?" Torrin asked, striding through the door onto the bridge.

Smythe held up a tablet in answer. He'd taken it from the *Melisende* with the recording of Crimson. Somehow, his tech team had been able not only to extract the information but also to upload new information to it.

"Good." She reached for it and opened up the root directory, looking for new files. "Tien, sync in the new information from the tablet. I need you to run a full diagnostic on it. I need geographical and chronological sorting and cross-indexing. I want you to parse the data however many ways you can manage and I'll need you to give me a rundown of any and all connections you find, no matter how small or seemingly insignificant."

"Understood Torrin." Tien paused for a moment. "It will take some time, the data is extensive and rather complex. I will report to you when I have completed my analysis."

"Good." Torrin turned to fix Smythe with a penetrating stare. He'd plopped himself into the second chair and gazed back at her blandly. "So what was it you couldn't talk about back at the hospital?"

Smythe nodded in approval. "You caught that. Good." He swiveled his chair back and forth. "How do you think Crimson knew we were there?"

"I hadn't really thought about it," Torrin admitted. "I had other things to worry about at the time. It does seem awfully convenient, now that you mention it."

"That's what I thought. It's the same conclusion the Command Council came to." He stopped swiveling his chair and looked at her. "We have a mole. Someone's feeding information to the Orthodoxans. From there, it's getting to Crimson."

"Do you have any idea who it might be?"

"We don't. It could be someone at almost any level. We didn't exactly keep your presence under wraps. You're a little hard to hide."

"I didn't think I'd have to."

"We've already had enough sideways glances from the men who remember your trial and execution. That you're not dead was bound to tear its way through the grapevine in a hurry."

"What about Jak?" Dread gnawed at Torrin's insides. Jak would never forgive her if she'd tipped off the Haefonian public at large about her true identity.

"I've heard no rumors about her. It's probably the only good thing to come from how much notoriety you're getting. She's actually being overlooked. But then, Sergeant Stowell was never officially dead, only missing in action. There's news footage of your death."

"Good." Somewhat relieved, Torrin collapsed back into her chair before sitting bolt upright when another thought occurred to her. "So you have no idea who your traitor is?"

Smythe shook his head, face weary. "We've known someone was getting information out to the Orthodoxans about troop movements and planned raids. This is the first time they've gotten really specific intel on something that wasn't a larger scale operation. The timing of it is also worrisome. In order for Crimson to have had the time to get to Hill 372, the traitor would have needed to get the information to him almost immediately."

"I have to go." Torrin stood abruptly. "Tien, keep up your analysis. I expect to have your results when I get back."

The lieutenant bounded out of his chair and trotted after her, almost jogging to keep up with her long strides. "Where are you going?"

"Can I trust you?" The question was as much for her as it was for him. Could she trust him? She wanted to, very much. She got the feeling he'd always been straight with her, but he'd also known about their trip to the hill.

"As much as you can trust anyone."

"That's not very reassuring." But true. He hadn't tried to plead his case. Instead, he'd admitted that he could be a liability. Surely, if he had been the mole, he would have tried to convince her that he was completely trustworthy. With Jak out of commission, she needed to trust somebody. Smythe looked like he was going to have to be it. She would keep an eye on him, and if she did catch him out in a lie, then she would simply kill him. He was a small guy and she was confident she could take him. It was amazing how cold-blooded she'd gotten. Torrin had prided herself on staying above the frays she supplied. This was one she was neck-deep in. That she was capable of coolly deciding to end a man's life, and one she liked, if it was expedient was an indication of how much her moral compass had shifted. It might be time to back off some of the more unsavory smuggling contracts. For a while.

"Okay, here's the deal. I need somebody on this planet that I can trust. I'm going to call in reinforcements."

"How are you going to manage that? Our very occasional communications beyond the surface of the planet all have to go through the League ship on picket."

Torrin stared at the lieutenant for a moment. His statement triggered a half-formed thought. She worried at it mentally and wanted to curse when it didn't quite come together. Frustrated, she filed it away for later. Whatever was giving her pause wasn't revealing itself to her. Hopefully, it would come to her if she set it aside. Maybe she would talk to Jak when she'd recovered. Sometimes talking it out with someone else jarred things loose for her.

With a start, Torrin realized that Smythe was waiting patiently for her. She had paused at the top of the ladder to the lower deck and was staring at him. With a grimace, she slid down the ladder, her feet braced along the outside, bypassing the rungs. He took the ladder in the same way, landing in the spot she'd vacated.

"I need to get out of the system," Torrin finally explained, "which means getting past the picket, which won't be easy since the League ships know I'm down here."

"Ships? How many are there now?"

"Only two, but it makes it that much harder to get past them undetected. There's nothing for it though. I have to try. Hopefully, I'll be back before Jak wakes up."

"You're not going without me," Smythe said, though he looked a little pale at the idea of leaving the planet's surface.

"Oh, yes, I am." Torrin's tone held no room for objections, but the lieutenant paid her no attention.

"No, you're not. You're my responsibility right now. You and that data."

"Then you can keep the data company. You stay on the *Calamity Jane*. I'm taking the *Melisende*. The League bastards aren't as familiar with her as they are with the *Jane*."

"Then you need to tell your ship to let me know the results of the data analysis as soon as it's complete. Whether you're back or not."

"Deal." Torrin and Smythe eyed each other smugly, each convinced they'd gotten the better end of the bargain.

"Besides, I need someone back here to buy me some time. We have two League ships. Let's give them two targets."

Discomfort writhed across Smythe's face. "There's no way I can pilot your ship."

"Don't worry about it." Torrin flapped a hand blithely in his direction. "Tien will be doing most of the work. Your job is to get the timing right and have her break for it at just the right moment so they follow you and I can make my own break out of the system."

"I'm not sure this is such a good idea." The poor man was getting paler and paler, but Torrin didn't feel too much sympathy. He was the one who'd wanted to stay with the data. She ignored his objections.

"Tien, I'm transferring temporary control to Lieutenant Smythe. You'll be doing the heavy lifting, but on his mark."

"Understood Torrin." The AI's voice was preoccupied and distant.

"Here's what we're going to do," Torrin said, bringing up the display on her console. With a resigned sigh, Smythe bent his head to watch as her fingers danced across the screen.

Less than an hour later, Torrin fired up the engines of the *Melisende*.

"Eowyn, keep our power signature as small as possible, please." Tien's instructions had been the opposite. Torrin wanted the *Calamity Jane* to draw as much attention as she could. The League captains would still be smarting over the fact that she'd slipped through their grasp on the way down to the planet's surface. She was counting on their irritation to blind them to the smaller power signature of the other ship.

The *Melisende* had smaller engines to begin with. She was the standard vessel model in Troika Corp's small fleet and didn't have the advantage of the modifications the *Jane* had. She was still a fast little thing, but she didn't have the raw power that the *Jane* was able to muster when necessary.

Next to them, the *Calamity Jane* roared to life. Tien was apparently taking her instructions to heart. A basso profundo rumble started at the far range of her hearing, then increased in intensity until her teeth rattled, even though she was in the other ship. Tien was pulling out all the stops and Torrin winced slightly. There was no point in blowing out the engines. She would have to trust that Tien wouldn't cripple herself in an overabundance of enthusiasm.

"Tien," Torrin said through her subdermal transmitter, "let her rip."

"Affirmative Torrin." The ship's voice was tinny in her ear.

"Remember my instructions. Make them think you're making a break for it, but play it safe. I don't want any more damage done than already has been done." Her last-minute assessment of the damage to the *Calamity Jane* had been both disturbing and relieving. She'd felt relief that none of the damage was major, but it was more than merely cosmetic. She would need to take the ship in for repairs when they returned to Nadierzda. Until then, the *Jane* was flyable, but she had some disturbing blind spots where some of the sensors had been melted to the hull by glancing plasma weapon strikes.

"Affirmative Torrin," Tien repeated, an edge of exasperation to her voice. Was it really there or had Torrin projected it instead?

"I mean it, Tien. You are not to engage them, and make sure you stay over land so they don't decide to take any potshots at you."

In answer, the *Calamity Jane* lifted off and sped away to the north. Torrin tracked the progress of both of the ships in orbit. It took a few moments but first one, then the other changed their orbital paths to match the *Jane*'s trajectory. She couldn't tell from the sensors which League ship was which. For the safety of her own ship, she hoped the *Icarus* wasn't the nearest ship, but for the success of her mission, she hoped it was. She'd seen a shrewd mind in the maneuvering she and the unnamed captain of the *Icarus* had engaged in.

Another long minute ticked slowly by, and it was clear that both ships were tracking the *Jane*. Gently, Torrin eased the *Melisende* off the ground. The key was to keep her movements smooth, to avoid any surges in power that might betray her gambit to the orbiting ships.

So far, so good, she thought, chewing on her lower lip.

"Eowyn, monitor the progress of the League ships and tell me right away if one of them breaks off its pursuit of the *Calamity Jane*."

"Understood Torrin."

She headed in the opposite direction from Tien and Smythe, putting as much distance between them as possible, hoping the curve of the planet would camouflage her from the sensors of the *Icarus*, to a greater degree, and less so to the other ship.

The deception was working; the League bastards were none the wiser for it. She hit the upper levels of the atmosphere and punched it to break free of Haefen's grip.

"One of the ships has turned away, Torrin." Eowyn's interruption was unwelcome in the extreme, and Torrin swore sharply, the invective flying off her tongue.

"Which ship?"

"I am unable to ascertain that information, Torrin. The planet still obscures their signature."

"Good." Torrin disengaged the safety harness and hurled herself out of the captain's chair. "Ready a cryostasis pod, and keep us on this course." She turned her shoulders to slide between the barely opening doors to the bridge and pounded down the short corridor to the cryochamber. Once again, she turned sideways and slid between doors that were barely open.

One pod was open and waiting for her. Torrin made a beeline for it, shedding her clothes as she did so. To her disappointment, the pod wasn't outfitted with even the most rudimentary of bridge controls. She made a mental note to have all the ships in the Troika fleet retrofitted with that enhancement.

"Eowyn, I want to see the League ship's progress onscreen."

A screen to her left flickered on. Sure enough, it showed the League ship still in pursuit. Torrin stepped into the pod and tried to keep an eye on the viewscreen. She had to crane her neck uncomfortably to see it from the cryopod. *We'll have enough time*, she thought. *I hope.*

"Get me hooked in, Eowyn." She drew a deep breath at what she was about to do. AIs weren't known for their split-second decision-making abilities. They could parse thousands of processes at a time, but they still had to run each one of them. Torrin was about to trust her and Nat's lives to a computer and one that she didn't even know that well.

"As soon as we've cleared the atmosphere by the minimum amount for transfer to peripheral space and I'm safely in cryostasis, I want you to make the jump. After you've made three jumps, bring us back to normal space and revive me."

"Affirmative Torrin." Large-bore needles sank into her flesh, drawing a pained whimper from her throat. She hadn't been expecting them, craning her neck as she was to catch another glimpse of the viewscreen. "What is our heading?"

"I don't have time to calculate that," Torrin gasped. "You're going to have to use your best judgment. I'm counting on you."

"Are you certain, Torrin?"

"I am. Make sure you don't take us toward Nadierzda, and get us as far from Haefen as you can."

"Understood Torrin." The AI sounded doubtful and Torrin couldn't blame her. She doubted the computer had ever been given that much latitude. Her thought processes began to fuzz; Eowyn must have pushed the sedatives. She snickered a bit. The decision had been a hard one, but if it didn't work out, at least she'd never know. If this hare-brained idea went as pear-shaped as it probably would, the chances that she would ever regain consciousness were pretty slim. Oddly, the thought comforted her as she slid feetfirst into oblivion.

CHAPTER ELEVEN

The ceiling was too high. Jak stared at it, unsure of where she might be. Sunlight slashed a bright swathe across the far wall and bleached out the light blue paint until it was almost white. She raised her head and looked around. Blue blankets covered the bed and a white curtain separated her from the rest of the room.

Haefen. She was back on her home planet. Out of reflex, she raised one hand to her chest. Her heartbeat tripped, then raced so hard she felt like her entire body was shaking. What was she doing without her breastbinder in a strange room on Haefen?

Panicked, she looked around and spied the footlocker against the wall under the window. Her boots were next to the locker. Hopefully, the rest of her clothing was as well. Carefully, she sat up. A split second of light-headedness swirled through her, and she froze, but it passed quickly.

Why was she there? From the machinery in the bed, she assumed she was in a clinic or hospital, but she didn't feel injured or sick. Aside from that quick flash of vertigo, she felt fine. Jak took another moment for a quick physical inventory. All her limbs seemed to be intact and she didn't detect any new holes in her body. Her last memory was of…what exactly? Darkness studded with thousands of points of light. That was strange.

There was a redhead and she smiled. Torrin. Where was Torrin, anyway?

Satisfied that she wasn't going to do herself more damage by moving, she swung her legs over the edge of the bed. Fortunately, very little of the bed's machinery was actually hooked up to her. The diagnostic equipment monitored her vitals, but none of the treatment equipment was hooked up, not even the fluids array. If something bad enough had happened that she'd ended up in the hospital, why wasn't she being treated?

More mysteries. She needed to put on some clothing and find whoever was in charge. The hop off the bed reassured her that whatever her problem was, it wasn't an injury. She had the presence of mind to switch off the monitoring machinery before she pulled the leads off her extremities. The machine emitted a muted chirp, then went dark.

The footlocker held clothing, including her breastbinder. Hurriedly, she pulled on underwear and then fastened down the binder. Even though she was still mostly naked, Jak immediately felt less exposed. The rest of the clothes were a new Devonite uniform. She pulled the pants on and shrugged into the shirt, buttoning it all the way up to the top. Now there was no way for anyone to tell she was a woman. She heaved a sigh of relief.

The uniform jacket stole back that sense of relief. Her sergeant's stripes were gone. Jak ran her fingers over the right arm's upper sleeve. It was completely bare. Since there was no way they could have overlooked that she was a woman, maybe this was her punishment. That couldn't be right. If she was being punished, she wouldn't have been allowed to stay in the Devonite uniform. The first thing that happened to Devonite soldiers who'd been discovered in a crime was that they were stripped of their uniforms so they would cease to disgrace them. Besides, she would be in the stockade if they planned on trying her.

The sniper insignia on the jacket's raised collar were also gone. Jak had to sit down when she noticed their absence. That hurt even more than the demotion. She didn't even recognize the insignia left in their place. What was the logo supposed to be? She squinted at it, trying to distract herself from the fact that she was no longer a sniper. Were those two hands? Or maybe a squashed bird? It made no sense. She needed to find out the answers to her questions, and she wasn't going to be able to do that by sitting by herself on the bed.

As she pulled on the jacket, she craned her neck to stare into the footlocker. There was no sign of her weapons. Another blow. Her life was turned upside down and she didn't have any way to defend herself. She wasn't Torrin, able to flip enemies about with her bare hands. If she'd had even a combat knife, she would have felt a little more secure. She was no slouch with a blade. Torrin's presence would have gone a long way toward reassuring her. Where the hell was her lover?

It was time to face the music. She pulled back the curtain and was a little disappointed at what it hid, a small sink and mirror in one corner and a door in the other. To her surprise, the handle turned in her hand. She pulled the door open and stepped into the hall.

The long hallway bustled with people. Nurses and doctors in the uniforms of the Medical Corps hurried past her. Though none of them gave her more than a cursory glance, she felt as though they were staring at her. The room she'd exited was halfway along the corridor and she glanced both ways, trying to decide which way she should try first.

With a start, she realized that she hadn't needed to try thinking her way through the map of Sector 27. How long had it been since she'd been able to do that? she wondered. When she tried to bring up her memories of the map, they were sketchy at best. She remembered no more than she would have if she'd studied it a few times, only vague outlines and impressions.

"Sergeant Stowell?" A female voice startled her and she looked toward the source of the voice. A small woman with laugh lines around her mouth watched her closely, her mouth set in disapproval. The expression looked a little strange on her, her face looked made for smiles, not frowns. She had major's insignia on her epaulets and Jak snapped into a salute, only lowering her arm when the woman returned the motion.

"Yes ma'am."

"If you'll follow me. The lead doctor on your surgery team wants to examine you."

"Understood ma'am."

The major strode off down the hall. Jak was taller than she by a few centimeters, but she had to scurry along behind her. The woman moved quickly, but somehow unhurriedly.

She was taken down two flights of stairs and over a pedestrian bridge into a neighboring building. It seemed to contain offices. The amount of hustle and bustle was minimal compared to the activity level of the wards.

The major knocked on a door in a long hallway lined with them. This door, like all the other anonymous doors along the hallway, had nothing remarkable about it. Frosted glass filled a large pane, but there wasn't even a number to distinguish it from the others.

"Come," said a man's voice from the other side. The nurse opened the door and gestured for Jak to proceed inside. "Ah, here's the sergeant now." A trim man with captain's insignia on his shoulders raised an eyebrow at her.

Jak saluted, as did the major who'd come in after her. For the first time, Jak wondered why a woman was forced to salute to a man who should have been her subordinate. The major outranked this captain, yet the nurse's rank was considered separate and unequal.

"You may take a seat, Sergeant. Or I should say, Captain."

"Excuse me, sir?" Jak dropped the last few inches into the seat. She'd already started sitting when he'd made the comment about her rank.

"Central Command has seen fit to give you a promotion." The officer looked somewhat irritated. "He's also seen fit to allow me to give you the good news. You've been promoted to captain and are the first officer in a new branch of the service." He pushed a small lumpy envelope across the desk toward her.

Jak opened it up and stared at the silver double bars that winked back at her. "I see, sir." She didn't actually, but she wasn't sure how the captain would take questioning.

"Call me Dr. Graham. I'm sure Nurse Major Tarrik told you that I performed your surgery. She assisted me along with a small team of equally qualified individuals. I'm glad to see you up and about. We expected you to have woken up almost a day ago. You gave us a bit of a scare."

"So you know, sir?" Jak hated the hesitancy in her voice and cleared her throat. Her voice came out rougher than she meant it to. "Is that going to be a problem?"

He blinked at her, surprised at the vehemence of her tone. "You don't need to call me sir," Graham said, not answering her question. "We're of the same rank."

Jak glanced at Nurse Major Tarrik, then back at the captain. "But she…"

"Isn't in the same position you are," Tarrik interrupted. "Yes, Captain Stowell, we know you're female. Everyone on the team knows your secret. General Callahan handpicked us for our discretion and flexibility. You don't have to worry that any of us will betray you."

"But you don't like me." Jak dropped the gravel in her voice.

"Not because of your gender, Captain." Tarrik smiled at her, utterly devoid of humor.

"I see," Jak said, though once again she didn't. Was this what being an officer was like? Trying to understand what people were saying to you as they talked around the edges of an issue?

"That's neither here nor there," Graham announced. "I have some tests to run on you, Captain. Then you are to report to Central Command, as long as I can determine that you have regained your full mental faculties."

"All right. I do have one question though. Where's Torrin Ivanov?"

Tarrik looked like she'd bitten into a juicy plum only to find half a worm in the fruit. So that was her problem. She disapproved of Jak's relationship with Torrin. How did she even know?

"I'm afraid we don't know, exactly," Graham replied, his face grave as he held her eyes with his. Jak thought she detected a glimmer of empathy in their depths. "She left the surface to contact her home planet for help. Lieutenant Smythe said she expected to be back before you regained consciousness, but she hasn't been seen yet."

"Help for what?" Jak's mind raced. Torrin was overdue. What exactly was going on around here?

Graham nodded at Tarrik. "Make a note, Captain Stowell appears to be experiencing some medium-term memory loss. Not unexpected after this kind of data corruption." He looked back at Jak. "Your memories should return gradually over the next few days. If that doesn't happen, come see me."

"Help for what?" Jak repeated, standing up and leaning forward across the captain's desk.

"I think it best for the general's staff to fill you in on recent events. We need to proceed with your testing."

"You won't be testing me for anything without some answers."

"Stowell," the captain fixed her with a steely glare. She might be on even footing with him, but he clearly felt he could order her around. "You won't get any answers from me. I don't have any for you. The only reason I knew what Lieutenant Smythe had to say is because he stopped by to relay the reason for Miss Ivanov's absence."

Jak stared at him a moment longer before taking her seat again. If he did know what was going on with Torrin, then he was a very good liar. "Let's get those tests out of the way then."

She sat in the chair and answered his questions for as long as she could stand it, her answers getting more and more clipped the longer it took. After that, he hooked her up through the jack in her hand and ran her through a number of simulations. The longer his testing took, the more she chafed at the delay. Finally, after the fifth simulation, Jak pulled the cord out of her palm.

"I'm done," she said flatly.

"That's too bad, Captain," Graham said, his voice equally as uncompromising as hers, "because I'm not. You've gone through barely two-thirds of the simulations."

"Well, I'm walking out of here, whether you like it or not."

Dr. Graham glared at her, dark eyebrows drawn low over his eyes. Surprisingly, it was Nurse Major Tarrik who broke their impasse.

"Doctor, how has she performed on the tests so far?"

"She's the picture of mental fitness," he grumbled.

"Then perhaps she can return to complete the simulations at a later time?" Tarrik addressed Jak directly. "I need to collect your vitals, then you'll be able to go."

"That's fine."

In the face of their agreement, Graham was left with no other choice but to go along with it. Jak decided that Nurse Major Tarrik was a formidable woman who shouldn't be crossed. Technically, the captain might outrank the nurse, but she didn't appear to let such things get in her way.

"I'll be compiling my notes," Graham said and pulled a long cable out of the wall before plugging himself in.

The nurse was all business and rebuffed each of Jak's poor attempts at small talk. She'd never been good at it and she wished that Bron, or better yet Torrin, was there. People had seemed incapable of resisting their charms. Not for the first time, she told herself she would work on improving at engaging with others.

"So how did I do?" she asked after Tarrik was finished.

"Pretty well." The petite nurse frowned slightly. "Your lung function is diminished from what we have on record. We noticed the same problem before your operation, but we weren't sure if it was attributable to your data corruption. In some advanced cases, people start to see physiological disturbances as the corruption spreads to the parts of the brain that handle autonomic functions."

"No surprise there. I picked up a nasty virus before I left the planet. It led to…complications." How did she explain cryostasis to those who had never experienced it? Better to gloss over the details and leave it at that.

Dr. Graham's vision sharpened and lost the inward focus of someone plugged into the net. "The captain's lung function is still compromised? Did I hear that right?"

"Yes Doctor."

"Is it still within acceptable parameters?"

"Barely Doctor. Frankly, previous tests showed her lungs functioning at exceptional capacity. If her lung function hadn't been so high before, I believe she'd be experiencing significant impairment now."

He nodded. "If she's still within normal parameters, then make a note of it. Let's keep an eye on it though."

"The doctor on Nadierzda was very confident that I wasn't going to lose any more capacity," Jak said. "She's pleased with the recovery that I've made."

Graham wrinkled his nose, apparently not impressed by the diagnosis of a doctor he didn't know. He probably didn't appreciate that she was female either. Jak was beginning to understand Torrin's impatience with the men of Haefen, even the Devonites. Since she'd experienced the benefits of a non-gender-restrictive society, it was proving difficult to reacclimatize to the repression of her home planet.

"If you've gotten what you need from me, then I'll be on my way."

"Yes, yes." Graham still looked put out over her skipping out on the last of the simulations. "I expect to see you back here to finish testing."

"Yes Doctor."

"Follow me," Tarrik said to Jak and left the room. She led Jak down the corridor and into a room at the far end of the hall.

The room looked like a lounge of sorts. Couches and cots lined the walls. At least two people were making use of the cots. A few men sat at a table in the center of the room, conversing quietly. A man in a lieutenant's uniform made his way over to them before saluting Jak. That wasn't right. He didn't salute her, she was the one who was supposed to do that. Memories of the man tickled at the underside of her brain for a split second before surfacing.

"Lieutenant Smythe." It took her a moment to realize that he was going to hold the salute until she responded, and she did so in a hurry, a little embarrassed.

"Congratulations on your promotion, Captain," he said quietly.

"I'll leave you two," Tarrik said. "Captain Stowell, if we don't see you back here within three days, I will come and find you and drag you back to complete the tests." She didn't wait to see if her warning had registered; she simply turned with complete confidence that Jak would comply and left the room.

Smythe gave her an amused grimace. "I'd listen to her, if I were you. I don't think I'd want to be on the bad side of that one."

"Tell me about it." Jak rolled her eyes. "I'm pretty sure if I don't listen to her, she'll knife me, then drag me back here. Not only would I have to finish her precious tests, but I'd have to be nursed back to health by her." She gave a small shudder that was only a little more theatrical than she really felt.

"Let's get you back to General Callahan."

"Good. Maybe you can fill me in on what I'm missing."

He nodded and waited for her to precede him through the door. The moment was a little awkward before she remembered that officers of higher rank always left a room before those of lower rank. Her face red, she stepped through the doorway and waited for him in acute discomfort.

"So what's going on?"

"Do you remember anything?" Smythe asked.

"Not much at all." Jak grimaced. "My memories are trickling back, but it's slow going. It was a complete surprise to wake up on Haefen. And in a bit of a delicate position." She watched the lieutenant to see how he'd react to her statement.

He simply nodded, his face giving away nothing. "That must have been difficult."

"It was." Two could play that game. She would admit to nothing unless he initiated the conversation.

He waited for her as she preceded him through another door and they stood under the piercing blue of the Haefonian sky. A military truck waited for them and she climbed into the back. The private in the driver's seat gave her a horrified look and exited the vehicle with unseemly haste.

"It's all right for you to ride in the front now, Captain," Smythe said, mild amusement coloring his voice.

Jak grumbled under her breath and stepped over the break between the front seats and settled herself in the passenger seat. The private climbed into the backseat and Smythe took his spot behind the wheel. With a grind of gears, he put the truck into motion.

"We don't have too far to go," Smythe assured her. He glanced back at the enlisted man in the backseat and ventured nothing further.

Jak chafed at the delay and tried to bring up the subject. Her inquiries were politely diverted by comments about the weather and other inanities. Finally, she lapsed into irritated silence and brooded for the remainder of the ride. Where was Torrin and what was going on?

"Here we are." True to his word, the ride had been very short, less than ten minutes all told. Smythe hadn't pulled up in front of the hulking edifice that housed General Callahan's offices. Instead, they were at a large house. At three stories, it was bigger than most houses she'd seen on Haefen, though much smaller than the monstrosity Hutchinson had called home. That was another one she hadn't realized she'd forgotten until it came back. *Hutchinson.* She tasted the name in her mind, not liking the bitterness that came with it. The holes in her memory were frustrating, though they seemed to give up their secrets more readily when she wasn't trying to force them.

Keeping an eye on the house, Jak climbed down from the front passenger seat. It was much easier to negotiate than climbing out of the back of a truck. She could get to like being an officer, she thought. Smythe also climbed down and the private waited until they were both clear before maneuvering himself into the driver's seat and driving off.

"So what is going on?" Jak burst out, unable to hold it in any longer. "What's going on with Torrin?"

"Too many ears out here," Smythe said, his hand raised in a mollifying gesture. "Let's go inside."

She looked around and didn't see anyone remotely close to them. There were a number of men in officers' uniforms hanging around closer to the house, but none were within earshot. Jak ground her teeth but held her tongue. Her usual patience was deserting her, as it tended to with anything involving Torrin.

"I'll show you your room, then we can talk." Smythe jogged up the front steps of the house.

There were a decent number of stairs and Jak was slightly winded when she reached the top. Her lung capacity was diminished, that much was obvious. There had been an illness, she'd known that much when the nurse uncovered her lung issues. The details were sketchy, but she had flashes of the forest and a clearing full of dying Orthodoxans. Those must have been some crazy fever dreams...

Some of the officers greeted Smythe by name as they entered the house; others nodded to him in passing. All of them eyed her curiously. A few of them seemed to recognize her and seemed to be wondering what she was doing in their bastion against the unwashed enlisted. She wished she'd taken the time to affix the captain's insignia to the epaulets of her jacket. Her shoulders had always been empty, and here she was wishing there was something on them. The thought produced an inner snicker at her hubris. She'd never thought highly of those officers who insisted on wearing their insignia on the front lines, especially not the newly minted ones. She understood a little better the reasoning behind their choice. It was a stupid and suicidal choice, but one that she could now sympathize with, at least a little bit.

Up the stairs and down a hallway well-lit with large windows, Smythe led her to a bedroom. It wasn't huge, but compared to the room she'd shared with Bron in the snipers' barracks, it was palatial. A small bathroom with gleaming fixtures was visible through an open door and the brilliant mirror was devoid of pits and cracks. A real bed, not a cot, graced the center of the room. Wonder of wonders, she had a dresser, not just a footlocker and duffel bag in which to store her belongings. A large viewscreen took up part of one wall and there were multiple cable plug-ins around the room.

"So what do you think of your new room, sir? A bit of a step up from your last quarters, I'd think."

Jak fixed him with a hard glare. "Don't try to distract me. What's going on?"

Smythe sighed and sat in a chair by the window and gestured for her to take the seat across from him. "You and Torrin came here to fix your data corruption problem, but we thought you were here because of what happened to the latest set of her suppliers." He carefully studied her face for a long moment then continued. "One of them was shot and the other kidnapped by the sniper known as—"

"Crimson," Jak finished for him. "I know his work."

"I thought you might."

When he stopped and showed no signs of going further, Jak bored in for more detail. He was definitely holding something back, and she was starting to feel rising nausea. "So who was killed?"

"Not Torrin's sister."

Relief washed over her and Jak felt momentarily lightheaded. Dread returned in a heartbeat. "So she's the one who's kidnapped? Do you have any idea where she is? What's being done to recover her?"

"It's too bad you've got some memory loss. So far, you're the one who's done the most to get her back." Smythe filled her in on their ill-fated trip to Hill 372 and the ambush by Crimson. Her mind wandered while he talked, chased itself in circles, really. It always seemed to come back to the sniper with her, and she didn't think it was all coincidence. He'd killed her father, her brother and had now kidnapped her lover's sister.

"Wait, Collins died?" She caught Smythe's words a little late and looked at him, stricken. He'd been a tie to her former life, one that was getting further and further away. At the lieutenant's confirmation, she clenched her jaw.

"So now we know we have a traitor in our midst," Smythe continued. "It's something we've suspected for a long time, but the speed of the attack confirmed it. When Torrin found out about the mole, she decided to call in reinforcements. She left the surface in her sister's ship and said something about heading to the nearest relay. She was determined to get back before you came out of sedation."

"When was that?"

"Almost two days ago. She had to escape the League ships manning the blockade. The last we saw of her, she was trying to outrun one, then she up and disappeared."

"Disappeared?" Jak was suddenly standing. Her voice was shrill and she ruthlessly throttled her rising panic. "What do you mean by 'disappeared'?" she asked in a more moderate tone.

"Only that one second she was on the *Calamity Jane's* sensors and the next she wasn't. Her ship didn't say much. The computer, Tien was it?" Smythe continued after her nod. "Tien didn't think her ship had been destroyed. She is of the opinion that Torrin probably translated to peripheral space, though she's not completely certain."

"But she's reasonably confident?" Jak grasped at the small piece of encouraging news.

"Yes. Though, she's also concerned that Torrin hasn't returned yet. Apparently the nearest relay is only about ten hours away, which means she should have been back over a day ago. We have no means of communicating with her."

Unable to quell the nervous energy that swelled within her, Jak paced the floor in front of the window. "I need to help her."

"I don't know how you're going to do that," Smythe said, voice gentle. "Not unless you know how to pilot a spaceship."

"I don't," Jak admitted. If she couldn't help Torrin, then she had to help the one person she could. Nat was relying on her and there was no one else better suited to finding her. "I'm going out."

"Don't go for too long. The general wants to speak to you first thing tomorrow morning. He needs to fill you in on your new position."

"Got it," Jak said. "I'll be there." The lie sat easily on her tongue. As far as she was concerned, keeping Callahan happy was the least of her priorities.

"Good. I'll let you get settled then. Your gear's been brought in. You'll find everything you need here." With a final salute, Smythe left the room, closing the door gently behind him.

Jak pulled open a few drawers and found fatigues inside. She pulled out a full set. Smythe had said her gear was all here, so where was her weaponry? The knife and pistol she found in another dresser drawer, but her rifle was nowhere to be found. A little more poking around revealed it leaning in the room's small closet.

She pulled off her jacket to change into the fatigues and heard clinking in one pocket. Remembering the rank insignia, she pulled them out. They were very shiny, she thought, as she ran a finger over the edges. Aware of exactly how much she was giving up, she placed them on top of the dresser and went back to changing.

CHAPTER TWELVE

"Fuck," Torrin yelled. Her ears rang from where she'd hit her head on a pipe. She raised the spanner in her hand before thinking better of it and lowering it again. If she gave in to her impulse to bash the nearest object, who knew what else she would damage. The ship was a hunk of junk. She was embarrassed to have it in her fleet and it was costing her valuable time.

"Are you all right, Torrin?" Eowyn asked.

"Fine," Torrin grumbled. "Just fucking fine. How the hell did you end up in such disrepair, anyway?"

"Apparently my last retrofit was delayed, Torrin." The AIs voice didn't betray any satisfaction, but Torrin felt like she might have been gloating, at least a little bit. The decision to delay upgrades wouldn't have been Torrin's, but she felt guilty nonetheless. She was going to have a long talk with Mac when she got back to Nadierzda.

The power coupling finally lay open in front of her, its innards exposed. The conductive gel inside had deteriorated so much that it had hardened and then crumbled into burnt orange sand. She was careful not to let the crumbs come in contact with her skin. Even in its poor condition, the gel was highly corrosive and she had no desire to view the muscles of her hands up close. Only the specialized silicone coating on the interior of the ship's conduits and couplings kept it from eating through her ship's innards.

With a shake of her head to dispel the last of the pain, Torrin carefully laid aside the spanner and pulled on a pair of mesh gloves. They were heavy and lined with thick silicone; the outside was a fabric of woven carbon-steel. With extreme care, she pulled the gel-dregs out of the coupling with a metal scoop. It looked like a soup ladle, if the ladle had a handle that was three feet long and the bowl was protected by yet another thick layer of silicone. She gingerly placed the dregs in a container beside her where they hissed when they came in contact with the bottom and sides. Slowly, she cleared out the decayed gel, then sealed it securely in the container. They would be able to reconstitute the conductive gel, but that would have to wait until the *Melisende* got back to Nadierzda.

The coupling was clear of the old gel. Torrin had cleared the final crumbs by hand, moving with deliberate speed so they didn't eat through the material of her gloves. The gloves' only sign of damage was scorched fingertips. She examined them carefully before deciding they were all right.

Another container lay a short way down the dark crawlway. Power to the entire section had been cut and the only light came from the small, but bright, lamp Torrin had clipped around her neck. Torrin dragged the now-full container of desiccated gel behind her down the crawlway. It wasn't the gel that made it so heavy. No, what made it so heavy was the shielding that prevented the gel from eating through the container, then through the floor, then through the deck below and finally out through the hull, exposing the ship to hard vacuum.

With the other container, Torrin crawled back to the coupling and paused, making sure her hands were rock-steady before opening the lid. Unlike the dried gel that had still been hissing in the container, even before she closed it, the liquid gel bubbled. It sounded like champagne as tiny air bubbles broke its surface. Her eyes watered at the acrid vapors it released. It cast a muted orange glow through the cramped passageway. Carefully, she lifted the heavy container and poured its contents into the exposed coupling with agonizing slowness. As soon as the void in the coupling was filled, she slapped the top back on the container and attacked the exposed coupling with a vengeance. As fast as she could, she closed the coupling back up.

"That's done it." Torrin mopped at her sweating forehead with the crook of her elbow and exhaled loudly with relief. "Turn the power to this section back on."

"Affirmative Torrin," Eowyn replied.

Torrin held her breath. The lights came back on smoothly, without the slightest flicker. She sighed again and crawled back down the cramped passage, picking up the second container at the junction where she'd left it. It took some wriggling, but she managed to get both containers out of the crawlway and past the bulk of the port engine without having to drop one and go back for it later.

Of course it was the power coupling to one of the engines that had failed. Torrin was glad it had failed on the translation from peripheral space to normal space. If it had failed going into peripheral space, no one would have ever known what happened to them.

But that meant they were nowhere near their original destination. Not only had they not made it to their final jump, but the power surge before the engine failed had pushed them through the fabric between spaces hard enough that they'd overshot their jump. It was miraculous that they hadn't been pushed out into a planet or a star or the path of a comet. The only silver lining was that the surge would have made it almost impossible for the League ship on their tail to follow them.

Torrin secured both containers in a specially designed cabinet in the workroom. The metal of the cabinet was three inches thick and further buffered by silicone, then another layer of metal. Short of an explosion right inside the cabinet, the caustic cargo was safe.

"Run the engines through a full diagnostic, Eowyn," Torrin said. She climbed up the ladder to the upper deck and strode down the hall, not taking the time to change out of her soot-marked and grease-stained coveralls. The bridge door hissed open and she dropped into the captain's chair. The engines whined as the AI put them through their paces and Torrin watched the diagnostic levels on the screen. Everything seemed to be functioning within normal parameters.

She swiped the diagnostic results into a small corner of her console and brought up a star chart of the area. They'd come out of the periphery into an area of space she wasn't familiar with. It appeared to have been largely unexplored and Torrin could see why as she perused the charts. If she was correct, the area was almost completely inaccessible via peripheral space. That they hadn't ended up in a black hole or a supernova was ascribable only to luck. She shuddered when she realized how close they'd come to disappearing without a trace.

"Eowyn, I want you to do your best to recreate exactly how we ended up here through peripheral space." It could be very handy to have a little bolt hole that could be accessed through FTL only by those who knew exactly what they were doing. Unfortunately, at the moment it meant they would have to navigate out of the area the long way. Until Eowyn had properly charted the trajectory, there was no way she was going to try reverse engineering their trek.

"Affirmative Torrin. Also, I have completed the diagnostic and both engines are back at full capacity."

"Excellent." Torrin marked the relay they'd been aiming for on the chart and calculated the fastest way over to it. Their best bet was actually to head away from the relay until they got to a sector that was clear enough to allow them to make their next jump. The black holes that littered this little corner of the galaxy were strong enough to pull a ship into them even when it wasn't traveling in normal space. She brought the engines on line and plotted her course. This time, the *Melisende* obliged her and they were moving swiftly toward the jump point.

Torrin was loath to coax the engines anywhere near their standard safety limits. The last thing she needed was another blowout. When they got the ship back to Nadierzda, she would have the entire power system overhauled. She'd noticed other spots along the conduits that were less luminous than they should have been. All the same, she chafed at the delay. Jak was probably already awake. She'd promised to be present when Jak woke up and she'd already broken that promise. There wasn't much she could have done about it, but she was bothered by it all the same.

She caught herself running a hand through her hair and smiled. It was one of Jak's nervous habits, and it seemed she'd picked it up. Whether she would have the same habit when her hair had grown out to a more acceptable length remained to be seen. The strands curled around her chin and jawline. When it was this short, there was some curl to it. It had been so long since she'd had hair so short, that she'd forgotten how curly it could get.

Why was she obsessing about her hair? Didn't she have better things to worry about? Like Nat? Torrin grimaced and pulled her mind away from considerations of what her sister could possibly be going through. Knowing the Orthodoxans, whatever it was couldn't be good. They had to get her back. She reached over to the console and nudged the speed up. She had to override the safety limits to go faster, but only by a little bit.

"At our current speed, how long until we reach the jump point I've marked?" Torrin asked.

"My calculations show about eight hours, Torrin."

Unacceptable. Eight hours, then at least another twelve or so to reach the relay. Torrin bumped up their speed even further. Urgency rode her now. They could have another blowout, but it was time to make the gamble.

Six and a half hours later, Torrin was back in the cryopod preparing for the jump to peripheral space. Soon after, they would be close enough to the relay that she could send out a communications burst. The message should bring the cavalry in a hurry. She wanted the best, someone she could rely on in addition to Jak. With some outside help, there was a chance they'd be able to get Nat back in one piece.

There were no sounds of movement from the hall and there hadn't been any for some time. Sunset had been hours ago, but activity in the large house had continued until about thirty minutes ago. Jak had checked the window, but there was no good way to climb down and she wasn't going to risk jumping and injuring herself. She was going to have to sneak out through the building instead.

Slowly, she turned the handle and pulled the door open. She held her breath and cringed as she did so, waiting for the hinges to give her away. Thankfully, the door opened noiselessly. She slipped through the doorway, closing it carefully behind her. The floorboards beneath her feet squeaked slightly, and Jak froze before moving forward slowly. She worked to spread the weight on her feet across as much surface area as possible as she tried to avoid giving herself away. Bron had always claimed it was the only way to keep from squeaking floorboards. He would have known, she supposed. He was constantly sneaking out after lights out on one assignation or another. That had never been an interest of hers, though if she'd known... Her ears heated as she thought of Torrin and the last time they'd made love.

And then Torrin had gone and slept with someone else.

Jak came to a momentary stop. That was something she hadn't remembered until right then. And it wasn't quite right. Torrin hadn't slept with another woman. That had been a deception engineered by Tanith. Tanith, who was dead, Jak remembered with some satisfaction.

With deliberate caution, she continued forward toward the head of the stairs.

The darkness of the stairway yawned before her and she engaged her implant. The shadows gave way to sharp contrast and she negotiated her way down the steps.

Where is Torrin anyway? Sadness swamped her and she fought not to burst into tears. Torrin was missing and Jak didn't even know what her last words to her lover had been. The stairs swam in her vision and she blinked rapidly to dispel her tears.

The last step successfully negotiated, Jak whispered a small sigh of relief as she hit the bottom floor.

Her night vision disappeared in a painful flare of white. With a muffled oath, she squeezed her eyes shut, tears streaming from the abused orbs.

"What have we here?"

Jak recognized the voice. She gritted her teeth and switched off the overloaded implant. With deliberate slowness she cracked one eye open and glared in the direction of the voice.

"McCullock." Her voice was flat, almost dead. It gave her grim satisfaction not to have to acknowledge his elevated rank. They were now peers, if only in name.

"I'd heard you were back." He moved closer, the ginger mustache twitching below his nose.

"What of it?"

"It's an interesting choice," he said. "Your first day at a higher rank and you're sneaking out of here. You're a bit of an ungrateful whelp, aren't you?"

"What are you doing here?"

"Put in for a transfer, didn't I? I seem to remember you being very adamant about that." He beamed at her and she stared at him. She'd never seen that look on his face before. "Best move I ever made. The intel here is far more interesting. You wouldn't believe some of the rumors I hear. Really, I should thank you."

Floored by his sudden shift in mood, Jak stared at him. She closed her mouth with a snap.

"Why don't you come with me, kid?" He drew near her and moved to throw an arm around her shoulders, but she moved out of his reach. He dropped his arm and studied her, his head cocked to one side. "You might as well come with me. I could turn you in right here, but there are some things I think you need to hear instead."

"I don't have much choice, do I?" Jak made sure to roughen her voice. After witnessing one of this man's last interactions with a woman, she really didn't want him to realize her real gender. Or was he trying to tell her that he already knew?

"Not at all," he said, voice actually cheerful.

"Lead on then."

"We'll go to my room."

Crap, *did* he know she was female? Was this a ploy to get her up to his room where he would take advantage of her? Briefly she considered bashing in the back of his head as he preceded her up the stairs. Her hand twitched on the butt of Bron's pistol. The heft of the pistol would easily be enough to knock him out. But then how would she explain her assault of a fellow officer?

Her hand on the pistol's grip soothed her. She released the catch on the holster and eased it slightly. He wouldn't catch her unaware if he tried anything. While she preferred the rifle, her accuracy was still damn good with a pistol. If he decided to attack her, she would make sure he regretted whatever twisted impulse had set him after her.

With some apprehension, Jak followed McCullock to his room. His quarters were on the top floor. The fourth floor's hallway was dark, the walls lined with unfinished oak and there was a decided lack of adequate lighting. Many more doors lined the hall here than where her quarters were.

McCullock opened the door into a cramped room that was even darker than the hall had been. He slapped his hand on a light panel next to the door. There wasn't much improvement and Jak considered activating her implant again.

"Have a seat," McCullock said, indicating a seat by the room's tiny window.

"I'm fine here." Jak leaned against the doorframe and waved him toward the chair. There was no way she was going to let him stand between her and the door. She watched him carefully while he fussed with the chair before finally sitting in it.

He cleared his throat nervously and looked back at her.

Jak got tired of waiting. "So what is it you want from me?"

"A couple things." The captain fiddled with the corner of his mustache. Silence stretched between them. "I was wrong about you," he burst out after too much silence. "I thought you were some kind of fairy and I treated you like crap because of it."

"You thought what?" Of all the things he could have said to her, this was not one she'd expected. An apology? For being right, no less, though not in the way he thought.

"Well, you never had a girl or seemed interested in finding one. Your brother obviously didn't have that problem. He was constantly on report for sneaking out, but not you." He grinned at her conspiratorially. "I should have known when you showed up in Miss Ivanov's room that you had something going on with her."

"What makes you think I did?" She didn't want knowledge of her relationship with Torrin to become common knowledge. Only a fool would believe that the truth of her gender would remain a secret forever and she was no fool. Lesbians didn't fare any better than gay men in Devonite mores.

McCullock laughed out loud at her evasion. "It's over half of Fort Marshall." He watched shock chase across her face and pointed a finger at her. "Take it from an intel officer, if you want to keep a relationship secret, then don't go in for a tongue lock in front of your escorts."

The scenario seemed unlikely. She couldn't imagine permitting Torrin to kiss her in front of Devonite witnesses. She barely let Torrin kiss her in front of the other women of Nadierzda. Years of deception had made her very secretive about her personal life. But if McCullock knew, it must have happened.

"So what was the other thing?" Jak asked after realizing the silence had gone on too long once again.

"I need to tell you that our command structure has been compromised." He leaned forward, elbows on his knees. "When they accepted my transfer, they put me to analyzing the patterns of Orthodoxan movements in relation to our own. The Orthodoxans know things they shouldn't unless someone high up has been feeding them information." He grimaced and gestured to the room. "Popular opinion of me isn't exactly glowing at the moment, as you can tell by my current accommodations."

"What does that have to do with me?"

"I think we can help each other. If I can break open who the traitor is, I can feed you the information. That could help you get your lover's sister back."

"Why should I trust you? After what you tried to do to Torrin, I should put a bullet between your eyes and dump your body in the woods." Jak still didn't trust him, but it sounded like he had a better line on the mole, better than anyone else she knew about. Or he was the traitor and was trying to lull her into complacency. Taking Torrin out would certainly help the Orthodoxan cause.

"You need me." McCullock's face had a strange look and it took Jak a moment to realize he was going for sincerity. It made him look as if he were trying to combat a case of the runs. "I've got a bead on the intel and I know what to do with it. You need that kind of information to go after Crimson. Smythe might think he has a lock on everything, but there are people who talk to me precisely because they know I'm not well thought of at the moment."

"And what's in it for you?"

"No one listens to me." McCullock's voice was petulant. This was definitely more in line with what she was used to hearing from him. "If I can crack this, you can get it to the people who need to hear about it. You're in much better odor with the brass right now. Your room used to belong to a major. Usually captains don't move below the third floor. Lieutenants are relegated up here. Second floor is for majors, colonels and the like."

"So what you want is to get a more comfortable room?"

"It's not the comfort, you little…" McCullock didn't look sincere anymore, he looked angry. His mustache twitched beneath his nose. "It's the status. They still salute me, but the lieutenants are pretty damn slow about it. I know what they think of me, but if I can expose the mole, they'll have to take me seriously. Besides, taking out the mole means that our men stop dying needlessly."

Jak hesitated. Could she afford to blow him off? If she agreed to help him, at least she could keep an eye on him. He seemed to have gotten past some of his hatred of her, but how much of that was a front and how much was the convenience of the situation? But if she could find the leak and follow it to the next link in the chain, she could use that information to draw out Crimson. If it turned out that McCullock was the traitor, then she would happily kill him after slowly extracting the information she needed.

McCullock recoiled slightly at her smile, and she softened it to something that appeared more genuine, or so she hoped. "You've got yourself a deal," she said.

"Excellent," he said and bounded out of his chair and crossed the room to her in two steps, his hand outstretched. Jak half-drew her pistol from the holster at his abrupt movement but jammed it back in when she realized he wasn't attacking her. Hopefully he hadn't noticed. He grabbed her hand and shook it vigorously before pulling her close to him and thrusting his face in hers.

Jak tried to pull her hand back, her heart pounding in sudden panic.

"Don't you screw this up for us," he hissed. His sour breath washed over her. Jak turned her head to get the stench out of her nostrils. "You can't let them know we're onto them. So no unauthorized operations in the dead of night." He let go of her hand and she massaged it where he'd crushed her fingers. "That's right, I know what you were up to tonight. I won't let you throw this opportunity away for both of us."

"You don't have any say."

"Maybe not." He shrugged. "But I can spike your plans pretty easily. I'm not saying you can't go running around in the woods looking for your brother's killer or to rescue Ivanov's sister, but you have to play this one straight. That means following orders. If you're out there doing whatever, I won't be able to tell if the Orthodoxans are responding to leaked orders or if they're lucking out."

He made sense, but Jak didn't know how she'd be able to stand sitting around without doing anything. She stared at him, her jaw set in defiance.

"You're not going to do anybody any good if you get killed," he pointed out. "Follow your orders for once. If you get killed before we can figure this out, you'll be killing more than Ivanov's sister. You'll be killing countless of our men."

"Fine," Jak ground out. "I won't go after him tonight."

"You won't go after him until you have orders to do so."

"We'll see." She raised a hand when he opened his mouth to argue further. "It's the best you're going to get from me, so save your breath."

"It'll have to do." He stepped back and she straightened from her defensive half-crouch. "I'll contact you when I have something. Oh, and we need to keep our partnership secret."

"You don't have to worry about me advertising it, believe me."

"Good." He smiled again. It was amazing how normal he looked when he smiled. When his venom was directed elsewhere, he almost seemed like a regular human being. "Our bad blood is actually excellent cover. No one will ever suspect that we're working together." His face darkened again. "Unless you fuck it up." And there he went again, back to subhuman in five little words.

"Got it." Jak let herself out of his room before he could say anything further. She moved quietly down the hall. The turn of events was surprising to say the least. That was one of the longest conversations she'd ever had with McCullock. Unlike her other interactions with him, she hadn't come out of it ready to set herself up in a blind and wait for him to expose himself so she could blow his brains out.

The stairs were dark and she crept down them, keeping to the outside of the steps where they would be less likely to creak. She didn't trust McCullock. As far as she was concerned, there was as much chance that he was the traitor as not. But if he was, she would use the situation to her advantage. If only Torrin were there. The hollowness in her chest threatened to choke her as she worried about her lover. Where could she possibly be? She needed Torrin and not only to help her figure out the undercurrents of intrigue.

Jak let herself back into her new room and locked the door behind her. She pulled the rifle out of the closet and leaned it within arm's reach of the bed, then collapsed backward onto the soft mattress. The tears she'd been holding in finally overwhelmed her and she curled up in a tight ball. What was she going to do? Once again she was all alone. She was walking a thin branch high above the forest floor and it was getting thinner. She couldn't go back and any misstep would kill her. There was no one there to catch her.

CHAPTER THIRTEEN

Masculine laughter jerked Jak from her fitful slumber. Sitting up, she looked wildly around the room. For a few panicked moments she couldn't remember where she was. Then it came back... She'd been with McCullock last night, and he'd almost been a regular human being. Surely she'd been dreaming. Sure, he was being a decent guy because he needed something from her and because he no longer thought she was gay. She snorted in amusement.

A sharp knock on the door sent her scrambling under the covers before she remembered that she was mostly clothed and still wore her breastbinder.

"Captain Stowell?"

"What is it?" She roughened her voice. Her throat had started to feel raw from all the gravelly talking she was doing.

"General Callahan has sent word that he wants to see you by 0900."

She grunted in response as she scrabbled under the bed to find her boots. "I'll be there."

"You can request a driver downstairs, sir."

"Fine, fine." Jak hauled one boot out from under the bed. She had to get up to find the other where she'd kicked it over the end of the bed. She tutted to herself. There was no excuse for the mess.

She hauled herself into the small bathroom. A quick glance at the mirror over the sink showed that she was in no condition for an audience with the general. Her fatigues were rumpled and creased. There was nothing for it; she would have to put on the service uniform. The room's closet had revealed a set of dress blues, but there was no way she could wear those. It probably wasn't appropriate for the meeting, and only McCullock wore his dress uniform around the camp. Besides that, she wasn't even sure how all the different pieces went together.

There was no time for a shower either; she had only a little more than half an hour to get prepared. She stripped off the jacket and shirt of her combat uniform and scrubbed down her face, chest and arms. At least she didn't have to shave. Men really were unobservant, she thought as she patted her hair dry. It had apparently never occurred to any of them to wonder why Sergeant Stowell had never needed a shave. No wonder they'd allowed an Orthodoxan sympathizer, or worse an Orthodoxan, to infiltrate their ranks.

The swiftness of practice was hampered somewhat by the unfamiliar service uniform. She was on her way out the door when she remembered the rank and unit insignia. The pins slid smoothly through the grommets in the material.

The man who stared back at her from the mirror was wholly unfamiliar. Bron would have laughed his ass off to see her. Jak had barely worn the service uniform as an enlisted soldier; she'd pretty much lived in fatigues. Seeing herself in it now brought her up short. There was a certain gravitas to her now, even though she felt like a stuffed shirt. She looked at the peaked cap in her hands in discomfort. For so long, officers had symbolized so much of what was wrong with her life. They'd told her where to go, whom to kill and when to do it. They'd been her targets. Orthodoxan officers were the ones locking their people into the straitjacket of the messed-up morals they'd been laboring under for centuries. And now she was one of them. It should have given her a sense of freedom, but all she felt was the weight of unwanted responsibility pressing down on her shoulders.

Jak pulled her bowed shoulders back and stared at herself in the mirror. Responsibility had never been something she'd shirked and she wasn't about to start now. Glaring at her reflection in defiance, she settled the cap on her head and left the room, stopping only to snag her rifle and settle it over her shoulder. It wasn't part of the uniform, but she wasn't going to let her rank change who she was.

She passed a major and a lieutenant colonel in the hall on the way to the stairs. They nodded to her and returned her salute without making her wait. What had she done to deserve so much respect? she wondered. All she'd done before her promotion had been her job. There were dozens of enlisted soldiers who were more deserving of the elevation in rank than she was.

With wary eyes, she watched the men she passed, but none of them seemed to harbor any ill will or hard feelings for the suddenness of her promotion. They greeted her with cheeriness and affability. To escape their approving stares, she headed right out the front doors. She would flag down a vehicle on the way to the general's office, or she'd walk the entire way if she had to. Her mood had soured considerably since she woke up and it had been dark to begin with. It seemed disagreeable Stowell was back with a vengeance. *Good*, she decided. Maybe it would keep some of them away from her. The last thing she needed was to make nice with anyone. She had work to do and they were all keeping her from it with their promotions and their niceties.

It was surprisingly easy to flag down a transport vehicle. The new uniform had its advantages, though she caught some of the men giving her unfamiliar unit insignia second and third looks. Jak didn't enlighten the inquiring glances; she was still waiting to find out.

"Sir!" A frantic sergeant came pelting out of the truck's cab when she tried to climb in the back of the truck with the enlisted men. "It's all right, sir. I'll ride with the men, you can ride up front."

"I don't mind," Jak said, determined that she was going to damn well ride with some real soldiers. She looked up to find twelve men staring down at her with varying expressions of consternation. It dawned on her that she wasn't one of them any longer. The realization hurt more than she'd thought it would. She'd never really considered herself one of the guys but being further alienated from them was a bigger blow than it should have been. "Never mind, Sergeant. I'll take the front."

"Very good, sir." The man hauled himself into the truck's covered bed and Jak made her way around to the front. The cab was raised, but there were adequate footholds and she climbed in to join the driver.

"Sir," the driver said. He shifted the truck into gear as she closed the door. "Where are you headed?"

"I need to get out at the admin building."

"Yes, sir, it's on our way out of the fort."

"Good. I don't want to put you out. If it's at all out of the way, let me out as close as you can and I can hoof it the rest of the way."

The driver's glance was less horrified than the sergeant's had been, but it was still concerned. She was never going to get the hang of this command bullshit. She'd been a sergeant, but that had meant very little actual command in the sniper regiment. As a spotter, Bron had been a corporal, though he hadn't let the technical difference in rank stop him from giving her hell when he thought she deserved it, which was most of the time.

One thing she did know was that officers didn't apologize. She wasn't sure if she would be able to hold to that, but she wasn't going to apologize for being who she was. The Devonites were going to have learn to deal with it.

The ride was quiet and uncomfortable. Her one attempt at conversation had made the driver visibly nervous so she stopped trying to chat. Bron would have put the man at ease with a well-timed quip and they would have been chatting away like they'd known each other for years after only a couple of minutes. The only person she felt particularly glib with was Torrin and a few of the women she'd met on Nadierzda. She wished they hadn't left Torrin's home planet.

Coming back had been a mistake. Torrin was missing, Nat had been kidnapped and she was back where she'd been at the start. The only thing Jak could show for any of it was a snazzier uniform.

"Here we are, sir." The driver jammed on the brakes and the truck jolted Jak out of her unwelcome introspection.

"Thank you." Jak opened the door and hopped down without checking to see if her politeness had thrown the man for another loop. She took a moment to gather her thoughts in front of the unprepossessing structure before heading inside.

"Captain Stowell." A private with the insignia of the general staff on his collar waved to get her attention.

"Yes?"

"Come with me, please, sir. The Command Council wants to speak with you."

"I thought I was here to see the general only."

"I was told to take you to the council, sir." The private shrugged and trotted off down the hall. Jak didn't have much choice except to follow. Her irritation grew with every step. The council meant she would be spending even more time on pleasantries and bureaucratic bullshit.

"In here, sir. They'll call you when they're ready." She was waved into a small antechamber. A few uncomfortable-looking benches graced the dim room. Satisfied that he'd discharged his duty, the private left Jak to her own devices.

After a quick turn among the benches, she finally chose a seat where she could keep an eye on both of the room's doors. She sat and allowed herself to slip into the semimeditative state she usually employed when on a stalk. There she would be beyond the reach of her worries.

The far door opened and Jak snapped back to herself. She hadn't been waiting long, maybe fifteen minutes if her internal clock was anything to go by. It would have been nice to have some view of the sky. From that, she would have been able to tell almost to the minute how long she'd been within herself. The call of the forest tugged at her.

"Captain Stowell?" A clerk stood silhouetted in the doorway. She stood. "Central Command Council is ready for you now." He stood to one side and held the door open for her.

The room beyond the antechamber was enormous, the ceiling rising high above their heads. General Callahan sat at the head of a horseshoe-shaped table, his clerk sat to his left. Colonels Wolfe and Elsby were also there with their aides. Another half dozen high-ranking officers and their aides were arrayed along either side of the horseshoe.

"Captain," Callahan rose in his chair and returned her salute before gesturing to a chair that sat halfway between the ends of the table.

"Sirs," Jak said, nodding to the officers around the table. Judging from their insignia, they ranged from majors through lieutenant-colonels and colonels. The Devonite army had only one general. By contrast, she'd heard that the Orthodoxans had anywhere between twenty and thirty generals, depending on their ability to avoid political disfavor. Orthodoxan generals who found themselves on the wrong side of politics or who lost too many engagements tended to be summarily executed.

"Captain Stowell, you are the first member of a newly created special branch." Callahan looked her in the eye. She was a little surprised that he hadn't beaten around the bush, and she appreciated his willingness to get down to business. "We're calling you the Liaison Corps, though the name could change."

"Sir? What does that mean?"

"Your main duties are to assist in coordinating the receipt of goods from Troika Corp."

From his explanation, she figured she would be helping Torrin, but that would make her little more than a glorified quartermaster.

"For now, you'll be reporting to me and Colonel Wilson, head of Supply and Logistics."

At one end of the table, a bluff man whose service uniform strained against his portly frame half-rose from his chair. "That's me, Stowell."

"Sir." Jak nodded to him. She didn't know much about him. That in itself was probably a good sign. If the man had been an unmitigated asshole, it would have been all over the armed forces. She hoped. "What exactly will I be doing?"

Wilson settled himself back in his seat and crossed his arms across his substantial chest. He regarded her for few seconds before responding. "The first thing we need is an analysis of how we can continue to receive our shipments should Miss Ivanov not return."

Nods from around the table greeted his pronouncement even as Jak's stomach plummeted. If they were asking her for such an assessment, then they believed there was a good chance that Torrin wouldn't be back.

"Miss Ivanov's unexpected disappearance only underscores our dependence on her," Elsby said. "We need to know how we can continue to receive the materials we've paid for even if she's no longer...in the picture."

"Very true." Callahan nodded. "She will likely return, but this sudden disappearance on top of the weeks there was no Troika Corp representation after the unfortunate death and kidnapping, well, it only reminds us that we need some contingency plans in place."

A major with an impressive handlebar mustache stood and addressed Jak. "Captain Stowell, when do you think we might have the next shipment?"

"I don't know, sir." Her palms were starting to sweat. She hadn't been prepared to become the point person of a brand-new unit nor to be grilled about her lover's activities. "I'm not privy to Miss Ivanov's business plans."

"Are we supposed to believe that Miss Ivanov hasn't confided in you at all? From what I've heard, you two are very close."

Mentally, Jak cursed whatever impulse of Torrin's had led to that damning kiss. The only thing worse than knowing Torrin had kissed her in public was not being able to remember it. She would have at least liked to enjoy it.

"Crandon!" The general's voice was a whipcrack of reproach. "Captain Stowell is here to offer his opinion, nothing further. There is no reason to believe that any rumored personal relationship might give him special access to Ivanov's plans."

"Apologies sir." Crandon said. He ran a finger over his mustache. "And to you as well, Captain."

"That does bring up an interesting point though," another major said, a little aggressively. "How sustainable is this business relationship? It seems to me that having a supplier from offworld is a major liability."

"Of course it is," Wilson blustered back. "That's why we've created this new unit. It's high time we accept that there are others out there, off our world. They can help us or hinder us, but we need to be prepared to explore those options regardless. Don't forget about the League of Solaran Planets."

Jak tuned out the argument as it unfolded. Most of it was far above her head, if no longer so far above her pay grade. She should have been paying attention, but all she could think about were the call of the forest and Nat all alone out there. When addressed by one of the council, she responded and the meeting dragged on. Finally General Callahan stood up to dismiss them.

"Captain, you'll stay with me and Colonel Wilson. We have some specifics to go over."

"Yes sir." Jak stood. She wished she'd ignored McCullock and left when she had the chance.

More meetings? *How does the brass get anything done?* Jak wondered. So far all she'd seen them do was talk. There was no chance she could slip away, not when Callahan and Wilson were standing right there. She tried not to seethe too visibly as she followed the men up two flights of stairs and down the hall to the general's office.

"I know you want to get out there, Captain," Callahan said as soon as the door was shut.

"Yes sir. I do."

"You have a greater responsibility now than to only one person, I hope you realize that."

"And I hope you realize, sir, that if Miss Ivanov's sister isn't found soon, you will most likely lose your contract with her."

"That was part of what we wanted to discuss with you, Stowell." Wilson sat down on a chair that creaked alarmingly under his bulk. "Will the woman be unreasonable about this?"

"Unreasonable sir?" Jak resented the man's insensitivity. "Respectfully, sir, I hardly think it's unreasonable for her to be concerned about her sister's disappearance. And if the Devonite army isn't willing to show there are serious efforts being made to recover her, you're going to lose her business."

"This is your opinion from the time you've spent with her then?"

"This is my opinion based on being a decent human being, as well as some insight into what makes her tick. Sir."

"I don't know that I approve of your tone, Captain."

Before the discussion could deteriorate further, Callahan jumped in. "Colonel, the captain is saying that in order to continue our business relationship with Ivanov, we need to make the effort to find the girl. I happen to agree."

He glanced at Jak to make sure she'd gotten the message. Jak thought so. She was certain the general was letting her know that Colonel Wilson didn't know the truth about her gender. Maybe. Torrin was so much better at reading these kinds of messages and for the umpteenth time that day, Jak wished that she was there with her.

"Yes sir." Jak nodded vigorously, not only agreeing with Callahan but trying to let him know that she'd understood his message. "That's exactly what I'm saying. Can you tell me what efforts have already been made?"

Wilson cleared his throat. "The woman's overdue. There's a good chance that she won't be returning at all. I think our efforts will be better directed at finding a way to continue receiving her goods if she has been killed. Can you continue in her stead should that become necessary?"

"Me, sir?" His effrontery blew her mind. For a moment, she was speechless. "I wouldn't know where to start, sir. It seems to me that if Torrin…isn't coming back, then we need to concentrate doubly on finding Nat. Not only would Nat be the only one who could get us back in contact with Torrin's company, but rescuing her would raise our standing in the eyes of her people."

"Her people?" The colonel folded his hands atop his belly and considered her. "I thought they were a company."

"That's what I meant, sir." Jak could feel her face growing hot at the slip. She wasn't used to having to watch her tongue like that.

She knew Nadierzda's existence was a secret. The vast majority of the galaxy had never heard and would never hear that name. Troika Corp was a known entity and served as a public face for the planet's secretive populace.

"Your next steps, Captain Stowell," Callahan said, "are to draft a plan for us to continue to work with Troika Corp even if Miss Ivanov is out of the picture. Also, you are to work with Lieutenant Smythe to track down the younger Miss Ivanov. Covering both our bases will put us in a better position all around. The technology that Miss Ivanov has provided us with has already given us an edge over the Orthodoxans and we don't want to lose our advantage."

"An excellent plan, sir," Wilson said. "Stowell, you will concentrate on the Troika Corp plan first. Lieutenant Smythe has been detached from his normal duties to work with you. You may direct him as you see fit, though I suggest you play to his strengths. You have offices on the top floor of this building in the new Special Liaisons Office. At this point, you have no staff, but personnel are being reassigned to you."

"Thank you, sir." What was she going to do with a staff? It sounded like she would be stuck behind a desk creating reports and drafting plans while her people would be doing the actual work. Suddenly, her woods seemed worlds away, on a different planet. She thought longingly of her sailplane back on Nadierzda, of being able to fly above it all.

"Talk to Lieutenant Smythe about delegation," Callahan suggested. "I know you're being asked to jump right into something for which you have very little background. You wouldn't be in this situation if we didn't think you were up to it."

"Thanks for the vote of confidence, sir." The encouragement didn't actually make Jak feel any better. If anything, it made her feel worse. If she couldn't pull this off, she would be letting down the supreme commander of her army. The only more powerful being she could disappoint was Johvah, and she was pretty sure she'd already managed that. Her guilt at that thought was almost nonexistent these days. Seeing all those women in happy, productive relationships with each other and Torrin's periodic lectures on the subject had finally convinced her that there was nothing intrinsically evil in her tendencies. The lingering guilt she attributed to the fact that she would never be able to tell her family. Though if they were around in some way, watching over her, she was pretty sure they already knew. Bron, at least, she was sure approved, if not of the idea in general, then of Torrin in particular.

"Good. You're going to have to hit the ground running. Don't be afraid to ask for help from Ops and Intel. They've both been instructed to assist you in any way possible." Callahan dismissed her with a wave of the hand. "My clerk will take you to your offices."

Jak followed the general's clerk up flights of stairs, her hands fisted at her sides. She quivered with suppressed anger, feeling like if she didn't hit someone, she would fly apart. When the poor clerk stopped in front of a door on the top floor, she nodded curtly to dismiss him. There was no point in beating up on the poor man. Her issues weren't his fault, but it took everything she had not to unload on him.

She strode through the door and slammed it behind her before taking a look around. They'd given her some pretty decent offices, it seemed. They might be on the top floor, but they were roomy and clean. By the amount of space, the general was planning on expanding her operation greatly. The idea didn't please her at all. It was even more proof that she would be stuck managing the operation instead of doing the work. Idly, Jak wondered what she would have to do to get a demotion.

"Good, sir, you're here." Smythe stuck his head through an open doorway. His face betrayed no consternation at the noisiness of her entrance. "We can get started."

"Yes, we can, Smythe." Jak crooked her finger at him, beckoning him closer. He bounded over to her and saluted. With an internal sigh, she returned his salute. And here she'd been thinking that as an officer she wouldn't have to salute nearly as often. Her arm was going to fall off from constant use. "At ease," she snapped when he brought himself to attention in front of her. He dropped into parade rest and cocked his head at her. A wicked gleam lurked at the back of his eyes. "You shit." Jak laughed, some of the tension draining from her.

"Sorry sir."

"Ugh, don't call me that."

"Why not? It's the truth. You are now my superior officer."

Jak rolled her eyes. "In name, maybe. I'm not an officer. I never wanted to be one. Letting other people go out and get killed in my place is not my idea of a good time."

Smythe regarded her, the amusement gone from his face. "Did you know that's one of the reasons you were promoted, sir? The general appreciates an officer who doesn't consider his, or her, life to be more important than that of his men. He feels it leads them to better decisions, less wasteful ones."

"I don't care. Let him pick someone else then. I've served with plenty of men who could meet that criteria."

"But he picked you, sir, because he admires you and what you've done."

"What I've done is what I'm being paid to do. Forty credits a week."

"Plus dental." Smythe echoed her on the last line. "Not everyone would have had the presence of mind that you did. What you did in bringing Torrin back to us has the potential to halve the length of this war, if not more."

"Torrin's the important part here. And her sister. I haven't been able to get a straight answer about what's being done to get Nat back."

"That's the thing, sir." Smythe had the grace to look embarrassed. "Not much is being done. They tracked Crimson's tracks to where he crossed the fence, but they weren't able to do anything beyond that. No one wanted to risk sending someone across the fence after him. Not to go after just a girl."

"And that was how many weeks ago?"

"Almost three now."

Jak fixed him with a hard glare. "I don't ever want to hear you say 'just' and 'girl' in the same sentence again."

Smythe blanched slightly. "You have being an officer down better than you thought, sir. And it's not the way I feel. All I'm doing is passing along the general consensus."

It wasn't that Jak didn't know how to be an officer. It was that she didn't like being one for the Devonites. She hadn't felt so hemmed in by her duties on Nadierzda. Not to mention that she'd related so much better to the women under her command. Here she felt painted into a corner. She nodded grudgingly to the lieutenant.

"So what do you want to do first, sir?"

"Our first priority is to find Nat Ivanov."

"Then may I suggest we adjourn to the *Calamity Jane*, sir? The ship's AI has some interesting results to share."

"Results?"

"Yes sir." Smythe disappeared into his office and emerged settling a soft cap on his head. Jak wished she was also in combat fatigues, but she wasn't going to waste time heading back to her room to change. There would be time for that later.

CHAPTER FOURTEEN

"Greetings, Jak and Lieutenant Smythe." Tien's cool, slightly alien tones washed over Jak. The lack of concern was somewhat comforting, and Jak wondered if the AI was capable of anxiety.

"Tien." Jak was still somewhat nervous around the AI. She was never quite sure how to act around it. Torrin interacted with the AI as if it was a real person, but Jak was always very aware that she was speaking with a computer.

"How may I be of service, Jak?"

"Have you heard anything from Torrin?"

"I have not, Jak." The little hologram on the main console lifted both shoulders in apology. "But that is to be expected without a communications relay in the system. To communicate directly with me, she would have to be well within the system. Of course, she would show up on my sensors well before that, unless she is working very hard not to be seen. With a League of Solaran Planets ship still in orbit, she would likely be making herself very difficult to spot."

"Aren't you worried about her?"

"I have no true emotions, Jak. Though, I do confess her absence is uncharacteristic. However, I would not worry this early. This is not the first extended absence I have experienced from her."

The AI wasn't trying to make her feel better, not really. Jak got the feeling that Tien's words were only to make sure that it was thoroughly, though dispassionately, explaining the situation in as full a context as she could. However backhanded the reassurance was, it did make Jak feel better.

A thought occurred to her and she cursed herself for not having thought of it sooner. "Can't you bring Nat up on her subdermal transmitter?"

Again the hologram lifted its shoulders. "Regretfully, no, I cannot, Jak. There are no local communications arrays that I can use to expand my broadcast range. Without such things to tap into, my range is limited to about forty kilometers."

"What about the laser array that Torrin's people were helping the Devonites set up?"

"Unfortunately, Nat Ivanov was never patched into that network, Jak."

This time Jak cursed out loud. It had been too much to hope for. If it had been possible, surely Tien or Torrin would have already thought of that.

"Tien finished running her analysis of Crimson's attacks a couple days ago, sir," Smythe said.

The main viewscreen blinked and a detailed map of the Devonite side of the isthmus materialized. As Jak watched, colored dots spread out on the map. To her eyes, they looked like a random dispersal of dots, but Smythe was smiling and nodding as he looked over the results.

"She really is fantastic," Smythe said, fondness warming his voice.

"It doesn't look like much to me," Jak admitted.

"I can understand how you might think that, sir, but if we look at the incidents over time, an interesting picture emerges." Smythe stepped closer to the viewscreen. "Tien, remove all the dots that relate to Captain Stowell." A small number of dots disappeared, but they changed the overall look of the map. The incidents were separated into two almost completely distinct clusters, one to the northern end of the isthmus, the other further south.

"Why are his hits so separate?"

"This is where it gets interesting, sir." Smythe was really enjoying himself. He rubbed his hands together with glee. "Tien, please indicate the dates of the incidents." The dots shaded into different colors from dark to light. "The darker dots are the oldest ones, the lightest ones are the most recent. Excepting of course the incident on Hill 372. Because it related to you, it's been removed as an anomaly."

"All the older ones are further north," Jak said. She studied the map closely. There were some darker ones further south, similar to the lighter ones to the north, but the bulk of the most recent ones were concentrated on a relatively small area immediately to the south of Camp Abbott.

"Exactly, sir. I think he was stationed up there until about six months ago. He must have been reassigned to one of the Orthodoxan camps to the south around then. It's my opinion that aside from the attention he's paid you, the outliers represent specific assignments he was given."

"I need all the information we have on the Orthodoxan camps in that area." Jak focused on the area. She quivered with tension and she took a deep breath, forcing herself to relax. She needed to be under control to pull the trigger or the shot would go wide. Nat was in that area. She finally had somewhere to focus.

"I have that information back in our offices, sir." Smythe cleared his throat nervously. "May I remind you sir, that you are to be coming up with a plan to keep our people in contact with Troika Corp even if Torrin is out of the picture?"

Jak closed her eyes. According to Colonel Wilson, that was her main priority, but with something to point them in the right direction for Nat's kidnapping, it was the last thing she wanted to do. She understood Wilson's position that keeping the flow of goods from drying up was of utmost importance to the Devonites. However, she disagreed with his tactics. Nat was what everything hung upon. Torrin would be back, but if they couldn't get her sister back, she would probably turn her back on the Devonites. Still, it went against the grain for her to ignore a direct order.

"Tien, do you have a communicator on board?" She'd been assigned one on Nadierzda, for all the good it had done. She had a flash of the communicator half-buried in sand on the bend of the river while Tanith searched for her.

"I do, Jak. There are a couple in the work area in the cargo bay. If you take one of those, I will be able to reach you at Fort Marshall without any problem."

The work area was mostly as she remembered it. After a few minutes of digging in one of the cabinets, Jak unearthed the transmitters. She snagged two, one for her and one for Smythe. On her way out of the cage, an item on the work bench caught her eye. She picked up the small, red-vaned dart. It looked familiar, but she couldn't remember why.

"What is this?" Jak asked Smythe when she rejoined him on the bridge.

"You found that up on top of Hill 372, sir."

"Umm." Jak held up the dart. "Maybe that's why it seems so familiar. I wonder if my memories are coming back."

"That can't be a bad thing, can it, sir?"

Jak became aware of the furrow between her brows. "Not at all."

"Should we get back to the office, sir?"

"Yes, let's. I want to take a look at the Orthodoxan camp emplacements." She looked over at the hologram that still hovered an inch above the main console. "I need you to let me know the second you hear anything at all from Torrin or Nat."

"Yes Jak."

Deep in thought, Jak strode from the bridge. She bounced the small tranquilizer dart in one hand. The small projectile's significance worried at the back of her mind. The sensation was maddening. It was like talking to someone whose name she should have known but couldn't quite remember. The harder she tried to grasp at the memory, the more elusive it became.

The ride back to their offices was quiet. Smythe seemed to sense that Jak was in no mood to chat. Her inability to winnow out the dart's significance had left her irritable and she was glad for his silence. If he'd said anything unfortunate, she was likely to snap at him. With a grim smile, she acknowledged that she might be more Devonite officer material than she would like.

Once in their offices, Jak waited with barely concealed impatience while Smythe brought up a map of the area to which Crimson's recent activities had been pinpointed. She took the opportunity to take a look around her office. It was bare, but the furnishings were good quality. Her office was bigger than the room she'd shared with Bron in the snipers' barracks. She could have had a bed in there and the room wouldn't have felt significantly smaller.

She opened drawers and lockers while Smythe fiddled with the viewscreen in the main room.

"It's up, sir." He waited for her, sitting at a small conference table in the middle of the room.

"Good. So what camp do you think he's based out of?"

"There are a few options, sir."

"Of course there are."

Smythe shot her a rueful glance as he stood to indicate four points on the map. "We have Camps Bravo-II and -IV, as well as Romeo-VII and Whiskey-I. None of the camps have full-time sniper units stationed at them, at least not that we know of."

"That isn't good news." Jak leaned forward and clasped her hands together, drumming the fingers of her right hand on the back of her left. "Does one of them seem like a better bet than the others?"

Despair flowed through her at Smythe's noncommittal shrug and she slumped back in her chair.

"We'd need to get up close and personal to find out, sir," he said.

"What do you mean by up close and personal?"

"I mean infiltration, sir. Get someone into the camps to ask the right questions."

"I can do that." Jak sat up, excited to have a role.

"Begging your pardon, sir, but no, you can't." Smythe looked her in the eye, his adamant refusal chilling her anticipation.

"Why the hell not? I fooled all of you for years."

"Yes, you did, sir. But you fooled us in a specific way. We don't need you to convince the Orthodoxans that you're a man. We need you to convince them that you're one of them." He kept his eyes on hers. "I can do that. I have done that."

"You've been in their camps?"

"More than once, sir."

"If you're going in, then someone needs to cover you." It was her turn to be adamant. He was too important to risk needlessly.

"Not you, sir."

"You don't have any say in that, Smythe." She smiled unpleasantly. "Someone has to make sure you get back with your hide in one piece. While I don't have the experience in Orthodoxan camps that you do, I'd bet that I've logged far more hours in Orthodoxan territory than you have." Besides, if he did track down Crimson or Nat, Jak was damn well going to be positioned to act. She would either save Nat or avenge her.

It had been four days since he left. Her food was gone, finished off the previous night, and her stomach growled weakly. Even it no longer had the energy to make its needs known. Nat patted it soothingly, like it was one of her cats. As with her cats, the gesture only served to calm things down for a couple of moments. Soon it was back to producing weak murmurs.

This is it, she thought. She'd promised herself that if the sniper didn't show up by morning that she was going to make a break for it. The board was slotted loosely back into its spot on the wall. Once it had come free, it had been very useful as an ersatz crowbar and she'd used it to lever a bigger space between the boards of the wall. Nat had babied the board along, not wanting to snap it against the others. It had taken three days, but she had a gap wide enough that she could squeeze through.

It probably hadn't been his intention, but the weeks of reduced diet had left her skinny enough to squeeze through the narrow opening. If she'd tried this right after she'd been captured, there was no way she would have made it.

With a deep breath, Nat stood up from her pile of rags. She balled a few of them up and stuffed them into her pockets. She had nothing else to take from this place.

The board popped easily out of its spot. She swung the loose boards as far from each other as she could and slid one shoulder between them. The edge of the boards scraped along her clothing, tearing small holes in a few places. She stopped. Her pelvis was getting hung up. Damn her breeding hips! Her mother had teased her when she'd hit puberty, saying she had wide hips which were perfect for birthing babies. The idea hadn't thrilled her then and now they prevented her escape. Try as she might, she couldn't get her pelvis through the narrow opening.

It took a lot of grunting and yanking before she was able to pull herself back into the shack. All she needed was a few more centimeters. Once again, Nat applied the board to the opening and pushed on it. Slowly the opening widened, first by a few millimeters, then a centimeter. The wood squealed in protest. *A little more, come on.* Nat threw her entire weight behind her improvised crowbar. With a final screech of tortured nails, the planks opened up before her.

She stumbled forward as her board snapped. The splintering was the last thing she wanted to hear and she looked down in dismay. It had finally given out, cracking about halfway up its length. The pieces were too short to be used for prying now. She stared at the two shards in glum silence. It had been her only tool, something she could rely upon, but it had failed her.

Not before doing what she needed it to though. The opening now looked wide enough that she'd be able to slip through. She dropped the shorter piece of board; the longer one might still prove to be useful.

Once again, her shoulders and rib cage fit through the narrow opening with some wriggling. For once, she was happy that she was relatively flat-chested. Not so much as to be mistaken for a boy, certainly, but she didn't have to worry about her breasts getting in the way. Angling her pelvis through took more work, but finally she was able to work her way free. Fabric tore as she pushed herself the rest of the way through, but she was out.

A quick glance around revealed only trees looming over the small clearing. The sun was rising in the east. She had no idea where she was, except that she must be east of the Orthodoxan force field. If she headed west, hopefully she would eventually find the fence. It was as good an idea as any she had and Nat struck off in the direction opposite the rising sun.

A path went off in roughly the same direction, but she avoided it. There was no sense in placing herself right back in the hands of her captor. It was only a short way through the trees before a clearing opened up before her. Moving through the woods had been difficult. She'd done her best to be quiet, but the dead branches and leaves, not to mention small bushes and other plants, seemed designed to make noise.

Bushes lined the trees at the edge of the clearing. She crouched down in them and looked out onto a beautiful sight. It was the biggest vegetable garden she'd ever seen. Food! Her stomach growled loudly and her mouth flooded with saliva. Nat found herself rubbing a hand across her mouth to keep from drooling. Her first instinct was to leap out and stuff her face, but she restrained herself, with difficulty, when she realized that the plants closest to her were probably tomatoes. It was hard to tell, since the fruits were blue, but aside from that little detail, they looked like tomatoes to her and big healthy ones from what she could see.

Poking her head above the bushes, she glanced around. There was no one within view. The clearing was huge. Far across it were some low buildings, but they were far enough away that she couldn't tell what they might be for. It seemed safe enough.

Nat took a moment to tear a small piece of fabric off one of her rags. She wrapped it around the end of her splintered piece of wood.

The fabric would keep her hand from getting torn up with splinters. The splintered edge was sharp enough for her to separate whatever vegetables she needed from their stalks.

With another furtive glance around to make sure the coast was still clear, Nat sidled out from the bushes. She made a beeline to the tomato plants. The first fruit she tried came off easily in her hand. She took as big a bite from it as she could manage and hummed happily as juice ran down her chin. The color was strange, but there was nothing wrong with the flavor. She'd never tasted a tomato so good. As quickly as she could, she finished off the tomato, not even waiting until she'd finished chewing before cramming another bite in.

Beyond the tomato plants were some sort of gourd. They could have been cucumbers or zucchini from the shape. They would travel better than the tomatoes. Nat pulled a couple more tomatoes off the plant in front of her and chewed on one as she made her way forward to the low vines. The long, skinny vegetables littered the ground and she picked a likely one. Definitely cucumber. She squatted in dirt and gathered as many cucumbers as she could reach. One of the rags would work really well as a sack, she decided.

Placing a piece that was roughly square on the ground, she piled her pilfered vegetables in the middle of the cloth. The last cucumber was barely within her reach and she stretched out to grab it. A booted foot came down on the back of her wrist, pressing it painfully to the dirt.

"What do we have here?"

Nat looked up into a leering face. The man's eyes crinkled nastily as he surveyed her. His grin sent fear rippling down Nat's spine, leaving a spreading chill in its wake. It sat on his face as if it had been pasted there, never reaching his eyes.

"Where did you come from?"

She simply stared up at him, her eyes wide.

"I asked you a question, bitch." He ground his boot on the back of her hand, the heavy tread pushing her hand into the dirt. She hissed in pain as his grinding broke her skin, but she refused to cry out. "So you have some spirit then. Hollister, Simmons!" He shouted back over his shoulder.

Nat took the opportunity and yanked her hand out from under his boot, tearing the skin further until blood ran down the back of her hand. She tightened her grip around the makeshift handle on her splinter of wood and threw herself at the soldier.

"What the–" He put up a hand to defend himself and deflected her aim. The sharp end of the board missed his neck and sliced through the shoulder of his combat fatigues. With the weight of her desperation and her entire body behind the attack, the sharp piece of wood tore open the top of his shoulder. Blood welled up instantly, coloring his jacket with a spreading scarlet stain. Shocked, she stared at the damage she'd wrought and missed the backhand he was aiming her way.

"Bitch," he yelled.

Stars burst across her vision and every sound was muffled, like she was suddenly in hard vacuum. She sprawled sideways, landing on her shoulder. With a grunt her head bounced off the ground and she lay there for a moment, stunned. Nat became aware of a weight on top of her and she looked up into the soldier's sneering face. Two other men peered at her over his shoulder.

"Whatcha got there, Johns?" The voice floated over her from far away.

"A hot little piece of ass. She's got some spunk to her." Johns licked his lower lip. "She's about to have some spunk in her too."

A low snigger met his sally. "Not like the bitches in the pens. Where do you think she came from?"

Johns shrugged and continued to stare down at her. "Don't know. Don't rightly care. Might as well take advantage of the opportunity."

"Aren't we on a deadline?" The third voice was a little worried. "Do we really have time for this?"

With a wave of his hand, Johns dismissed the concern. "We'll always have the chance to kill more Devonites. When's the next time we'll have the chance at one like this."

"I don't know…"

"If you want to keep on toward the tunnel and not take a break, then that's up to you. If you decide not to be a complete fucking pussy, then give me a hand here."

Nat threw herself to one side when she realized what they had in mind. Johns shifted with her and slammed her shoulder back to the ground.

"That's right," he said. "Keep struggling." She'd thought his smile was cruel before, but there was nothing human in it now. Nat knew she was giving him what he wanted, but she couldn't stop herself as panic rose within her, choking her. If he touched her, she would die, she knew it in every fiber of her being. Planting both feet against the ground, she shoved against him. Once again he rode her easily. When he came back down on her, she grabbed his head with both hands and brought it down towards her. His face bounced off her forehead and his nose gushed blood over his mouth and down off his chin.

"Fuck!" Johns grabbed his face and reeled to one side.

Nat twisted under him, got her feet under her and pushed off. She took off at a full sprint, heading for the safety of the trees. Terror gave her wings and she vaulted over the bushes in one bound. Something hit her hard in the middle of the back and she went down awkwardly. The breath burst from her lungs in an explosion of air and saliva. Sobbing, she tried to pull herself forward, grabbing hold of branches and plants. They tore at her hands, lashing them open as she was drawn inexorably back by hands wrapped like iron bands around her ankle. Another hand grabbed the waistband of her pants and pulled down roughly. She whimpered as her rump was exposed to chill air.

"Nice," a voice sneered from behind her.

"Get them down further," the third voice urged. Apparently he'd gotten over his reticence. The hands complied and her pants and underwear were shoved down to her knees. Rough hands around her hips dragged her ass into the air then roamed over bare skin. Her skin crawled at the contact and she threw herself forward, trying to get away from the heavy weight at her back.

"Hold her down," Johns said. A hand between her shoulder blades shoved her face first into the ground and a weight settled on her back. It felt like someone was kneeling on her, immobilizing her. She felt like an insect mounted on a card. She kept struggling but couldn't get anywhere and was tiring out rapidly. Pain exploded in her side and she cried out.

"Give her another," Johns urged and she turned her head in time to see the Orthodoxan soldier there pull back his foot. He slammed it into her side and she cried out again.

"Yeah, give it to her, Johns." The words, filled with sick glee, came to her from the end of a long tunnel. Her mind fled away from what was happening to her body. Eyes screwed shut, she lay in comforting darkness, blind and deaf to what the animals were doing to her. She had no idea how long she cowered in the darkness of her mind…

Distant peeping intruded on the silence. The local birds had no interest in her plight, it seemed. Trees branches squeaked together high above her while the leaves rustled quietly in the breeze. It took her a while to realize the pain had stopped. The weights between her shoulder blades and against her ass were gone. She didn't hear anything else, but kept her eyes screwed shut just in case. She was cold. Scrabbling for her pants, she pulled them up, sniffling quietly. Finally covered, she looked around. An Orthodoxan soldier lay next to her, half his face missing. Behind her, Johns had a gaping wound where his neck used to be. Further away, a third body was slumped on its side.

They're all dead? Nat looked around in confusion. When she looked back, he was suddenly there. Her kidnapper materialized out of the forest.

"That was incredibly stupid," he said, his voice emotionless.

"What happened? Why did you…?"

"I should have left you to their fun." He squatted, bringing himself to her eye level. "You try this again and I will. If I didn't need you, you would still be entertaining your new friends."

Nat stared at him. She loathed him. Only his threat to leave her kept her from spitting in his face. Her captor sneered, looking exactly like Johns for a moment, and Nat shied away from him.

"You didn't look like you were enjoying yourself. You a dyke like your friend?" He stood and yanked Nat to her feet. She bit back a whimper, her abused flesh protesting the sudden movement. "You probably are. You've infected her, all of you."

The venom in his voice subsided and what replaced it sounded very much like regret. For some reason his sudden change of mood frightened her more than his anger. "There's nothing for it now." He sounded like he was about to cry, his voice hitched and went hoarse. "She's not worthy. Change of plans. I'm going to have to kill her." Nat twisted her head to look up into his face. His voice was full of emotion, but his face might have been carved in stone. The sniper stared at her for a long time before shrugging. "You're going to have to take her place. Someone has to."

He yanked her along but not back toward the shack.

CHAPTER FIFTEEN

The planets of the Haefen system winked mockingly at Torrin. Their bright colors hung against the impenetrable blackness of space. In one corner of the system, the nebula still floated, tranquil with its hidden depths. She drifted, power cut to all systems except life support.

The *Icarus* roamed the outer edge of the system, cutting off Torrin's path to Haefen. Apparently they'd gotten wise to her people's comings and goings; Tien might have gone a little overboard with her distraction. Torrin chafed at the delay. Every minute kept her from rejoining Jak and tracking down Nat. She was powerless and could do nothing but watch as the League ship patrolled right inside the orbit of the furthest planet.

If she were closer to Haefen itself, she could have asked Tien to fire up the engines and draw the League bastards off again, but at this distance she had no choice except to sit and wait. The *Icarus* showed no sign of leaving. They knew she was out there.

How had they known she would return so soon? The other trips had weeks between them. She couldn't afford to wait any longer; she needed to act now.

"Eowyn, bring us up to full power."

"Are you certain, Torrin?" The AI's voice held the same mechanical doubt she'd heard in Tien's tone on previous occasions.

"I am." Her racing thoughts had calmed now that she had a course of action. "The captain of the *Icarus* doesn't know it, but she and I have an appointment."

"Very well, Torrin." Around her, lights flickered on and the deck plating vibrated. The engines coughed to life.

"Unidentified vessel," the comm spat out a strident warning, "this is Captain Mori of the League of Federated Planets spaceship *Icarus*. Heave to and prepare to be boarded for violating the blockade of the sovereign planet Haefen."

"Eowyn, give me visual." A handsome female face filled the screen. One dark brow lifted in surprise to see Torrin. "Captain," Torrin said, unconcern in every line as she lounged in her chair, "I think you'll find I'm not moving."

"Indeed. And you are…" Far from being irritated by Torrin's lack of concern, the captain of the *Icarus* twitched her lips in amusement. It was too bad she belonged to the League of Solaran Planets space corps. In another time and another place, Torrin would have been very interested in this self-assured woman.

"Captain Allilueva. I've been contracted by the Devonite government to relay some messages. Apparently they have interests outside of their system."

"I…see." Full pink lips had thinned at the mention of the Devonites and they thinned further at the mention of their possible intersystem interests. "You and I have much to talk about, Captain Allilueva. I'm going to have to insist that you join me."

"Very well, Captain." Torrin had gotten her attention, that was for sure.

"I'm sending over a ship. You will admit my people without any problems. I have no problems reducing smugglers to atoms."

Torrin affected a wounded expression, being careful not to overplay her hurt. "Smuggler, Captain? I'm a courier, nothing more."

The captain's lips twitched again. At least she had a sense of humor. Hopefully she also had a sense of outrage. If she did, Torrin would be able to play on that to get back to Haefen and the women there who were depending on her.

"You have nothing to fear from me."

The look the Leaguer gave her was flat with disbelief. This time it was true. In another set of circumstances, things might have been different, but Torrin needed her. What she didn't need was the captain knowing how much Torrin needed her right then. Torrin shrugged in response to the League captain, playing up her lack of interest again.

"Ready a boarding party for the ship," the captain said to someone off-screen. She graced Torrin with a thin smile. "You'll be enjoying our hospitality in no time, Captain."

"Then I'll go prepare." Torrin sat forward and was halfway out of her chair when the captain's voice stopped her.

"I would prefer if you didn't, Captain. I want you right where I can see you."

"Very well." She settled back into the chair and studied the Leaguer with polite interest. For her part, the *Icarus*'s captain sat in her own chair and directed her attention to one of the officers on her bridge. The man sneaked glances at Torrin, unable to affect the cool composure that his captain was pulling off without any effort.

Mori might have been playing up ignoring Torrin, but every time she so much as twitched, the captain's unwavering gaze snapped back to her.

A short while later, a chime sounded through the *Melisende's* bridge.

"That'll be your people, Captain. I'm going to have to disconnect now."

For her personnel, this was the most dangerous moment, but the League captain simply nodded with remarkable sangfroid. "Don't try anything, Allilueva." Her voice was unyielding and cold. In that moment, Torrin believed that she would have no problem opening her ship up to space.

Rather than reply to Mori's warning, Torrin switched off the comm. It was a calculated risk. Mori could take the move as a threat, but Torrin needed to maintain a position of strength. Or at least stay away from a position of weakness.

"Let them in, Eowyn." She pushed herself out of the pilot's chair and strode down the hallway to the hatch. There was no point in antagonizing the other captain any more than she had to and she wanted to make sure the troops from the *Icarus* could radio back to the ship to confirm that she was cooperating before Mori's bloodlust for smugglers got the better of her.

Two marines stepped through the hatch in full body armor, plasma rifles raised. Torrin waited calmly while one pointed his weapon at her and the other scanned both ways down the corridor.

"It's clear," the marine barked over her shoulder. Her partner brushed past Torrin and took up a position behind her. He moved with a businesslike economy of motion that she recognized in Jak. That was all that reminded her of Jak. This man towered over her and the woman was almost as tall. Torrin wasn't used to feeling short around other women, but the marine with her multitude of braids spilling out from under her helmet made Torrin feel tiny.

A lieutenant, by the shield on his left shoulder, stepped through the hatch. Two more marines took up the rear. The short hallway was beyond cramped with all of them standing there. The marines in their body armor took up an inordinate amount of room. Thankfully they weren't wearing power armor, or there would barely have been enough room to breathe. It was interesting that they weren't in power armor though. Either Mori hadn't wanted to wait for the time it would take for the marines to don the armor, or she had never really planned to fire on Torrin's ship. There might be something Torrin could use there, and she filed the information away.

"Ma'am." The lieutenant nodded jerkily at her but didn't salute. "I'm Lieutenant Savard. I've been sent to escort you to the *Icarus*." Savard was as tall as the biggest marine, but slender to the point of being painful. He reminded her of a long-limbed water bird.

"Understood Lieutenant."

"You should bring some effects with you," he said, rubbing his hands together nervously. "The captain didn't say how long you'd be our guest."

"I see." Mori was taking her seriously. If she'd been instructed to bring clothes along, that meant she wasn't going to be imprisoned right? On the surface, this was looking like a polite interaction.

"No weapons."

"Got it." Torrin moved away from Savard toward her cabin. The hulking mountain of a marine and his not-quite-as-hulking partner shadowed her. There was no question about locking them out of her room; they followed right inside on her heels. They were taking no chances. The female marine pulled opened Torrin's closet door and checked inside before allowing her to pull out some articles of clothing to pack.

Though having the two of them watching her every move was a little unnerving, it took her very little time to get squared away, if only to get out from under their watchful eyes. More occupied with watching them watch her, she paid very little attention to what she was actually stuffing in her soft-sided bag. There was only one item she really needed to bring along, and she was able to conceal it from the marines. Thank goodness for the concealed compartment at the bottom of her satchel. No smuggler worth her salt would be without her hidey-holes, and Torrin was one of the best.

A few minutes passed and she was packed. With no more words than they'd spoken, Torrin was escorted back out to where the nervous Lieutenant Savard and the rest of his escort waited.

"I'm ready," Torrin said dryly. She held up her bag by way of demonstration. It was far less preparation than she'd had at the start of this whole mess. To think that everything had started when she'd stepped foot off the *Calamity Jane* on Haefen all those months ago. This time she knew who she was dealing with, at least.

"Excellent. After you." Savard gestured her toward the open hatch.

"Eowyn, put all systems into standby mode after I leave the ship," Torrin said aloud. She wasn't sure if the League had the same type of subdermal transmitters she did. If they didn't, she wanted to keep that to herself. "Power them back up when I return."

"Very well, Torrin," the AI said.

Had she told Mori her first name, the real one? She hoped so, because if she hadn't then Eowyn had busted her in a big way. Keeping her face a bland mask, she stepped through the hatch. The shuttle the Leaguers had come over in was attached to the hatch by way of its belly. There was a moment of disorientation as her senses told her she was falling to one side. She stumbled slightly and turned to watch as the rest of her escort joined her in the small shuttle. The marines gave no indication that anything out of the ordinary had happened; they flowed from one gravity to another. Savard stumbled as she had and looked a little sick.

The shuttle was as cramped as the hallway had been. The lieutenant made his way forward to the pilot's chair. She was left to find a seat along one of the benches, under the attentive eyes of the marines.

The benches were hard and the marines stared through her impassively. She tried to catch the eye of one of them, but it was like tossing stones at a cliff face. Thankfully, the ride to the *Icarus* was short.

Torrin watched through the front window as they came up on the League ship. From up close, it was very impressive. It dwarfed her little ship many times over, and the hull gleamed stark white. It was completely impractical for skulking in space. A blind person could have picked it out from among the stars.

A crack in the ship's hull opened in front of them and yawned wider. Savard deftly maneuvered the ship into the hangar bay. Torrin was glad that his nervousness hadn't extended to his piloting skills. He was really very good, with a deft touch on the yoke.

As one, the marines stood when the shuttle touched down. Torrin stared up at them. She wasn't going to move until she was good and ready. There was no point in letting them know exactly how intimidating a sight they were in their wall of matte black body armor. Lieutenant Savard squeezed his way out of the pilot's chair and through the small group.

"We have atmosphere on deck," he said. "It's time to go, ma'am."

While one marine opened the exterior hatch, another came over and stood at Torrin's shoulder in an unsubtle hint to get moving. "Since you asked so nicely," she said dryly, looking up at the marine. She thought she detected a faint glimmer of amusement in the woman's opaque gaze, though the marine's face didn't even twitch.

"Umm yes." Savard twitched nervously and headed out the hatch. Torrin followed at his heels, trying to look like she really wanted to be there. More accurately, she tried to look like someone who didn't want to be there trying to look like she wanted to be there. Let them think that being on the ship made her uncomfortable. And it did, though not for the reasons the Leaguers might have thought.

The marines escorted Torrin through the ship in a loose box, two ahead and two in back. The League personnel they encountered gave their strange group a wide, if curious, berth. This was Torrin's first time on the inside of a League ship, and she kept her eyes peeled for anything she could glean that might come in handy later. Unfortunately, all she learned during their trip from the hangar was that the League of Solaran Planets had an unfortunate propensity for uniforms with tight pants and that they kept their featureless corridors immaculately clean.

The marines said nothing to her or to the lieutenant on their walk, though Savard gave her plenty of nervous glances. If he thought she was going to attack him under the watchful eyes of their marine escort, then he was insane. She would have to be severely deranged to consider such an action. Her latest gambit was a bit of a risk, but she wasn't crazy. Not yet.

Their little group stopped in front of a door that gleamed white against the utilitarian gray of the walls.

"Lieutenant Savard escorting your guest, sir." A small panel lit up next to the door and the lieutenant placed his palm on it. After a moment, the door shushed open. It made almost no sound and Torrin was impressed despite herself. The lieutenant made no move to accompany her, instead standing aside and motioning her forward. With a final glance up at the impassive marine faces looking through her, Torrin stepped through the doorway.

"Torrin Allilueva." Captain Mori stood in front of an oval conference table. Windows in the hull looked out into space. The windows were small and if Torrin wasn't mistaken, they seemed to have some sort of iris closure that would armor them closed.

"Captain Mori." She eyed the League captain while Mori blatantly did the same. The other captain was shorter than she'd expected. Her hair was so black it had blue highlights. It was cropped short and fashioned into a stiff crest. She looked good in her uniform, though the pants were as tight as the others she'd seen. Not to her detriment, Torrin decided when Mori turned away to pull out a chair.

"Have a seat, Captain," Mori said.

"Thank you, Captain," Torrin replied politely, sitting in the chair.

Mori settled herself across the table and pulled her sidearm out of its holster and placed it on the table, the muzzle pointing at Torrin. "So we're clear," she said.

"I'm hurt, Captain. Don't you trust me?"

"Not hardly. Though perhaps you'd like to tell me why I should be talking to you at all and not locking you up in the brig and taking you with me back to the nearest League planet for trial?"

CHAPTER SIXTEEN

Torrin cooled her heels in a small cabin. Lying on a soft bunk, she stared up at the ceiling. Small by the standards of the League ship, though still larger than the one on *Calamity Jane*, it had the same institutional feel to it as the rest of the ship. At least her ship looked like it was used. Her negotiations weren't going well. Mori didn't trust her, and she was right not to, but Torrin was running out of time. This whole thing was costing her days rather than the few hours she'd envisioned. Torrin tapped fingers on the back of her leg, fretting over Jak. Had the procedure been a success or was her love lying in a Devonite hospital bed as a brainless vegetable? She turned over, restless at the direction her thoughts were taking her. Again. Much as it pained her to admit, she might not be able to negotiate her way out of this situation or at least not under current conditions. She wanted to get the best possible deal, but that might not be an attainable goal. Simply getting back to Haefen might be the best thing she could negotiate.

Her mind made up, Torrin rolled out of bed and strode to the door. A League marine stared at her impassively from across the hallway. The constant presence of her marine guards was another reason for her mounting feeling of claustrophobia. She felt like she'd been here before and she felt Hutchinson's phantom breath on the side of her neck. With an irritable swipe of her hand, she wiped the feeling away and strode down the hall.

"Ma'am," the marine's voice followed her down the hall. Torrin ignored her and kept going. An iron grip closed around her elbow and jerked her to a halt. Torrin stepped back into the woman but stopped herself before she planted an elbow in the marine's solar plexus.

She looked over her shoulder, up into the soldier's grim face. "You're going to have to drag me back to my room. I don't care how tall, dark and foreboding you look, I'm going to see the captain."

"Captain Mori will send for you when she's ready to meet with you again."

For a moment, Torrin considered taking on the imposing woman. Her hand-to-hand combat skills were very good and she'd never had the opportunity to try them out against some of the League's finest. Was she crazy? There was no way she should even consider getting into an altercation with League marines. They would take her apart, not to mention the damage it would do to her case. But she wasn't going to budge.

"You can throw me over your shoulder and haul me back, but it's not going to get you what you want from me." Torrin winked at the woman. Again she thought she detected the little glimmer of amusement she'd observed two days previous. "We haven't moved for a couple of days. The captain can't be that busy right now. I need to see her and I'm not going to wait. So unless you want to take me back to my room, tie me down and finally admit I'm your prisoner, not your guest, then I'm going to find her."

She stared up into the marine's eyes, her face as impassive as the soldier's. After another moment, her arm was released. Torrin stomped off with the marine on her heels. The woman spoke into her wrist as she followed Torrin through the halls.

"Understood sir." With a few long strides, the marine passed Torrin and preceded her through the spotless corridors. "This way, ma'am."

Torrin didn't gloat; there was no point. She followed the tall soldier, not to the conference room where she'd been meeting with Mori for two days now, but to another area of the ship. There were more doors along the corridors of this deck and Torrin thought perhaps they were in the *Icarus*'s living quarters. That was interesting.

The marine stopped in front of a door no different than any of the others and tapped deferentially upon it. The door shushed open and Captain Mori stood in the doorway. She was out of uniform for the first time that Torrin had seen her. Clad in a loose robe and flowing pants, she looked ready to turn in.

"Thank you," Mori said to the marine before transferring her attention to Torrin. "What did you need to see me about that couldn't have waited another few hours, Captain Allilueva?" Inside, Torrin winced. She hated giving away her hand, and letting the captain know that she was in a hurry wasn't going to help her position, but she had decided that this negotiation needed to move forward. As foreign as it was going to be, perhaps honesty was going to have to be the best policy for dealing with the League. In this one instance, she felt she had to make an exception.

"Captain Torrin Ivanov, actually." Torrin gave Mori a half smile. "I'm afraid I haven't been completely forthcoming with you, Captain."

The eyebrow Mori raised held less surprise than it did an invitation to go on. Taking a deep breath and ignoring the feeling that she was making a huge mistake, Torrin forged ahead.

"I need to get back to Haefen. My sister has been kidnapped by a member of the Orthodoxan military. Every hour I spend here with you prevents me from finding her and taking her back. Frankly, Captain, I no longer have the time for this little dance of ours."

Mori sat down in an overstuffed chair and indicated for Torrin to take the one across from her. "I knew you were holding something back, but this is not what I anticipated. How did your sister come to be on the planet?"

"That's not really important. What's important is that I need to get back there and you need to let me through your blockade."

"Captain Ivanov, why on Earth should I do that? You're asking me to break a dozen different military protocols and for no other reason than to help someone else who broke through the Haefen blockade?" She eyed Torrin. "There's a reason the planet is off-limits. There's a civil war going on down there. It isn't safe for civilians."

"That's the thing, Captain." Torrin leaned forward, her eyes boring into Mori's, willing the captain to see things her way. "If that's what your blockade is for, then why are the Orthodoxans carrying League weapons?"

"There's no way they have our weapons. If they have weapons at all, I'm certain you're the one supplying them."

"The Orthodoxans don't take kindly to women, you may remember. If you don't believe me, send out a transponder ping. You'll notice a signal in my quarters. I was given the weapon on my last trip to the planet's surface."

Mori watched Torrin for a long moment. She gnawed carefully on her lower lip, the only sign of uncertainty Torrin had seen in her façade so far. She got up and tapped a few commands into the console on the wall. Her face paled considerably at what she saw there.

"Your people can find that on the table in my room," Torrin said. "I didn't think it was a good idea to try getting through the ship carrying it. You'll find the League markings have been removed."

Mori leaned into the console and spoke a few words that were too indistinct for Torrin to hear.

She returned to the table. "If this is another one of your lies, we'll be heading to the nearest League planet, and you *will* stand trial."

"How long have you been on the picket out here, Captain?" Torrin pushed the point inexorably.

"Almost a year." The answer was pulled from Mori almost against her will. "We relieved another ship who had been on picket for five years."

"I received notice about eight months ago that the Orthodoxans needed supplies."

"We left the picket to resupply around that time. Part of the resupply run also includes a run to the nearest relay to send info dumps back to regional HQ. Many of my people send out personal messages at that time as well."

"So my question for you is, how badly do you want to find the person on your crew who's selling weapons to the Orthodoxans?"

"There might be another explanation." Mori paused as she cast around for another way to explain the Orthodoxans' missive and the presence of the weapon in Torrin's quarters.

Torrin snorted her contempt. "You can't possibly believe that. There's no reasonable way the request could have gotten out. And then there's the pistol in my quarters. If you track the transponder log, you'll see I'm not lying."

"You're asking me to believe that one of my people has conspired against the League not only to break the blockade, but to engage in illegal arms dealing."

"I have reason to believe the same person has been acting as a conduit between a traitor within the Devonite command structure and the Orthodoxans. Whoever this person is, they've been doing their best to see that the Orthodoxans prevail in this little war."

"How can you possibly know that?" Mori stood up and paced in agitation in front of the room's small windows.

How did she know that? This was where everything hinged. Torrin wasn't fond of putting herself in the line of fire but if she wanted to get back to Nat and Jak, she was going to have to put herself on the line. "I know because I've made my way through your blockade on more than one occasion. I've been in communication with the Devonite military and they've told me about their little mole problem. Information is getting back to the Orthodoxans in pretty damn close to real time. Until a few months ago, the only way of doing that would have been to relay the information through your ship."

"So you admit to smuggling goods to a League-blockaded planet."

Torrin shrugged, trying her best to project an attitude of unconcern. "I have no allegiance to your League. But the person who has been doing this, he does."

"He? You know who he is."

"Hardly. I have no idea who your traitor is, but I do know the Orthodoxans. There's no way they would deal with a woman, not even when it's to their advantage. Their misogyny runs way too deep."

Mori slumped back into her chair, an expression of supreme dissatisfaction on her face. "You're asking me to take a lot on your word here."

"It's all backed up easily enough. Talk to your Devonite contacts and they'll corroborate everything I've told you. Check the logs on the weapon in my room. They'll tell you what you need to know." She watched Mori closely. The League captain was almost there, she could feel it. "How much are you really risking in letting me get back to Haefen? Even if I am lying, which I'm not, all you have to do is pick me up next time I try to leave the surface. Isn't the risk worth it to find a traitor on your crew? Someone who's working against the League's interests here. I doubt your League will be happy with the Orthodoxans coming out on top."

Captain Mori leveled a finger at Torrin. "You've talked me into a nice little corner here, haven't you? If this is you being honest and forthcoming, I never want to match wits with you over something where you could really make a difference against us." She shook her head ruefully. "I'll agree to allow you back to the planet if you'll agree to one condition."

Torrin cocked her head inquisitively. "What's your condition?" She was wary of what the captain would ask of her. She'd laid her cards on the table and Mori had to know that she would agree to almost anything. The captain might think Torrin was playing her, but the truth was its own best advocate in this case.

"You help me find out who my problem is, then you leave him to me. I don't know what method you're going to use to expose him, but I'm assuming you're going to draw him out."

That's it? Torrin kept herself from slumping with relief, but only barely. "You've got yourself a deal, Captain."

She stood up and extended her hand to the League captain. Without hesitation, Mori stood and grasped her forearms right below the elbows and clasped them. The move surprised Torrin and she took half a step back.

"What are you doing?"

"This is how we seal bargains on the inner worlds." Mori looked at her, their faces separated by little more than half a meter of space. "It shows I trust you enough to let you in close to me. You've never made a bargain with a member of the League?"

Torrin's smile was a little sickly; she could feel it lying limp on her face. "You're my first." She cut off the end of her statement before she insulted the captain. This was indeed her first League bargain. With any luck it would also be the last.

The rustling of leaves set Jak's teeth on edge. It was bad enough that she was set up on the outskirts of the Orthodoxan camp and not in it, but they'd saddled her with a partner. She'd made it very clear that she didn't want anyone there with her, but her protests had been turned aside by Smythe's impeccable logic. At the end, she'd finally agreed, but only because she was starting to feel like a petulant child.

With her promotion, apparently she'd become too important to be risked on solo expeditions on the other side of the fence. Smythe had politely but firmly refused to allow her out on her own. She'd actually gotten the impression that if she pushed the notion he would report her to their superiors.

"Alston," she hissed. "Be quiet."

"Captain," he protested, voice hushed, "there's no way they can hear us down there. We're a klick away from the bastards."

He had the right attitude, at least, but that didn't stop her from resenting his presence. At least Smythe had the intelligence to assign her a spotter. There was no way she was going to entrust his life to someone else. If Smythe got into trouble in the camp, he needed the best watching over him and that was Captain Jak Stowell.

"I don't care if we're four klicks away." Her voice took on an unaccustomed tone of command. Trying to command men was an exercise in frustration. There was no reasoning with them; they had to be forced to see things her way and to fall in line. The women of Nadierzda's militia had been less formal, but at least she could trust them to recognize common sense when it smacked them in the face. "You will treat every moment we're in hostile territory as if the enemy is right on top of us. Do you understand?"

"Yessir." Alston looked properly chastened and ducked his head to watch the far-off camp through his scope.

Jak dropped her head as well. There wasn't much to see. The walls were barely two meters high. They would have barely slowed down a proper Devonite assault. The Orthodoxans didn't believe the Devonites would ever go on the offensive. After all, for thirty years they'd been content to protect their own territory and to mount the occasional raid, but never a sustained assault. Jak hoped she would be there to witness the day the Devonite military threw off its policy of defense and swung the pendulum back into the Orthodoxans' teeth.

The walls were high enough to block her view inside the camp. She couldn't see Smythe. He'd entered through the north gate. It had been educational to see him put on the persona of an Orthodoxan conscriptee. As he'd donned the uniform, he'd slouched into an attitude of defensive swagger. She'd never really thought about it until seeing it on him, but he'd nailed the prevailing Orthodoxan mindset. The men were full of swagger and power over a portion of their population, but they also expected abuse at any moment. Jak felt an unexpected—and unwelcome—pang of pity. Their national psyche was completely screwed up by generations of indoctrination. It was no wonder they were messed up. Shit flowed downhill, after all. Unfortunately, it was Orthodoxan women who sat at the bottom, and there was nothing to stop them from being buried beneath an avalanche of excrement centuries in the making.

She unlimbered herself and settled in, preparing for a long haul. There was no telling how long Smythe would be down there. He'd cautioned her not to expect rapid results.

Alston sighed next to her. She ignored him. A few moments later he sighed again.

"Something wrong, soldier?" Jak didn't bother hiding the bite in her voice.

"Sorry sir," Alston said. He glanced sideways at her before putting his eye back up to the spotter's scope. "I'm not used to being out here without my partner."

"There's no reason for you to come out with me again after this." *Please say you're not coming back.* He was so young, unseasoned. "You'll be back with your partner then."

Out of the corner of her eye, she saw him lower his head and she looked over at him. Pain painted his face. It was an expression she recognized; she'd felt it often enough herself over the past couple of years. All at once, she felt about a centimeter tall.

"I'm sorry," she said, her voice quiet. "I didn't know."

"No reason you should. I lost my partner while you were…away. An enemy sniper took us by surprise, killed Hans before we even knew he was there. I only survived because he missed the second shot." He was quiet and the silence stretched as Jak wracked her brains for something reassuring to say. "I ran. Didn't even get his dog tags. He's still out there somewhere."

"Was it Crimson?"

"Nah. Some run-of-the-mill Orthodoxan sniper." He smiled, though no humor touched the rest of his face beyond the lips. "When we get that bastard, I'll pretend it's the guy that got Hans."

"Do you think that'll help?" How many times had she done something similar? For every Orthodoxan she killed, it felt like she was balancing it against Bron's death. There were days when she thought she'd have to drown in their blood before even coming close to making up for her brother's death.

He shrugged. "Can't hurt."

"No, it can't." Maybe he wasn't such a bad kid, after all. All Alston needed was a little guidance. Fortunately for him, she was one of the best. "Do me a favor, scope out all the possible exits on the camp, then talk me over to them."

"Yes Captain."

With something to work on, Alston peered through the scope and concentrated on the camp. They passed the rest of the afternoon into the evening plotting out Smythe's possible exit routes from the camp. It wasn't an enjoyable way to spend the day, not exactly, but it gave Jak the sense of accomplishing something. If nothing else, it was far better to spend the time doing this instead of sitting around with their thumbs up their butts, waiting. The boy turned out to be a quick study. His partner had laid a good foundation for his training. Jak hadn't known a sniper named Hans, but if he hadn't been in her unit, she wouldn't have. Bron might have; he'd been much more prone to socializing than she ever had been.

A damp chill crept over them where they hunched on the hillside. Jak was glad for her ghillie suit. It had been waiting for her in her office with a note from Lambert when she and Smythe had returned from the *Calamity Jane*. She smiled again in genuine pleasure. It was good to know the grizzled quartermaster was still looking out for her. Alston wore a cloak, but this one hadn't started glitching out, at least not yet. Still, she kept an eye out for the telltale shimmer.

As happened most nights, clouds rolled in. The night's rain was a steady mist, not a downpour. The moisture clung to them and soaked through every non-water-repelling piece of clothing they wore. Miserable, Alston shivered next to her. Jak did her best to ignore her own discomfort and concentrated instead on watching the camp. Nothing happened to indicate any issues and they whiled away the night in cold comfort with each other.

The rain slowed, then stopped. The mist melted into fog.

"Shit," Jak said.

"The fog?" Alston asked.

She grunted in agreement. "Tell me what you see down there."

He trained his scope on the camp in the valley and cursed. "Pretty much nothing is what I see."

"Exactly." She rolled her head on her neck and sighed when the joints popped, giving her some relief from the stiffness that had crept in while they kept watch. "We need to get closer."

"Is that a good idea?"

"Not really, but we don't have much choice. We'll never see Smythe on his way out, let alone be able to cover him if he comes out hot."

"What if the Orthodoxans find us?"

"We'll have to be careful is all." She sat up slowly, all her senses stretched out and sensitive to any sign of danger. Nothing tipped her off, and she stood. "Come on, we need to move quickly but carefully. Keep an eye out for Smythe's flare. We should be able to see it, even in this soup."

Jak kept them to a crawl as they made their way down from their ridge overlooking the camp. Alston could move quietly when he wanted to and one glare from her was all it took to convince him that it was time for stealth. Their vision had been reduced to less than half a kilometer, which put them much closer to the Orthodoxan camp than she was really comfortable with.

The fog clung to low-lying areas in great banks and their passage through these ground-bound clouds sent swirls eddying away from them in their wake. It would have been pretty if it hadn't been so dangerous. The dense mist also muffled sound, and Jak kept herself on high alert as they forged through another bank.

Voices floated over to her from within yet another fog bank and she held up a hand, then gestured to the side. Alston went to ground immediately, crouching behind a large stump. In his cloak, Jak couldn't see him, but the fog flowed away from him as he moved. Jak flattened herself in a small depression. If she could hear someone, they had to be almost on top of them, and she wasn't going to risk stepping on a branch and alerting whoever it was to their presence.

"Three of them, this time." A small patrol of Orthodoxan soldiers emerged from the fog, gossiping among themselves. The fog moved away from them, disturbed by their passage, and Jak could see she and Alston had gotten dangerously close to a narrow dirt road. She hunkered down further, trusting her ghillie suit to keep her concealed from her enemies.

"Lucky bastards," said another soldier. "I wonder if they'll make it over the fence."

A tall man leaned over and spat into the weeds on the other side of the road. "Fucking deserters," he sneered. "I hope the Devonites fill them with shrapnel. Serve them right for taking off. Damn cowards."

"C'mon, Sarge," the first man said. "You mean to tell me you wouldn't take off, given the chance?"

"No chance, not for the Devonites. Now if I could get myself a nice patch of land somewhere, a place to farm and get the hell away from this bullshit, that chance I'd jump on."

Jak tensed and slowly reached for her pistol as the group drew abreast of her position. She needn't have worried as they were completely oblivious to the danger they were in. Instead they kept walking and grousing. The fog swallowed them up; they were visible one moment and gone the next. She exhaled a small sigh of relief and stood, her senses on edge.

"That was close," Alston said, his voice almost impossible to hear.

"It was." Jak squinted to one side and brought up her map of the area. She'd downloaded it the night before. There seemed to have been no ill effects from her little episode. Besides, prepping for the mission had allowed her to keep her mind off Torrin's absence, something she needed to keep ignoring if she was going to get her work done. Firmly, she put Torrin out of her mind and concentrated on the map. The road they were on, little more than a track really, was barely visible on the chart. "We need to swing east to get away from the road. There's a hill a hundred meters on that'll give us a decent view of the camp."

"Yes sir." Alston moved off, ghosting through the fog. It parted easily around him and the negative space made him look like some sort of spirit—a malevolent spirit, at least to the Orthodoxans. She fretted that the cloak was actually a liability in their current circumstances, but there was nothing she could do about it except get them to their next observation point as quickly as possible.

They climbed the hill without further incident and set up. As an observation point, it was all right—as long as the fog kept up. If the sun came out and burned the mist away, they would be exposed if they tried to leave the hill. There was very little vegetation surrounding it. The weather report had called for fog most of the day, though, and Jak now hoped it would stick around. It was funny how the fog was both working for and against them.

"Check out the landmarks and talk me over to them," she instructed Alston after she'd gotten settled.

"Got it, sir." He settled in next to her and started his careful perusal of the camp. Jak waited patiently while conducting her own survey.

They spent the rest of the morning watching the camp. Jak was getting nervous. Smythe had thought he wouldn't need more than the night and had been expecting to slip out in early morning. As the sun climbed higher, Jak became more and more anxious. She did her best to keep her concern to herself, but Alston had picked up on it.

When a flare went up from the camp and a sharp report tore apart the silence, it was as much a relief as a concern. Jak's adrenaline kicked into overdrive and she glued her eye to the scope.

"Where is he?" she snapped.

"I don't see him, sir." Alston was tight with tension. His voice shook slightly with it.

"Keep looking." Jak took her own advice and swept her scope over the camp below them. The walls kept her from seeing much of use. "Wait! Watch the men along the top of the wall."

Three men were running down the walk at the top of the battlements toward the nearest corner.

"I see them," Alston said. "Do you think they're after the lieutenant?"

"They're certainly reacting to something going on inside the walls. We have to assume it's him."

"If we could create a diversion, would that help?"

"Absolutely. What are you thinking?"

"I can barely make out fuel tanks on the far side of the camp. Think you can put a bullet in them?"

"Hell, yeah." Jak swiveled her rifle, trying to see where Alston was looking. "Talk me over to them."

"Okay." Strangely, the tension had left his voice now that he had an objective. There was hope for the kid yet. "Follow the line of the wall to the left and back. It's a coupla hundred meters beyond the far corner."

"Gotcha." Jak stuck her tongue out between her teeth and followed his directions. They were spot on. Two cylindrical tanks gleamed white, almost disappearing against the fog that still blanketed the area. That Alston had seen the tanks was nothing short of amazing. She dialed in the distance and adjusted for the wind as he murmured his readings to her. Shouts rose from inside the camp and drifted over to where they hid. Smythe's situation wasn't getting any better. He didn't have much time.

"Take the shot, sir!"

She ignored him. He wanted it to be over, but she knew that rushing the shot could result in missing the target and compromising their position. When the pressure was on, it was time to be more deliberate than ever.

There—she was now sure of her shot. She'd compensated for the bullet's drop and for the sluggish crossbreeze. She bit down on the protruding tip of her tongue, exhaled and pulled the trigger. The rifle's stock kicked and she rode the recoil, resighting in one smooth, unconscious motion. She needn't have worried; the far tank went up in a blinding flash. Moments later the explosion's concussive blast rolled over them, followed quickly by the thump of the shockwave. Even from their position, the sound made her ears ring. The blast was followed in the same instant by a second explosion as the other tank went up on the heels of the first.

"Holy Johvah." Alston touched his forehead, then his lips in reverent prayer. The back corner of the camp was gone. It had ceased to exist. A large chunk of wall was missing, flames licking at its edges.

"I guess that counts as a diversion. Keep an eye out for Smythe."

"Yes sir." Alston stopped staring with a shake of his head and trained his scope back on the front of the camp. Jak watched for a moment longer as men rushed into the breach. From here they didn't look so different from her people. The two of them had really done a lot of damage. This wasn't the time for weakness. She hardened her heart and turned her focus back to the wall in front of her.

"He's out." Jak could hear Alston's smile and she responded with one of her own. She'd picked Smythe up on her scope. He looked none the worse for wear and was headed away from the camp at a rapid clip. His trajectory was taking him away from their position, but they would be able to head him off easily enough.

"Let's go get him."

CHAPTER SEVENTEEN

True to her word, Mori allowed Torrin to go back to her ship, then escorted her through the system to Haefen. Flying past planets with a League ship on her tail that wasn't chasing her felt very strange. She checked the ship's power signatures constantly to make sure the *Icarus* wasn't preparing to fire on her. The *Bonaparte*, the other League ship on the blockade, didn't harass her when she slipped into Haefen's orbit, but she didn't breathe a sigh of relief until she had entered the blue planet's atmosphere. Mori had upheld her side of the bargain; it was up to Torrin to reciprocate.

"*Melisende*, come in please." The comm crackled to life as she approached Fort Marshall.

"*Melisende* here, Torrin Ivanov on the comm."

"You are cleared to land, Miss Ivanov. Central Command requests that you attend him immediately upon landing."

So much for seeing Jak right away, not that Torrin knew where to look for her. She would have to ask Callahan where Jak was recovering. *That's right*, Torrin told herself; she was going to see him because it would get her to Jak faster, for no other reason.

"Affirmative. Inform the general that I will see him within twenty minutes."

"Understood. Marshall Flight Command out."

She landed the *Melisende* next to the *Jane* without a hitch.

She knew the route to the general's offices and made her way there at the fastest clip she could manage, arriving at the building sweaty and gasping. Taking only a moment to regain her breath, Torrin entered the building and took the stairs two at a time up to Callahan's floor.

"Miss Ivanov," Callahan's clerk greeted her with reserve. "The general will see you soon. You may be seated." He waved vaguely in the direction of the chairs while looking inward. Torrin recognized the look on his face; he was hooked into the net.

I don't think so. Confident that she would have a moment before he realized she was heading right in, Torrin pushed past his desk and through the door to Callahan's office.

"Torrin!" Callahan seemed pleased to see her. "I had no idea you were here. Have a seat." He pressed a button on his desk. "Anders, hold all my calls."

"So what's the big rush?"

"I thought you might want to know that Captain Stowell has come through his surgery successfully." Catching Torrin's questioning look, he smiled wryly. "I find it easier to keep Stowell's secret intact if I continue to refer to him in the masculine."

"I see." Torrin wondered what Jak would think of that.

"He's been assigned as your liaison with the Central Command Council." His normally genial facade dropped. "Recent events have taught us that we need to engage in some contingency planning. We aren't willing to lose the equipment you've contracted to provide us, not when we've paid such a steep price."

"That's an excellent plan, General. I'll make sure I talk it over with her. Contingencies need to be set up on my end as well and I want to make sure they mesh well with your plans."

"Excellent." He was all smiles again.

"Now that we're on the same page, where can I find Jak?"

"He hasn't returned from his current assignment."

"Assignment?"

"He and Lieutenant Smythe have identified some possible areas where Crimson may be based and where your sister may be held. They've left to inspect the first of their leads."

"I see." Torrin sat back. How did she feel about this? It hadn't taken long for Jak to insert herself back in the action and Torrin worried what it would do to her. While she trusted Jak more than she did anybody else when it came to tracking down her sister, she didn't want Jak to do it at the expense of her life or her sanity. "When do you think she'll be back?"

"We don't know for certain, but the captain and the lieutenant indicated they thought it would be a short mission. They left two days ago. The earliest they'll be back is another couple of days or maybe a day or two beyond that."

"Very well." Torrin stood up. "I'll return to my ship. If you would be so good as to notify me when she returns."

"By all means. Thank you for stopping in, Torrin."

Torrin nodded and left the room. Frustration burned in her chest. After working so hard to get back, she'd missed Jak again. Were they ever going to be on the same page at the same time? Her relationship with Jak was starting to feel like a series of missed opportunities. They came so close and then were pulled in opposite directions. The universe had given her a woman she would be proud to call partner— wife even—then did its damnedest to keep them apart.

"Miss Ivanov." The cool tones pulled her from her introspection and she looked up to see the clerk staring at her.

"No need to thank me, Anders. I let myself in. The general seemed surprised to see me."

He flushed an ugly red and mumbled something. Torrin was too far away to hear what he said, but the tone wasn't flattering. *I don't have time for this shit.* She decided to let it go and flashed him a breezy smile instead.

"General Callahan knows he can reach me at my ship if he needs me."

"Very good, Miss Ivanov." His lips barely moved as he acknowledged her words.

"Have a great day."

"Indeed. You as well."

Rattling his cage made her feel a little better, and she left the office in a slightly better frame of mind.

The *Calamity Jane* was quiet and cold. She wished Jak was there with her. Her presence had brought the ship to life. On their last trip, she'd asked a ton of questions about the *Jane* and about space travel.

Torrin hadn't tired of answering her queries, and it had been nice to have the company. Torrin hadn't realized how much she would enjoy having somebody other than Tien to talk with.

Depressed by the silence in the ship, Torrin headed for her quarters. She was tired; she hadn't slept well during her time on the *Icarus*. It had been so alien from what she was used to. Since Jak wouldn't be back for two days at least, she might as well work on catching up on her sleep.

The wait reminded her of the day those months ago when she'd waited for Jak to return from the front's trenches. A chill raised goose bumps on her arms. That had turned out so well. Jak had almost died as a result of the infection she'd picked up there. At least then Torrin had known where Jak was; now she didn't even know what the sniper was up to. If something went wrong, would she even know? What if things had already gone pear-shaped?

She stared up toward the ceiling, unable to see it for the oppressive darkness of the room. Each room on the ship was completely contained, sealed off from the rest of the ship. Light had no way of penetrating those seals. Fretting about Jak stopped her from dropping off to sleep and she watched the darkness with prickling eyes.

"Torrin." Tien's mechanical tones woke her. When had she fallen asleep? She didn't feel like she'd slept at all. "Torrin. Someone is approaching us on foot."

Rubbing sandy eyes, Torrin pushed herself up in bed. "Lights." Tears streamed from her light-sensitive eyes and she blinked to clear them. "What time is it?"

"It is 2537 local time, Torrin."

She'd been sleeping for almost eight hours then. With that much sleep she should have felt rested, but she was still as tired as she had been when she'd gone to bed.

"What's the status on our visitor?"

"He appears to be a Devonite army captain, Torrin."

"Did you know he was coming?" She stood and stretched, trying to work persistent kinks out of her back and limbs.

"Negative Torrin. I received no notification that we were to expect him."

"Huh. Let's have a look at him then." The viewscreen in her quarters lit up in shades of green. Even through the distortion of the infrared spectrum, Torrin recognized the errant captain immediately. "McCullock."

What is he doing here? Her upper lip curled away from her teeth. She was in no mood for him. She was tempted to have Tien blow him away, to reduce him to a smoldering pile of ash. Adrenaline surged through her in an eerie reminder of the night she'd spurned his advances and he'd attacked her.

The figure onscreen moved around the base of the ship. He walked first one way, then the other, searching for something. Finally, he shrugged and wandered over to a hatch. She watched in confusion as he raised a hand and rapped on the ship's hull.

"Miss Ivanov?" His voice was tinny through the ship's exterior speakers. "I need to talk to you."

What in frozen hells could he possibly have to say to her? She doubted he'd come all this way to apologize. The Jagger McCullock she'd gotten to know the last time she was here didn't have any extra room in his pathetically limited worldview for the feelings of others, especially not those of a woman. McCullock disgusted her. On some level he frightened her. It wasn't even as if he'd been the first man to try forcing himself on her. Somewhere in all of this, he'd become a symbol of everything that was wrong with this world. Hutchinson, the Orthodoxan colonel she'd encountered when she'd first arrived on Haefen, was bad enough, but his particular brand of evil had been up front. He was the product of a society where a callous disregard for female life was the norm. She wasn't excusing the Orthodoxan and she was glad he was dead. McCullock should have been different, but Devonite misogyny was simply dressed in prettier trappings than that of the Orthodoxans.

"Miss Ivanov!" He rapped harder against the hull with his knuckles. His voice had dropped in register. It no longer wheedled; it commanded.

Torrin bared her teeth at the image onscreen. "Tien, lock weapons on that little shit."

"Do you mean the man rapping at my hull, Torrin?"

"Yes Tien. I mean the man rapping at your hull."

Weapons readouts appeared on the main viewscreen. McCullock's face was suddenly framed in concentric circles. They contracted for a moment, dialing in the distance. It was hard for the ship's weapons to focus on something so near to the hull. They almost never had to deal with a threat this close. Fortunately, McCullock didn't know that. His face paled within the targeting matrix at the same moment it lit up.

Tien had locked on and all of the ship's weapons would have turned toward him in what Torrin hoped was an extremely menacing fashion.

He raised his hands slowly over his head. "I can see you're not in the mood to chat. My apologies." Locked in as she was, Torrin could see his adam's apple bob as he swallowed. "I will speak with Captain Stowell instead." Hands still held high, he backed away from the ship until he was under cover of the trees, or so he thought.

The viewscreen kept his figure outlined against the backdrop of night. The weapons were still locked on. All it would take was the swipe of one finger or one word and Tien would reduce the Devonite and the area around him to smoking ruin. The urge to do so was almost impossible to resist. Torrin's hands trembled, and she finally crossed her arms to keep from reaching out.

"Tien, disengage the weapons."

"Affirmative Torrin."

Where was Jak? Wherever she was, Torrin hoped she was safe and that she'd made some decent headway. They needed to get Nat and get out of here. She looked down. The arms she'd crossed were now wrapped around her body in a cruel mockery of what she needed from Jak.

"Come back to me soon, Jak."

"Four hundred and two meters," Alston shouted in her ear, straining to be heard over the roar of water. "Wind's all over the place. It's almost completely still in here, but it's blowing hard at the mouth of the canyon, twenty-two klicks from the southwest."

"Got it." Jak lined up her shot, tracking to her left and up a bit to adjust for the bullet's fall. A quick bite of her tongue and a squeeze of the trigger and an Orthodoxan's face disappeared in a burst of gore. His body toppled sideways from the narrow ledge he'd been inching along. She was able to squeeze off another round, but in her haste she missed the kill shot on the man behind him. It didn't really matter. With a hole through his shoulder, the Orthodoxan followed his buddy into the gorge with a despairing cry.

There were no other targets. The other Orthodoxans who'd been inching their way along the narrow precipice had retreated.

"That's it for now," she yelled, putting up her rifle. "Keep an eye on the entrance, Alston."

"Yes sir."

"That was very impressive," Smythe said from behind her, his words barely distinguishable from the white noise of the waterfall below them. "So do you have a way for us to get out of here?"

"Not at the moment." She glanced back at him. The bruise on his cheek had darkened quickly. He was developing quite the shiner. "I guess our diversion didn't work as well as I'd hoped."

"If you hadn't blown those fuel tanks to kingdom come, I'd be entertaining some very testy gentlemen right now. I'm very glad you pulled the trigger on that one."

"But we're still trapped and the Orthodoxans know where we are. We don't exactly have many options."

She looked behind her. The canyon ended a couple hundred meters behind them in a wall of water. A powerful waterfall dominated the back wall. Their perch was significantly wider than the tiny ledge they'd traversed to get into the canyon, the same ledge the Orthodoxans were trying to use to get at them. Still, they weren't going to last long. They had few supplies and their exposed position was going to be a liability come nightfall. The only good thing that could be said about their position was that the Orthodoxans had almost no chance of getting to them. They could be picked off at will as they tried to reach them.

"Neither do they," Smythe said, echoing her thoughts. He peered over the edge down thirty meters to the river below them. "Do you think we could get down there?"

Jak stuck her head over the edge and followed his gaze down. "Maybe. But where do we go when we get there? We'd have to swim out." The banks of the river were the sheer edges of the canyon. "Not to mention we'll be totally exposed on the way down."

"It looks to me like there's an overhang behind the waterfall. Maybe even a cave. If we climb down there and hide in it, maybe the Orthodoxans will think we climbed up and out."

"So you want us to hide behind a waterfall where you think there might be some shelter? And if they find us there?"

Smythe snorted. "Come on, they're Orthodoxans. We'll lay a bit of a false trail and they'll leap to the easy conclusion."

"Sir, they're giving it another try."

"Dammit." Jak pushed herself up and aimed her rifle at the far-off blob. Through her scope, she made out a man struggling with a bulky burden. He settled himself and raised the burden to his shoulder.

"Shit!" The curse dropped from both of their mouths at the same time. Without waiting for Alston's information, Jak trusted her instincts and squeezed off a round. The bullet ricocheted off the wall next to the soldier's head. He flinched and swayed, almost falling off the ledge. Barely conscious of the calculations, Jak corrected her shot and put a bullet between his eyes. He toppled to join the half dozen other Orthodoxans who'd already gone over the ledge.

"What happened?"

"He had a rocket launcher, sir." Alston filled him in without looking away from the ledge.

"Shit, indeed."

"If they get a couple of men on the heights with a launcher, we're in deep trouble," Smythe said. Jak could feel his eyes boring into her. "I think it's time we considered throwing them for a loop, Captain."

She sighed. She didn't like his solution, but it was the best of a bad lot. Their other options were to fight their way back out along the ledge, exposing themselves to Orthodoxan fire. In those circumstances, even they couldn't miss. The other choice was to climb down and swim out. The river had looked deep and who knew what the current was like. They could kill themselves in the attempt.

"Fine. But we have to do this right. That means under cover of night and we need to throw them off the trail. Alston, you help the lieutenant out with whatever he needs. I'll cover the canyon and make sure we aren't interrupted."

"Yes sir." Alston crowded past her to join Smythe. Jak took up her vigil over the ledge. It was a long afternoon. Jak had to knock more Orthodoxans off the ledge every few hours. When night fell, it was a relief.

"So what's the plan?" she asked Smythe. He sat next to her munching away noisily on an MRE.

"We did our best to make it look like we climbed out. Alston was able to make it halfway up the cliff face and climb back down without disturbing too much. It should be enough to throw them off." He paused and swallowed his mouthful of food. "It's funny though."

"What is?" She knew she was hungry when even the MRE smelled good, but she couldn't keep watch and eat at the same time. As soon as Alston finished with his meal, she would have him take over.

"It looks like there's already a path down. At least it looks like some of the hand and footholds have been enhanced for easier use."

Surprised, Jak glanced over at Smythe. "That's weird. Why would someone be climbing up and down there?"

Smythe's eyes glittered in the darkness. "Who knows? But I'm sure we'll get the chance to find out."

With a rueful shake of her head, Jak put her eye back up to the scope. Trust an intel officer to get a mental hard-on over the chance to uproot a random secret.

"So now all we need is to slow the Orthodoxans down when they come after us." It had been an hour or so since they'd last tried. If the pattern held, they would finally be getting their nerve up in another hour or so. "I think we need to give them something to hold their attention while we slip away. Torrin taught me this one."

"A formidable woman, your Torrin."

Jak smiled. It was true, after all. "We need a heap of everything that will burn. I think there are enough shrubs up here that we can build a bonfire. That should give them something to think about."

"They'll know we're up to something." Jak could tell from the warmth in Smythe's voice that he was grinning. "When they get past the fire, they'll find the tracks up and they'll assume we were distracting them for that purpose."

"Exactly." Jak was proud of herself. She wasn't especially gifted at diversion and distraction. The bulk of her gifts lay in stealth. Torrin was rubbing off on her, it seemed. Thinking of her lover sent a tightening through her chest. She missed Torrin with an intensity that surprised her. It was an intensity that wouldn't allow her to bury herself in her work to avoid the pain. That tactic had worked occasionally as she dealt with the realities of Bron's absence in her life. The faster they got out of there, the faster she could get back to Fort Marshall to see if there was any news of Torrin.

The pain twisted in her chest, wringing a grimace out of her. She needed to stop thinking about Torrin until she could afford to have a messed-up head. Right now she needed to be as clear-headed as possible.

"Alston, watch the ledge and let me know if you see any movement." She moved away, allowing Alston to take her spot. The MRE that had sounded so good a few minutes earlier crumbled like ash in her mouth. She managed to choke down half the package before giving up.

While she tried to eat, Smythe worked on hacking up the shrubs that had managed to scrabble out an existence on the almost bare rock. He wielded his combat knife deftly; before long there were piles of bushy debris on their ledge.

The ledge narrowed as it led away from their perch toward the mouth of the canyon. One of them would have to brave it again to lay their bonfires. After a harsh, whispered argument, Smythe bullied Jak into letting him put down the fuel for their fires.

Grumbling, Jak joined Alston in keeping watch on the ledge. With Smythe out there, it would make any shot much harder and she needed to be at the top of her form. Fortunately, no Orthodoxans came to test her aim. Before long, the bushes burned merrily. Smythe had staggered them into three piles so each one would have to be cleared separately, slowing their enemies down even more.

"That's lovely," Smythe said, rubbing his hands together gleefully. "Shall we?"

"Yes let's." Jak sat on the ground, working her way out of her ghillie suit. There was no way she could wear it climbing thirty meters down a cliff face. There were too many opportunities for her to get caught up in the trailing pieces. She would roll up the suit and stow it in the webbing she'd had made to transport it. She wasn't about to lose another one. "You guys go on. I'll catch up when I'm done here."

Smythe made a move like he was going to dispute her order. Jak stared at him, daring him to push her. She'd let him get away with too much, had let him be too familiar. He smiled at her and levered himself over the edge and disappeared out of sight with surprising quickness.

Alston glanced at her. "You next," Jak said in a tone that allowed no room for disagreement. He nodded and waited another few minutes before following Smythe.

Jak slung the webbing with her ghillie suit over her backpack. She took one final pass over the ledge with her scope. There was still no sign of Orthodoxans. So far the bonfires were doing their jobs. At least something was finally working out. She slung her rifle over her shoulder and lowered herself from the ledge, feet searching for footholds. Smythe and Alston were already almost halfway down to the water.

He'd been right, she thought. Someone had gone to some trouble to carve out holds for hands and feet. Her going was still pretty slow. Whoever had made the path down the cliff face had been taller than she was. Her arms ached from having to suspend herself while she scrabbled around with her feet, toes blindly seeking for the next foothold.

Smythe noted her predicament when he hit the bottom of the cliff and she was still barely a quarter of the way from the top. Alston splashed down next to him very soon after and Smythe grabbed him and pointed to her, saying something she couldn't make out.

"Another few centimeters down and to the right, sir." She almost sobbed with relief as her foot was finally ensconced in a stable area. She found another hold quickly and rested for a moment, taking the strain off her trembling forearms. With Alston's assistance, she was able to negotiate the rest of their vertical path with much more speed and assurance.

"Thanks Alston," Jak said when she finally stood next to him in calf-deep water at the edge of the basin formed by years of erosion from the waterfall. "I owe you one." She clapped him on the shoulder and he colored at her words of praise. "Where's Smythe?"

"He went over to check on the waterfall, sir."

"He's been gone a long time."

"Maybe he found something."

Jak pushed herself forward toward the waterfall. She had to be careful; the basin's edge sloped away quickly. Based on the deep blue of the water, the bottom was a long way down. She didn't want to slip into the depths, to be pulled under by the currents created by the waterfall. Alston followed along behind her, being equally careful.

As they approached the waterfall, Jak saw no sign of Smythe. The space he was hoping to find had to be at least big enough that he could squirrel himself away. The rocks by the waterfall were especially treacherous, wet as they were from the constant spray. She tried to steady herself using protrusions from the cliff face, but there was little to hold onto. The closer she got to the waterfall, the less she was convinced that there was any space at all behind it. She certainly couldn't see anything through the heavy curtain of water. Maybe Smythe had slipped off the rocks into the water and had drowned while Alston was still directing her down the cliff path.

Finally she stopped a few steps shy of the curtain of water and stared at it hopelessly. She was hesitant to try going through it. Who knew what waited for her on the other side?

A hand broke through the wall of water and grasped her collar, yanking her forward. With a muffled yelp that turned into incoherent spluttering, she flew into a dark cave to find herself face to face with a grinning Smythe.

"Surprise," he said. More splashing heralded the entry of Alston into their dank alcove. "The cave goes back for quite a ways. I'm pretty sure it joins up to a tunnel or gallery. Someone's been using this as an underground highway."

CHAPTER EIGHTEEN

The cave stretched before them into darkness. It was long and narrow, more like a tunnel than a true cavern. The walls and floor were rough, though wide enough that they were able to pass through easily for the most part. They'd come far enough that the night vision their implants provided was useless by itself. In the cave, there was no ambient light to be collected and amplified. A couple of light sticks helped, but when those died they would have no light source and would be truly blind. The floor was uneven and they had to move slowly; even with their meager light source, it was still difficult to tell where the dips and lumps were.

Jak tried not to think too hard about being trapped down in the dark without any hope of finding their way out. She could feel the walls closing in. Not for the first time, she wondered if it was too late to head back and try to swim out. Cold sweat trickled down her back. Drowning in the river might be preferable.

"I see light ahead," Smythe said, his voice hushed but sharp in its urgency. "Stow the light sticks."

Peering ahead, Jak could see the glow he was referring to. It didn't look like natural light; it was too warm. She crammed the light stick into one of the deep pockets in the pants of her combat fatigues.

"I'll take a look," she said. Smythe shot her the look. She recognized it from all the other times he'd disagreed with her plans. "Neither of you moves as quietly as I do. I'm going on ahead. You wait here."

Without waiting to see if he would follow her orders, Jak laid her pack and rifle on the ground. She pulled her pistol from its holster and moved forward, keeping low and to the side of the tunnel. She did her best to disguise her silhouette with the edges of the large rocks and small boulders that littered the floor of the tunnel. If someone came down the passage, they would see her immediately, but she hoped anybody glancing in would overlook her.

Slowly and with great caution, she kept moving toward the light. It definitely wasn't natural. It was warmer than sunlight, though not as warm as firelight. The tunnel narrowed where it met the source of the light. Jak hunkered down behind the corner and cautiously stuck her head into the junction.

The ceiling of the passage their little tunnel had met up with was furnished with light panels. Not enough to make it bright, but enough to see by. By contrast to the rough, twisting tunnel the three of them had been following for almost an hour, this passage wasn't a product of nature, at least not completely. Tool marks stood out as white blobs on the too-smooth walls. And unlike their little passage, it was a pretty straight shot. Across the passage, their tunnel continued on.

There were no signs of anyone else. She listened intently for any signs of life, but even with her audio implant engaged, she heard nothing. She crept back down the tunnel to where Alston and Smythe waited for her.

"It's a tunnel carved into the rock. I didn't see anyone."

Smythe gave a quiet whistle. "I think I know what this is." He looked excited. "I've heard rumors of an Orthodoxan tunnel under the fence. I'd bet this is it."

"It makes sense," Jak said. "The tunnel runs almost directly east-west."

"We need to follow it, see where it comes out."

Alarm bells jangled along Jak's nerves. This was the last thing she needed, more time trapped underground, away from the sky. "The corridor's not that wide and there's nowhere to hide. What if we run into Orthodoxans?"

"It may be our only option, aside from heading back and taking our chances in the river."

"If the Orthodoxans fell for our bait, they might have cleared off the ledge," Alston said. "We can probably head back."

Jak gave the boy a half smile. Hearing the justification from him made her realize how thin the rationale was. Going back would put them in as much danger as moving forward, and without the potential payoff of discovering where the tunnel's mouth came out. Who knew how many lives they could save by shutting down this pipeline to Orthodoxan territory?

"The lieutenant's right. We need to follow the tunnel to where it comes out." How bad could it be? Surely by now they were close to the fence.

"Thank you, sir." Smythe nodded, pleased with her support. "We'll need to be on our guard, of course, but the tunnel isn't likely to be too heavily traveled. From what I've heard, it's been used over the years as a way to introduce snipers into our territory."

"How far are we from the front?" To answer her own question, Jak brought up her map of the area. She found the small canyon and waterfall where they'd holed up. They'd traveled an hour north through the narrow cave. Of course the cave didn't show up on her map and she had to estimate their progress. The going had been slower than it would have been over regular terrain. If her estimations were correct they were about… "A day or so still," she said, her heart sinking.

Smythe nodded. "That's what I figured also."

"This had to already have been here," Jak said. "There's no way they could have dug this out from scratch. Portions of it have to be natural."

"Does that help us?" Alston asked.

"I doubt it. This passage probably isn't a straight shot to the border. I wouldn't be surprised if it takes us longer than a day to get back." She quirked a bitter smile. "We need to break out the stims." Torrin would be pissed, if she'd turned up by the time they got back.

"Agreed," Smythe said. Alston nodded.

"We might as well get moving." Jak shouldered her pack on and headed back up to the corridor, the two men behind her. She waited at the junction again before moving forward, but there were still no signs of Orthodoxans. With a look both ways along the passage, she stepped out and headed west, toward the border.

The passage wended its way unsteadily west and Jak's fears were rapidly confirmed. The only dug-out portions were from one set of caves to another. Not only was the route sometimes circuitous, but it also wasn't easily passable. Some effort had gone into easing passage in the caves, but their progress was still slow. At least the way was well lit.

There were signs of Orthodoxan activity, though little of it looked recent. The equipment they occasionally found stacked in corners was covered with layers of dust.

"Why go to all the work to dig this out, then not use it?" Jak asked.

Smythe shook his head. "I don't know. I don't think anyone on our side knows about it. At least, not that I've heard."

"It really doesn't make sense."

"I agree."

They passed from another dug-out hallway into a huge gallery. Jak looked around her, open-mouthed. The cave ceiling soared into darkness. Huge columns of striated blue stone grew from the floor and disappeared into the shadows. It was like being among her trees. Her claustrophobia disappeared and for a moment she imagined that she could feel the wind upon her face. She smiled when they passed a stream wending its way between the columns. Here and there clusters of crystals grew from the base of the columns. The crystals didn't glow from within like the shelf-fungus found in the depths of Haefen's forests, but they reflected hundreds of points of light back from the light panels that lined the path.

"Can we stop for some food soon?" Alston asked.

At his quiet request, Jak's stomach tightened in sympathy. She nodded. "Let's keep an eye out for a good spot. We need somewhere that'll give us some cover."

"What about over there?" The young spotter pointed past a small mound of cerulean boulders a short distance off the trail.

"That'll do."

They picked their way across the rocks and sat in the shadow of the mound. It was a good spot; no one would see them from the path. The only way they could be discovered was if someone climbed over the rocks to join them.

Jak pulled out an MRE without bothering to see what flavor she was in for. As she ate the warm glop, she consoled herself by remembering that Orthodoxan MREs were worse. She was fairly certain that the one she was eating was chipped beef. Even after living on them for almost a week in the wilderness, she hadn't been able to tell one flavor from another. She smiled. It had been an ongoing joke between her and

Torrin, trying to guess the flavor without looking. As uncomfortable as they'd been, both with the circumstances and with each other, they'd had some good times out there. If only they hadn't been separated so much lately. If there was any justice in the universe, Torrin would be waiting for her when she got back to Fort Marshall.

"Do you hear that?" Alston's harsh whisper yanked Jak from her musings. She sat up and increased the sensitivity on her audio implant. The only sounds she heard were water dripping and ripples from the stream that ran along the path on the other side of the mound.

"I don't hear anyth–" She cut off when Smythe held up a fist, his palm toward her. It was the signal to stop everything and get down. He tapped his ear and nodded. He'd heard something also. She listened again, then heard it. The sound of boots over stone. Lots of boots. He tapped a finger on his forearm. Jak nodded, enemies indeed. It couldn't be anybody else out here.

Jak turned and pointed to Alston. She cupped a hand to her forehead and pointed around the hill. *Watch for enemies from behind the mound.* He nodded and moved to slink off. She grabbed his arm and gestured low. *Be stealthy.* She turned to Smythe and pointed at Alston and touched the top of her head. He flashed her a thumbs up. He'd understood and would cover the kid. Finally she gestured to herself and peered at him through the curled hand up to her eye. She then pointed to the columns behind them. They formed a little rise. Smythe flashed her the thumbs up again. Jak would cover both of them with her rifle from higher ground.

At her nod they broke carefully to their positions. Jak crept into the darkness behind the columns. From there she would be able to cover a larger area. Smythe would keep the kid as safe as he could. She had to trust that they would stick to their assignments. That was one reason why she preferred to work alone. She couldn't rely on anyone but herself. Well, and Torrin. Mostly.

From her higher vantage, she checked out Alston and Smythe. The kid wasn't doing too badly. He'd picked a position where he could see whoever was coming, but where anyone on the trail would have a hard time picking him out of the shadows. Smythe was in fine position to cover him. Her only gripe was that she wouldn't be able to cover him from any Orthodoxans who ended up right in front of him.

She could hear the tromp of boots clearly now. Even when she turned the sensitivity of her audio implant back to normal levels, she could still hear them coming. It was impossible to tell where they were coming from; the acoustics in the cavern bounced sound all around them.

After what felt like an eternity, the Orthodoxans appeared along the path. They headed east, opposite the way her little group was going. She bent her eye to the scope and watched them. Bandages were visible on limbs and under helmets. Overall they seemed somewhat worse for wear. This group had seen action and recently.

Her finger hovered over the trigger. They didn't even have their weapons out. It was as if they were out for an evening stroll in some city park without even a care in the world. She could have wiped out half the group before they even knew what hit them. The taste of iron flooded her mouth; she'd bitten into her lower lip. Her finger twitched. If she shot now, Alston and Smythe would follow suit. They could annihilate the group.

How had the Devonites not destroyed the Orthodoxans long ago? They really were too stupid to live. Thirty years of conflict should have been enough to sweep their miserable society off the face of the planet. The Orthodoxans sent wave after wave of men against them, a seemingly inexhaustible supply of machine gun fodder, and were beaten back more often than not. They needed to shut down those breeding pens. The war wouldn't be over until their enemy ran out of expendable bodies. If she'd been in charge, she would have given the order to invade a generation ago. She would make every single Orthodoxan share the price of Bron's death.

Movement caught her eye. Smythe was facing her, one arm waving over his head. Attention. What did he want? He flashed a thumbs down, then held up two fingers. A problem? Two problems? She swept the line of men. There were fewer than twenty Orthodoxans, so what was he getting at? Wait, what was that? She focused far behind the last stragglers attached to the column. Another column followed. She had been comfortable with them taking on fourteen to sixteen men, but another group changed the dynamic.

Jak grimaced in frustration, then shot Smythe a thumbs up. She understood his warning. She didn't like it, but even she couldn't justify taking on that many men with just the three of them. They'd have to hole up until the two groups passed and hope that none of the Orthodoxans stopped to take a leak at an inopportune moment.

She watched as more Orthodoxans streamed by their hiding place. She tried to relax. If they were discovered and she was this tight, she would be no use whatsoever. She worked on her breathing exercises and tried to divorce her mind from what was unfolding in front of her. It was difficult to achieve the semitrance in which she was most effective, but eventually she got there. Her churning thoughts slowed and her head was filled with blessed silence. No more worries, no more cares; it was only her, the rifle and the Orthodoxans, who were still blissfully unaware of their presence.

The last enemy soldier passed their hiding spot without even a glance in their direction. Jak stayed put and watched the column flow away from their position. A straggler or someone glancing back could blow it for them. She signaled to Smythe to stay down.

Minutes flowed by without any more Orthodoxans, and finally she signaled the all clear. Smythe tapped on Alston's shoulder and said something in his ear. She climbed down from her vantage point and joined Smythe.

"I'd really like to keep our presence under wraps if we can manage it, Captain," Smythe said.

"No kidding. The last thing we need is a firefight in these conditions."

"Of course, sir. And if they know we've found out about their little secret, then they'll stop using it. I'd rather use this to our advantage."

"If we can. I'm going to concentrate on getting us out of here in one piece. I won't risk the safety of any of us to stay undetected."

"Understood sir." Smythe snapped her a crisp salute.

Jak stared at him with suspicion. She couldn't tell if he was mocking her, but Smythe watched her with complete seriousness.

"Let's get moving," she finally said. Smythe nodded, and they met Alston by the path and started out again.

CHAPTER NINETEEN

"Now what?" Alston asked, voice muted.

The three of them were parked on a rock ledge looking down on a large cavern. They'd finally found the evidence of Orthodoxan occupation they'd been expecting. From Jak's calculations, they were in Devonite territory; it couldn't be much further to the entrance of the network of caves. She yearned to be out of there, to see the sky. It had been over a day since they entered the caves and she wasn't sure how much more she could take. Claustrophobia was her constant companion, never far away.

The collection of rude buildings were all that stood between them and open skies. She was tempted to start picking off Orthodoxans and her finger itched toward her trigger.

"We need to get past them," Smythe said.

"Oh really?" Jak sniped. "How do you expect us to do that?"

Smythe shot her a look of mild reproof, his brows slightly furrowed. Ashamed of her outburst, all Jak could do was shrug uncomfortably.

"We do have one advantage, sir," Smythe said. He plucked at the front of his Orthodoxan uniform. Jak had gotten so used to seeing it on him that she'd completely forgotten he still wore it. "I can easily infiltrate their little outpost."

"You could do that and draw them out. Then Alston and I can pick them off."

Smythe winced. "I'd rather not do that. We'll completely expose that we know about the route. Let me scout them out and see what I can find."

Jak shut her eyes. He had a point, but her body screamed for blue skies and trees. *A little longer, you can do this.* She could hold on if she had to—after all, she had two men counting on her.

"That's fine. See what you can figure out. But if I think anything's about to go wrong, we're going to rain a shit storm down on their heads."

Alston nodded in emphatic agreement.

"I understand." Smythe gave them a crooked grin. "More than that, I'm counting on it."

"Good. Now get going. The faster we get past them, the better."

"Understood sir." He gave her a completely unnecessary but crisp salute. Jak had to smile, though she felt like a coiled spring about to snap.

She and Alston watched as Smythe picked his way down from the ledge and onto the path below. His progress across the cavern was tortuous and Jak had to force herself to relax.

"Do you think he'll be okay, Captain?" Tightness in Alston's voice betrayed his nervousness. Her heart rate increased in sympathetic response to his anxiety.

"If anyone can do it, Smythe can." The answer wasn't as reassuring out loud as it had been inside her head. For someone who had spent so much of her life living a giant lie, she sucked at being dishonest. Her skills at deception apparently extended only to hiding her gender. Most of the time she felt like she spent so much time lying that she didn't have the stomach for it when it wasn't completely necessary. Jak flashed Alston what was supposed to be a reassuring smile. From his sober appraisal, he didn't believe the reassurance any more than she did.

"Let's keep an eye on him. He might need us to get him out of a tight spot again." She was being brusque, but with the weight of the mountains pressing in on her, she had room for little else.

"Yes sir." Alston peered through his scope at the makeshift buildings across the way. Jak followed Smythe's progress as he knocked on the door of the biggest building. The door was answered by a soldier in Orthodoxan uniform. After a short exchange, he was allowed inside.

"Well, that's it," Jak said. "Not much to do now except wait."

Hours passed without incident. There was no movement from the buildings below. It was about 1030 hours by her internal clock when the lights visible through cracks in the buildings went out. They still hadn't seen anyone enter or leave the small installation.

Alston yawned beside her and Jak felt her jaws crack open in response.

"Time for more stims," she said. Alston nodded and produced a small packet from his pocket. He popped a pill into his mouth and passed one over to her. She swallowed it dry with a grimace at the bitter taste. Almost immediately adrenaline coursed through her body, wiping fatigue away before it.

They passed another hour in silence.

"Sir, something's happening by the big building."

Jak focused in on the largest of the three shacks. Someone was slipping out a side door. She zoomed in and breathed a small sigh when she recognized Smythe.

"Finally," she said. Alston gave a small grunt of agreement.

"So what's the plan?" Jak asked as soon as Smythe joined them.

"These." He tossed a bag at their feet. Jak opened the sack to find it full of clothing.

"Orthodoxan uniforms?"

"No way, sir," Alston said. "Ain't no way you're gonna get me in one of those."

"You don't have a choice, Private." Smythe glared at the young spotter. "The Orthodoxans think we're a small strike team and that you two were delayed so I went ahead. They're expecting you first thing in the morning."

"But, sir…" Disgust covered Alston's face.

"He's right, Alston." Jak didn't like the idea any better than the kid, but she also understood where Smythe was coming from. "It makes sense and it explains our weapons and equipment."

"It does." Smythe looked grim. "But they were expecting me, or rather who they think I am. We don't have a whole lot of time. You need to be at the outpost at 0600 hours. The longer we wait, the better chance there is the Orthodoxan team will show up." His worry cut a furrow in his brow. "I'm Lieutenant Johns, and you're Privates Simmons and Hollister. I wish I knew what the real strike team is meant for. The men down there don't know. They spent the evening trying to pump me for information."

"Alston, you get changed first," Jak ordered. "I'll watch the outpost."

"Sir." His voice was sullen, but he complied. She could hear the rustle of clothing as he changed. When the rustling stopped and she looked over, she had to work hard not to laugh and couldn't prevent a smirk from escaping. His uniform was ill-fitting in the extreme. It had been made for someone a half dozen centimeters shorter. His wrists and ankles were exposed.

"Sir, won't the Orthodoxans wonder why my uniform doesn't fit?"

"Not at all." Smythe was also grinning at the sight of the spotter. "Uniforms that fit are much rarer than ones that don't. You'll blend right in, trust me."

"Awesome." Alston's sour tone threatened to pull out the laughter that bubbled in Jak's chest.

"My turn," she said, quashing her amusement. "Keep an eye on them."

She waited until Alston turned his attention to the Orthodoxan outpost before hurriedly starting to change. Disrobing in front of others was something she'd avoided at all costs and while she wasn't stripping to her skin, going down even to her underwear in the presence of others made her nervous. Smythe didn't worry her—he already knew her secret—but she wasn't ready for Alston to know. Years of practice had made her adept at flying through a wardrobe change and before long she was uncomfortably situated in the uniform of her enemy.

Where Alston's uniform was too small on him, Jak's was too large on her. It seemed the Orthodoxans ascribed to a one-size-fits-all philosophy, though one-size-fits-no-one would have been a more accurate description. To keep the cuffs from spilling over her hands, she rolled them back. The same treatment to the cuffs of her pants took away the chance of her tripping and falling on her face.

"I look ridiculous," she groused. Alston gave her a sunny smile, and Smythe turned the grin on her.

"It's fine." He glanced over at Alston. "Anything look out of place down there?"

"No sir."

"Good." He sat on the edge of the ledge and prepared to lower himself down. "Remember, 0600 hours. At the latest."

"Got it. We'll be there."

Jak watched as Smythe made his way back to the small grouping of buildings. There was no sign that he'd been missed, but she still held her breath until he'd made his way back inside.

"So we have seven hours to kill," she said to Alston. He nodded glumly. She didn't blame him; it wasn't like she was the best company. So far she'd rebuffed all his attempts at conversation. They'd been gentle demurrals but firm nonetheless. She didn't feel up to making conversation. With everything she had on her mind, even the attempt at casual conversation put her on edge or even more on edge.

After a little struggle with her recalcitrant mind, Jak was able to slip into a semimeditative trance. Normally she could keep it up for hours at a time, but Alston's fidgeting kept pulling her back to herself. The hours passed very slowly. Finally, after about six and a half hours, she'd had enough.

"All right, we're out of here," she said. She double-checked the cuffs of her pants, stood and shouldered her rifle, and they made their way carefully down from the ledge. When they finally reached the path that ran through the cave, they strode along it like they didn't have a care in the world. The skin between Jak's shoulder blades itched, but she refused to act furtive. Their success depended on them being able to sell that they belonged.

She was confronted by a sleepy sentry who stepped out in front of them when they arrived at the buildings. Up close, the structures were even more ramshackle than they'd appeared from the ledge.

"Who goes?" The sentry looked them up and down, eyes strangely incurious. His uniform fit as poorly as theirs did.

"Privates Hollister and Simmons. We're here to hook up with Lieutenant Johns."

The Orthodoxan grunted and gestured toward a near door with his thumb. "He's through there."

Jak turned away from the sentry, ignoring him now that she had the information she needed. Over the years she'd noticed that Orthodoxans were very brusque with each other. Unless they were personal friends, they didn't trust each other. Even then, the trust only went so far.

The door creaked as they went through it. The shack's interior didn't disappoint. It was filthy and smelled of burned food, sweat and something else her mind refused to identify. A group of men sat quietly at a long table. Only a few of them talked; the rest ignored each other. Smythe sat by himself at one end of a rude bench.

"Lieutenant," Jak said, taking care to roughen her voice. This was the last place on the planet she wanted to betray her secret. She wished she were back up on the ledge, taking a bead on each man as he walked outside.

"Simmons, Hollister." Smythe's greeting was distant. He barely looked up to acknowledge them. He scraped the spoon around his bowl a few more times before he stood up. "Wait for me outside."

"Sir," she and Alston chorused. They stepped back through the rude door. Jak was glad to be out of the shack's oppressive atmosphere. She hadn't thought being back in a cave could feel so much better, but it did.

After a few minutes of ignoring and being ignored by the sentry, Smythe stepped out through the door. Another man followed closely on his heels.

"The corporal will be joining us," he said.

"But–" Alston shut up at Smythe's glare.

"I'm your guide on the other side of the fence," the corporal said. "Name's Weller. Used to be with the Devonites, but things here appealed to me a little more." He grinned at them.

Jak glared and turned her back on him. Alston looked offended. Weller must have been used to the treatment; he said nothing.

"Let's go," Smythe said, pushing past them.

The sentry passed them through with a disinterested wave of the hand. A short way beyond the buildings the cavern narrowed to a passageway barely wide enough for two of them to walk abreast. Jak took point while Smythe and Weller walked behind her and Alston took up the rear.

"So I'm to get you to Camp Braier." Jak kept her ears peeled to hear what else the corporal had to say, but Smythe's response was too quiet for her to make it out. After that, Weller lowered his voice and all she heard were indistinct murmurs as the two men talked. They proceeded down the carved out passageway for five minutes before it widened into a natural cavern once again.

"This is it," Weller said. "We're about to head into Devonite territory."

Jak looked around the small cave. Along the far wall were a couple thin sheets of duracrete.

"The entrance is beyond there, I take it?" She pitched her voice low. Weller nodded and picked his way across the cave. Someone had gone to great pains to litter the floor with rocks so it appeared more natural. She wasn't sure why they'd bother since the duracrete sheets weren't in the least bit natural, and neither was the passageway whittled into the rock.

"We need to make sure we put this back into place after we leave," he said with a grunt as he hefted one of the sheets.

Jak caught Smythe's eye and tilted her head toward the Devonite deserter. What were they going to do with him? He shook his head slightly, which could have meant anything. Surely he didn't intend them to take Weller along? He seemed to have some sort of plan, though, so she let it be. She looked over at Alston and gestured him forward to give Weller a hand. As close as they were to the outside, she felt her claustrophobia keenly. To calm herself, she took slow, even breaths through her nostrils and exhaled through her mouth. Her nerves twanged and popped and she wanted to scream at the two men to hurry. Instead she diverted herself by watching back the way they'd come.

More quickly than it probably felt like, Alston and Weller cleared the door. Jak volunteered to take point again and ducked through the small opening before anyone could contradict her. She had to turn sideways to squeeze through the opening, which was barely more than a gash between boulders. A cool breeze dried the sweat beading her brow, and she drank in the scents of the forest. The earthy smell promised relief and safety. She stepped to one side of the cave mouth and allowed the others to exit behind her. The mouth of the cave was barely visible through the jumble of boulders. Weller turned and pulled the duracrete sheets back into place. They'd been textured with small rocks, stones and moss and disappeared almost seamlessly into the rock face.

"Okay, we're good to go," he said in a cheery voice. "Follow me."

Again, Jak caught Smythe's eye, trying to figure out what his plan was, but as before he shook his head at her. Smythe fell in behind Weller, and Jak took the spot behind him, leaving Alston to take the rear. The spotter seemed happy to be as far from Weller as possible. Jak caught him sending dark glances into the traitor's back.

They moved quickly from the small clearing at the base of the rock face and into woods. Soon they were surrounded on all sides by the cathedral-like majesty of Haefen's forests. The silence that surrounded them was broken by the occasional rustle as the wind whispered through the branches around them.

Without any landmarks, Jak wasn't sure exactly where they'd ended up. The series of caves had meandered enough that she'd been unable to track their progress with any accuracy. Happy though she was to be back among the trees, she craned her neck in an attempt to find something that would help her pinpoint their location.

Weller was taking them on a southwesterly course and Smythe seemed happy to follow along behind the turncoat. Finally, they reached a break in the trees. Jak looked out over the vista and noted a nearby hill that jutted out of the surrounding trees. It was curiously flat at the top. Flat and devoid of trees. That wasn't something they saw very often in that area of Haefen.

"Is that...?" Jak allowed her voice to trail off when she remembered Weller's presence. The hill looked familiar. She'd been there before and recently.

"It sure looks like it," Smythe confirmed, voice quiet.

Jak glanced at their guide. He was ahead of them, already heading down an incline. "What are we going to do with him?"

"I want to get him back to base. As soon as we can, we'll overpower him. I'm not going to miss out on the chance to gather more intel."

"Fine." Jak shrugged. "Let me know when you want us to move on him."

"You'll be the first to know."

"Good. Oh, and keep him away from Alston. The boy looks like he's ready to cosh him over the head just for breathing. Can't say as I blame him."

Ahead of them, Weller stopped and they caught up with him as he waited. He gave them a big grin and continued on.

They'd barely crested the top of a ridge when Jak caught a flash of something out of place among the trees ahead.

"Get down," she yelled half a breath before shots rang out. She threw herself to the ground and rolled to one side to fetch up behind a half-buried boulder. Around her, the men scattered. A man's scream rose above the sounds of gunfire.

"Devonites," Weller yelled. With his assault rifle held out at an awkward angle, he fired blindly around the tree that provided him scant cover.

Jak looked around to see who was injured. Smythe was to her left, fetched up behind a rotting log. Alston lay half on top of a bush, clutching at his leg, which was bleeding from a wound right above the knee.

"Alston, over here," Jak hissed. He rolled his eyes wildly to see who was talking to him before they settled upon her. She gestured to him and he slowly crawled her way, leaving a trail of blood behind him.

"It's time," she yelled at Smythe while Alston made his way painfully over to her. Smythe nodded and Jak stuck the muzzle of her sniper rifle over the boulder and took a few shots into the air. She didn't want to harm any of her own men, but she needed to give them a reason to keep their heads down while Smythe worked to get closer to Weller.

Intermittent gunfire from the Devonites up the slope slowed when she took the shots. Smythe vaulted over the log and dashed a few meters up the incline to join Weller behind his tree. Jak took a look through her scope at the Devonites. They'd had the misfortune of running into a fairly large patrol. They needed to move before the patrol organized a flanking action.

A soldier popped up and Jak put a bullet into the tree behind him. The man disappeared in a hurry. She could suppress the entire group for a short while. A grim smile crossed her face as she squeezed off round after round, being careful not to hit any of them. She'd never worked so hard not to hit anyone before.

"What are you–?" Weller's incredulous voice cut off sharply with a sick thunk.

"He's down," Smythe yelled.

"Good," Jak yelled back. "Now let's get those guys up top to stop shooting at us."

Smythe pawed through the Orthodoxan's pockets until he found a square of white cloth. He tied it to the barrel of Weller's assault rifle and waved it back and forth. For a moment, the rate of fire increased and bullets passed through the small white flag, ripping it to shreds. Shouts filtered down to them through the trees and the gunfire slowed to a few sporadic cracks before finally stopping.

Jak tensed. They weren't safe yet. It wasn't unheard of for Devonite soldiers to save their superiors the cost of housing prisoners of war. She looked down to see Alston with his hand pressed to his leg. His growing pallor spoke of blood loss. Jak kneeled over him and put her fingers inside the hole in his pants leg. With a quick jerk, she tore a long rent in the fabric and he paled even further. She wasn't sure how he was staying conscious. It probably would have been better for him if he'd passed out. The hole in the front of his knee was small and oozed blood sluggishly. She slid her fingers around the back and encountered a much larger hole. Blood flowed freely from the back of his leg.

"I need a tourniquet," she said to the boy. He stared at her without comprehension. "Tourniquet!" Understanding slowly dawned on his face and he reached into a pocket on his jacket. They were all supposed carried rudimentary first aid supplies, including tourniquets. Some men conveniently forgot their first aid packs, preferring to lighten their load whenever possible. Jak was glad Alston wasn't one of those.

Jak snatched the item from his hand and wrapped it around his leg at mid-thigh. She pulled a cord and the tourniquet deployed with a soft hiss, air pressure slowing the flow of blood.

"Pull out your dog tags." Jak followed her own instructions. Smythe was shouting back and forth with the Devonite patrol.

Smythe stood and raised both hands above his head, stepping out from behind the tree. Jak quickly put her eye to the rifle's scope and watched the Devonites. If any of them looked ready to take a shot at the lieutenant, Jak would take him out. There were plenty of places she could hit them that shouldn't be lethal.

He walked forward a few paces. Standing alone in a small clearing, he was as exposed as it was possible to be. Jak didn't think she could have done the same. It showed a lot of trust for his fellow soldiers, and Jak had kept her fellow Devonites at arm's length for so long there was no way she would expose herself to them in that way. With an intensity that tightened her chest, she wished she was back on Nadierzda. After only a few months, she trusted those women far more than she had ever trusted the men of Haefen. When she got back to Nadi, she was going to burn the damn breastbinder and never worry about it again.

She kept watch through the scope with one eye and tracked Smythe's progress with the other. The Devonites looked tense, but none of them seemed ready to pull the trigger. One of them stepped hesitantly from the bushes. He had every right to be worried. The Orthodoxans had been known to employ all sorts of nasty surprises and tricks to gain an advantage over their hated brethren. Jak hoped the men from this patrol had never met with any such tactics. She didn't need one of them putting a bullet through Smythe because he'd decided the lieutenant might be wearing a jacket of explosives and was simply waiting for someone to get close enough to detonate. At least they had the advantage that, to her knowledge, no Orthodoxans had ever claimed to be Devonites disguised as their enemies.

Smythe stood there, arms upraised, dog tags in one hand. "My name is Lieutenant Evin Smythe. I'm stationed at Fort Marshall in the Intelligence Corps. My identification number is sierra-echo-niner-niner-five-seven."

The Devonite soldier edged closer as Smythe repeated his personal information as a mantra. Jak cleared her mind and exhaled. She swept the Devonites again but saw no signs of treachery. The men were tense, but none of them looked ready to pull the trigger.

In the clearing the soldier reached out a hand and Smythe deposited a dog tag in it. With one wary eye on the lieutenant, he scrutinized the ceramic disc.

"We're all good," he called back up to his line of men. The men relaxed and stood, though they never let down their guard completely. Jak approved of their vigilance.

Jak stood up and stepped out from behind her boulder, her rifle held to one side. "We have injured."

"Medic!" The patrol leader pointed at Jak. One of the men hurried down the slope toward her. He skidded a little as he navigated the underbrush and rocks. A few more men followed at a slower pace. Jak indicated Alston and the medic knelt at his side.

"You'll be okay," Jak said, clasping Alston on the shoulder. He gave her a grateful look. Jak walked over to join Smythe. As she passed Weller, she noticed that he was stirring slightly. She gave him a prudent tap behind the ear with the butt of her rifle.

"Weller needs to be secured," she said upon joining the two men.

"Sergeant Ivarsson, this is Captain Stowell."

"Sir." The sergeant didn't salute, for which Jak was just as happy. Knowing there was a secret Orthodoxan highway into Devonite territory left her feeling exposed. There was no way of knowing if an Orthodoxan sniper, maybe even Crimson, was watching them.

"Thanks for taking the lieutenant's word for it, Sergeant." Jak gave the sergeant a wry smile.

"No sweat, Captain." Ivarsson's shake of the head belied his breezy words.

"We need to get back to Marshall," Smythe said. "I want to see what the prisoner has to say."

"Yes sir." He turned to the men who stood a little apart from them in the clearing. With a few snapped orders, the men scattered. Two went over to help the medic with Alston. Four grouped around the Orthodoxan. One of them nudged him roughly with the toe of his boot. When Weller didn't stir, the Devonite drew his foot back and gave him a solid kick to the ribs.

"Don't do anything permanent," Smythe yelled.

"Yes sir." They hoisted the unconscious traitor under the arms and started back up the slope, half carrying, half dragging him.

The two men with Alston and the medic were much gentler. They took either shoulder and helped him hobble up the hill.

"Good job, sir," the medic said as they passed. "You kept him from bleeding out. The surgeons'll be able to patch him right up. He'll probably be back in the field in a week."

Jak nodded. She was relieved that Alston would be all right. The kid had grown on her. Despite his relative youth, he'd done a good job as her spotter. She wouldn't mind working with him again.

She followed Smythe and Ivarsson up the hill. They were finally heading back to the fort. It would be good to be back in friendly territory. Maybe Torrin was home. At the thought, Jak quickened her pace. She certainly hoped she was. That Torrin might be out in space, dead or worse, still lurked at the back of her mind, but she refused to acknowledge the concern. In her version of events, Torrin was waiting for her.

CHAPTER TWENTY

Torrin became aware when a weight dipped her mattress. She tensed, then relaxed when an arm snaked around her and Jak's earthy scent filled her nostrils.

"You're back," she said. She tried to roll over, but Jak was pressed the length of her back and held Torrin firmly against her body.

"So are you," Jak whispered in her ear, spreading goose bumps down her neck. Torrin relaxed against Jak, glorying in the feeling of her lover's warmth as it wrapped around her. Jak pressed her lips to Torrin's neck. "I missed you."

Torrin moaned, delectable fire spreading down her spine to settle in her groin. "Me too." Fully awake now, she pulled herself from Jak's grasp despite the small sound of disappointment the movement wrung from her. Looking over, she saw Jak was still clad in her underthings. "That won't do."

Jak gave her a lazy half smile and propped herself up on one elbow. "Why don't you do something about it?'

"Don't think I won't." Torrin pushed Jak down onto her back and straddled her hips. She reached out and slid her hands beneath Jak's undershirt. Her hands encountered the breastbinder and she grunted in irritation. "Lose it," she ordered.

With hooded eyes, Jak watched Torrin as she lifted the shirt over her head. She grinned when Torrin said, "The binder goes, now."

Jak reached to the top and undid the first of the multitude of fasteners.

"Keep going," Torrin said, licking her lips. Slowly, Jak undid the next one, revealing a hint of curved flesh. Unable to wait any longer, Torrin attacked the breastbinder as Jak laughed. Her laughter turned to gasps when Torrin ran both hands over her chest, filling her hands with Jak's breasts, teasing and pulling at her nipples. Torrin lowered her head and worshiped Jak's right nipple with her tongue, pulling the erect nub of flesh into an even harder point before biting down on it. Jak gasped and arched against Torrin.

"Johvah, Torrin," she groaned. "That's so good."

Torrin smiled around the mouthful of nipple before kissing her way over to the other breast and lavishing the same attention on it.

"The shorts," she mumbled, her mouth full. "Lose them." She leaned forward on her knees while Jak fumbled hastily with her underwear. As soon as the offending clothes were down to Jak's knees, Torrin rocked back, pressing her mound against Jak's. Both women moaned in unison at the contact, damp curls grinding together in delicious and damp heat.

Torrin ground her center against Jak while bringing her head up to capture Jak's mouth for a searing kiss. Jak slid her tongue into Torrin's mouth, teasing and coaxing as she explored Torrin's lips and tongue with long, slow licks. Heat continued to build between Torrin's legs and she moaned into Jak's mouth.

Torrin was unable to stifle the yelp when Jak took her in her arms and rolled them over.

"Better," Jak said. She settled between Torrin's legs, moving hard against Torrin, who threw back her head. She wrapped her legs around Jak's hips, panting as she sought to increase the contact. She was rapidly reaching her peak; it had been too long. When Jak reached between them and dragged fingertips across her throbbing clit, Torrin couldn't hold herself back any longer. The pressure in her groin exploded outward and tingles like thousands of points of light moved through her and washed over her skin. Torrin came in a breathless scream at the ceiling.

Jak didn't slow down as Torrin came but kept stroking her. Sensations continued to pour through her, centering from the fingers on her clit. Torrin was being wound back up already and she whimpered at the relentlessness of her arousal. Jak's eyes, normally so light, were dark with desire.

"Jak baby," Torrin gasped out. "Let me–" She groaned as Jak slid the length of two fingers into her.

"Not a chance." Jak's voice was rough with passion and Torrin thrilled to hear her. "You're mine."

She'd never heard such a declaration of ownership from her lover. Torrin had the dim feeling that she should object to Jak's claim on principle if nothing else, but she couldn't do anything except moan and gasp as Jak thrust fingers into her, hitting all the right spots on the inside while continuing to stimulate Torrin's clit with her thumb. She couldn't believe how quickly Jak had drawn her back to the edge of orgasm and for a moment she sat deliciously on the brink, teetering.

When Jak slid another finger into her alongside the other two, the fullness as she stretched to accommodate was her undoing. A hoarse shout and arching back accompanied her orgasm this time. Torrin clamped her thighs around Jak's hand, holding her lover in place inside her as she shook and rode out her release. Finally, she collapsed onto the bed, exhausted and wrung out.

Jak looked down at her, grinning.

"Proud of yourself?"

"Damn right, I am." She wiggled fingers still buried in Torrin's pussy. Her belly clenched as Jak's fingertips stroked along her sensitive inner walls. Torrin closed her eyes and shuddered at the sensation.

"Jak, I need a second."

"No problem, lover." Jak drew her fingers out with excruciating slowness and Torrin sighed. The sensations had threatened to overwhelm her, but now all she felt was aching emptiness.

Jak glanced back down at her and smiled. The wicked glint in her eyes took Torrin's breath away. Before she knew what was happening, Jak was straddling Torrin's head while her own head hovered over the juncture of Torrin's thighs. Her pussy clenched again at the feeling of Jak's warm breath brushing over her most sensitive skin.

Jak's pussy was revealed when she reached down and spread her labia, exposing herself to Torrin, damp and glistening. Torrin raised her head and licked along Jak's slit. She was rewarded with a loud groan that muffled quickly when Jak spread her open, taking her clit between her lips and sucking Torrin into her mouth. Torrin licked along Jak's labia and curled her tongue, dipping into Jak's opening and pulling another moan from her lover. It vibrated deliciously along her clit.

Not to be denied any longer, Torrin wrapped her arms around Jak's hips and brought Jak down firmly in contact with her mouth. She attacked Jak's pussy with a happy vengeance, nibbling and licking her way along Jak's opening and up to her clit. As she swirled her tongue around the focus of Jak's pleasure, Jak tried to flex her hips against Torrin's mouth, riding her hard, seeking even more friction. Thrilled at the effect she was having on her lover, Torrin tightened her grip and laved the flat of her tongue along Jak's clit.

Jak's hips jerked and she lifted her mouth from Torrin's pussy, resting her forehead on Torrin's thigh.

"Johvah, Torrin." Jak undulated her hips against Torrin's mouth again. "I'm almost there…"

Encouraged, Torrin nibbled her way back down to Jak's opening. She licked her way around wet flesh, then pushed inside her lover with stiffened tongue. Jak thrashed on the bed until Torrin held her immobile. She redoubled her efforts, sliding her tongue in and out of Jak.

Jak's thighs trembled with the effort of holding herself together. For long moments, she clutched Torrin's thighs and rode her face. Unable to contain herself any longer, she shouted a wordless exhortation before stiffening and collapsing across Torrin's body. A moment later, she rolled off Torrin to lie gasping beside her.

Torrin crawled up to lie beside her. She stroked Jak's side idly with one hand.

"You're a little sweaty."

Jak gasped out a little laugh. "And you're not?"

"I never said that." Torrin laughed along with her. "That was a nice surprise."

"I was so happy to see you back that I couldn't help myself. I was worried about you." Jak's face resumed its customary sober expression, and she gazed earnestly into Torrin's eyes. She seemed to be on the edge of saying something, and Torrin rubbed her palm in soothing circles over Jak's belly.

"I won't share you," Jak finally burst out.

Torrin stopped her rubbing and looked back into Jak's eyes, surprised at the outburst. "Jak…"

"No Torrin." Jak's eyes were determined and bored into hers. "I can't do it. I thought maybe I could, once, if that was the only way to keep you. But I can't. When I thought you'd been with that Breena, I couldn't handle it." She shook her head to forestall Torrin when she opened her mouth. "I know you've always had lots of lovers and I thought that I'd be okay being one of them. But when you were overdue and I didn't know if you were dead or alive…Torrin, it ate me up. I love you, Torrin. But I won't settle for being one of many. I have to be your only, or I need to move on."

Torrin waited a moment after Jak finished her speech. It had clearly been difficult for Jak to get out, her hands trembled slightly and her eyes were suspiciously wet. Torrin took one of those trembling hands in hers and brought it to her lips, kissing Jak's open palm.

"Jak, honey…" Torrin trailed off. It was hard to speak around the large lump in her throat. "Jak, I don't want anyone else. Since I met you, there's never been anyone else. The way I was in the past is over. How could you even think that you'd have to compete for me?"

"Well, everyone on Nadi always says how many lovers you have and how you hate to be tied down. I thought…" Jak trailed off.

"You thought? I never asked you for that. Jak, all I want is you. Since I met you, you're all I've wanted. Since before I knew you weren't a man, you're all I've wanted."

A tremulous smile crossed Jak's face and her eyes shimmered. Torrin watched, astounded as tears spilled forth. Worried, Torrin reached out and cupped Jak's face between her hands. She drew her thumbs over Jak's cheeks, eradicating the tear tracks.

The sound her gesture pulled from Jak was deep and heartrending. Horrified, she watched as Jak dissolved into heaving sobs. Torrin sat up, pulling her lover into a tight embrace.

"It's okay, love." Torrin rocked her back and forth as she cradled Jak to her chest. She felt Jak's arms wrap around her back and shoulders holding her tight as Jak continued with deep, wracking sobs. She sat with Jak, holding her and soothing her while Jak cried out years of pent-up anguish.

Many long minutes later, Jak's tears waned and she quieted in Torrin's arms. She shuddered gently and made an obvious effort to bring her breathing under control.

"Better?" Torrin stroked the side of Jak's cheek tenderly.

"Yeah." Jak looked a little embarrassed; pink tinged her cheeks. "I don't know what that was about. I'm sorry."

"No need to be sorry. I wish you'd done that sooner."

Jak lifted one shoulder, then let it fall. "It's hard for me."

"I get that, but it doesn't have to be hard with me. You can tell me anything, I hope you know that."

With a yawn that threatened to crack her jaws, Jak settled herself more comfortably in Torrin's arms. She nuzzled in and sighed, her eyes drifting shut. "I do…know that."

Torrin had to strain to hear Jak's response; it was practically inaudible. Her breathing lapsed into the even rhythms of sleep and Torrin shook her head. With Jak in bed with her, she might finally be able to get some decent sleep herself. She settled herself more comfortably among the bedclothes and laid her cheek on the top of Jak's head.

The warmth was seductive and it took all Jak's willpower to open her eyes. She'd been lying in the bed, not quite sleeping, but more than dozing. She luxuriated in the feeling of having Torrin's body wrapped around her. There was too much work to do for her to be lazing around in bed, but she really didn't want to leave Torrin now. Her cheeks heated as she remembered breaking down in front of her lover the previous night. It wasn't something she'd planned on, but after being so happy to see Torrin in one piece and with the insanely fantastic sex, she'd been unable to keep her feelings under wraps any longer.

It was such a relief not to have to worry about sharing Torrin with anyone else. After seeing Torrin's astonishment that Jak could think such a thing, she felt a little ashamed for not having trusted Torrin sooner. Trust was such a hard thing, so fragile and with the power to hurt so badly when broken. Her heart was in Torrin's hands now, and she reveled in the feeling of letting somebody else in. She didn't feel exposed like she'd thought she would. Quite the opposite, in fact. For the first time in years, Jak felt safe, cradled by Torrin's love for her.

Jak gazed at the length of neck that was exposed to her. The curve of Torrin's jaw beckoned her. Unable to resist, she stretched and placed a featherlight kiss on the corner of her jaw, right where it met her neck. Up close, she could see Torrin's pulse and she covered her gently throbbing skin with her mouth.

She was rewarded with a soft murmur and a quiet rustle as Torrin turned her head to look down at Jak.

"Hi," Jak said.

"Hi yourself." Torrin stretched like a cat but managed to keep Jak anchored to her side. "What time is it?"

"0530. I should be going soon."

"So soon?" Disappointment shrouded Torrin's face, and Jak reached over and cupped her cheek.

"We're still working on finding Nat. This trip wasn't successful, but we have three more solid leads."

"Really?" Torrin looked guardedly hopeful.

"Yep. Tien helped us track down the four camps that Crimson was most likely to be based out of. Smythe infiltrated one. That leaves three more to check."

"How long is that going to take?"

"We're going as fast as we can, Torrin." Jak gazed at her, willing Torrin to see how badly she also wanted to find Nat.

"I know. It's just so incredibly frustrating." Gently, Torrin disengaged herself from Jak and pushed herself up in the bed. "And I might have blown an angle."

"What do you mean?" Jak had felt Torrin's absence keenly, but something about the way she was holding herself made Jak wary of getting too close.

"McCullock was here." Torrin watched her closely.

"Okay."

"You're not surprised."

"I guess not. He talked to me a few days ago. He's trying to track down the mole in Central Command's office."

"How can you even work with him?" Torrin drew herself up and looked away from Jak.

"Well, I–"

Torrin cut her off. "How could you? He tried to attack me. Who knows what he would have done if you…If we…" She turned anguished eyes on Jak, who ignored Torrin's attempts to pull her hands from Jak's grasp and kept them trapped between her palms.

"Torrin, I didn't see how we could afford to turn him down. He's been working on the problem for months, and if the mole has a line to Crimson, then exploiting that could be how we get Nat back."

"Nothing good will come of working with that man. You can't trust him."

"I don't." Torrin had stopped trying to get her hands back, but the crushed look on her face tore at Jak. "I doubt he's the traitor, but I wouldn't put it past him. If he is working against us, then being close to him will help us smoke him out."

"So, do you think he's the spy or not?"

"I don't think so, but I can't rule the idea out completely. The only people I *know* aren't traitors are you and me. I'm pretty sure it's not Smythe or General Callahan. Everyone else in Fort Marshall is fair game."

"You need to keep him away from me. If I see him again, I'm going to do something permanent."

"Don't worry, baby mine." Jak stroked a finger down Torrin's cheek. "I'll take care of him myself if it comes to that."

"Did you find anything on your mission?"

Glum, Jak shook her head. "Smythe is reasonably certain that Crimson wasn't based there. Apparently, he would pass through every now and again, but never for very long and not on a regular basis. We're looking for his home base." She shrugged, trying not to let Torrin see her frustration. "Only three more to go."

Torrin squeezed her eyes shut. "I wish we had her back already."

"Me too. But we're doing everything we can, I promise."

"I believe you, but I don't trust the others."

Jak patted Torrin on the shoulder and leaned in for a quick kiss. Torrin clung to her and pressed desperate lips to hers. The kiss lengthened until Jak had to gently disengage herself from Torrin while they gasped for breath.

"I have to go." Jak's breath came in short pants. There was nothing she wanted to do more than to crawl back into bed with Torrin, but duty called. She understood Torrin's desperation. Grief and worry both numbed and sharpened her emotions. Feeling anything reminded her that she was alive and that there was more to life than despair.

Jak stood and dressed in quick movements, no motion wasted. She sent Torrin a reassuring smile that felt wooden even as she gave it.

"Love you," Torrin said.

Jak's smile deepened and became genuine, instead of a pale imitation meant to reassure. "I love you too."

She stopped for a quick kiss on the lips, then snagged her rifle from where she'd deposited it in the corner and continued out of Torrin's quarters into the corridor. From there it was a short trip through the ship, and moments later she was standing in ankle-deep grass that was wet with morning dew while Tien closed the cargo bay ramp behind her.

Because of the early hour, there were almost no men on the street. She made her way through the quiet streets as quickly as she could. She could have stopped and requested a ride at the fort's guardhouse, but trusting in her own legs felt good and she let physical exertion burn away some of her cares. She hadn't slept through the entire night; the stims making their way out of her system had seen to that, though she knew better than to tell Torrin. She'd laid next to Torrin, holding her and worrying about their next step. Clearing three more camps would take a couple weeks, at least. And that was if nothing went wrong. Nat had already been in Orthodoxan hands for fourteen days, which was fourteen days too long. What was she having to endure at their hands? No, she couldn't think about it, not and focus on finding her. Though her breath was catching in her throat, Jak lengthened her stride.

She passed her office quarters and made her way to a long, low building. Concertina wire topped a chain fence. Right inside the fence a force field hummed and flickered. A Devonite soldier stopped her at the gate.

"Papers sir?"

Jak produced a thin data pad from the breast pocket of her combat fatigue coat and thumbed it on. A quiet whine was the only sound as the small device powered up. She plugged the jack from the device into her palm and accessed her identification papers and orders. After only a split second, the required documents appeared on the small screen. She waited in mute approval while the soldier jacked in and perused each document before handing the pad back to her.

"You're cleared, sir."

She nodded to him and passed him at a more moderate clip. Now that she was closer to the building, she could see that it had no windows. The only feature that relieved the stark duracrete facade was a huge metal door. She walked up and pounded on it. A viewscreen over a keypad flickered to life. Jak plugged the datapad into the port below the screen. There was no response, but the door clanged dully a few times before popping open, swinging slowly toward her. As soon as it opened far enough, she slipped through it.

"Captain Stowell." A crisply uniformed NCO awaited her. "I'll conduct you to the prisoner, sir."

"Thank you, Sergeant." Jak fell in behind him. They stopped in a room full of secured lockers and he waited patiently as she checked all her weapons and locked them up.

"Is that everything, sir? They'll be checking."

"Got it. And yes, that's everything." How would they be checking? She'd never been privy to an interrogation, not at this level. She'd only ever delivered prisoners; she'd never been involved in questioning them. Still, she couldn't take off now, that would raise all sorts of awkward questions. There was nothing to do for it but continue and hope for the best.

The sergeant nodded and preceded her out of the room. They made their way down two flights of stairs and through three checkpoints where she had to access her orders and credentials all over again. Finally, they stopped in front of a door with no more distinguishing characteristics than any of the others she'd seen so far. Two guards blocked their progress.

"Sir." One guard moved up to her. He gestured to the wall across from the door. A white rectangle was painted on the wall opposite the door. Resigned, Jak put her hands at either end of the rectangle. It was a little tall for her and the reach was awkward.

Here goes nothing. The guard ran professional hands over her, searching for hidden weapons or contraband. She appreciated the level of security, but she worried about discovery, just as she had for every other pat-down she'd received since joining the Devonite army. She blew out an almost imperceptible sigh of relief when the guard finished. Fortunately, the breastbinder felt enough like the light body armor many of the men wore beneath their fatigues that no one had ever remarked upon it.

"You're good to go, sir."

"Thank you, soldier."

The other guard opened the door for her and she saluted as she passed through. The room was unrelieved white. Walls, ceiling and floor were the same stark white, marred only by the occasional dark smear. In the center of the room, Weller sat, trussed to a chair. Smythe stood in one corner, deep in conversation with a man Jak had never seen before. He was small, almost as short as she was. Ropy muscle ran down his exposed arms, every inch defined in stark relief beneath his skin. She couldn't tell what rank he held; he'd stripped down to his undershirt and his fatigue pants.

At her entrance, the two men looked up.

"Oh good," said the small man. "We can get started." He crossed the floor to the room's center and casually backhanded Weller.

* * *

The agony between her thighs had long since receded, though Nat imagined she could still feel it when she dwelled on it, which she tried not to. It should have been an easy enough solution, she told herself. *Don't think about it, whatever you do.*

The sniper hadn't left her alone for more than a few hours at a time since she'd made her break for it. He was no help in keeping her mind off the attack, not with the considering way he'd started watching her. He never looked at her with lust in his eyes. He rebuffed her every attempt at conversation. Not cruelly or angrily, but with a complete indifference that chilled her to the core. When he looked at her, Nat was convinced he saw nothing more than a tool. She'd seen a kinder regard on his face when he looked at his rifle.

The look on his face as he paged through the water-stained album in his hands held more emotion than she'd seen from him before. She looked around the cabin again, with its unfinished log walls and the open living area. No one had been there for a very long time. The only tracks in the thick layer of dust aside from their own belonged to animals. They weren't tracks she recognized, but Nat had given up her curiosity about the planet. For as often as she'd wished she were anywhere but Nadierzda, she would have given anything to be back home again. This certainly wasn't the adventure she'd anticipated.

Hot tears prickled in her eyes and she closed them rather than let the liquid spill over her cheeks. When Nat opened her eyes again, she was astounded to see tears tracking through the accumulated grime on her captor's face.

"Are you okay?" Nat quickly regretted her soft query. She'd offered it out of a shared sense of misery, but the white-hot glare he turned on her told her louder than words that he shared no such feelings. Rage stared back at her.

"Okay?" The sniper all but hissed at her. "How can I be okay? She was perfect. She was…" He looked down at the page in the album. Tears added to the already stained page. "Look what they did to her."

Nat tried to stop herself from recoiling as she took the book that was shoved into her hands. His anger was terrifying and unexpected after countless days of a complete lack of emotion.

She looked down at the page and couldn't stop the smile that broke free. "Jak." It was such a relief to see a familiar face and her throat tightened painfully at the sudden reaction. She traced the edge of the photograph. On the opposite page was the faded picture of a little girl. With a start, Nat recognized her as Jak also.

The sniper's face was suddenly nose-to-nose with hers. "Jakellyn!" he screamed.

Nat leaned away from him. Spittle dotted her face, but she didn't dare lift her hand to wipe it off. He moved in closer to her, shoving his face in hers.

"Jakellyn," he repeated, voice barely above a whisper. "You call her that again, and I'll…" His voice trailed off, and Nat waited for him to finish the threat. Instead, he carefully took the album back from her and headed across the room. Halfway up the stairs, he turned and looked down at her.

"Don't go anywhere. I'm going to be a while. If you do try to run, I'll track you down and stake you naked outside the nearest guard post." The sniper didn't wait to see if she'd heard him. He simply continued his slow trek up to the second floor.

Nat stood, frozen. She had no doubt that he would carry out his threat. Her mind skittered away from the events in the field. Crashing and banging noises from the upper story pulled her attention back to the present.

Wood splintered overhead and the ceiling shook when something hit the floor with a resounding thud. Something else hit the floor above her head, followed by more sounds of snapping timbers. The ruckus continued for a long time. When it finally ended, there was a long period of almost complete silence. She could hear him moving around on occasion, but that was it.

Exhausted and without the noise to keep her awake, Nat put her head down on her arms where they were crossed over her knees. She settled herself back into the corner of the room. It wasn't ideal, but no one was going to sneak up on her there. She couldn't keep her eyes open, but she couldn't quite drop all the way off either. Small movements overhead kept filtering through her consciousness. Trapped on the edge of dozing, Nat drifted and twitched.

CHAPTER TWENTY-ONE

Jak was filthy. Her fatigues were encrusted in mud, and even though it had been half a day since they'd been caught out in a deluge, portions of them were still damp. The fourth Orthodoxan camp had been a bust, and she was having to fight to keep her thoughts from spiraling into despair…again.

The trek back to the fence had been quiet; Smythe seemed as despondent as she was. When the first three camps had come up empty, Jak had been eager to try the fourth, figuring they would finally track Nat down there. She'd fantasized about the various ways she would take out Crimson. Did she want to go with the bullet to the throat? It had a certain poetic justice to it but was unnecessarily showy. The most prudent shot was the one to the torso, though that didn't seem nearly painful enough. She really wanted him to suffer as she had. Maybe a gutshot would do it.

But it was all for nothing. They were no closer to finding Crimson or Nat. In fact, they were now further away than ever.

"I want to get this straight," Jak said to Smythe. He glanced over at her as they walked from the transport to their building. "Torrin's going to ask, and I need to know exactly what to tell her."

"The last camp was our best bet," Smythe said, his voice weary. She'd been grilling him for two days. "He was based there and recently. No one's seen him there for a couple of weeks. Word is he's been reassigned."

"But we don't know for sure?"

"We're as sure as we can be without seeing his transfer orders. My sources all agreed they hadn't seen him for a while. Apparently, he was acting strange before he disappeared." Smythe shrugged and shook his head. "But he's a sniper, strange comes with the territory."

"Hey!"

Smythe smirked at her. "Oh, come on. If you guys weren't a little crazy already, you wouldn't do what you do."

"So that's it then?" Jak left the sniper comment alone. She was happy Smythe had unbent enough to treat her like a regular person again, instead of overcompensating with formality.

"For now. It was a promising lead, but it didn't pan out. Maybe if we'd gotten the intel a month sooner."

"A month sooner, we weren't here."

"True."

They arrived at the door to the office. Jak took a deep breath before pulling it open. On her arrival, chair legs scraped across the floor as the room's occupants jumped to attention. No matter how many times she tried to convince them to tone down their enthusiasm, they ignored her. Torrin had shrugged off her discomfort when she'd looked for some commiseration.

"They're proud of you," she'd said. "Everyone knows who you are and that you're going out and tracking down the dreaded Crimson. Not to mention what you did to bring me back with you. Did you know someone actually wrote a song about your exploits?"

Jak had groaned and hidden her head in her arm. "Great. That's fantastic." For someone who'd survived on anonymity, the attention made her intensely uncomfortable.

"You might as well go with it," Torrin had advised. "The song is pretty entertaining, though a little inaccurate. It's catchy as hell. Did you know that you dispatched a squad of forty Orthodoxans from close range, with your rifle?" She'd rubbed Jak's back in small, soothing circles.

"You'd think they could work on being a little realistic."

"Let them have their mythology. Every conflict needs its heroes."

Jak surveyed the room; the men watched her expectantly, every last one holding onto their crispest salutes. Smythe was rigidly at attention at her side as well. She returned their salutes.

"As you were." The din repeated, in reverse this time as the men seated themselves. She fled into her office, closing the door behind her.

She'd barely taken a seat at her desk and pulled off her boots when she was interrupted by a knock at the door. Her socks were soaked and she pulled them off as well.

"Come."

A young clerk opened the door part way and stuck his head through it. "Apologies sir. The colonel ordered me to tell you to check your messages. He was very insistent."

"Thanks Caldwall. I'll check that out. Is there anything else?"

"One other thing, sir. A Captain McCullock wants to go over a shipment lading from Troika Corp. He was concerned they shorted us on something."

McCullock wanted to speak to her? He wanted to talk badly, if he was willing to approach her in the office.

"I see. Set something up for us before the end of the week. No particular priority. Work it around my schedule." She didn't want to betray the importance of the meeting by moving things around to fit him in, but she also didn't want to wait too long. Now that they'd exhausted their leads, working with McCullock might be the only way to get Nat back. Torrin wasn't going to be happy, but she had to understand that sometimes you had to dirty your hands to get what you needed accomplished. Like Jak had with Weller. Thanks to that filthy business, the passage under the fence was being monitored and Orthodoxans were being followed as they came through. Smythe hadn't wanted to close down the passage completely. He thought there might be more to come.

Jak had pointed out that closing the passage would make it impossible for the Orthodoxans to do any damage there. Smythe had only smiled and asked her if she knew the next place they would pop up. When she'd asked why the Orthodoxans hadn't closed down the tunnel when their strike team didn't show up, he'd shrugged. As much as he'd tried to play it off, she thought he might have been puzzled by that also. To her mind, either the Orthodoxans were too lazy to close down their back door into Devonite territory, even if it had been compromised, or the three men had been late because they'd deserted. With the Orthodoxans, it was even odds as to which one was the right answer. "Got it, sir." Caldwall saluted and pulled his head back around the door, closing it behind him.

Jak stared at the cable protruding from the wall next to her desk. She had no desire to hear from Wilson. She'd managed to avoid him quite well since he'd become her immediate superior. It helped that she'd been away, checking out Orthodoxan camps, for the past two and a half weeks. They had come back to Marshall to regroup after each failed attempt, but it had been barely long enough to get a good night's sleep and resupply before they were out again.

She got up and walked to the door, locking it behind Caldwall. She pulled a fresh set of combat fatigues from the closet in the corner and quickly changed out of the damp, smelly ones she was wearing. It only took her a few minutes and she felt better for the change. She plopped herself back down behind her desk.

With a sigh, she plugged the cable into the port on her left palm. Immediately, she was assaulted by images and sounds. It took her barely a second to acclimate and she shook off the momentary disorientation to access her message files.

"Stowell!" Wilson's voice thundered in her ear. She winced and lowered the volume. "You owe me a report! I expect to have it in my in-box before you take off on your next excursion. I will have you confined to quarters if I think you're trying to leave the fort without completing it." Angry breathing filled her mind and Jak could easily picture Wilson's florid face, bright red with angry veins pulsing at his forehead. "Get it to me by end of day tomorrow or I'll have someone else take over the search for Ivanov's sister. Don't test me on this!"

The message cut off abruptly and Jak leaned back in her chair. She sorted through her files before pulling up the report she'd started, the one that would keep her from searching for Nat. Wilson's insistence on getting the report finished was aggravating in the extreme. So far she'd managed to get one line written. The text blinked at her mockingly.

She hated writing. Words had never been tools that came easily to her. Bron had been much more successful with them while they'd been in school, and when they'd joined up, she'd relied on him to write out their after-action reports. With his death, she'd been forced to take them on. They hadn't gotten any easier to write in the intervening two years.

At the end of a couple of hours of laboring, Jak had two paragraphs, neither of which was overly useful.

"Fuck this," Jak said out loud, ripping the cable out of her palm. "I'll work on this tomorrow." She stood up and stretched. Sitting in the chair for so long had given her a crick in the neck and her back was stiff.

The rest of the office was quiet when she opened her door. The men had gone home an hour before. There was still a light on in Smythe's office, and she stuck her head in to say goodnight.

Smythe started when he saw her and blinked at her in owl-like confusion. "Captain. I thought I was the only one left in here."

"I'm heading out," Jak said. "You should think of doing the same."

"Got it, sir." Smythe shuffled together a small stack of papers. "I only have a couple more things to do, then I'm out."

"Good." Jak left the office and headed down the street to the exterior gate.

The streets were full of men. It was the right time of night for many of them to start hitting the bars around Fort Marshall's perimeter. Steady streams of soldiers flowed from the various barracks to the surrounding bars. Jak mixed in with the flow and allowed it to carry her toward the gate. A small space opened around her as men became aware of her rank. When they realized who she was, the whispers inevitably began. The space she didn't mind, but the whispers she could have done without. They made her self-conscious and the feeling that everyone was staring at her made her skin crawl. As the whispers swelled, Jak picked up the pace, pushing her way through the crowd when she had to. No matter how hard she tried, she couldn't outrun the murmurs.

Jak had a moment of panic at the gates. Would Wilson make good on his threat to keep her confined to the fort until she finished her report? To her intense relief, the guards waved her through. The fence and Orthodoxan territory lay in the opposite direction, and she wondered what would happen if she'd tried to leave through the gate on the far side of the fort.

The cargo bay ramp lowered as she approached the *Calamity Jane*. She entered the cargo bay.

"Finally," Torrin's voice rang out. Jak had less than a second to brace herself before Torrin threw both arms around her and squeezed. She lowered her head and covered Jak's lips for a searing kiss that made Jak's lips tingle, matching the excitement she felt further down.

"Mmm, that was nice." Jak licked her lips, missing Torrin already when she pulled back.

"You were gone too long." Torrin gave her another quick kiss. "Did you have any luck?" Her voice was so hopeful. Jak hated to disappoint her.

With a grimace, Jak shook her head. "It was a dead end. Smythe said no one's seen Crimson for a few weeks."

"So right after he ambushed us on Hill 372?"

"I guess so. The timeline's about right for that."

"So what now?"

"I have one other option, but you're not going to like it."

"McCullock?" Torrin's voice was expressionless, and Jak could tell from the tenseness of her muscles that she was not best pleased.

"I know you don't want to, but if he's found something, I don't see how I can discount it." She looked into Torrin's eyes. "He tried to see me today."

"What do you want from me? I can't change the way I feel about the bastard." The anger and fear in Torrin's gaze made Jak's heart ache.

"Look at it this way, without him we never would have gotten together."

A brief smile met her sally. "Nah, I would have gone after you sooner rather than later." Torrin laughed at Jak's surprised look. "I was so hot for you. I'd almost gotten to the point where I was ready to jump you, penis or no."

"Really?" Jak was at a loss for words.

"Yes really. You have no idea exactly how hot you are, do you?" Torrin grinned and the expression looked almost natural on her face. "Don't answer that. I know you don't believe it."

"I might not believe it, but I will let you prove it to me." Jak slid her hands under the hem of Torrin's shirt. Torrin captured her hands and turned, pulling Jak onto the elevator. For a while, at least, they could make each other forget the cares heaped upon them.

Torrin lay on her back, staring into the dark. Jak was curled beside her, back pressed to Torrin's side, and she ran her fingers idly up and down her torso. Her rib cage moved in gentle rhythms of deep sleep. Torrin envied her. She'd gotten a little sleep after they'd made love, but after less than two hours she was wide awake. Guilt gnawed at her. How could she be holed up with Jak, making love while who knew what was happening with Nat. Was she being unreasonable, refusing to work with McCullock?

A shudder ripped through her at the idea. McCullock and Hutchinson were linked in her mind. Memories of the night McCullock had tried to attack her brought the same feeling of helplessness she'd had during Hutchinson's attempted assault. Her legs flexed restlessly on the bed while she remembered the Orthodoxan colonel's breath on the side of her neck. She turned her head at the memory of how he'd ground himself against her. Without Jak, she didn't know how things would have turned out. Would she have fought him? Would she have been willing to die before allowing him to touch her like that, or would she have submitted to him to keep from being hurt? Was Nat being confronted with a similar choice?

The line of thinking wasn't helping her get any sleep. Carefully, she slid from the bed, making sure she didn't disturb Jak. She didn't want to worry her lover; Jak already had so many things riding on her. Torrin snagged a robe from the back of a nearby chair and left the room. She made her way to the bridge.

"Tien, bring up a chart of the system." She slid into her chair. Sitting there made her feel better. When she was at the ship's helm, she always felt in control. The *Calamity Jane* was something she could affect, something that would move to her commands, unlike the situation with her sister.

"Affirmative Torrin." The viewscreen flickered into a view, Haefen dead in the center.

"Highlight the League ships."

The AI obliged and the two ships were outlined in brilliant orange. For a few minutes, Torrin watched their orbital paths.

The door opened behind her and Jak's arm was around her shoulder, warm and comforting.

"I woke up and you were gone."

Torrin smiled up at her. "I couldn't sleep."

"I know." Jak squeezed her shoulders comfortingly. "I'm sorry. I wish I had more to show for our efforts the past few weeks."

"You're trying. I know that. It's just so…"

"Frustrating?"

"Yeah. And all I can think is that Nat is out there all by herself. I'm her big sister, I'm supposed to protect her, keep her safe." Torrin's eyes prickled, and she cleared her throat, trying to keep her composure.

"It's not your fault." Jak barked a bitter laugh. "I talked you into giving her a chance to get off Nadierzda. And now that things have gone down the tubes, I can't even find her for you."

"I don't blame you. You were right. Hell, she was right. I blame that bastard who took her." Despite her best efforts, hot tears coursed down cheeks.

Jak rested her cheek on the top of Torrin's head and held her. She didn't say anything else, and Torrin finally allowed herself to cry, to really feel the pent-up anguish she'd been carrying since hearing that Nat had disappeared. Torrin leaned on Jak, absorbing her strength.

"Torrin," Tien's mechanical tones interrupted her quiet sobs. "We have a new power reading in the system."

"What?" Torrin looked up, surprise halting her tears. "Show me."

Tien highlighted the new power signature on the screen. It was definitely coming in from outside the system.

"Give me specs on the ship."

Numbers appeared as an overlay on the screen, detailing power fluctuations, drive mass and density.

"It can't be..." Torrin leaned forward to get a better view.

"What is it, babe?"

"They shaved four days off the trip." Exultation colored Torrin's voice. "I don't know how they did it. I don't want to know." She stood up and grabbed Jak, hugging her close. "It's the *Nightshade*."

Jak's face lit up in a broad smile. "Well, they'll definitely help."

"Yeah, they will." A thought occurred to Torrin. "Tien, open a channel with the *Icarus*."

"Yes Torrin."

Torrin waited, tense minutes passing as Tien tried to raise someone on the *Icarus*. If she could see the *Nightshade*, she had to believe the *Icarus* could as well. While she wouldn't bet against the *Nightshade* in a fight, the outcome would be too close for comfort. There was no point in even chancing it, not when they were on the same side, if only for the moment.

Torrin shrugged off Jak's comforting embrace and paced back and forth in front of the viewscreen. Minutes crawled by in tense silence. Finally, Captain Mori's face filled the viewscreen.

"This better be damn important, Ivanov." She looked behind her and gestured to someone they couldn't see. "We're a little occupied at the moment."

"I thought you might be, Captain." Torrin smiled, trying to project an aura of ease. "The ship that appeared on your scanners a few moments ago is with me."

"They're with you? They aren't responding to our hails."

"That isn't too surprising. They aren't used to dealing with the League. I called them in to help with my situation before I had the opportunity to speak with you."

"I see." Mori's eyes narrowed. Torrin wished the League captain was as stupid as the rest of her ilk, but so far all evidence pointed to the contrary.

"I'm going to hail them and let them know you're here. That should help avoid any misunderstandings."

"You do that. It's past time for a meeting, Ivanov. Tomorrow, all the players in our little drama are going to meet. You still owe me and the convenient appearance of your friends makes me wonder if you intend to make good on your end of the bargain."

Torrin cringed inwardly. Mori had hit the nail on the head. She'd hoped to be able to sew things up without involving the League. Their help would put her in their debt. She didn't like owing anybody, but knowing the League had a marker they could call in put her especially on edge.

"Of course, Captain Mori. I'll arrange things for a meeting tomorrow. I'll be in contact first thing in the morning with the details."

"See that you do." The screen went dark for a moment then was filled by the system chart. The *Nightshade* was moving steadily through the system, toward Haefen. The *Icarus* and *Bonaparte* had paused in their intercept course.

"Tien, hail the *Nightshade*."

"Affirmative Torrin."

Axe's face replaced the system chart almost immediately.

"Torrin! Hell, woman, what's going on down there? We got your packet. Your sister's missing?"

"Axe, I'm glad to see you. It's true, the natives have Nat and we're having issues tracking her down. I really need your help finding her."

"You got it, Torrin. Major Stowell." Axe nodded to Jak.

"It's still Jak, Axe. I'm only a captain on Haefen."

"No can do, Major. You're carrying the honor of the Nadierzdan military now. We're going to claim you for every bit you're worth to us, and that's a hell of a lot."

Torrin could hear Jak's sigh from across the bridge. She wasn't comfortable in the various roles of prominence into which she kept being placed. Her expanded role was working to Torrin's advantage, but she wished it was easier on Jak. It didn't help that Jak was so good at it, which was why she kept finding herself in the role. Jak was a natural leader. Like the best of them, she didn't expect anyone to do something she hadn't done. She led from the front, she didn't push from the back. Her people would follow her into the jaws of hell; some of them already had.

"The League picket is aware of your presence in the system," Torrin said. "They've agreed to let you through unharassed."

"You're dealing with the League?" Axe's face creased with concern. "Things must be really bad."

"When I sent the message out to you, they caught me like I had my hand in a Sonoran merchant's cashbox. I had to make a deal to get out with my hide intact." Her attempt at a smile felt brittle.

Every path to Nat felt like it was littered with shards of broken glass. Finding Nat was going to be a matter of choosing the least painful path, for Nat and for the rest of them. The longer they spent negotiating their way toward her sister, the more Nat would suffer. She longed to cut through all the crap and take the shortest road. They were in the middle of the long con now, but there were too many balls in the air, too many pieces on too many boards. If she had any hope of finding her sister alive, she had to trust in those around her. She filled Axe in on the situation.

"That's some deal." Axe sat back in her chair and Torrin could see Olesya over her shoulder. The lieutenant gave them a small nod, her usual sunny smile suppressed by an icily professional demeanor. "If the League keeps its promise and stays out of our way, we'll be able to rendezvous with you in a couple of hours."

"Good. That'll give us time to get things moving down here. Maintain a position in orbit. There are people down here I'd rather didn't know about you."

Axe flicked her eyes over to look at Jak. When she gave a small nod, Axe echoed it. "Understood, I'll see you shortly. Axe out."

The transmission ended before Torrin could say her goodbyes. She wasn't offended, she appreciated the seriousness in Axe's voice and face. She glanced at Jak over her shoulder.

"I hope you're ready to go. Things are really going to start moving now."

Jak pushed herself up from the arm of the pilot's chair where she'd been perched for the duration of her conversation.

"That's how it goes. I need to head in to the office. There are things I need to get done before I can leave Marshall again."

"You're coming with me tomorrow." Torrin wasn't asking, and she knew her voice fell a hair short of ordering Jak. The only response she got was a raised eyebrow and a nod.

"I know." Jak closed the distance between them in two steps and pulled Torrin's head down for a kiss. Her lips seared Torrin's before she pulled back and rested her forehead against Torrin's. She stared deep into her lover's eyes, boring deep into her. She seemed to be trying to console Torrin through sheer force of will. "We're going to get this figured out. With the Banshees here, we can't fail. I'd put them up against half the Orthodoxan Army."

"All we need is for them to beat one sniper."

Doubt flitted across Jak's face but was replaced almost instantly with grim resolve.

"We can do this," she said quietly. "We will do this."

CHAPTER TWENTY-TWO

The briefing room on the *Nightshade* was too small for the tension and veiled hostility it contained. Jak looked around the room. Such a gathering had never happened in the history of her people. She suspected it hadn't happened in the history of Torrin's people either.

On one side of the table, the serious Captain Mori was accompanied by a couple of lieutenants. The captain hadn't bothered to introduce them to the rest of the gathering, but they surveyed the group without bothering to hide their suspicion. The big one whose uniform strained across the huge shoulders it covered was probably Mori's chief of security. A slender woman who was taller than even Torrin would be whatever passed for an intelligence officer in the League. Her searching gaze was suspicious and it weighed everything it touched. Jak thought she caught a look of recognition passing between Smythe and the unnamed lieutenant.

Across the table from the Leaguers were the Devonites. They were crammed in along their side. General Callahan had insisted on going to the meeting and when his staff had found out it was to be held in orbit, they'd insisted he bring a sizeable retinue. So much of a retinue, in fact, that they weren't all capable of sitting on their side of the table.

Colonel Wolfe and Smythe sat with Callahan. To Jak's discomfort, she did also. She would much rather have shared a spot along the wall with the soldiers who made up the general's personal guard. He was so informal that she hadn't realized he had a guard. Most of the guard she recognized as the clerks from his office.

Torrin sat at one end of the long table with Axe and Olesya at the other. There were a few Banshees in the room. The Leaguers had pressed her on why she needed them, to which Torrin had glibly responded that a woman in her line of business couldn't be too careful. Let them assume the Banshees were bodyguards. The women were all business, displaying none of the traits she'd come to know when spending time with them while on liberty. They watched the entire room while not seeming to see anything. They were easily as impressive as the League of Solaran Planet Marines who lined the wall behind Captain Mori.

"General Callahan," Mori said, her low voice cold. "I'm surprised to find you retaining the services of someone like Torrin Ivanov."

Jak bridled a little bit at the implied insult and glanced over at Torrin. She seemed unaffected and Jak clamped her mouth shut on an angry retort. As it was, she was under strict instructions from her superiors and her lover. Torrin didn't want her betraying their relationship and possibly weakening their position. Colonel Wilson had made it clear that she was only along to provide background. He'd made it even clearer that if she hadn't managed to finally produce her report, she wouldn't have been along at all. She'd gotten very little sleep in the thirty-four hours since the *Nightshade* had entered the system, but she had finished the report in the nick of time.

"I'm in a delicate situation, Captain," Callahan replied easily. His mask of affability was firmly in place today. "I can't afford to turn down help from any quarter. We didn't make first contact, but we've had no problem with the assistance Miss Ivanov has been able to offer us so far."

The answer was pure politics. Callahan was signaling the Devonites' interest in continuing to work with Torrin, while distancing themselves from any of the blame in reaching out to her. Jak was only dimly aware of how far she'd come, that she could read the subtext beneath the general's words. Before meeting Torrin, she would only have read the surface meaning.

"I'm so glad, General." Torrin's amused smile showed that she'd received the message also. "I thought we'd already been through all this, Captain." She turned her smile to the League captain and was rewarded with a slight thawing of Mori's demeanor.

"Then why aren't we any closer to resolving our bargain?" Mori's smile was hard-edged. She was a woman who had run out of patience and had the military might to back up her displeasure. "I kept up my side." She flicked her glance over to the Banshees. "Twice now."

"Miss Ivanov has apprised us of your bargain," Colonel Wolfe said. "Though it was struck without our knowledge, we are in favor of a solution that allows us to unmask the traitor in our ranks. Of course, we're also happy to support any deal that keeps more League weaponry from piling up in the armories of our enemies."

What Wolfe wasn't saying was that Torrin had told them about the bargain only hours earlier. Wolfe wasn't best pleased at being on the hook for something he hadn't signed up for. Callahan hadn't been overjoyed either. If the plan hadn't been exactly what they needed, Jak was sure they would have turned her down. Torrin had maneuvered them neatly into her corner. Not only did the Devonites need to find out who the mole was, they also needed Torrin.

"Excellent." Mori's thin smile said she suspected Torrin had been playing fast and loose with the terms of the bargain. There wasn't much she could do about it at the moment. Mori needed to find whoever it was on her crew that was profiting on League weapons—weapons that had likely come from her own armory. "I suggest we move on this ASAP."

"Agreed," Wolfe said, his smile mirroring Mori's. They turned as one and looked at Torrin, who stared back at them without displaying the slightest hint of concern.

"I'm only here to facilitate," Torrin said. "The specifics have to come from you."

"And yet you're the one with the most to lose," Mori pointed out.

The corners of Torrin's eyes tightened for a moment. It was the first outward crack in her armor. Jak didn't think anyone else would pick it up—none of them knew the smuggler as well as she did—but she was surprised that anything could puncture Torrin's negotiation armor.

"We need to draw your man out," Jak said, trying to come to Torrin's rescue. Every eye in the room was drawn to her like iron filings to a magnet. She wished she'd kept her mouth shut except for the flash of gratitude in Torrin's eyes.

Wolfe cleared his throat. "Indeed. Contact with the League goes through my office, so we'll coordinate with you."

"How do we know the leak isn't in your office?" Mori was still staring at Jak, though she addressed Wolfe. Jak felt like the League captain was weighing her, testing her mettle. She looked back at her, trying to school her features into the same unflappable mask as Torrin. She had the feeling she was failing miserably.

Wolfe shrugged. "We don't." He sounded angry. "If it is coming from my office, I want to know. I'm going to kill the bastard." He colored slightly at the small noise Callahan made. "I mean, he's going to stand trial to answer for his crimes. Then I'll kill the bastard."

Smythe leaned forward. "We need to draw the two of them out in person. Correct me if I'm wrong, Captain, but your communications equipment has the ability to alter voices, does it not?"

"It does. You're absolutely right. We need to catch them both at it."

"And you're capable of hacking our new comm system, aren't you?"

Mori's eyes flickered toward the tall woman at her side. From the glance, Jak surmised that they'd already cracked the Devonites' comms.

Smythe smiled. "Of course you are." He hadn't missed the look either. "So our problem is even bigger than we thought. Your leak has access to even more information on our troop movements than he had before the new comms came online."

"That can be taken care of," Torrin said. "A software upgrade and the League will lose their ability to watch you."

"Actually, Miss Ivanov, this works to our advantage right now."

"We'll want that upgrade down the road," Callahan added, watching the Leaguers with a small smile. Torrin nodded and sat back.

"We need to turn up the heat on our conspirators," Smythe said. "Right now we have all the tools we need to do that."

"Go on," Mori said when he paused.

"Certainly. It isn't going to be easy, but I think we can make this work." He quirked a sly smile at Mori. "Am I correct in assuming you've been recording our comm transmissions?"

She glanced at the woman next to her again and received the same flicker of assent she had before.

"Excellent!"

Callahan pushed his head forward. "How is that excellent, Lieutenant? The League has no business in what's going on down here."

"It means we have our mole, and likely Captain Mori's arms dealer, on file. We have their voice prints, and if we can pull those out of the chatter, we have a point of comparison." He looked over at Torrin. "Captain Ivanov, once we've pulled out those voice prints, can your AI run through the recordings and look for matches?"

Torrin looked up at the ceiling. "I'll have to ask Tien, but I'm sure she could do it even if she were missing half her vital systems."

"Excellent!" Smythe beamed and rubbed his hands together. "Once we get the rest of those transmissions pulled out of the mix, we're sure to hear our mole identify himself."

Mori leaned forward and stabbed at the table with her finger. "And what makes you think I'm going to turn over League property?"

Callahan laughed. "Because Mori, we're not very happy about the League's interference in sovereign Haefonian matters. It seems to me that you need to make us much happier than we need to make you."

Mori leaned back in her chair and surveyed the general over steepled fingers. Her gaze slid sideways to Torrin. The smirk on Torrin's face said she was enjoying the League Captain's discomfort. Jak wished she'd at least made an attempt to hide the grin. When the Orthodoxans were gone, her people might need the League, and it wouldn't do to make an enemy of them right away. She wasn't exactly happy that the League had been listening in on the Devonites, but she also knew it made good tactical sense. If she'd been in their shoes, it would have been almost impossible to give up that advantage.

"We'll turn over our recordings, but I want a crack at your mole. You turn him over to me. We have some plans, and I will find the scum on my ship. He will be dealt with according to strictest League of Solaran Planets policies."

"Fine by me." Callahan shrugged. "I'm not in the habit of telling my allies how to deal with their internal policies."

The tension in the room dissipated, and one of the Banshees whispered in Olesya's ear. The lieutenant nodded and looked back at the table. Suddenly, the room was full of competing voices as others raised questions or tried to make a point regarding the plan. The noise level was deafening compared to the deathly quiet when Mori and Callahan had been locked in their struggle.

Jak was having problems keeping her eyes open by the end of the planning session. The night spent working on her report was catching up with her. She offered her opinion when it was asked for, but she was only there as an expert on Crimson. Their plan touched only peripherally on the Orthodoxan sniper, so her contributions were minimal.

By the time they wrapped up the session, Jak was half-asleep in her chair. It took her a moment to realize they'd finished and people were filing out of the briefing room. A hand on her arm brought her fully back to herself.

"Do you have a moment, Captain Stowell?" Mori was leaning across the table, touching her.

Axe tensed next to her and Jak shook her head slightly. She didn't want the Banshee exposing her or Nadierzda by jumping in. The only ones left at the table were Jak, the League captain and the two Banshee officers. Everyone else was out the door or very nearly so.

"What is it, Captain Mori?"

Mori looked over at the Banshees. "I'd like to speak with the captain in private."

Axe and Olesya hesitated, and Jak wanted to scream at them to move.

"I'm all right," she finally said, hoping the statement was innocuous enough not to rouse Mori's suspicions.

The Banshees stood and moved away from them, but they didn't leave the room and loitered by the door instead.

"They seem very protective."

Jak shrugged. "Perhaps they know better than to leave me alone with League personnel. It's their ship. They're responsible for our welfare, just as they're responsible for yours." After all, it wasn't the Devonites' potentially hostile ship floating a bare few hundred meters off the bow.

"True enough." Mori sat back and regarded her over steepled fingers. "I've heard a lot about you."

"I find that hard to believe."

"Not at all. Your people's communications are filled with your exploits. The stories grow in the retelling, but by all accounts you're extremely resourceful." She grinned, the expression surprisingly youthful on her face. "Of course, you're also rumored to be two hundred centimeters tall. I was a little disappointed to find out you're not."

"My height has nothing to do with my abilities."

Mori waved a hand dismissively. "Of course not. Have you given any thought to what you'll do when they find out you're a woman?"

"Excuse me?" Jak narrowed her eyes at the League captain. "You've known our people long enough to know that your last statement is extremely insulting."

"That's very good. You're very convincing, I'm not surprised you've managed to keep your secret as long as you have."

"What is it you want from me, Captain? Are you thinking you can blackmail me with your ludicrous accusations?" She wanted to laugh. Finally, some good was coming out of the brass's knowledge of her gender.

Mori's eyebrows climbed up her forehead in a look of genuine concern. "No. Nothing like that. I'm trying to offer you a job. The League can use people like you. You're obviously good at what you do. I would love to have you on my crew, but I'm sure your prospects would be even better among the Marines."

It took everything Jak had not to look over at Axe and Olesya where they lurked at the door, in quiet conversation. "I'm quite happy where I am."

"I see. Well, when things come to a head, remember that you have a friend on the *Icarus*. You won't be turned away when you have to leave Haefen."

"Thank you for the offer, Captain Mori, but I won't be taking you up on it."

"Keep it in mind, that's all I ask." She stood and nodded formally to Jak. The marines peeled themselves away from the wall and followed her out the door. Axe and Olesya parted to allow them to pass.

Jak waited a few moments before following. The Banshees fell in step with her as she walked the corridor toward the docked shuttle.

"What did she want, Major?" Olesya asked.

"She wanted to offer me a job." Jak laughed, though there was little humor in the sound. "I guess I'm not as good at this as I thought. People are picking me out all over the place."

"Don't worry about it," Axe advised. "Some people know what to look for. All it means is she's had some experience with your situation at some point in the past. Besides, you're good enough at it that you fooled Torrin. You would have fooled most of us. My guess is that Mori's been in your shoes."

Jak nodded, though she continued to fret inside. She could feel the strain of her deception closing around her again.

"Before you go," Olesya said, "we brought you a present." She bent down and fixed a mobile transmitter around her neck. "Try not to lose this one." Her grin split her face and Jak realized how much she'd missed the Banshee. She smiled back up at Olesya and tucked the transmitter under the collar of her uniform.

"We'll loop you in on as much as we can," Axe said. "It's good to have you back with us again."

"You have no idea how happy I am that you're all here."

Olesya clasped her shoulder and gave it a brief squeeze. "We'll find her."

"I know. I should get going." The Banshees saluted her as she ducked her head to get through the hatch to the docked shuttle. She returned their salutes with a smile. It was good to know she had friends close at hand.

"There you are," Torrin said when Jak joined her on the bridge. "What took you so long?"

The only other person on the bridge was Smythe. Jak trusted him as much as she trusted any of the Devonites, more than pretty much all of them, really. Still, she didn't want to talk to Torrin in front of him so she shook her head instead.

Torrin caught the way Jak's eyes cut over to the lieutenant and she narrowed her eyes. "Smythe, would you go let the general know we're ready to head back to the surface?"

It was a thin excuse to get him out of the room, but he left without any comment. The doors hissed closed behind him. Torrin looked at her, one eyebrow raised.

"It's nothing. Captain Mori offered me a job is all." Jak watched the main viewscreen over Torrin's shoulder as she turned to the console in front of her. The stars rotated on the screen then slid to one side before being blocked out by the brilliant blue curve of Haefen.

"What did you tell her?" Torrin's voice lacked any inflection.

"I told her thanks, but no thanks."

"Good." Relief overwrote the tension in Torrin's shoulders. "Because I'm no good at sharing either."

"Johvah, Torrin. She wanted me to work for her, not to sleep with her."

"Getting in bed with the League means getting out of bed with me."

Torrin was adamant. She clearly meant every word that she said. Jak was floored. "What is that supposed to mean? If I'd said yes to her then we would've been over? You'd let your politics run our relationship?"

Torrin kept her eyes on the viewscreen. "Well, when you put it that way…" Jak had to strain to hear the muttered words.

"I can't believe you. I'm ready to–"

The doors to the bridge hissed open and Smythe came back in. He took a careful look at the two of them and wisely didn't comment on the tension that vibrated through the bridge. "The general has been apprised of our impending arrival."

"Good," Torrin snapped, "then let him know that we're about to hit the atmosphere and he should be strapped in."

"I'll do it," Jak said. She pushed past Smythe before he could move.

"Jak, let Smythe do it!"

Ignoring Torrin's order, Jak stormed down the hallway.

"Jak!" Torrin's voice rose behind her, but Jak pushed on. Anger simmered through her veins. Here she was, ready to leave her people behind for good in order to be with Torrin. She'd been willing to go against the teachings that had been drilled into her since childhood about the evils of same-sex unions, and Torrin couldn't even put aside her political misgivings.

It was a good thing they'd disengaged from the *Nightshade* or Jak would have been tempted to go back and catch Mori to let her know she was interested. So far she was the only one sacrificing anything for their relationship. All Torrin had sacrificed was fucking a different woman every night, big deal. Torrin had been the one to spill the truth of her gender to Callahan, Wolfe and Elsby as well. Shock stopped her in her tracks for a second before anger spurred her on once more. She'd forgotten about that, but there she was, standing stock still in Callahan's office, trying to keep herself from running out the door and not stopping. Never stopping.

She slid down the ladder to the lower deck, anger spiking her movements.

"We're about to hit the atmosphere," Jak growled at the head of Callahan's security detail. "Secure yourselves."

The squat soldier nodded. He was almost as short as she was, but almost twice as wide.

"You heard the captain," he said. "Let's get everyone tied down."

The men who'd been milling around the cargo bay assumed sitting positions upon metal crates along the bay's walls. They secured themselves to the cargo netting on the wall. Callahan strapped himself in and waited patiently while his head of security tested the restraints.

When they were secured to his liking, the wide soldier strapped himself in beside Callahan.

Jak headed to the jump seat in the small work area. It took her only a few moments to secure herself.

"Tien, we're secured down here. Let her know she can take us in." Saying Torrin's name was more than Jak could manage in her current state.

"Affirmative Jak." Tien's dispassionate tones soothed her somewhat, and she exhaled, trying to let go of some of the anger.

Moments later, the ship lurched and vibrated as it made its way into the buffeting winds of Haefen's atmosphere. The first time they'd made landfall, Jak had been nervous in the extreme. The jostling and shaking had unnerved her, but now that she'd been through it a few times, she didn't worry. Torrin knew what she was doing and Jak trusted her.

If only she could trust me. If only I was the first thing she thought about instead of her business, her precious money. The thought was uncharitable, Jak knew that, but she was in no mood to give Torrin the benefit of the doubt. She'd been doing that all along.

The shaking continued, and Jak sat there, listening to the silence of the men right outside the work area. This was the first time any of them had experienced reentry. She wondered if some of them would crack under the strain. The buffeting always seemed to go on a little longer than what felt necessary. Jak could feel the tension rising in her belly as she waited out the turbulence.

The *Calamity Jane* lurched hard to one side and a flash of red caught her eye. Something rolled out from under the work bench. It was small, with something red and vaguely furry-looking sprouting from the top. It was out of place in the small area. Jak couldn't remember Torrin having any tools that looked like that. For all of that, it looked familiar.

The shaking finally eased, and the object rolled back under the bench while the *Jane* righted herself. Jak unclipped her safety harness and dropped to her knees. She felt around under the bench's lip until she came in contact with the small cylindrical object and pulled it out.

It was a dart, one she'd seen before, and she stared at it. It made her think of a hill, the top devoid of vegetation. At the same time, it reminded her of cool forests and a valley with a creek running along the bottom, shrouded in mist and trees. She slid it into her pocket and took her seat again. Her anger had dissipated, to be replaced with hurt. What was she going to do about Torrin?

Torrin watched Jak storm off the bridge.

"Jak!" There was no response except the fading sound of boot heels pounding on metal. "Shit." She kept her eyes on Haefen growing steadily larger on the viewscreen.

"Problems?" Smythe asked.

"Stay out of it."

"Got it," he said and held his tongue. His silence felt reproachful and bored into Torrin.

"She can't expect me to get over years of hatred for the League overnight," Torrin burst out when she couldn't stand it any longer.

"Excuse me?"

"Never mind." Torrin wished Olesya were there. She needed some serious girl talk and she wasn't going to get it from anyone on board.

She concentrated instead on maneuvering them into Haefen's orbit. It felt strange but also rather refreshing not to be concerned about the League ships. The *Icarus* still floated behind them and Torrin had a moment of hot anger when she thought of Mori's nerve. Jak had no place with the League; her place was with Torrin.

Shame washed over her. That was what she'd meant to say, but instead she'd burst out with an ill-timed order not to go anywhere near the League. No wonder Jak had stormed away. If she'd been in Jak's shoes, she would have done worse than leave.

"Everyone is secured for reentry, Torrin," Tien said. Was it Torrin's imagination, or did her voice sound reproachful? She knew she'd screwed up; she didn't need to hear it from others.

"Good." Torrin danced her fingers over the main console, adjusting their speed and trajectory enough to slip them into orbit. She rode them down with only half a mind on her piloting. It was a good thing the League ships were giving them temporary amnesty. If she'd piloted the ship this absentmindedly when they were after her, she would have been caught for sure.

Touchdown was a little rougher than usual and Torrin blushed. No one else would even notice, but she knew. Her distraction was unacceptable. As soon as the *Calamity Jane* was settled, she jumped up and left the bridge without even a word to Smythe.

By the time she made it to the cargo bay, the door was down and General Callahan's security detail was marching off the end of the ramp. Torrin stuck her head into the caged-in work area, but there was no sign of Jak.

"Shit." She leaned her forehead against the cage's metal doorway. She'd been an ass and now Jak was avoiding her.

"Miss Ivanov." The last voice on Haefen that she wanted to hear came from behind her.

"McCullock." Torrin whirled around to stare at the captain, who was walking slowly up the ramp toward her, hands raised over his head. He remembered the welcome he'd received the last time he tried to approach her. Torrin flexed her fingers as she watched him. What did he want? He was making no attempt to be stealthy and looked her straight in the eye.

"Miss Ivanov," McCullock said. "It's important that I speak with you. I know we didn't leave things very well in hand, but we have more important matters than that little misunderstanding."

His attempts at entreaty sent a hot spike of rage through her body. She vibrated with it. Torrin snatched a spanner from the wall of the cage and rushed McCullock, slamming him into the unyielding metal of the ship's deck with a resounding clang. He grunted at the unexpected attack and pushed back against her.

"What the hell?" McCullock froze as he felt the end of the spanner being jammed up under his chin.

"That's it," Torrin said, her voice hard. "Give me an excuse."

"Miss Ivanov." He lowered his hands to his sides and looked up at her. "I need to talk to you."

"You aren't on my list of dinnertime conversationalists, Captain. You've made another list altogether." She jabbed him in the ribs again. "I'm here, so talk. It better be worth my time, or I will be taking it out of your hide, one strip at a time."

Torrin felt the spanner move as he swallowed hard against it. His voice was hoarse when he continued, "Can we take this into the ship? It's not safe out here."

She laughed without humor. "I'm not making the mistake of being alone with you again. And you're starting to bore me, Jagger."

He flinched at her cutting use of his first name. "I need to get a message to Captain Stowell. He hasn't been getting back to me and what I've found can no longer wait. Things are rapidly coming to a head and if we don't move now, the results could be disastrous."

Now it was Torrin's turn to freeze. "What do you know about that?"

"I'm one of the people working on trying to figure out the mole's identity."

"I already know that. Tell me what you've found out and I'll tell Jak."

"I can't do that, Miss Ivanov. You wouldn't understand. As a woman, there is no way you would know the realities of warfare." He managed to shrug from where he lay. "I can't trust you."

He can't trust *me?* The ship tilted beneath her and she put her hand on his shoulder to steady herself. Terrified that he would take advantage of her weakness, she shoved him back hard against the floor and raised the spanner. His mouth opened in dismay before she brought it down on the side of his head with a sickening crack and he went slack. Dismayed, she stared down at him. Blood dripped from his head, pooling scarlet on the deck.

"Get the med bay running, Tien. It looks like we have a guest."

McCullock was out cold…still. Torrin watched him, bored. He'd been out for fifteen minutes and showed little sign of waking. Blood still oozed sluggishly from the laceration behind his temple.

"What do you think, Tien? Is he worth a trip through the autodoc?"

"I do not know, Torrin. Is your question rhetorical?"

Torrin barked a humorless laugh. "I guess it is." She'd bounced the tool off the side of his head with some authority. She hadn't meant to injure him quite this badly, but she wasn't sorry, at least not for injuring him. Her actions had been overly impulsive however. If it would help them find the mole, she needed the information he had. Torrin leaned forward and peered at him in the harsh lights of the med bay. His face was very pale beneath the ridiculous mustache. "I suppose we'd better get him checked over."

Leaning over him where he lay in the diagnostic bed, Torrin slapped him lightly on the cheek.

"McCullock." She slapped him again, harder this time. "McCullock!"

There was still no response. Torrin drew back her arm to deliver an even harder slap but stopped herself. It was doubtful that further head trauma would wake him any faster. Instead, she sighed and settled back onto her heels.

"Wake him up for me, Tien."

The autodoc's diagnostic arms unfolded from the table and scanned his body. Torrin stood by, tapping her fingers on her forearms. Patience wasn't her strong suit and she had more important things to be seeing to. By all rights, she should have locked him in the med bay. Tien would take care of him, awake or unconscious. But she had to know if he'd been telling the truth about Jak. Could her lover have been so insensitive as to join forces with this piece of human excrement? She hoped not. Surely he'd said so to put her off her guard. It had to be an effort to get her to agree to whatever his current scheme was. If it turned out to be another attempt to get into her pants, she was going to give him a permanent place in orbit.

"He has some significant head trauma, Torrin. Not only does he have a concussion, but you appear to have cracked his skull."

"Whoops." Torrin didn't bother to hide the ugly grin that she could feel smeared across her face. "Any chance you can fix him up but leave him with one hell of a headache?"

"I'm afraid that won't be possible, Torrin. I must fix him completely or not at all."

"Pity. Could you at least render him impotent while you're tinkering around in there?"

"I am afraid not, Torrin."

"How about making him incontinent?" When Tien didn't dignify her suggestion with a response, she huffed in irritation. "A little stutter then?" More silence met the sally, and she stomped out of the med bay. "Fine then. Fix him up. I need to find out what the hell he was doing skulking outside the ship. Let me know when he's conscious again. Make damn sure he's not capable of attacking me."

Torrin stepped out of the med bay and headed down the hall to the bridge. She needed to touch base with the Banshees. They would be wondering what was taking her so long.

A chime sounded from her subdermal implant. Speaking of alien life…

"What is it?"

"Torrin, it's Axe. We're going to offload to meet with you."

"Give me a bit. I had something come up and I need to take care of it first."

"Anything you need a hand with?"

Torrin laughed. "I think I have this one handled. I'll let you know when you can come down."

"All right then. Hurry it up if you can. The Banshees are restless. So am I, frankly."

"I'll do what I can."

"Axe, out."

Torrin settled herself in her chair and stared moodily out the main viewscreen. It showed a lovely view of Haefen's trees all around her. Nat was still out there alone and she had to wait on the puffed-up jackanapes in her med bay.

"He is awake, Torrin." She was still staring blankly out the viewscreen when Tien's voice came over the speaker in her room.

"I'll be right there." Torrin hopped up and jogged down the short hall.

She paused in front of the door to the medical bay and took a deep breath. Her heart tripped and nerves jangled; she needed to calm herself. Settling as serious a look on her face as she was feeling, she walked forward, the doors parting before her.

McCullock lay half-reclined on the autodoc. Tien had raised it so he could be in a seated position, but the autodoc's diagnostic arms were still engaged, preventing him from leaving the table.

"Torrin." Her face froze and McCullock swallowed, his adam's apple bobbing as crazily as she had when she'd hit the river those months previous. "Miss Ivanov, I mean." He tried a tentative smile, but the expression was chased off his face by her continued silence.

Torrin stared at him, drawing the silence out even further. Usually her weaponry of choice was words, but silence could be equally effective and now she wielded it with grim pleasure.

"You lost the right to call me that the night you attacked me." Her voice was flat and rimed in ice. McCullock shivered as if the room's temperature had suddenly plummeted. "Tell me why I should bother listening to anything you have to say?"

"Uh yes. That." Color suffused his face and he coughed, discomfort palpable. Good. He'd made her extremely uncomfortable. Between his attempted assault and Hutchinson's predation, she'd lost a sense of confidence, of invulnerability. She'd found herself stooping to actions she would never have contemplated before. Her deliberate torture of Monton sprang to mind and for a moment her mind lingered over doing the same to McCullock. The gangster from Tyndall had deserved the agony she'd visited on him. There was no other way he would have spilled about his partnership with Tanith. Part of her was horrified at her cavalier attitude, but the rest of her refused to shed a tear over the man who had targeted her people. Aware of the dark direction her thoughts were taking, she pulled herself away from the fantasy. Her stomach roiled uncomfortably.

"Well?" Torrin prompted when McCullock seemed to have stalled out.

"I was a fool to do what I did. Would it help if I said I was sorry?" He stared at her, eyes imploring.

Fury exploded in her breast. How stupid did he think she was? "Talk is cheap, especially from a man like you. I don't want your apologies." Her lip curled away from her top teeth, and he recoiled, terrified at what he saw staring at him from her eyes.

"I'm sorry, but we don't have time for this," McCullock said. He cringed, leaning as far away from her as he could while still restrained in the autodoc.

She stepped forward, looming over him and thrust her face in his. "We have as much time as I'll give you. Think carefully because it may be the last of it for you. Now tell me what you know of the mole."

"I-I can't." Sweat beaded on his brow and trickled down the side of his face.

Her voice was a whisper, hissed in his ear. "Then why are you wasting my time? I have someone to rescue from the clutches of your repulsive 'cousins.'"

"The Orthodoxan who has your sister is the least of our problems."

Torrin's ears roared and her vision grayed out for a moment. Without conscious thought, she backhanded him across the mouth. His head snapped to the side and blood sprayed from his mouth in a messy arc. Her hand twitched toward the vibroknife clipped at her waist. She held her fist behind her back before she could do what she really wanted to.

"You're free to go." She didn't recognize her own voice. "I'd better never see you again. If I do, they'll never find your body. Do. You. Understand?" Torrin breathed the last word directly into his face. She stared deep into his eyes and watched him to make sure he understood how serious she was. The pallor of his face increased by a few shades and he managed a jerky nod. "Good."

Sick to her stomach at her loss of control, she left the med bay. Her left hand throbbed, and she hoped she hadn't broken it.

"Put him out, Tien, then dump him outside."

"Affirmative Torrin."

Back on the bridge, Torrin activated the subdermal transmitter behind her ear.

"Axe, I'm ready to go."

"About time. We'll be right down."

"Fine." Not in the mood for idle chitchat, Torrin terminated their link. She tracked the *Nightshade's* progress. When they were overhead, she pushed away from the console and headed down to the cargo bay.

With both the *Calamity Jane* and the *Melisende* docked in the clearing, the *Nightshade* had nowhere to land. She watched through the cargo bay door as dust and vegetation kicked up while the *Nightshade* hovered overhead. Moments later, a group of Banshees landed with heavy thumps. They disengaged their antigrav packs and trotted up the ramp toward her.

"Exciting, isn't it?" Olesya said, her faced creased by the ever-present grin.

"It's a blast." Torrin tried to grin, but the expression felt foreign. She gave herself a mental shake. She needed to be fully present and ready to go. Nat's life depended on it. "Go on up. I need to touch base with Jak quick. I'll be right there."

CHAPTER TWENTY-THREE

Nat wrapped her arms around her legs, trying to tame the shivers that shook her entire frame. She felt like she would never be warm again. The sniper had dragged her down into these caves days ago, she was sure of that. How many days had passed exactly, she had no way of knowing.

The darkness in the cave was oppressive and absolute. It weighed her down with inexorable pressure. The sniper had left her again, taking with him the only source of light. He didn't bother to tie her up or try to confine her in any way. The dark would keep her put. That was his assumption, and it was a good one.

It had been a while since the last whisper of boot against stone had dwindled into the distance. Longer still since his dim light had disappeared in the direction of the main passage.

Unlike during her previous captivity by him, Nat had no food. He'd taken to keeping the rations with him at all times. He wasn't usually gone for longer than a day, not like he had been when she'd been locked in the shed, and the first thing he did upon his return was to feed her. He didn't want her to get too sickly, it seemed, not now that he'd decided she would serve the purpose he'd imagined Jak in. His attentions weren't as brutal as the Orthodoxans who'd found her during her disastrous escape attempt. At least when he took her, it was over quickly. He used her with less thought or care than he gave his weapon, but he didn't actively try to hurt her.

Nat swallowed around the lump in her throat. It felt like the size of her fist and it ached. She didn't know how much more of the sniper's indifferent mercies she could take. There was nothing else for it. She had to escape. It was a long shot. Chances were good that she would die down here in the dark and damp. Even so, dying free of the sniper was by far the better option than staying with him.

Had it been long enough since he left? Nat had no way of knowing. Time had little meaning when she was alone in the dark.

The chamber he had chosen as her prison was large, and he kept her near the center, where it was difficult to orient herself. She hadn't wasted the time when he'd been there. While the light was on, she'd committed a path of rock formations to memory.

Nat stretched out her hand and groped along the floor until she felt a small formation with three lumps on top. Sliding her hand beyond that, she encountered a slightly higher, narrower sliver. It was smooth and wet, not muddy like she'd thought it would be.

Emboldened by her success, Nat moved forward, shuffling awkwardly. The ground was rough enough that she worried she would shred her knees if she were to crawl. It wasn't long before her hands were raw from being run over stone surfaces. Some of them were surprisingly smooth, while others were as rough and porous as they had appeared in the dim light of the sniper's lamp.

Her progress was painfully slow. Moving in a crouch took a lot out of her, especially in her weakened condition. Still, it paid to take her time instead of rushing the process. If the sniper's pattern held up, it would be quite some time before he came back, and the last thing she needed was to get lost in the dark.

If the map she'd constructed in her head was right, she should have been close to the cave wall. When she hit that, Nat knew she would be able to shift to the left to find the passageway that led from the large chamber.

With a splash, Nat's hand came down in a puddle of water. She pulled her hand back with a soft curse. *Shit, that's cold!* It was so cold her hand ached almost immediately. She reached out again and groped around to the side of the puddle. Her fingers encountered more frigid water. Beyond that was still more water. This was more than a puddle. As she explored the edge of the small body of water, she became aware of her breathing. It was loud, especially in the underground stillness. It rasped in her ears and Nat wrestled down her rising panic.

There was no large puddle or rivulet or stream or whatever this was on her mental map. She sat back on her heels and closed her eyes. It made no difference in the level of darkness, but she felt a little better. Panic was her greatest enemy now. If she allowed it to get to her, she would make a mistake, and she had a feeling that errors made underground were punished as harshly as those in made in space.

Thinking about the cave in the same way as hard vacuum was oddly comforting. Nat had training on survival in space. Anyone with her spacer's papers from Nadi did. Torrin wouldn't have allowed her to sign on as half the crew if she hadn't.

Nat needed to orient herself, determine her goal, then move carefully and deliberately toward it. In space, haste would kill as surely as inattention.

Now that she had a plan, Nat could feel her pulse slowing. Her harsh breaths no longer overwhelmed her hearing. There was a quiet trickle coming from the right. It seemed the puddle was a rivulet after all. She didn't know the way back, but it stood to reason that the trickle of water had to come from somewhere. With any luck, she could follow it around to the cave wall, then follow the wall to the exit passage.

It was a good plan and Nat was heartened as she groped her way through the darkness again. It wasn't like she had much to lose. If she got lost and starved or froze to death down in the dark, at least it would be on her own terms. Better a death by her own doing than life as the sniper's breeding machine.

The thought was more comforting than it should have been. She held onto it as she crept deeper into the unknown dark.

The sun tracked along the wall through Jak's open window. She stared at the dappled spot without really seeing it. Her deep anger at Torrin was finally giving way to low-key irritation. Torrin was under a ton of pressure. She'd dealt with Jak's lack of progress without so much as raising her voice. Maybe Jak could cut her some slack, at least until they could talk about it again.

Jak made no move to get up and find Torrin. She needed to cool down some more to make sure she wouldn't say something she'd regret later. She lost herself in her thoughts instead, mentally cataloging the progress they'd made with Nat. Or rather, the lack of progress they'd made. Something still tickled the back of her mind, a couple of somethings, actually. The niggling thoughts stubbornly refused to become more than vague misgivings, and she finally sat up, snarling in frustration.

A quick glance at the clock panel on the wall let her know that it had been only a few hours since she'd come back to her room, and it was still the longest chunk of time she'd spent in it since Torrin returned. The sun was setting and the sky outside had deepened to a royal blue. There were no clouds to break up the unrelieved blue of the sky. The rain would come late tonight.

She reached over and pulled the net cable out of the wall, then plugged it into her palm. There was a flash of light in her mind and she was accessing her in-box. The messages were as she expected. The one from Wilson pulsed an angry red; he'd coded it high priority. Not that the priority told her anything—he coded almost all his messages to her as highest priority. In her experience, there couldn't be that many emergencies in the world.

Her schedule for the next few days beckoned and she opened it up. Most of the appointments and meetings would need to be rescheduled, but discreetly. Jak toyed with the idea of rescheduling them herself, then discarded the idea. Having her clerk do it would be more in keeping with her position and would occasion less comment than doing it herself. There was an appointment with McCullock for the next day.

A chime sounded from the transmitter around her neck. One of the Nadierzdans was trying to contact her. Jak hesitated. She wasn't sure if she was ready to talk to Torrin, not yet. Still, they rarely tried to get hold of her through the transmitter.

"Jak here."

"Jak." Torrin's voice issued tinnily from the transmitter. She didn't sound apologetic at all. There was none of the cajoling tone that she got when trying to talk Jak around to something. Instead, she sounded distracted. "Are you there?"

With a start, Jak realized that she hadn't answered yet.

"I'm here."

"Good. Look, I'm sorry about earlier." The perfunctory apology out of the way, Torrin rushed on. "Something really strange is going on. McCullock tried to find you here. He seems desperate to track you down."

"I'm supposed to see him tomorrow."

"That isn't soon enough, apparently. He was very insistent. For a bit, anyway…"

"That doesn't sound good."

"It wasn't, not for him. I sent him packing, but he's a little worse for wear. I thought you should know."

"Thanks for the info." Was that all Torrin was going to say? A quick sorry, then go check out McCullock? Something had her normally chatty girlfriend spooked.

"I have to go," Torrin said. "The Banshees are here."

"Okay, I'll see you soon then."

Jak disabled the transmitter and sat up on the bed, jerking the cable from her palm. That couldn't be good at all. It was dark in the room; there was barely any sunlight visible outside, only a faintly lighter shade to the west. Most of the officers would be at the mess getting dinner. If she was going to see McCullock, she either had to move now or wait until after midnight.

She slipped out her door and headed down the hall. Her floor was mostly empty. The soft rumble of male voices issued from behind one door, but the remaining rooms were silent and dark. She made her way to the fourth floor, not hurrying and making no attempt to hide. Moving furtively would make her stick out in the mind of anyone who saw her.

The top floor hallway was even quieter than hers had been. She walked to the end of the hall. McCullock's was the last room, tucked up under the eaves. He really had pissed someone off. The room would be one of the coldest in the building, exposed as it was to the wind on two sides and furthest away from the furnace.

His door was slightly ajar and light spilled out into the dark hallway. Jak slowed down. If he had someone in there with him, she didn't want to be seen. She would come back. Engaging her aural implant, she turned it up as high as she could. There was no noise from the room.

A familiar smell assaulted her nostrils when she drew up outside the door. A metallic tang hung in the air and she squeezed her eyes shut.

Not good. Jak pushed the door open a little further and cringed. McCullock was slumped over the room's small desk, his back to the door. A massive pool of blood had collected under his chair, soaking into the cheap rug. She started forward and stopped. What was she going to do? Someone had killed him, a Devonite most likely. If he'd gone to Torrin again after the way she'd brushed him off the first time, he had to be desperate. If the mole had gotten him, had she been exposed as well?

She dithered in the doorway before moving carefully through it. Taking great care not to disturb anything, she made her way to his body. His eyes stared sightlessly to one side. She touched one fingertip to the edge of the pool of blood. It wasn't even slightly tacky and was still warm. He'd been killed not long before, probably soon after his ill-advised visit to Torrin. She sat back on her heels and studied the body. What the hell was she going to do?

A floorboard creaked outside the door and Jak spun, drawing her knife from its holster on her thigh. A familiar form appeared in the doorway. Smythe moved into the chamber and stopped, staring at her, then over at McCullock's body. He closed the door behind him.

"What did you do?" His voice was pitched low enough not to carry.

Jak straightened and moved toward him, and he flinched away from her. *Right, the knife.*

"It wasn't me," she said. Jak held the knife out toward him, handle first. "See, no blood." She gestured to her clothes, which were also free of blood.

"If not you, then who?" Smythe waved away the knife. "He left me a message saying he needed to see me."

"He tried to get to me through Torrin."

"Only someone who knew what his assignment was would understand the significance of the messages." Smythe started pacing. "His assignment wasn't common knowledge."

"He told me." Jak stared at him. A terrible suspicion formed in her mind. "How did you know?"

The look Smythe shot her way told her that he knew exactly which path her thoughts had taken. "I'm not the mole."

"And why should I believe you?" She put her hand on the handle of her combat knife. "You have plenty of contact with the Orthodoxans. It would be the perfect setup."

Smythe took a breath as if to answer her. He shut his mouth and was silent for a long moment. Jak watched him closely. "You can't tell anyone else about this, but you can confirm it with General Callahan."

"Tell anyone else what?"

Resignation crossed Smythe's face. "I'm the head of the Intelligence Corps, not Elsby."

"Pigshit. You're a lieutenant, and you report to me."

"I report to you for now because it gives me access to our two most important operations and because I can keep an eye on you."

"I don't believe you."

"Think about it. Everyone knows Elsby is in charge of Intel, so they all watch him. I'm a lowly lieutenant so I can come and go pretty much as I please. There's no surprise when I get reassigned, which makes my movements almost untraceable. I know McCullock was on the trail of our mole because I put him on it."

Jak stared at him, searching his face for any trace of duplicity. He looked open to her, and she hesitated. Bron had been able to read others so much better than she ever could. She was going to have to make the decision on her own, and all she had to go on were her instincts. If they were good enough in the Haefonian woods, they had to be good enough here. She nodded once. He'd held her life in his hands more than once out there, and she trusted that.

"So what now?"

"We get out of here before someone stops in and decides we did this." Smythe gestured to the door and Jak crossed the room quickly. The hall was still empty and she looked again to make certain.

"Let's go to my room. We need to talk."

"Agreed." Smythe took the lead down the hall. He moved silently on the balls of his feet, and Jak followed in his wake, trying to be as quiet. She could move like a ghost through the forest, but a world of creaking floorboards was not one she was used to. She managed to keep it down.

When they reached the stairs, Smythe dropped stealth and moved unhurriedly down them. It took her a few moments to realize that he was talking to her about a report he'd filed a few days previous and she nodded, trying to look as if she were engrossed in their conversation. Inside, her mind raced.

When they entered her room, she plopped down on the bed and gestured him toward the desk.

Smythe dropped into the chair. "We need to figure out why the mole killed McCullock now. Who knows how long the mole has been watching us. What made him decide to move tonight?"

"He knew McCullock wanted to talk to me. Whatever McCullock found out, he was scared. Desperate even. Desperate enough to contact me when he knew the mole might be watching."

"Something forced the mole's hand." Smythe drummed his fingers on the desk top. "What would be worth drawing so much attention to himself after this long? He's been at it for months, whoever he is."

"So something moved up on his schedule maybe?" Jak's head ached as she tried to force her mind down the twisting turns of trying to think like someone whose mind was completely foreign to her. "Something had to change." She stared up at the ceiling, willing the situation to snap into focus. Her eyes traced over the ceiling and down the wall to the floor.

"The mole can track our net movements. He must have seen something there, and it can't have been McCullock or at least not directly."

"The only thing I've done differently lately is finally get all my reports filed with Wilson." Jak had meant the statement as a weak attempt at humor, something to defuse the tension in the room. What had she seen? She moved her eyes back along the trajectory they'd just followed and froze.

"When did you do that?"

Jak stood up and moved toward her dresser. "When did I do what?"

"File your report."

She crouched in front of the dresser and cocked her head. The middle drawer was barely open. Something glistened on the surface. "Right before we headed up to the *Icarus* so?"

"You mentioned the tunnel, didn't you?"

"Of course I did. It was a big deal." She touched the wet spot and her fingertip came back a brilliant crimson. "Smythe!"

"Blood? What the hell!"

Jak jerked open the drawer. Blood was smeared on the shirts. This definitely wasn't the way she'd left them. One shirt was wadded up around something. Licking lips suddenly dry and already knowing what she would find, Jak unwrapped the shirt from around a bloody knife.

"Shit!" Smythe was at her elbow, looking down into the drawer with equal horror.

"I've been in here for hours. This wasn't here when I left to see McCullock."

"What is he doing? Why frame you? He'd have to know it wouldn't hold up."

Jak ran her fingers over her scalp. "But what would happen when they arrested me? My secret would be all over. Everyone would know!"

"And it would be all anyone would be able to talk about. Think about it. Gossip keeps soldiers from going crazy with boredom. The brass would be pulled in, especially with your recent promotion. All eyes would be on you."

Her lips were suddenly very dry and Jak licked them nervously. "He can't only be trying to expose me. There has to be a reason."

"That's it!" Smythe slammed his fist into his palm. "Why didn't I see it sooner? The tunnel! The Orthodoxans are going to come in through the tunnel. The mole's trying to cover his tracks, to throw up enough confusion to pull attention away from his target. He needs McCullock to be discovered, and he needs you to be found out. We can't have you arrested now. I need to get that tunnel covered, and you need to get out of here."

Smythe tore open the door and disappeared into the dimly lit hallway. His running footsteps faded down the hall. Jak stared out the door for a split second longer before heeding his advice. The hairs on the back of her neck prickled. She slipped into the corridor and moved confidently down its length, keeping her ears peeled. If a contingent of MPs showed up at the door to the officers' quarters, she wanted to know.

She needed to reach the *Calamity Jane*. It was the safest place on the planet, especially now. Urgency built within her, spurring her to drop caution and move with alacrity.

Taking the steps two at a time, Jak was surprised she didn't take a header. She was so concerned with pursuit that she almost bowled over a major making his way up the steps from the officers' mess.

"'Scuse me, sir," Jak muttered as she sidestepped the surprised major and hopped up on the banister to slide around him. She hit the stairs at a run and dashed out the front door before he could even muster a surprised grunt.

Jak leaped from the top of the mansion's front steps and took off down the street at a trot. Her lungs already burned from the exertion. She cursed her reduced lung capacity; she wasn't sure how much longer she was going to be able to keep up the pace. As she ran down the street, a truck pulled up beside her, horn blowing.

"Need a ride, Captain?" a private she didn't know yelled at her.

She nodded and veered over toward him. He slammed on the brakes and she jumped in before the truck had come to a complete stop.

"Where to, sir?"

"I need to get to the main gates." Jak grabbed the roll bar around the truck's exposed cab. "Floor it."

"Yes sir." The private took off in a squeal of tires and the stench of burned rubber filled the air. "This sounds serious, I'm glad I saw you running down the street like a scalded skunk."

"Thanks Private." Jak gasped, trying to catch her breath. "I'm in your debt."

The private simply nodded, his eyes on the road ahead as he drove at breakneck speed. There was another squeal of tires when he took a sharp turn into an alley between two office buildings. There wasn't much light and Jak switched on her implant's night-vision capabilities. They continued down the alley for a ways before the private turned them down another road. Jak didn't know Fort Marshall very well, but she was pretty sure they were heading the wrong way. Alarm started to build deep in her chest.

"Where are you taking us?"

"Shortcut sir."

"No way in hell, soldier. We're going the wrong way. Pull over. Now!"

The private ignored her and jammed his foot on the gas. The truck lurched forward, pinning Jak back into her seat. They were going much too fast for her to consider jumping out. Buildings flew by on either side, so close that she could have touched the ones on the near side with her outstretched hand.

She thumbed open the release on her holster and pulled the pistol on the driver.

"Stop the truck." Jak released the safety and the sound seemed to get through to him. He glanced over at her and his eyes widened.

"Holy shit!" He stood on the brake and the truck's wheels locked. Smoke billowed out of the wheel wells. Jak was thrown violently forward, and her forehead hit the windshield with a loud crack that she felt as much as heard. Nausea flowed through her at the sound and she dropped the pistol. Her vision swam and refused to clear, no matter how many times she blinked in a vain attempt to clear it. Indistinct shapes slowly approached the truck; they resolved into figures in Devonite uniforms, three of them.

She cast down her gaze, looking for the pistol but couldn't immediately find it. She shifted against the dash and a hard object poked into her chest. The transmitter. Bless the Banshees for their foresight! The next time she saw Olesya, she was going to kiss her. With fumbling fingers, she pulled it out from under her collar. She barely had time to activate the device before one of the men reached into the truck and grabbed the hand holding the transmitter. He squeezed and wrenched. Jak kept her fingers locked, refusing to let go, though it felt like the bones in her hand were grating against each other. If the Devonite got it and destroyed it before Torrin and the Banshees could triangulate the signal, she'd be on her own. Pain radiated from her wrist through her fingertips.

"Here now, 'Captain.'" Jak winced at the sneer she could hear in the man's voice at the mention of her rank. "Let's have a little lesson in why girls don't serve." He jerked against her, yanking her out of the cab.

She drew her knife. There was little hope that she could hold her own against four attackers, especially not in her weakened condition, but she would make sure they didn't escape unscathed. She bared her teeth and turned to face them.

"Do you think the Leaguers will keep their word?" Olesya asked Torrin quietly. Torrin wasn't sure why the lieutenant was trying to keep their conversation discreet; they were all crammed onto her bridge. Banshees leaned or perched on every available surface as they pored over charts and made plans. The room rumbled with the overlapping murmurs of many quiet conversations.

"For now," Torrin replied. "Mori really wants to know who's running weapons from her ship. Once they've found him, all bets will be off. Especially if they can connect me to…Well, the more I can stay off her radar, the better."

"Something you want to share with the rest of the class?" Olesya grinned at her.

"Umm, no. It's ancient history and–"

A chime sounded in her head and she stopped. The only people on the planet with subdermal transmitters were in the room with her. Who could be pinging her now?

"What's wrong?" Olesya had picked up on Torrin's consternation.

Torrin held up her hand. No one was addressing her through the comm and all she could make out background noise. "Everyone, shut up!" Torrin yelled. The room dropped into silence, every eye on her. She barely noticed, she could finally hear voices through the transmitter, right in time to hear a snarling male voice say "–a little lesson in why girls don't serve."

The words made her blood run cold and goose bumps erupted on her arms. It could only be Jak.

"It's Jak?" Olesya moved toward her. Torrin realized she must have said Jak's name out loud. She nodded and kept concentrating on the transmission. There were no more words, but she could clearly make out the sound of a scuffle. A scream jolted her into action.

"Tien, can you locate where Jak's transmission is coming from?" The watching eyes widened in concern as the Banshees realized one of their own was in danger. They were too well-trained to say anything, but room filled with tension, crackling electric along everyone's nerves.

"Yes Torrin."

"Good, then get us in the air and get us over there." Torrin paused and when she didn't hear the engines immediately spring to life, she screamed, "Now!"

The ship tilted as the engines came online and it leaped into the air almost in the same action. Torrin grabbed the console to keep from being thrown to the floor. Around her, Banshees weren't so lucky as they were hurled from their perches. They bounced up almost as quickly as they went down.

"Banshees," Axe's voice rang through the bridge, "get down to the cargo bay and prepare to drop."

Almost as one, the women turned and streamed through the door that opened before any of them were near it. In moments, Torrin was left alone on the bridge. She stared at the main viewscreen, watching as Fort Marshall streaked by beneath them. *Calamity Jane* came to a bone-shuddering halt above a cluster of buildings. Try as she might, Torrin couldn't make out anything on the ground.

"Tien, get me eyes on the ground."

"I am trying, Torrin. The buildings are blocking my external sensors."

Torrin realized the noises from the transmitter had stopped and she cursed. Figures appeared on the viewscreen, drifting down toward the buildings below.

"The Banshees are away, Torrin."

There was nothing she could say. Torrin was left to watch and hope her lover would be okay. How much time had elapsed since the transmission had come in? It seemed like an eternity, though the small part of her brain that could still think rationally knew it couldn't have been long at all. Any time at all was too long for Jak to be alone with those bastards if they knew her secret.

A chime rang inside her skull and she opened the transmission.

"Jak, is that you, baby?" Panic rode the edge of her voice and she forced herself to slow down. "Speak to me."

"Sorry, Torrin, it's me." Olesya's voice filtered through the transmitter, the normally cheerful burble replaced by impersonal professionalism. "We're about to touch down. I'm sending you a feed from my helmet."

One of the consoles flickered, switching from the map it had previously displayed to a grainy image in shades of green. Even with the Banshee's infrared camera on, it was still difficult to see. They were on a narrow street, dark and claustrophobic. There were no lights and the walls loomed high above them. A group of three, maybe four, men was visible about fifty meters further on. The still form of one person was crumpled to one side. For a second, Torrin couldn't breathe. To her relief, she saw the body was much too large to be Jak. The terror she'd felt turned into fierce pride. Jak had managed to take at least one of them out.

The men seemed oblivious to the approaching women, their attention taken up by something they were gathered around. As Olesya got closer, Torrin could see they were fighting to get at someone much smaller than they were. They weren't doing so well. She had her back to the wall and was fending them off with a knife that gleamed dully in the dim light.

"Jak..." Torrin breathed her lover's name. Her jaw ached from clenching it, but she was barely aware of the pain as she watched Jak dodge the fist of one man and drive him back with a wicked slice at his face. Her leg shot out and swept the Devonite's legs out from under him, and he went down in a heap. She noted with satisfaction that another man was down, a little further beyond the group, close to a truck that was stopped, both doors open, in the middle of the road. A number of the remaining men sported dark patches on their fatigues, mute evidence of the fight Jak was giving them.

One man, his fist raised and about to strike at Jak's face, went down. Plasma burned through the back of his jacket. The rest of the men turned as one and froze. Jak edged out from behind them, never turning her back on them. She was limping a bit, favoring one side, but from the helmet feed, she didn't seem too badly banged up.

"Fuck, more of them?" The soldier turned toward them and pulled a pistol out of the back of his waistband. "Waste them." He went down before the pistol was more than halfway up.

The Banshees moved forward as one, cold and efficient, almost mechanical in their motions. One man turned to run and tripped over Jak's outstretched foot. He pulled his own foot back to give her a vicious kick and howled as three plasma bursts hit him in the extremities.

"We need one alive." Axe's voice rose above the diminishing sounds of fighting. The men were down, except for one. The last man stared at them, terror in the whites of his eyes. His hand shook as he pulled the pistol from his holster.

"I...I..." He stopped and swallowed hard. "Sorry. I'm so sorry. I'll tell you whatever you want to know. Don't hurt me, please." His last words were so faint Torrin couldn't really hear them through Olesya's feed. She gleaned his meaning from his lips, then watched in horror as a crater exploded in his forehead, blood spraying in a sudden arc.

Silence dropped over the area and the Banshees crouched, pointing their weapons in all directions. One of them pushed Jak down onto the ground and covered her body with her own. Torrin made a mental note to find out who that was and thank her.

"What's going on here?" The man's voice shattered the sudden quiet and Torrin watched the feeds as a few Banshees turned to glance down the alley. A Devonite soldier stood there, silhouetted against the light filtering through from the street. She switched Tien's sensors over to sense heat and watched as men crowded in behind him, drawn by the sound of their brief firefight.

The rest of the Banshees still scanned the rooftops for the source of the last shot. It hadn't come from one of their rifles. To a woman, they were all packing plasma weapons. The only woman in the Nadierzdan Armed Forces who used a projectile-based weapon was Jak. For tense seconds they surveyed the area, but no second shot was forthcoming.

"Jak, are you okay?" Olesya turned her attention to Torrin's lover. The Banshee covering her had rolled off her and was helping her up while somehow still managing to survey the area. Jak sat up slowly.

"I'm okay. A little banged up. One of the bastards got me in the leg." Jak pulled fabric away from a wound on her leg. Blood oozed sluggishly from a deep puncture wound.

"Olesya," Torrin radioed. "You need to go. It's going to get crowded there in a hurry." There was no telling if there were more hostile Devonites in the crowd. "Bring her along quickly, I'll have the autodoc ready to go." Torrin pushed herself out of the pilot's chair. "Tien, bring the med bay online, and get the lift doors open in the cargo bay."

"Affirmative Torrin." The AI's answer came as Torrin sprinted down the hall toward the ladder to the lower deck. She wanted to be there when Olesya brought Jak back on board. Two Banshees squatted at the edge of the cargo bay ramp, covering their squadmates from above. Bulky headgear gave them the ability to see in the smothering darkness.

Torrin paced back and forth where the ramp met the cargo bay. What could be taking so long? She felt more than heard the whine of the Banshees' personal antigrav units. It started as an ache among her back teeth. There was a low rumble beneath the whine of the antigrav and Torrin realized that the crowd of Devonites had swelled. Some of the soldiers were shouting at them, wanting to know what was going on and not recognizing the armored Banshees.

"Tien, I want floodlights on that crowd. Let's make it harder for them to hit us if they start shooting."

A brilliant finger of light reached through the night, bathing upraised faces below. Those faces turned away rather than be blinded. Torrin held her breath, hoping Jak and the Banshees would get up to the *Jane* before the mood of the crowd boiled over.

Finally, Olesya and another Banshee landed on the ramp, Jak held between them.

Torrin followed behind the little group as they supported Jak between them. The adrenaline flowing through Jak's system must have lessened, and the pain of her wound was slowing her down. She put very little weight on the injured leg. They crammed themselves into the lift and Torrin got her first good look at Jak. Her face was covered with red welts that were already coloring in mottled dark patches. One eye was swelling shut.

Rage flowed through Torrin, coursing molten through her veins. Her head pounded. She staggered slightly to one side as her vision grayed out. Olesya reached out and steadied her without letting go of Jak.

"I'm okay." Torrin shrugged her shoulder out of the Banshee's grasp. "When I find out who did this, I'm going to fucking kill them." She looked back over at Jak. "How are you feeling?"

"I'm okay." Jak's gritted teeth made a liar out of her. "It hurts a bit, but it could've been a lot worse. I'm going to have to thank Perez and Hamilton for the extra close-quarters combat training. That's the second time their moves have helped me out of a tight spot. The Devonites didn't know what to make of it." She grinned, but her reassuring smile was marred by the blood that outlined her teeth.

"What the hell happened down there?"

Jak shook her head. "I don't know, exactly. Someone tipped those guys off. They knew I'm female, and they had plans to do something to me."

The lift door slid open and Torrin led them down to the ship's small medical bay. The autodoc was already up and running, waiting for its occupant. With a series of smooth motions that spoke of years of partnership, the Banshees laid Jak on the bed.

"Tien, I need a full diagnostic. I want to know everything those bastards did to her. Every bruise, every cut, every abrasion." *So I can carve it out of the flesh of the bastard who set this up.*

"Yes Torrin. However, I am receiving communication from the Devonites. They wish to know why we attacked their men."

"Why we?" Torrin laughed bitterly. "Tell them we didn't start anything, but we sure as hells aren't afraid of finishing it. Oh, and get us up into orbit as soon as the rest of the Banshees are on board."

"Actually, you're stuck with us that are on here," Olesya said. "*Nightshade* came by and picked up the others. They're over there getting fully kitted up. As soon as we have a target on this, we'll take it out. *Nightshade* will rendezvous with us in orbit. Besides, you only have the one autodoc. We needed to take care of the two women who were hit down there."

A small flare of shame went through Torrin's mind. She'd completely forgotten that the Banshees might have also received casualties.

"Of course, I completely understand." She looked back over at Jak sitting on the table. The table's arm moved slowly back and forth over her leg. The sniper looked up and met her eyes. There had to be something Torrin could do to keep her safe. Jak wouldn't thank her for it, but Torrin wasn't going to risk losing her again.

CHAPTER TWENTY-FOUR

Jak floated in darkness. She'd been exhausted when she'd fallen into bed. Torrin was still up, trying to track down the gunman who'd taken out the last Devonite. It had been quickly evident to her that whoever had killed him had been a pro and that they weren't going to find much. The stress of the attack and being patched up by the autodoc had taken their toll, and she'd headed to bed. Exhausted though she was, her brain would not stop racing and she was having trouble drifting off to sleep completely.

Trees extruded from the shadows and suddenly she was lying prone on the ground. Jak looked over to see her brother grinning cheekily at her. As she stared at him, he lowered the scope and regarded her with concern. His face was distinct, crisp, but the background was faded and smudged. The blond of his hair and brilliant blue of his eyes were the only color, everything else was a faded-out sepia tone.

"What are you staring at?" she asked him.

"I can't believe you haven't figured this out yet." Bron raised the scope back up to his eyes and scanned a far ridge. "The answer's staring you right in the face."

"What do you mean?"

"Who Crimson is." Still looking through the scope, Bron frowned. "Once you figure out who he is, you'll know where he's gone."

"So tell me."

"I can't. It doesn't work that way."

Glowering, Jak lowered her eye to the scope on her rifle and peered through it. She knew what was coming; every time she had this dream it ended the same way. Somewhere out there the sniper stalked them. She knew where to find him now and she trained her rifle on the far ridge, the one where she kept seeing the strangely familiar boy.

"You need to turn on your cloak," she told him acerbically.

"Don't try to change the subject." Despite his words, he reached around to the front of his neck and thumbed on the control for the cloaking device. Abruptly, he disappeared from her view; all she could see of him was a faint shimmer, like the air over a hot roof in the summer. "You're running out of time."

"Your cloak is glitching out. You should reset it."

"I'm fine. Stop trying to change the subject." She could feel his disappointment and ducked her head to peer through the scope again.

"I know we're running out of time. I can feel it slipping away from me. There's something I'm missing, but the harder I try to get hold of it, the slipperier it gets."

He snorted. "Well, you need to get your shit together, otherwise the girl's blood is going to be on your hands. She's out there, all alone, and she needs you to pull it together and get the job done."

"I know, I know. I'm trying!" There was the flash of red she was looking for. There wasn't much time now. She could feel her heart thundering in her ears and willed her galloping pulse to slow. "It's really hard, like trying to catch smoke with a net." She continued to scan the far-off foliage. The boy snapped into focus at the same time as he raised the sniper rifle and fitted his eye to the scope. Jak felt like he was looking at her. Right at her. Like he knew her, the real her. "I think I understand. Bron? Bron?"

He didn't answer, and she slowly turned her head, knowing and dreading what would happen next. She made eye contact with him just as his throat disappeared in a fountain of gore; red was the only color to the landscape now. Gone were the blond of his hair and the electric blue of his eyes. A fine mist of blood coated her face.

"Bron. Bron!!!" Jak screamed. "BRON!"

* * *

Torrin watched over Jak in the darkness of her cabin. She perched on the edge of the bed, watching as Jak moved restlessly under the covers. Her careful perusal of Tien's records on the firefight had registered nothing. Olesya was going over the feeds from the Banshees' helmet-cams, helped by Tien. Torrin should have been with them, but she wanted to be close to Jak. She'd almost lost her. Again. This time, she'd barely gotten there before it was too late. She hesitated to think of what could have happened if Jak hadn't had that transmitter on her.

And then there was the asinine conversation she'd been forced to go through with Callahan and Wolfe. They hadn't been put off by the flip answer she'd had Tien relay to them and had insisted on speaking with her. Wolfe was no fan of Jak's and had tried to make it her fault. He'd even insinuated that she'd been the one to kill McCullock. Finding out that someone had taken care of McCullock for her hadn't saddened Torrin in the least, but she wasn't going to let Jak take the blame. All it had taken was Torrin threatening to cancel their contract and Callahan had put a muzzle on his colonel.

A low groan drew her attention back to Jak's prone form. Her head moved slowly back and forth on the pillow. Torrin leaned forward; Jak was muttering something too indistinct to be heard.

"Bron!" Jak sat up and screamed her brother's name. Torrin caught Jak as she came flying off the bed. This wasn't the first time she'd been there when Jak had awoken from one of these nightmares. They'd been happening less frequently, but their intensity had ratcheted back up since their return to Haefen.

"Shhhh, I've got you." Jak shuddered in her arms as Torrin rubbed small circles over her shoulder blades.

Slowly, Jak's fright subsided. "Johvah, Torrin. It was right there. I had him."

"I know, baby. Let it all out, I've got you."

Jak pulled herself out of Torrin's arms and shook her head. "No, you don't get it. I had him. I had…" Her voice trailed off, and she stared at a pile of objects on the table across the room. "I need to see that." She pointed at the table, her arm trembling.

Torrin turned to follow her pointing finger. As far as she knew, they were the odds and ends that had been in the pockets of Jak's combat fatigues. Torrin had brought them in from the medbay. She was glad she'd thought to check the pockets of Jak's ruined pants before destroying them. "See what, sweetie?"

"That!" The emphasis was loud and Torrin placed a placating arm on her shoulder.

"Okay, okay." She got up picked up the small pile of objects. What Jak thought she would find, Torrin didn't know. A firestarter, a small scope, a couple of rocks, some feathers and a length of string. She shook her head and brought the double handful of disparate materials back to her lover.

Jak plucked the red feathers from the group. Separated from the rest of the objects, Torrin recognized it as a dart of some sort.

"Yes, this is it," Jak breathed, her voice so quiet Torrin had to strain to hear her. "I remember."

"Do you remember when you found that on the top of Hill 372?"

"No. I remember when he taught me how to make these." Jak lifted shining eyes to hers. "Torrin, when I was little Crimson taught me to make little dart bundles almost like this." A tear separated from her eyelid and tracked down the side of her nose.

"He what?" Torrin drew herself back and stared uncomprehendingly down at her. "What are you talking about? You knew Crimson when you were young?"

"His name isn't Crimson. It's Lucian. Lucian Cummings." More tears joined the first and they trickled down her face, landing with little splashes on her outstretched hand. "Before I was Jak, when my family still called me Jakellyn, he lived with his family in the next valley. I played with him and his sisters. After Mom got sick, sometimes his family would watch me and Bron." Jak sniffled and rubbed her nose on the back of her sleeve.

"I don't understand, is he like that Weller guy? Did he desert? How did he end up with the Orthodoxans?"

"I'm not sure, not exactly. His family was killed, wiped out by an Orthodoxan raiding party. I thought he was dead too. They must have taken him back with them." Jak inhaled deeply. Her breath shuddered out of her body when she exhaled, and she wiped at her face, trying to bring her tears back under control. "It doesn't matter. I know where he is. I know where Nat is. And I'm pretty sure I know what he wants. We were as close as siblings, closer than I was with Bron, at least then. He liked to play house and I would tease him by being the mom who wouldn't stay at home." The smile on Jak's face held no amusement. Instead, it was sour with dawning realization.

Torrin grabbed Jak's shoulders and pulled her up to stare right in her eyes. "Are you sure? Really sure this time? So help me, Jak, I can't go off prospecting the wrong asteroid again."

"It makes sense, why we couldn't track him down on the Orthodoxan side. He's already here, and he's waiting for me."

Cold threatened to sap Torrin's strength, fear froze her to the marrow. "He's waiting for you? What the hell, we're going to give him exactly what he wants? No way, Jak. I'm not going to trade you for Nat. I can't. Don't make me choose." She squeezed her eyelids shut and blew out a quivering breath.

Cool fingertips traced the tears that coursed down her cheeks. "You don't need to choose. I told you I'd get her back, and I will. Or rather, we will. Now that I know the right place to look, he can't stop me. He's drawn me right to him; he had to know I would recognize the dart. He might be good, but I'm better. Besides, we'll have help."

Torrin opened her eyes and stared at Jak's beatific smile. There was no swagger, no bravado. Jak had made a promise and she was standing behind it, it was as simple as that. Torrin stood. "I'll radio down to the Devonites. We'll get Callahan on the comm."

Jak's emphatic head shake stopped her in her tracks. "No!" Anxiety widened her eyes, and she clutched at Torrin's forearm, drawing her to a stop. "You can't do that. Someone out there knows about me. Torrin, the soldiers knew I was a woman. Someone set me up. There are only a few people who know, and it could be any of them."

"What? Who do you think it is?"

"I'm not sure, but someone had McCullock killed. They're serious, and if they know I know who Crimson is and where he's holed up, we'll get ratted out for sure."

"Wolfe said McCullock was dead. He said you were the one who killed him." She didn't know if Jak was the one who'd killed the odious captain, though it would have surprised her. Jak had been covered with blood when she'd been brought up. It had been impossible to tell which splatters had been hers and which had belonged to her attackers. She supposed some of that could have been McCullock's blood. It didn't really bother her to think Jak might have done the deed, but Torrin did worry that Jak might be blamed for it.

Jak shook her head. "Someone killed him right after he told you he'd made a breakthrough. He said he thought someone was on to him; at least that's what he said in his message to me."

Shocked, Torrin sat on the bed next to Jak, who wound suddenly clammy fingers in hers.

"Smythe showed up right after I did. He knew McCullock's real assignment. Told me about how he's the real head of the Intelligence Corps. He thinks the Orthodoxans are cleaning house, sowing confusion while they prepare to invade through the tunnel we found. He told me to get out of the fort after we found a bloody knife in my dresser drawer. I took off out of there, but got scooped up by the private in that truck. My lungs were killing me; I wasn't going to make the run all the way back here. Anyway, you know what happened next."

Torrin listened in mounting horror. "Is Smythe the mole?"

"I don't think—"

Torrin held up a hand to forestall her protests. "Think about it! It sounds like he was right there when McCullock was killed. What if he did it? And if he did, what's the only possible reason?"

"Torrin, he could have killed me at any time when we were out on the other side of the fence, trying to hunt down Crimson. And especially when we found the tunnel! If it was him, I'd be long dead. No, it's someone else. Either there was someone watching your ship, or there's a backdoor into my in-box. Either way, we can't risk tipping them off, not now that I know where Nat is."

"Then let's get over there." Torrin was sick of waiting.

"I'm going to need some of the Banshees." Jak paused before continuing, her voice hesitant. "You need to hook up with the Devonites and draw out the traitor."

Torrin jumped to her feet. "No way in hell, Jak! You got hit on the head harder than I thought if you think I'm going to send you off to face Crimson by yourself, let alone pull my sister out of his grasp without my help."

"Torrin, listen—"

"No, you listen. You need to put that thought out of your head right now. Don't think I'm going to budge on this one."

"But they need you there. We don't know what kind of communication the traitor has with Crimson. And you can't rip off the League. You need to make good on your promise to them." Jak reached out to take Torrin's hands, but she twitched them out of Jak's reach.

Torrin turned her back on Jak. "They don't need me. Axe will be fine." Her shoulders shook, and she wrapped her arms around herself. *Jak doesn't understand.* To be away from both her and Nat would drive her around the bend. She was barely holding it together as it was. Jak's forays into Orthodoxan territory had stretched her nerves to the point of breaking.

"Do you not trust me?" Torrin cringed to hear the tears in her voice; she knew it was weak, but she couldn't stop the tears that fell.

Hands took her by the elbows and pulled her backward. Jak's arms enveloped her into a tender embrace.

"Of course I trust you." Jak hugged Torrin hard for a second. "I don't want to lose you, and I don't want you to get hurt while we're out there. There's no guarantee. Crimson could see us coming and kill us, then kill Nat, or the other way around."

Torrin turned in Jak's arms and hugged her back. "I know that, which is why I'm not letting you go without me." She leaned down and pressed her lips to Jak's, teasing and nipping along her lower lip. Jak parted her lips and Torrin pressed her tongue deep inside her mouth. She took her time and bent her mind to memorizing the feel of Jak pressed against her. After a long, leisurely kiss, Torrin leaned her head against her lover's.

"You're stuck with me, Jak Stowell. I love you, and I'm not leaving your side again."

"I love you, Torrin." Jak raised her hands and cupped Torrin's face. She kissed the corner of Torrin's mouth. "I don't want to be without you either." She stopped and blushed, then looked away in embarrassment.

"What's the matter?" Emotional displays of any kind were unusual from Jak, but Torrin couldn't remember a time when she'd seen her so flustered.

"Only that I can't think of how things would be without you. I don't want to."

"I know, sweetness." Torrin pressed a kiss back on Jak's mouth. "I don't want to think about that either."

"You don't understand." Jak looked down at Torrin's chest, seemingly memorizing the pattern of her top. "I want to be with you always, not only now. I want to grow old with you. I haven't thought beyond the next mission in years, and now I want a future with you. I want the whole future with you."

"I *do* understand. Really, I do. I've thought about what the future might be like, about settling down with one woman. Before, I could never bring her face to my mind, and now, you're the only one I can see. I want to have babies with you and get old and wrinkly together."

"Babies?" Torrin could see Jak swallow. Her eyes darted up to touch Torrin's face, then skittered to the side.

"Sure, why not?"

"I don't know. I never thought about it, I guess. Are you sure we're ready?"

"We'll know when we are. I can't wait to meet the kids we'll make."

"When you put it that way…" Jak leaned her head against Torrin's chest. "But there's still one thing that…"

"One thing that what?" Torrin wrapped her arm around Jak's torso, snugging her in to the curve of her body.

"Why did you tell Callahan and the others about me?"

Torrin cringed. This was a conversation she had been hoping they could skip, but there was no getting out of it. Besides, Jak deserved to know. "The truth is…I panicked. I was going to let you tell them in your own time, but I was so bound and determined to get them to take care of you that it slipped out."

"Oh." Jak paused. She looked like she had something else to add, but she said nothing.

"I wouldn't have done it if I'd been thinking straight. The story was yours to tell, not mine. I should have said that earlier, but…I was afraid it was something you wouldn't be able to forgive me for. It was a horrible thing to do."

"I thought you were trying to tell me I was being silly in keeping it in or something."

"Absolutely not! I screwed up. If I could, I'd take it all back."

"But you can't." The statement could have been accusing in tone, but instead it sounded to Torrin like Jak was trying to let her off the hook. "It had to come out sometime, I suppose, though I wouldn't have done it that way. Or that soon. What's done is done. I'm glad to know you weren't trying to force me out."

"Never. Even if I disagree with you, something like that isn't my place to reveal. If I hadn't been scared out of my mind that I was going to lose you, it never would have happened."

"Good. Because I want to be with you for a very long time, but I need to know you have my back."

"I will always back you up." Torrin dropped a kiss on the top of her head. "We're in this for as long as we have together."

"Longer." Jak wrapped her hands around Torrin's arms and squeezed.

"It's a deal." Torrin turned all her concentration on the beautiful woman in her arms. Jak was all hers and she'd never been happier.

CHAPTER TWENTY-FIVE

The valley was quiet. Jak scanned the trees, but it was impossible to see much through the dense foliage. Normally, the screens of branches and leaves made her feel secure and hidden, but not today. Not now that she was taking the fight to Lucian, a sniper who came close to her in skill. Jak was confident that she was better. At the very least, she knew she was more grounded than he was. His obsession with proving his skill with the throat shot demonstrated that. "One shot, one kill" was the mantra that had been drilled into her head during sniper school. She went for the best shot, the one that had the highest kill percentage, no matter the angle. That shot varied from one situation to the next.

Why was he so obsessed with the throat shot anyway? He was showing off, and since she'd made the connection, Jak had the uncomfortable suspicion that he'd been showing off for *her*. How much of what he'd done had been because of her? She hoped she wasn't his motivator.

Rustling from behind drew her attention. Perez finished covering the antigrav units with fresh-cut saplings and branches from nearby trees.

"That should do it," she said.

"I hope so. This isn't a high-traffic area." At least it hadn't been when she was a child. It had been years since she'd been back this way. Jak found herself torn between eagerness to see her childhood home and dread at being there again. "Let's go." Her tone was brusquer than she'd intended, and she cringed internally before looking guiltily over at Torrin.

"It's okay," Torrin said. She captured Jak's hand and squeezed it quickly.

"Oh geez." Perez rolled her eyes. "The girlfriends thing is getting old, you know."

"I don't see why it would," Torrin said, her voice teasing. "We've only been together a few months. Wait until tonight. I hope you brought some earplugs."

"That's right," Jak added. "I can't wait to get my hands all up on her."

"Ugh." Perez looked disgusted, then brightened. "I don't suppose you'll need me to tag in?" Her leer sent heat rushing to Jak's cheeks. "Hah!" She smirked at having drawn the blush out in Jak's face.

"Never mind," Jak mumbled. Why did she even try to one-up the Banshees? It only ever ended with her embarrassment. She pulled up the hood on her ghillie suit. Torrin followed suit. At least Lambert came through, she thought. Her old quartermaster was some sort of wizard. Finding a ghillie suit tall enough for Torrin had been difficult, but as she'd known he would, Lambert had managed.

Perez's form shimmered before receding into the bushes. She didn't disappear, not exactly, but portions of her body appeared to recede into the surrounding greenery while her fatigues shifted from black to green. The effect was startling but effective. Her outline was almost impossible to make out; the camouflage would be even more effective from a distance.

"Follow me," Jak said. "We need to be careful. Lucian…Crimson knows this valley almost as well as I do." She started off, her pace measured. If something was going to give them away, it would likely be movement. Nothing drew the eye out here like something moving in a way or place that was unnatural. Torrin would chafe at their slow progress and Jak longed to be able to push more quickly, but she needed to keep them alive so they could get to Nat. As they moved deeper into the forested valleys of her birthplace, every ounce of patience she'd ever cultivated was being pulled on and stretched thin. It would be so easy to rush in, but that wouldn't help them or Nat. Especially not Nat.

They'd been deposited a few valleys over from where she'd grown up so they wouldn't tip Crimson off. Somewhere above them, the Banshees were working with the Devonites and the League to draw out the traitor. If he was in constant contact with Crimson, then the traitor would soon have more problems than trying to report on their activities. Jak knew her absence would soon be noticed and remarked upon. The truth of her gender was probably working its way through the camps even now.

At their slow pace, it took most of the day to traverse the two valleys. Jak called a halt when the shadows started to lengthen. Darkness came quickly among the hills and trees. Torrin and Perez were both outfitted with night-vision headgear. She'd tested out the equipment and while it was an improvement over having no enhancement, the loss of detail was staggering when compared to her night vision. Crimson had implants similar to hers and she didn't want to engage him at night. Their only advantage was in numbers. He knew they were coming and had undoubtedly prepared accordingly. She wasn't going to take him on when they weren't at their best capacity, at least not if she could help it.

"Let's get settled for the night."

Torrin looked mutinous but she didn't say anything. They'd already been through it on the ship.

"At least this time we have real food," Jak said. The statement earned her a small smile.

Perez plopped herself down on a downed branch, and Torrin took a seat not far from where Jak stood.

"The suit is a pain in the ass," Torrin griped. "It gets caught on everything."

"I know, but if Crimson has a soft spot for me, I'd rather he thought you were me. That should keep you a little safer. Besides, you're almost impossible to see out here." Jak took a final look around the area. They were nestled in a hollow on the hillside. It would be incredibly difficult for anyone to sneak up on them and they were difficult to spot. She felt reasonably confident that they wouldn't be in any danger from the Orthodoxan sniper. There was an area devoid of ground cover next to Torrin's leg, and Jak sat down, leaning her back against her lover's legs. Torrin leaned forward and Jak looked up in time to receive a gentle kiss.

"Oh please." Perez mimed throwing up into her dinner.

"Jealous?" Torrin asked, disengaging from Jak's lips.

Perez lifted one shoulder. "Maybe."

Jak blushed, her face on fire.

"You know she wouldn't say nearly as much if you didn't blush so easily." Torrin wrapped her arms around Jak's shoulders.

"I know but I can't seem to help it."

Dinner passed in companionable silence. Both soldiers kept a sharp eye on the surrounding woods. The usual chirps and clicks of the local fauna told Jak that they were alone. It was good to be home again or close to it. She sighed.

"You holding up all right?" Torrin watched her with concern.

"Yeah. It feels so weird. It's like everything's come full circle. I'm going back to the place where I lost both my parents. We lost our home because of my father's choices."

"What do you mean?"

"Dad decided it wasn't safe for me to be Jakellyn anymore, not after an Orthodoxan raiding party took out Lucian—I mean, Crimson's family. We're pretty close to the border here and you know how easy it is to get across. The fence was thrown up so quickly that it has a number of structural flaws. Both sides take advantage of them. It's useful in that we know where to expect the Orthodoxans, which is what makes that tunnel so dangerous. Anyway, there's a weak point in the fence we've been trying to shut down for years. It opened up around the same time Crimson's family was taken."

Jak closed her eyes at the memory. Her father had woken her up one morning. She'd been confused. He'd let her sleep in a few extra hours, something he didn't do unless they were sick. Before the Cummings family was wiped out, most mornings they were up when he was so she could accompany him to the woods and they could drop Bron at Lucian's house on the way. But not this day. He'd made her breakfast and watched her as she ate.

"What's wrong, Da?" His behavior was making her nervous.

"We need to make some changes." His eyes caught hers and didn't let go. "Jakellyn Stowell doesn't exist any longer. From now on, you're my youngest son, Jak."

She was even more confused. His words made no sense. She wasn't a boy. "What do you mean?"

"It's simple, Jak." The pet name took on new significance. "We tell everyone you're a boy. No one else really knows the family, they'll never know. I'll take care of everything." He covered her small hands in his and gave her a reassuring squeeze. "We're going to cut your hair as short as your brother's. You already wear pretty much the same clothing, so that won't be a problem. You need to forget that you ever had any other name."

She blinked at him. Tears gave his eyes a wet shine which scared her more than anything he was saying. The only time she'd seen him cry had been the year before when Mom had died. Jak nodded, trying to make him feel better.

"It's okay, Da. I get it. I'm Jak now." She didn't really understand, but she would follow his instructions if it meant he didn't cry.

"That sounds hard," Torrin said.

Jak looked at her, seeing the clearing again. She shrugged halfheartedly, little more than a jerky twitch of her shoulders. "All I did was what he said to. It became second nature real quickly. Bron helped. He thought it was great fun at first, tricking everyone."

"It sounds like something he'd like." Torrin grinned. She'd heard enough stories about Jak's brother to appreciate the glee he would have gotten from pulling the wool over everybody's eyes.

"It wasn't too bad, not really. At first, I don't think it was a big deal for Da. Financially I mean. But then, I turned twelve. Actually, I turned fifteen. He'd been telling everyone that I was two years younger than Bron. I was always smaller than him and Dad thought it made more sense for me to be the younger one." She grinned. "Bron liked that too."

"So what happened when you were fifteen?"

"I had to get my implants."

Torrin nodded, understanding the dilemma. Because the nanomechs that built the implants did so using a great deal of the host's own tissues and nutrients, they had to be perfectly typed to the host and chromosomal markers had to be exact. Getting typed in preparation for receiving the implants would have blown Jak's secret wide open.

"He took me to an implant doctor in a town far from here. He didn't want anyone to know us. I guess he had to pay the doctor a huge amount of money to keep my secret. He borrowed the money against the house and our property. When he died, he still owed a ton of money."

"And Crimson killed him?"

"Yep." Jak flinched as she saw the spray of blood from his throat, the same spray she would see from Bron years later.

"You owe us one of your sons for the war effort." The Devonite sergeant's *hard tone put her back up and she clenched her fists behind her back. She wanted to slug him for talking to her father that way. Bron lounged against the fireplace and did his best to pretend he wasn't listening.* "By law, your *eldest should have come to us when he turned eighteen."*

Her father looked across the table at the sergeant. "My eldest doesn't turn *eighteen for another six months." He glanced over at Bron.*

"Our records show that your eldest is nineteen right now."

Jak stared at the sergeant. He was talking about her.

"That damn screw-up." Their father pushed away from the table. "Hold *on, I'll go get the records. This has been messed up for years and every time I think it's been straightened out…" He walked across the large common room and up the stairs to the second floor.*

"You're a likely looking lad," the sergeant called over to Bron. "You *looking forward to your service?"*

Bron managed a tight smile and a small shrug.

"Those your rifles?" The sergeant tried again to get a response from him.

"One of them. Other one's my brother's."

The sergeant's eyes flicked over Jak, dismissing her as inconsequential. "Little young, isn't he?"

"Two years younger than me. Better shot too."

The sergeant's gaze returned and lingered longer this time, weighing her. "He could join you in a few years then. Hopefully you'll have a few more *centimeters then, boy."*

"Guess so, sir." Jak roughened her voice as she'd been taught, pitching it lower.

"Jak's not going anywhere." Their father's stern tone shut both her and the sergeant up. He stalked back over to the table and tossed a couple of plastic sheets on the table in front of the sergeant. "I'll need him to help me out *around here while Bron is doing his duty."*

"A lot of families send all their sons."

"A lot of families aren't living practically on top of the fence and supporting themselves by hunting and trapping."

The sergeant held his hands up in surrender before dropping them to the table and scooping up their records. He examined the papers closely.

"I see what you mean." There was no indication that he'd noticed that one set of papers as a forgery. There was no reason he should have been able to tell.

Jak's father had paid a small fortune to get her new birth papers drawn up. They'd been produced by a man who worked for the vital records office. He'd used the same plastic sheeting for the new record and had inscribed the new information on it.

"Good."

"We'll expect Bron in six months then. I'll make sure the records are updated."

"I'd appreciate that." Their father showed no sign that he was lying. None of them did. It felt strange to Jak to even think of herself as a girl. She'd gotten some teasing from Bron when her body had started showing signs of puberty. They'd gotten into one of the few knock-down, drag-out fights of their life, and he hadn't bothered her about it again after she bloodied his nose and blackened both his eyes.

"You could send him early," the sergeant said as he pushed his chair away from the rough table. "A lot of families send us their boys before their eighteenth birthdays. Of course, usually it's the larger families that do that."

"Thanks for the information." Their father's voice was dry. He wasn't going to send his children into harm's way any sooner than he had to. Jak knew he still had nightmares about his own service. Some nights, they could hear him all the way down the hall in their rooms when he was caught back in the worst of it.

"Thank you for the hospitality." The sergeant saluted their father and after a moment's hesitation, he returned it. The three of them stood on the wide porch, watching the small squad leave. The sergeant raised his hand in a final wave right before they disappeared around the corner of the small path that led up to the cabin.

"Did he know you, Dad?" Bron asked.

"Not exactly." When her father didn't elaborate, Jak looked at him. He stared off into the distance. From the tightness of his eyes, Jak knew he was looking far into the past.

"What do you mean?" she prompted when he kept silent.

"It's more likely he knows of me. Or of who I was." The answer wasn't particularly forthcoming and Jak shared an annoyed look with her brother. She looked up in time to see an amused smile lurking around the corners of their father's mouth. Their adolescent irritation at his parental obtuseness never ceased to entertain him.

"What do you mean by that?" Jak expressed her exasperation with an obvious eye roll. His eyes twinkling, her father opened his mouth to respond. Red sprayed out of his mouth and his throat disappeared in a smear of crimson.

For a second he stayed upright, his eyes locked on hers, then he dropped to his knees, hands clutching at the ruins of his throat. By the time he keeled over to land face first on the porch, he was dead. Bron and Jak stood, staring and covered with strands of red from the last arterial spurts of their father's life blood. Bron dropped to his knees next to their father's body. He grabbed his shoulder and shook him.

"Da?"

"Leave him be, Bron." Jak's voice was harsh. "He's gone."

"That's terrible." Torrin had her arms wrapped around Jak. The story was hard to tell, even now, over four years later. Torrin's presence made it a little easier, but this was the first time she'd told the story since relaying it to the authorities.

Jak shrugged. "I hiked up to town the next morning and informed the magistrate. They came and took Da's body and we cremated him three days later. I took his ashes and spread them along one of his favorite runs.

"A few weeks later a man showed up and started poking around the place. I confronted him and he told me that our home belonged to the bank unless we could pay back the loans Da had taken out. When he told me how much they were, I kicked him off the land. There was no way we could pay it back. It was hard enough trying to figure out how we were going to make it through the next month. That night we decided to stop by the nearest Devonite outpost to see if they'd take us both on." Jak smiled sourly into the darkness.

"What's so funny?"

"We needed to move fast. When I kicked the bank man off our land, I kind of snapped and beat the crap out of him. If I hadn't done that, we probably would've had a few weeks to get out of there, but after that, I knew we needed to get out before he showed with the sheriff in tow."

"Bit of a temper there?" Torrin's voice was lightly teasing, and she squeezed Jak's shoulders encouragingly.

"Maybe a little bit." Jak sighed. "There's not much more to tell after that. We went to the outpost and talked to the quartermaster. We knew him from when we used to go with Da to sell them yterrencatte pelts. He was happy to get us signed up. We were sent out on a transport to the nearest camp with basic training facilities. From there, we moved into sniper school. That's pretty much it." Exhaustion dragged her head down. She hadn't expected the story to take so much out of her.

"You should get some sleep."

"I can't. I need to keep watch."

"You can't do it all yourself. You don't need to. I'm here, Perez is here."

With a stubborn frown, Jak shook her head. "You don't know these woods. I need to be the one to keep watch."

Branches rustled as Perez turned from her post to glance back at them, the night-vision headgear giving her head a strange profile. "Major, what are you going to do tomorrow when we're trying to take on this Crimson character and you're wrecked from lack of sleep?"

Torrin glared at Jak. "Hand them over."

"I can't." Jak glared back as fiercely.

"She's going to take more fucking stims," Torrin said to Perez. "Because they haven't caused enough crap already."

"Torrin, that's not fair. We aren't going to be out here for two weeks. They're fine to take for a few days."

"That's not the point, Jak. You don't have to take them. You can count on us. You're not on your own. Perez and I have your back."

Perez had turned back to keep watch over their surroundings. "She's right, Major. You can count on us."

"Fine. But at least let me give you some pointers. Keeping watch out here is a little different than you're used to."

"Major, I've run missions in all sorts of terrain. These aren't even the densest forests I've seen." Perez sounded overly patient, like she wanted to give Jak a piece of her mind but knew she shouldn't yell at an officer.

With a wince, Jak turned to Torrin. "Then I'll fill you in." She would say it loud enough that Perez would be able to hear. When Torrin's eyes started to glaze over, Jak realized she'd gone on long enough.

"I think she's got it, sir," Perez said. "Why don't you get some sleep? I'll take the first watch."

"All right. Wake Torrin up for second. I'll take the last watch of the night." If they wouldn't let her take all the night's watches, at least she could take the worst one.

"Excellent idea, sir." Like all good enlisted soldiers, Perez made her agreement sound neutral enough not to arouse Jak's ire, but dry enough to get across that there was no other way the situation would have gone down.

"Come on, Jak. Let's get some sleep." Torrin slipped down from her perch and leaned her back against the rotting log. After a little wiggling, she opened her arms for Jak. Without a word, Jak leaned back against her, content to be enfolded in her embrace.

"No nasty stuff." Perez's voice floated through the small hollow.

"You keep your eyes front, soldier," Jak said, voice stern. A snicker was the only response to her admonishment. She shook her head. Torrin squeezed her and Jak felt the tension of the day's trip and her memories draining from her body. As usual when she was in Torrin's arms, she had no problem drifting off to sleep. The only hurdle to deep sleep was squelching the tiny kernel of excitement that smoldered in her belly. Tomorrow she would free Nat and take care of her brother's killer. She cleared her mind. It didn't do to dwell on a shot she hadn't taken. The shot was lined up, then taken, not the other way around. With the reminder firmly in mind, she slipped into a dreamless sleep.

CHAPTER TWENTY-SIX

The cabin was rustic and quaint, but bigger than she'd expected from Jak's description. Jak ghosted from tree to tree ahead of her, and Torrin did her best to keep up without making too much noise. Perez took up their rear by about fifty meters. She was covering their six. Jak had insisted Perez stay far enough back to be out of range of any ambushes or traps they might set off.

The early morning woods were deathly silent and dense fog wreathed the trees. Occasionally, Torrin would lose sight of Jak. She hadn't lost her for more than a few seconds. Fortunately, her night-vision headgear was also configured to see heat sources, and she was able to pierce the fog enough to catch up to Jak. Torrin divided her attention between the ground and the trees in front of her.

The cabin had suddenly appeared out of the fog, and Jak had gestured for them to stop. Torrin immediately crouched in her tracks and toggled on the heat-sensing equipment on her headgear.

"I don't see anyone," Torrin said, voice pitched to carry to Jak's ears but no further.

Jak shook her head. She pointed to Torrin and patted her head.

What is that supposed to mean? Torrin looked at Jak and shrugged. Irritation flashed across Jak's face to be replaced by a too-calm look. She made her way back over to Torrin.

"I need you to hang out here and cover me. I'm going to go down."

"Got it. There are no heat signatures down there."

"That doesn't mean he hasn't left us a surprise or that he's not covering the cabin from the heights."

Torrin looked up at the valley walls rising to either side of their position. The cabin was nestled snugly at one end of a narrow valley, almost a ravine, really.

"You won't see him if he doesn't want you to."

"But you'll be able to find him."

"Maybe." Jak's face was stoic, but her hands tightened on the rifle and Torrin thought she saw a flash of doubt in her eyes.

"Hey." Torrin put a hand on Jak's forearm. "I believe in you. That was a statement of fact." The last thing she needed was Jak to doubt herself, not when Jak was the key to getting her sister back. Uncertainty could be lethal, and she wasn't going to be responsible for placing such thoughts in Jak's head.

Jak nodded. She looked up and caught Perez's eye and gestured for her to join them. The Banshee made her way through the underbrush with as little noise as Jak did. Torrin felt a moment of irritation at the ease with which the two of them navigated through the forest. She still made twice the noise they did while moving half as fast.

"Perez, I need you to make your way to the top of the ridge at the back of the house. Cover us from there. Crimson doesn't like to shoot from the heights. From what I've seen, he likes to be elevated, but not at the top. He probably thinks it makes him harder to find. From there, you'll be looking down at the level he prefers, so keep your eyes peeled. Whatever you do, make sure you don't silhouette yourself against the sky."

"Got it, Major."

"I'm going to give you twenty minutes before heading into the cabin. Torrin's going to cover the front of the cabin from here."

Perez nodded again and melted back into the trees. She was there one moment and between one blink and the next, Torrin lost her.

Jak smiled, little more than a grim baring of teeth. "She'll do," she said, more to herself than to Torrin.

"I'm not staying here," Torrin said.

"We don't have time to argue." Jak settled down behind a tree and rested her rifle on a large knot that protruded from the trunk near the tree's roots. She put her eye to the scope and perused the area around the cabin.

"Actually, we have plenty of time to argue. You told Perez you wouldn't move for twenty minutes."

"She's expecting you to stay put."

"No problem, I'll let her know through my transmitter."

A muscle popped in Jak's jaw. "Torrin, baby, I love you. But out here, we can't be lovers. Only one of us can be in charge, and right now that's me. If you can't accept that, then you need to go."

Torrin didn't say anything. Jak's words hurt, though she knew they weren't meant to. She only wanted to stay with Jak, to make sure nothing went wrong.

Jak sighed. "I'm not trying to hurt your feelings, but if you're right here with me, I'm going to be distracted. I'll worry about you, and I can't afford to have anything affecting my focus. I'm not saying this because I don't care about you. I'm saying it because I care so very much about you."

A lump welled up in Torrin's throat and she swallowed hard to clear it away. "I understand," she whispered. "I don't want to lose you."

"You won't." Jak smiled, her eye still watching through the scope. "Not if you do what I say."

"Out here, fine. But don't let it go to your head, and don't for a second think that it's going to extend to all parts of our life together."

Jak's smile widened into a grin. "Don't worry. Somehow I'm pretty sure you won't allow that to happen. Tell you what, as soon as I know it's clear down there, I'll let you know to come in."

"And if it isn't clear?"

"Then I'll expect you to cover my ass and pull it out of the fire. I trust you."

To her credit, Jak even sounded like she meant what she said. Torrin nodded. "It's a deal."

She hunkered down a few meters behind and above Jak. Not trusting her with a sniper rifle, Jak had tried to convince her to go with one of the Devonite assault rifles. Torrin had insisted on sticking with a weapon she was familiar with; she had her plasma rifle. The range was much less than an equivalent Devonite weapon, but it was something Crimson wouldn't be familiar with. Torrin hoped the unusual weapon would keep him off guard. Above them, Perez had a similar weapon, though hers had been recalibrated for longer distances.

The minutes ticked by slowly until Jak finally stirred from her post. She moved forward slowly, heading toward her childhood home. Torrin had to remind herself to breathe as Jak slid forward from tree to tree. In her ghillie suit, Jak was practically indistinguishable from the undergrowth. Her slow movement and her way of slipping from one piece of cover to the next meant Torrin lost track of her more than a few times. With a start, she remembered that she was supposed to be covering Jak, not gawking at her. Face burning, though no one had been there to witness her embarrassment, she extended her attention to the surrounding woods.

She lost track of Jak. Time crawled by as Torrin waited for her to reappear. Finally, she noticed a form separate from the bushes by the cabin's front deck. The shape vaulted over the railing and froze, waiting for something. When nothing happened, it proceeded to the front wall and peered into one of the windows. After a long moment, Jak moved to the front door and hesitated. Torrin tore her eyes from Jak's back and went back to watching the woods. It was hard for her to ignore her lover, exposed as she was on the cabin's porch, but she had to keep an eye out. She knew her chances of actually spotting Crimson were vanishingly small, but she had to try. She'd told Jak that she could be trusted and she was going to do her best to live up to that.

When nothing seemed out of place, she risked another quick look at the porch. Jak was no longer there. Torrin tensed and pressed fingertips to the back of her ear.

"Perez, any sign?"

Tense seconds passed. "Nothing yet."

"Any sign of Jak? She's not around front." Torrin swept what she could see of the surrounding slopes with her plasma rifle. Jak had hooked her up with a decent scope. The Haefonians had top quality scopes and part of her considered getting a line on them as a possible export.

"No sign." There was no tension in Perez's voice, simply calm professionalism. Not hearing any worry in her voice allowed Torrin to relax a bit. "Wait…Yep, there she is. She's checking out the cabin's perimeter."

"Got it. Torrin out." Satisfied that Jak was all right, Torrin went back to watching for Crimson. Another eternity passed before Torrin caught movement from the cabin. Her attention was immediately drawn as the front door opened. Jak waved one arm in the all clear. Torrin heaved a sigh, vapor clouding the air. She pushed herself up and made her way slowly down to the front of the cabin, trying to match Jak's stealth. She was sure her efforts were a poor match, but if Crimson was out there, she wasn't going to make it easy for him. *Let him work for it, at least.*

By the time she was up to the front door, Jak had disappeared back into the house. Torrin slipped through the half-open door, barely bumping it on its hinges.

The cabin's interior was shrouded in shadows, the light from the windows barely penetrating the thick layer of dust. Torrin pulled her headgear down over her eyes and engaged the night-vision. The room sprang into glowing green detail. A sturdy table dominated one end of the room. Rustic chairs with tattered cushions sat in front of a fireplace that was choked with debris. Beneath the unkempt and filthy surface, Torrin could see the bones of the house were sound. Someone had poured a lot of love and skill into its construction. The exposed timbers looked like a conscious choice, not an afterthought. Torrin found herself wishing she could have met the man who had built the cabin.

She looked down and multiple sets of footprints. Jak's were easy to pick out. The other set was much larger and by the amount of dust that had settled in them, a bit older. Crisscrossing that set was another that was as old as the large set, but smaller. Someone had been there recently, though not as recently as they. Excitement burbled up in the pit of her stomach. If the big set was Crimson, then the smaller set had to be Nat's. Torrin finally had proof she was alive.

"Jak?" Her voice carried strangely, getting swallowed up before it went very far. "Where are you?"

"Up here." Jak's voice floated down to her from the stairs.

"What's wrong?" Torrin didn't like the stiff tension she heard in Jak's response.

"You should come up here."

Keeping an eye out for traps or items that looked out of place, Torrin made her way across the living area to the stairs along the back wall. The living area had high ceilings that went the full two stories. She took the steps carefully, taking care to step in Jak's footprints.

At the top of the stairs, Torrin saw three doorways, the doors hanging askew in two of them. She followed the scuffs of Jak's footprints to the last door. Curious about her lover's home, she glanced into the rooms as she passed them. The furniture had been moved around; it looked like someone had tossed the place, but a long time ago. Probably the bank, she thought. It was likely they'd gone through the place and stripped it of anything valuable after Jak and Bron had fled. Dust, cobwebs and remnants of animal habitation were visible on what remained.

"What is it?" Torrin asked as she stepped through the last doorway. "I don't…" her voice trailed off as she surveyed the scene in front of her. Unlike the other two rooms, the damage here was recent. The smell hit her first—excrement, her nose said—and her gorge rose. She breathed through her mouth, trying not to throw up. It was smeared on the walls.

Someone with a deep and seething anger had torn the place apart. Nothing remained unbroken that was larger than her hand. The walls had been attacked, hacked at with a knife. Deep gouges carved their way from the ceiling almost down to the floor.

"Was this…"

"My room." Jak's voice was toneless.

"The other rooms didn't look like this."

"Crimson's trying to send me a message." She chewed on her lower lip as she looked around. Torrin was surprised to see unshed tears glistening in her eyes.

She put her hand on Jak's shoulder. "Are you okay?"

Jak shook her head. "I'm fine. I knew things wouldn't be pretty here. Honestly, I figured the bank would have cleared everything out. I'm not surprised they couldn't sell it. A lot of people thought Da was crazy to be living out here." She reached up and covered Torrin's hand with her own. "But seeing this, in my home. It hurts, you know? And from someone I knew. It's really hard for me to reconcile Lucian and Crimson. All I can think of is the boy I used to play with."

Her shoulder trembled a bit under Torrin's grasp and she squeezed it comfortingly. "Let's get out of here. He's not here."

"There's only one other place he could be. He must be at his old homestead."

"Then let's take the fight to him."

With a nod, Jak turned to take in the whole room. She paused and looked hard at an object under one of the larger piles of rubble. "I think that's my parents' wedding album. What is that doing in here?" She moved forward to pull the oblong book from the bottom of the pile.

A prickle of alarm rippled down Torrin's spine. "I don't think you should–" She lunged forward to snatch Jak's arm right as she grabbed the book. With a heave, she shoved Jak aside. There was a loud click and a whoosh. Bright light flashed out from the pile, burning a brilliant afterimage into her corneas. Torrin threw up her arm at the sudden explosion of heat.

Torrin struggled to breathe, but her chest refused to expand; it was wrapped in steel bands that would not give. Finally, she sucked in a breath—only to lose it in agonized coughing. She opened her eyes to see streamers of flame running along the ceiling. They grew out from the back wall and licked their way over her head. She tried to push herself up but couldn't.

"Stay down," Jak yelled in her ear. Torrin could feel Jak's arms looped under her armpits, pulling her away from the scorching flames. Smoke rapidly filled the room and Torrin could barely make out the door. She pushed with her feet to help Jak. With a few heaves, Jak had her through the door. The air in the hallway was a little clearer and Torrin was finally able to catch her breath. She whimpered in protest as Jak beat at the front of her pants legs. They had no time to rest. The flames already licked at the top of the doorway. Inside the room, the back wall and half the floor were already engulfed in flames. Most of the ceiling already burned fiercely, and thin runners raced their way across the floor.

Jak pulled her to her feet and they ran crouched down the hallway and to the top of the stairs. Behind them, she could hear the roar of the flames. They sounded like they were catching up.

"Come on," Jak shouted and pulled her down the stairs, two at a time. Torrin followed, keeping up easily with her long legs. In seconds they were across the living room and bursting through the front door.

Smoke-free air had never felt so good. Torrin staggered off the porch and sucked in great breaths of air. Jak coughed next to her.

"We can't stay here," she gasped between wracking hacks. "He'll know." Jak pointed up and Torrin followed her finger. A dark column of smoke billowed from the cabin. It stretched up toward the heavens, a black banner raised for attention.

"Torrin, is the major all right?" Perez's voice rang through her head on the heels of the introductory chime.

It was Torrin's turn to offer Jak support as she continued to cough. The woods would shelter them and Torrin swung Jak into her arms.

She was a good deal heavier than she'd been the last time Torrin had carried her, but Torrin staggered on.

"She'll be okay, I think." The muscles in Torrin's legs shivered from the strain. She needed to make it a little farther. "I'm all right too, thanks for asking."

"I'm coming down."

"No!" Jak looked up at her. "Perez wants to come down to meet us."

Jak shook her head. "Tell her to keep an eye out for him."

"Jak says to stay up there." They reached the shelter of the trees and Torrin put Jak down. Her coughing was lessening, but she still hacked out the occasional paroxysm. "The fire will tip off Crimson. He could be making his way over here."

"Got it. Let Major Stowell know I'm on it." Perez was gone and Torrin looked over at Jak, who sat with her back against a tree, her head hanging between upraised knees. She breathed slowly and deeply.

"Perez is keeping an eye out for him."

"Good." Jak looked up at her. "How are your legs?"

"They're fine. What do you mean?"

With a finger that shook only slightly, Jak pointed at her lower legs. Torrin looked down and sat down with a sudden thud. Her ghillie suit was burned away, almost to the waist. Below it, the legs of her pants were scorched and angry red skin peeked through burned holes. Pain jangled through her nerves, and she blinked stupidly at the ground. She was only dimly aware of Jak coming to kneel next to her.

"It's a good thing you were wearing that suit," Jak said as she carefully moved the burned fabric out of the way. "Otherwise, you'd be hurting bad right about now."

She hurt plenty as it was. Torrin stared at Jak, then back to her legs.

"Looks like second-degree burns. I don't see any charring." Jak pulled a small pack out of one of her ghillie suit's many pockets.

"Jak, it hurts." Torrin sucked in a deep breath through her teeth. "It really hurts."

"I know, babe." From the pack, she produced a small tube and squeezed the contents into her hand. "This will help with the pain." Carefully, Jak smoothed the ointment onto the angry red wounds on Torrin's legs.

Torrin clenched her fists and the ground dug into her fingertips. She panted, every movement of Jak's hands sending agony through her. After a few moments, blessed numbness chased away the pain and Torrin let out a pent-up sigh of relief.

"Better?" Jak looked up at her, forehead wrinkled with concern.

"Yes." Experimentally, Torrin moved her legs. There was still some discomfort, but it was manageable. She'd had more painful sunburns.

"Good." Jak stood up and stowed her first aid kit. "We need to get you out of here, ASAP."

"I'm fine. I can do this, it barely hurts at all."

"You don't get it, Torrin. He's on his way. We lit a nice big signal fire for him. I don't think he feels the need to spare me anymore. What he did to my bedroom was a nice big 'fuck you.'"

"So we get out of here and wait for him."

"You need medical attention, before your burns get infected. Crawling around out here will get all sorts of crap in them." Jak looked up at the sky. "I know you can reach the *Nightshade*. I want you to call for evacuation. Perez and I will get you humped out of here and over to the next valley where you can be lifted to safety."

Torrin laughed and Jak shot her a surprised glance over her shoulder. "It's perfect. Let's use that asshole's trap against him."

"I don't follow."

"We know he's on his way. What would draw him better than a nice, juicy target?"

"You want to draw him out with the *Nightshade*?"

"And with me. You wanted him to think I was you, that's why I'm in the ghillie suit right? So we wait a couple hours, then have the Banshees come for me. Hopefully, he won't be able to resist finishing you off."

Jak spun on her heel and stalked toward Torrin, her eyes blazing. "No fucking way. I won't permit you to expose yourself like that."

Her face an expressionless mask, Torrin stared at Jak. "So now it's your turn to tell me what I can't do? That didn't work so well when I tried it, if you recall." Frustrated, she ground her teeth. "You don't have a choice. You can't force me to call the *Nightshade* right now."

Desperation was evident in the taut lines around Jak's mouth and, with a sigh, Torrin reached out to touch her arm. "Honey, let me do this. I can help. I want to help, and you know as well as I do that he won't be able to resist. If he thinks you're being loaded onto an evacuation transport, he'll have to tip his hand. If he's as good as you say he is, you won't have a better chance."

Her brows drew down in a dark frown and Jak huffed an angry breath through her nose. Slowly, her face lightened and she reached down for Torrin's hand and squeezed it.

"Knowing you'll be exposed is going to kill me."

Torrin squeezed back. "I trust you." She gave Jak a crooked smile. "I know you can get him."

"All right. Call in the *Nightshade*. Let's get this set up. It better be soon, because I'm not leaving your side until there's someone here with you."

"I would expect nothing less." Torrin kept her fingers entwined with Jak's as she brought her other hand up to activate the subdermal transmitter. "*Nightshade*, come in."

The top of the ridge was cold. The worst of the fog had finally dissipated in the strong winds that had come up, but Jak had little shelter from the worst of the chilly gusts. From her vantage point, she could see most of the small valley below. Smoke still rose from the ruins of the only place she'd ever considered home. Her childhood had burned away in less than an hour. It saddened her, knowing that everything she'd come from was gone, but she felt curiously light. In a strange way, she felt unbound, like the cabin had been tethering her soul in place. With it gone, she was free to go where she wanted, to do what she willed. She had this one last thing to do and her future could finally exist again. Jak could almost, but not quite, feel it stretching in front of her, like a phantom limb of possibilities.

She took a quick peek down the valley through the scope. The smoke in the air made it a little hard for her to pick out Torrin, but she could make out her form in the midst of a few Banshees who clustered around, giving her medical attention. Perez and Hamilton had taken their places in other positions on the heights overlooking the valley. Between the three of them, they could cover the most likely routes into the ravine. Crimson knew the area, though not as well as Jak did, and she felt she could predict with a fair degree of accuracy which routes he might take.

Where had she gone wrong? She thought she'd read Crimson's intentions. They had gotten along really well as children and she thought that maybe he'd harbored some feelings for her, based on his actions. If he hadn't felt that way, then why hadn't he taken her out on any one of the number of occasions that he'd had her in his sights? And yet, the trap in her room had been set to eliminate her. A small shudder shook her frame. If Torrin hadn't been wearing the ghillie suit and it hadn't been damp from their trek through the woods, she would have been very badly burned. That she had been injured in Jak's place lit a slow-burning anger in her chest. It wasn't that she needed another reason to want Crimson dead, but he'd handed her another one anyway.

And what was he waiting for? They'd been set up for a couple hours. It had taken half that time for her father to drop her off at his family's house when they were children. Even taking his time and cutting through the woods instead of taking the game paths should have put him there by now.

Jak activated the transmitter clipped to her collar. "He's got to be here." She spoke quietly, trusting the sensitive microphone to pick up her voice. "Keep your eyes peeled."

She received two tones back in confirmation. Below, the Banshees moved with smooth assurance, never betraying they suspected someone might be watching

Jak started her sweep at the top of the ravine. It was the highest end of the valley and had a commanding view of everything below. The angle to Torrin's position wasn't great from there, but someone with Crimson's talent could easily manage the shot. She started there because it was the last place she expected to see him. In his shoes, she would have been looking for that last place.

As she reviewed the area, she let her eyes wander, keeping her mind open to anything that looked wrong, out of place. Even the subtlest feeling of wrongness drew her attention for a closer look. Each area turned out to be completely innocuous.

Methodically, Jak made her way over to the next point, a rocky outcropping two-thirds of the way down from the ridge. Her perusal again turned up no sign of Crimson. She struggled to keep her mind empty of worry, but concern writhed along the outside of her thoughts. If he got a shot off, Torrin was as good as dead.

She turned her attention to slowly clearing the slope on the opposite side of the valley. Frustrated, Jak turned her attention back to the head of the valley and went over it again. Now she focused her attention on those spots that wouldn't have given a decent vantage, but where the shot would still have been possible. Only years of discipline kept her from searching the quadrants covered by Perez and Hamilton. She had to trust that they knew what they were doing.

After the third circuit, Jak's anxiety was out of control. She throttled down the butterflies that mated in her stomach. This wasn't working. They had to get Torrin out of there. If Crimson was there, he would be getting suspicious that they weren't evacuating her to the ship.

"Take her up," Jak said into the transmitter. "Looks like he's a no-show."

"Roger." Olesya's voice came through her earpiece. Below Jak's position, she could see Olesya look up at the surrounding slopes. Jak cringed. If Crimson was there and hadn't been tipped off before, he was now. She swung herself around to check out the likeliest position.

"Jak, I'm not going up." Even through the transmitter's crappy speaker, Torrin sounded pissed. "We talked about this."

"You don't have an option," Jak said. She zoomed in her scope on the head of the valley. "Olesya, this isn't open for discussion. Get her out of here." Her anxiety had ramped up to a fever pitch and her instincts screamed at her. He was there, somewhere, and the longer Torrin sat out in the open, the greater the chance that she would catch a bullet in the throat.

"Yes sir." Olesya terminated the transmission, and drifting up from below, Jak heard the whine of the *Nightshade's* engines as they came online.

Frantically, she searched the closely packed trees on the slopes. Throwing discipline to the wind, she quartered her way across Perez's territory, then started surveying her way across Hamilton's. Finally, she caught her break. In the overlap between the territory being covered by Perez and Hamilton, almost out of view from her vantage, something was wrong. At first, Jak didn't even know what had drawn her attention, but she stopped over a nondescript stand of trees. One tree had gone down at some recent point, and bushes grew in the gap. For the barest moment, the leaves on one bush seemed to be blowing the wrong way.

She had him. Jak blew out a long, slow breath. After all these years, after all the pain he'd caused her—and to keep him from causing her further pain—she finally had the chance to take him out.

CHAPTER TWENTY-SEVEN

As soon as Jak pulled the trigger, she knew the bullet would fly true. It wasn't an easy shot; she was at an awkward angle to Crimson. The bullet lanced toward him and Jak's hopes went with it. Time slowed, and she floated with the bullet, down from her vantage point, spinning ever closer to the source of her misery.

Emptiness settled over her heart as leaves flew up from the bush. She lay, cold and waiting, hoping for some sign that Crimson was no more. Seconds dragged out and her scalp prickled. Something was wrong. There should have been an indication that she'd hit someone, but beyond the impact when she'd first sent her bullet in, the bush hadn't moved again. There was no blood, no body.

Jak pulled her rifle to her chest and rolled to the side. She had to move. In her haste to kill the bastard, she'd exposed her position. Only her stillness after the shot had gone out had saved her. At her first motion, she felt the air of the slug's passing, felt it tug at the tendrils of her ghillie suit. A sharp report shattered the air. That was way too close.

She needed to get away from the edge of the ledge, to melt back into the trees where he wouldn't have a clear shot. But anywhere he couldn't reach her, she couldn't reach him. If she was beyond his reach, then he was beyond hers. But unlike him, she wasn't out there alone.

Jak scrabbled at the transmitter's headset. Her fingers fumbled with it as she tried to keep moving, dodging and weaving, never giving him a clean shot. "Does anyone have a bead on him?"

Silence met her query and damp darkness enveloped her as she pulled further back into the trees. She crawled around a large tree and placed it between her and Crimson. She was safe, at least for the moment.

"I've got him." Satisfaction dripped from Perez's voice. "You almost had him, he was set up right near where you took your shot." She paused and when she continued her tone was subdued. "One more second… just need to…" Another report rang out. "Shit!"

"Missed him?" Jak was already moving; she knew the answer to the question. She pushed herself up from the ground and circled the base of the tree at a trot, hurdling over a downed log and heading parallel to the ridge.

"Yes Major. I can't believe I missed him." The shame Perez felt was palpable. "I didn't allow enough for drop, it went right over his head."

"It's all right," Jak gasped. She was sprinting now and her breath rasped in her throat. She ignored her laboring lungs. She wasn't going to let her damaged lungs slow her down; McCullock would not have the last laugh. "Hamilton, you're next closest to him." She slowed as she called up her map of the area. In the back of her mind, she blessed the planning that had led to her upload a sector map to her brain. She didn't need it to navigate, but it would help her direct the others.

"He's heading to these coordinates." She stopped and rattled off a stream of numbers, then took off again. "Have your AI direct you to them."

From his vantage, the best route back to his family's cabin was down the creek bed. It only filled up during the rainy season, which left it fairly dry for half the year. Surely, he would head that way. Fortunately, she was a little closer to it than he'd been.

Weaving in and out among the trees reminded her of games played with her brother and Lucian. How often had they roamed these woods, pretending to be chased by aetanberan or setting up pretend ambushes for infiltrating Orthodoxans? That game had turned out to be uncomfortably prescient. The woods hadn't changed much. In the details maybe. A tree down where it had once grown tall, a log they had once played on claimed by mushrooms and decay. The feeling remained the same, the trees waited, as they always had, impassive and incurious to the dramas that unfolded among them.

Jak crested the far ridge and angled to the south, heading for the creek bed. There was no way she was going to be sneaking up on anyone, but Crimson now knew she wasn't the only one out there. He would be running scared.

"Perez," Jak gasped into the transmitter. "Head to the valley using the coordinates I gave Hamilton." A rock rolled out from under her foot and she went down to one knee to keep from rolling her ankle with it. She slapped the ground with her left hand, keeping her rifle from hitting the dirt. The last thing she needed was to knock it out of alignment. Barely breaking her stride, she bounced back up. "Set up a good vantage." She panted. Running downhill was harder than running uphill. The smallest slip, the slightest loss of balance, and she would be rolling all the way down. "Scout the area out and report to me when I ask. See if you can figure out where he's keeping her."

The ground disappeared to her right and she headed toward the slight drop. All it took was a quick hop over a gentle bank and she was running down the creek bed. Haefen was so wet that even in the dry season, things didn't dry out completely. A trickle a little wider than her hand dug a narrow channel through packed dirt. She splashed through the water and tried to keep her eye on the ground in front of her and further down the slope at the same time. All she needed was a sign that she was on the right track. Going for the creek had been a gamble, a good one but a chance nonetheless. If he hadn't gone this way, there was no way of knowing where he would be.

Breath burned in her lungs, searing its tortured way in and out of her rib cage. Stubbornly, she refused to slow. Too many people were counting on her. Nat, Torrin, Bron, her father, Collins… The list felt like it weighed a ton, but she couldn't let it go. This one last task would set her free.

A footprint stood out in stark relief in the middle of a puddle of mud. Jak would have sobbed with relief, but she couldn't suck in enough breath to do so. She was on the right track. Lifting her eyes, she scanned the slope below her for any sign of Crimson. There was nothing and she pushed herself on.

Her foot caught in something and she went flying forward to land on her chest. Somehow, Jak managed to keep from landing on her rifle, but since she wouldn't break her fall, her body took the brunt of the impact. What little air she'd dragged into her lungs was expelled in an explosion of breath and saliva, and she slid on her front before fetching up against a young tree. At the last moment, she ducked her head and managed to avoid slamming her forehead into the trunk. For a second, she lay there, taking stock.

You're fine. She pushed herself up again and kept on. Her suit caught on branches that reached out and snagged her, hindering her progress. Her arms and legs were leaden and it was an effort to keep moving forward. The air was sand in her lungs and she wheezed. An audible rattle was all she could hear as her body tried to keep up with the demands she'd placed on it. She had to trust that the Banshees were following her instructions. If they'd tried to report back to her, she wasn't sure she'd hear them.

A flash of movement through the trees in front of her gave her flagging feet a burst of speed. There he was, further down the slope where the creek bed curled around a short bluff. She caught sight of him a moment before he disappeared around the bluff's corner. Jak's fatigue fell from her and she dodged through the trees. She hurdled over the creek's far bank and back into the thick of the woods. The creek bed ran along the bluff's bottom for a short way. Now was her chance to make up some ground on him.

The going was definitely slower—the underbrush was thicker here and she was still being slowed down by her ghillie suit. She wished she could shed it. The safety it brought in concealment was useless now and she needed all the speed she could get.

The trees thinned in front of her and she burst out along the cliff's edge. The terrain was rocky and she moved more easily, making up ground. Crimson was making no effort to conceal his passage; she could see him easily, sprinting along the creek bed, water and mud splashing up from beneath his pounding feet.

Being so close to her quarry gave her another burst of energy and she pushed herself, not caring about anything except getting to him. She drew abreast of him and grinned. He'd given no indication that he knew she was so close. He glanced back occasionally, but never up. Mostly he looked forward, raising his arms to keep branches away from his face.

It was now or never. Jak threw herself forward with one last burst of speed, then pushed off the cliff's edge, her arms and legs churning in empty air. For a second, she felt suspended in nothingness before falling forward. She slammed into his back and he went down in a heap. Her rifle, forgotten in one hand, went spinning off into the trees. Jak grabbed for the back of his head, intending to slam it into the ground. Crimson was too fast. She thought he would have been stunned, but he was able to flip over, squirming away before she could get a good grip on him.

Brown eyes stared into hers, dilated with shock. She recognized them. The eyes of her childhood friend stared at her out of the face of a stranger. They both hesitated and were still for the barest moment before Jak lunged, wrapping her fingers around his throat, digging her thumbs up under his jaw. Those familiar brown eyes blinked, then narrowed as rage crawled across his face, twisting his mouth until slightly yellowed teeth were bared at her.

He pushed himself up, dragging her along with him, and she was forced to let go of his neck. Crimson towered over her; he was huge. Lucian had never been a big kid. Where had the height come from? she wondered incongruously. The chances of gaining the upper hand in close-quarters combat with him were slim and she reached for her pistol.

Crimson's eyes narrowed and he lunged at her before she could raise the gun. He caught her with one arm around the waist, bearing her back to the ground with him, slamming her shoulders and back into the unyielding turf. Somehow, Jak kept her hold on the pistol. Lips pulled back into a snarl and teeth bared, she slammed the butt viciously into the side of his head.

He lost his grip and reeled away, holding both hands to his head. Jak scrabbled backward away from him, legs pushing her away and barely catching herself on outstretched hands. Something was wrong with her left arm; it gave out beneath her when she tried to put her weight on it. She fetched up against the hard-packed dirt of the bluff, unable to stop the cry of pain that forced its way past her lips.

Barely out of arm's reach, Crimson's eyes cleared and snapped over to her at the sound. Jak raised the pistol and pointed it at him.

"Try it," she said. She wanted him to. It would make things so much easier. Shooting him would have been easier from behind or from the comfortable distance of her rifle's scope. This close, she saw the eyes of her friend, and they pulled at her, reminding her of a time when life had been simpler, before her deception had complicated everything.

She needn't have wasted her voice. Crimson didn't seem to hear her. The brown eyes she knew held no sign of recognition. He moved forward, deliberately at first, and Jak squeezed the trigger, but then he was coming at her with the speed of a striking snake. His outstretched arm smacked into the pistol and knocked it to one side right as it went off with a thunderous roar. He had enough momentum that even though the bullet went through his shoulder, he still clipped her on the chin with her fist. Arms flailing, he disappeared backward down the hill.

Jak's head snapped back and light exploded across her vision when the back of her head impacted with the wall. Her vision went gray and she bit her lip. *No, I'm not going to lose it, not now.* She focused on the pain in her lip and bit down harder as the shadows at the edge of her field of vision threatened to overwhelm her. Blood ran down her chin.

The darkness receded. She thought she'd held it together, but when she raised her head, Crimson was gone.

"Fuck." Jak pushed herself up and the forest swam before her eyes. She shook her head and the trees settled into place with a nauseating snap. "Fuck!" Did she go after him now or try to find her rifle? She hesitated, then turned toward the creek bed. He was going to continue down there until he got back to wherever he'd stashed Nat. Jak had no illusions over what would happen if he got there before her. Nat was as good as dead unless she went after him. "Fuck, fuck, fuck!" She couldn't stop angry tears, and she dashed them angrily from her eyes and pushed on.

Jak was in bad shape and she knew it. Her left arm hung uselessly at her side and her back ached. She wondered if any of her ribs were broken. The beating she'd taken so recently had been healed, but how well? After a few deep inhalations, she went into a paroxysm of coughing. Her breath rattled through her throat, but her ribs didn't hurt that much more. Bruised, she thought, maybe cracked at worst. Her only encouragement was that he was in at least as bad a shape as she was.

A splash of scarlet caught her eye. Crimson was definitely in bad shape; he was leaving a blood trail. The hole she'd put in his shoulder would slow him down and lead her right to him. Jak smiled and ignored the small flash of pain and the renewed drip of blood down her chin as the bite in her lip opened further. Her quarry was injured and running from her, but she could feel herself closing in.

* * *

"Captain Yozhin, the captain of the *Icarus* is demanding to speak to you." The AI's impersonal tones filtered through the medbay and Torrin looked over at Axe.

"What's going on?"

"We had to break off our operation with the Leaguers to come to your rescue. They're a little put out with us right now." Axe shrugged, her face showing nothing but unconcern for the League's attitudes. "Some things are more important. They should understand about priorities."

"You're damn right, some things are more important."

The *Nightshade*'s autodoc was more advanced and much more powerful than the one she had on the *Calamity Jane*. The damage had been deeper than she'd known but was almost all healed now. Torrin itched to get back down to Haefen's surface. She needed to know what was going on.

"There's no need to worry, Torrin. We know where our sympathies lie. I do wish I knew what to do with the mole."

Torrin stared at Axe, astounded. "He's here?"

"I told you, we were in the middle of the operation. Once we isolated Crimson's voice, we spoofed it and set up a meet. When he showed, we picked him up."

"What happened to tracking him by his voice?"

"The Devonite Army is busy stopping a full-blown Orthodoxan invasion through a tunnel in the hills. We didn't have anyone who would let us run the voice print against their records, so we had to improvise."

"Who is he?"

Axe lifted one shoulder and let it fall. "No idea, but I don't know who any of these yahoos are."

"Is he Intel?"

"He doesn't seem to be. Doesn't say much except to threaten to do all sorts of terrible things to us." Anger twisted her mouth. "He tries any of that with my women, and he'll be left without the proper equipment to do what he's promising."

"I should see him." Torrin looked down in frustration at the mechanical arm that still passed back and forth over her leg. "How much longer?"

"Only a few minutes now." The medic looked up from the other side of the autodoc and smiled. "I'd heard you served with us a while back and it shows. You're like everyone else around here—ready to get back out there and throw yourself in harm's way."

"I've got people down there."

The medic's smile dimmed. "Don't we all."

At Torrin's questioning glance, Axe shook her head.

"Captain?" The AI's questioning tones floated through the room again. "How would you like me to respond?"

Axe exhaled a small huff of irritation. "Let's see how much longer we can put her off. I'm not going to break off now, not with Major Stowell down there after that asshole."

"Have you heard anything from her?"

"You're good to go," the Banshee medic announced. The autodoc's arm retracted and Torrin checked out her shiny new skin as it gleamed in the medbay's bright lights.

"Not that I've been told," Axe said, moving out of the way so Torrin could stand. She activated the transmitter behind her ear. "Has anyone heard from Major Stowell?"

A long pause met her query before Torrin heard Olesya respond, "Hamilton and Perez report that they haven't heard from her since she gave the order to head over to the next valley."

Torrin stopped in her tracks at the news. The medbay's doors waited patiently for her.

"I need to get down there now."

"And do what?" Axe activated her transmitter again. "Lieutenant, do we have a lock on the major?"

"Negative, Captain. Her transmitter hasn't moved for a few minutes. We think she lost it."

"Fuck, Olesya!" Torrin couldn't stop the expletive from bursting out of her mouth. She wished she had it back as soon as it came out, but it was too late. Nothing to do for it but push on and apologize later. "Either she's lost the transmitter or she's injured." *Not dead, not dead, not dead,* she chanted in her mind. *Never dead.*

She felt a hand on her arm and looked up into Axe's understanding eyes. The captain raised her hand in a mollifying gesture.

"Let's get a squad into a shuttle and down to the surface to check on the major."

"I'm going."

From the eye roll Torrin received, she needn't have bothered with the statement.

"I know. It's going to take the Banshees a few minutes to get ready. Let's stop by the brig so you can take a look at our captive before you head down."

"That works for me. Can we get me some body armor also?"

"We'll get you completely kitted out. The body armor won't be fitted to you though."

"That's fine, I can deal with a little discomfort while we're backing up Jak."

The captain led Torrin through the ship to its bowels. On the *Jane*, the area would have been part of the cargo bay. Here, it was devoted to storage space for military hardware and prisoners. Not that the Banshees had many opportunities to transport prisoners. Most of the time when they went out on a mission, they were rescuing women who'd been held captive. Their way of dealing with the women's captors was to eliminate them, not to imprison them. On occasion, however, they would pick up some piece of human refuse and turn him in to law enforcement on planets with more progressive codes of law.

Torrin wished that it was only men the Banshees had caught. On one of her last runs, the one that had convinced her to make a career change, the mastermind behind the slavers had been a woman. The conditions in which they'd found the poor women who'd been under her thumb were the worst she'd ever seen. She still didn't understand how a woman could do that to other women. The slaver queen hadn't been lucky enough to be offered a ride in the brig.

The man sat in the small cell with his back to them.

"Hey asshole." Axe knocked on the wall next to the cell's opening. He hunched his shoulders but didn't turn around. "Someone wants to talk to you." There was no answer.

"I don't have time for this," Torrin said.

"Don't worry about it. We'll get a few extra hands in here, he won't have a choice."

At Torrin's voice, the mole curled further in on himself. His shoulders relaxed in resignation and he turned his head enough for Torrin to see his profile.

"You?" She stepped forward but was stopped by the force field that stood in for the cell's front wall. "I thought it would be…"

"Who?" He stood and walked to the front of the cell and stood, barely half a meter separating them. "Wolfe? He was certainly vocal enough about his displeasure, but he couldn't be bothered to actually act on it. Or maybe McCullock. He was scum, but ultimately too honorable."

Torrin had seen the man a couple of times but had never spoken to him; she didn't even know his name, but she knew his position. "Colonel Elsby's clerk," Torrin said to Axe. "Elsby heads up Intel and is one of Callahan's right-hand men. Looks like McCullock was right about the mole being close to the top. He would have had access to pretty much everything Elsby did."

"A clerk? How could a clerk do so much damage? And why?"

"That's the real question." Torrin stared at the man. "So why did you do it? Why betray your people?"

The clerk leaned forward and spat at her, the glob of spit sizzled when it hit the force field and dissipated before it had run halfway down to the floor.

"I don't think we're going to get much from him," Axe said. "This is the most we've gotten from him so far. I'll have a couple of the Banshees…interrogate him." She smiled unpleasantly and the prisoner took half a step back before sneering at her.

"I'm not scared of any mere woman."

"Good." Her smile slid from unpleasant to terrifying. "We'll enjoy teaching you otherwise."

The clerk swallowed hard and retreated to the back of the cell where he sat on the room's narrow bed. He glowered at them.

"We don't have time for this," Torrin said. Axe took the lead again and led her away from the cell and out of the brig. Across the hall was another door; when Axe opened it, the sound of women talking at the top of their lungs rolled over them.

"Captain on deck," snapped a tall non-com, bulky in her matte black armor. Silence spread through the room as if someone had thrown a sheet over a cage of particularly talkative Myrrandian macaws. The women, in various states of dishabille, came to attention and saluted Axe.

"At ease," she said, saluting them in return. "Sergeant Shao, get Torrin here outfitted in some body armor. You should have been briefed that she would be accompanying you planetside."

"Yes Captain," Shao replied.

"Get her kitted up in a hurry. The shuttle's going to be ready in five minutes." Axe gripped Torrin's forearm. "Good luck, Torrin. And bring the major back to us in one piece."

"You know I will."

Axe smiled and squeezed her arm before letting go. She saluted Torrin before turning on her heel and leaving the room.

"I've been told you know your way around a suit of body armor," Shao said while leading her back to an unattended locker.

Around them, the noise level rose again as the women returned to the business of getting geared up for their mission. Torrin watched them engage in the rough-housing and bullshitting many of the women got up to as a way to relieve some of their premission jitters. Some women sat quietly by themselves with eyes closed in quiet contemplation. Everyone had their own way of dealing with the nerves that cropped up before it was time to get down to business, and it was good to see that some things didn't change. Torrin had been among those who got boisterous as her adrenaline level started ramping up, but not this time. She was focused on one thing: her family.

"I do. It's been a while though."

"You'll be borrowing Private DeFresne's suit. It's not powered. We don't have the time to get you hooked into all that." Shao pulled open the locker, pulled out a jumpsuit and handed it to Torrin. "She's close enough to your size that it should fit all right."

Torrin stripped out of her clothing and pulled on the undersuit. She had no qualms about getting naked in front of these women. Shao handed her a pair of boots, followed by shin guards. While Torrin strapped herself into the leg gear, Shao started strapping her into the bulky chest protection. Between the two of them, they got her outfitted with no time to spare. A two-toned chime rang through the locker room.

"That's our cue," Shao said. She handed Torrin a bulky helmet and plasma rifle. "Move it out, Banshees. You too, Ivanov."

The implication was obvious. Torrin might have been one of them a while back, and they were extending her certain courtesies, but she was still a civilian. She got the message and nodded to Shao. She would do her best to stay out of their way; the last thing they needed was someone else to cover, someone to pull them out of the rhythm of their training and experience.

Two abreast, the six women trooped out of the locker room, followed by Shao and Torrin. The armor weighed more than she remembered. It also bound and rubbed in a number of places. By the end of this, she would have some raw spots, but if the other option was to stay put up here while Jak faced who knew what on Haefen's surface, she would gladly make that trade again. Power armor would have been nice though.

Though she was crammed with the Banshees into a small shuttle, Torrin couldn't help but think back to the missions she'd been part of back when she'd still been in active service. Looking around the shuttle, she wondered which of the women wouldn't be coming back. The all-too-familiar sick dread settled into the pit of her stomach.

She watched out the window as they cleared the *Nightshade*. Haefen's beautiful blues shimmered in the lower half of the window. They flew along smoothly for a couple of minutes before the shuttle began to bounce around on atmospheric entry. The turbulence of the atmosphere was a fitting metaphor, she mused. Her own thoughts were easily as disordered and frantic. Trying to clear her mind, Torrin stared out the window and sorted through mental pictures of Jak and Nat, remembering them in happier times.

CHAPTER TWENTY-EIGHT

"The pilot ran a thorough scan as we came in," Shao said. She spoke to Torrin, but her eyes were on the trees, scanning for any sign of enemy activity. They might be in friendly territory, but Torrin approved of Shao's vigilance. She was never quite sure exactly how friendly the Devonites actually were.

"Anything?"

"None. The pilot picked up Perez and Hamilton, but no sign of Major Stowell, Nat, or the Orthodoxan sniper."

The Banshees were spread out around them, each as aware of her surroundings as Shao.

"They have to be around here somewhere. They can't all have disappeared." Torrin looked around. The small bluff rose above her, casting a shadow over the mostly dry creek bed in which they stood. "According to your AI, Jak's signal stopped moving right around here."

Shao nodded. "You three," she barked, indicating the closest Banshees, "you're on overwatch with me. The rest of you, see if you can find the major."

The Banshees didn't answer; instead they sprang into action. The first three fanned out even further, forming a loose perimeter around their group. The rest of them commenced a visual scan of the area. Torrin joined them in searching. Jak's signal was strong to within fifty meters. If she was around, she should have been easy to spot. The trees grew thick along the creek bed and the undergrowth was dense.

"She's wearing a ghillie suit," Torrin said, activating her subdermal transmitter. She didn't want to shout. "If she's here, she'll be difficult to find. Check every piece of vegetation."

There was no response, but Torrin hadn't expected one. One possible explanation for the pilot's inability to locate Jak was that she was dead, whispered the traitorous little voice in her head. Torrin ignored it and kept looking.

Methodically, they combed through the bushes and between the trees while the rest of the Banshees covered them.

"Ma'am," one of the Banshees called to her. From where the woman stood next to the creek bed, she held up Jak's transmitter. Torrin moved to join her, dodging bushes that threatened to trip her up. The other Banshees involved in the search joined them.

"Looks like she took a tumble," a long-haired corporal said. She crouched in the mud of the creek bed, paying no heed to the trickle of water that moved sluggishly around her feet. "She jumped up quick enough, it looks like. She was chasing someone, a man by the size of the prints."

There were two sets of footprints in the mud, even Torrin could see that.

"Petra, follow the tracks," Shao said. "The rest of you, patrol formation."

The Banshee nodded and pulled her dark braid over one shoulder before standing. She handled her weapon casually, and Torrin had no doubt that she knew how to use it. No one made it into the field with the Banshees without being well-trained. They were picky as hell and only the best were welcomed into their ranks. At one time, Torrin had been inordinately pleased to be counted among their number. She'd stuck it out for three years, but the grim reality of their work had ground her down. The nightmares had mostly faded, but being back among them, she could feel the tension deep in her bones again. Torrin was more on edge than she'd ever been during a mission. Back then, she'd known that women were in trouble, but they'd never been anyone she knew.

Petra followed the tracks quickly, almost at a trot. They were clear, even to Torrin. Neither Jak nor Crimson had been doing anything to hide sign of their passage.

"They had quite a scuffle here," Petra said, coming to a stop. She followed the tracks back and forth before kneeling next to a large patch of disturbed dirt. "Looks like the major injured the Orthodoxan, but she didn't get out scot-free. He went down over there." She pointed down the hill. "The major followed him. Neither of them was moving very fast after their encounter. I'd say they're both injured to some degree, and one of them is bleeding."

"Is it Jak?"

Petra shook her head. "I can't tell for sure. I think it's him, but the trail is confused."

"Nothing to do but follow them, is there?"

"I'm afraid so, ma'am." Petra stood and continued on, slower this time.

To Torrin's inexpert eyes, the trail meandered more now, sometimes disappearing for short stretches before she caught sight of another footprint further down the creek bed. Petra seemed to have no problem following the trail, though, even when there were no signs that Torrin could see.

They followed the trail down the hill and back to the creek bed where it wandered down one side of the valley. Eventually, the creek broke through the trees and into a large clearing. Or at least something that had once been a clearing. Haefen's trees were reclaiming the area and had been for some time. Saplings grew tall, competing with each other to reach the most sunlight. Some of the young trees were already close to five meters tall.

Torrin's transmitter chimed and a familiar voice spoke in her ear. "I see you," said Perez. "The coordinates she gave us puts us twenty meters from the Orthodoxan's old home."

"Got it," Shao said. "Did you see the major and Crimson come through here?"

"Negative, Sergeant."

Shao looked over at Petra.

"They came through here, Sergeant," Petra reported. "But it looks like they were doing their best not to be seen. At least he was. The trail follows the edge of those trees. I bet those blocked Perez's view."

Shao reached up behind her ear. "What about you, Hamilton?"

"I can't see you, Sergeant. I didn't see the major or the Orthodoxan, but I got into position after Perez did. They could have already been gone by then."

"Sergeant, the major asked me to scope out possible places where Nat could be hidden. Only place I see around here is the burned-out cabin."

Shao glanced inquiringly over at Torrin, who nodded. "Cover us, we're going to check it out." Shao turned to the Banshees, and after a series of gestures, they split into two groups and spread out. "Your choice, Ivanov. Do you want to go with the group that's checking out the cabin or follow the tracks with Petra's group?"

Torrin stood there, torn by indecision. This was the choice she'd been dreading, the choice she'd managed to avoid so far, but couldn't any longer. Her sister or her lover? She couldn't go after both. Shao watched her, eyes sympathetic and face impassive as Torrin glanced back and forth between her and Petra.

Taking a few measured breaths and forcing her pounding heart to calm, Torrin forced herself to look at the problem objectively. Flying off the handle into a nervous tizzy wasn't going to help anyone. If the pilot hadn't seen any sign of Nat in this area, then it wasn't likely that she was in the ruins of the cabin. Really, Shao was probably heading that way mostly to cover their bases. If they were following Jak who was following Crimson, then he would probably lead them to her sister.

"I'm going with Petra," Torrin finally said. "My money's on following the bastard to Nat. We can pick Jak up on the way." Her attempt at breezy confidence fell somewhat flat, but wisely, no one commented.

Shao nodded, her face impassive as ever. "If we don't find anything, we'll follow your group in." She joined the waiting Banshees.

"Ready when you are, ma'am," Petra said.

"Good. Let's move out then."

Petra peered back at the ground. "They went that way," she said, pointing along the tree line.

The other two Banshees spread out to flank her, watching the trees and clearing with equal intensity. Torrin was left to bring up the rear. As she followed along in their wake, her training was trickling back to her. She swept their backtrail, watching for signs of anyone following them. She wasn't able to manage the stealth the Banshees did and she smiled a bit, imagining Jak's amusement as she tried to play soldier again. Still, she didn't think she was doing too badly for herself.

The route they followed was circuitous and kept to the edge of the trees. Torrin had a hard enough time tracking the Banshees; the active camouflage of their body armor blended into the background. After the third time she turned around and had to stop to acquire them visually, she decided enough was enough. She decided to resort to the heat-imaging sensor in her visor to keep track of them.

When they passed back in among the trees, Torrin gave a mental groan. The ambient light dwindled quickly there, and the trees closed around them in a hurry. Torrin was reminded of the deep woods she and Jak had passed through on their way back from Hutchinson's compound. They were going uphill and she figured they were on the other side of the valley.

"Watch out for local wildlife," she said when Petra stopped to check the trail again. "It can be very aggressive and at least as dangerous as the Orthodoxans. More so, probably." The Banshees nodded and returned to watching their surroundings. Rocks and fallen branches conspired to take them down with every other step.

Petra pulled down the visor on her helmet. Torrin assumed she was engaging the helmet's night-vision capabilities and decided to do the same. Being able to see heat signatures wasn't helping her avoid natural obstacles in the darkness under the trees.

They followed the trail a short way before Petra stopped in front of a large rockfall. Above them, a cliff jutted out of the hillside. At some point, part of the cliff had come down, leaving a jumble of rocks with trees that stuck out at haphazard angles. The fall was old, the trees long dead.

"Trail leads up to the rocks," Petra said. "Watch my back while I try to pick it back up again."

Torrin and the Banshees set themselves up in a rough semicircle around their position while Petra combed the ground. "Any luck?" Torrin called over her shoulder when the waiting started to get to her. One of the Banshees threw her an amused look which she ignored.

"Yes and no." Petra's voice was disgruntled. "I didn't find their tracks, but I think I know where they ended up. There's an opening in the rocks. I bet they went down there."

"So we follow them then." Torrin wasn't asking; she was telling. She recognized that she had no authority to order the Banshees around, but if they didn't want to follow her orders, she would be going down there alone. Besides, it made sense. The pilot hadn't found any trace of them on the surface, but if they were underground, they wouldn't have shown up on a surface scan.

Pausing only to mark an arrow on the rocks, Petra ducked her head and stepped through the opening. The mark glowed in the low light; Shao would have no problems following them when she got to their position. Torrin ducked into the cave right on Petra's heels and the other Banshees followed them in.

"Rock floor," Petra said. "No good for tracking."

Torrin looked down. Petra was right. The ground was rocky and dry. Very little existed to be disturbed. They followed the passage for a short way before it opened up.

"Shit." Torrin looked around, the passage branched three ways. "Now what?"

Petra studied the ground but shook her head. "There's nothing for it. We need to split up."

Jak's shoulder throbbed and her lungs burned. Crimson wasn't moving any faster than she was, so at least she was able to catch her breath, but she couldn't seem to make up any ground on him. Somewhere along the way, he'd managed to slow the bleeding. She hadn't found nearly as many blood spots along his trail. Fortunately, he wasn't doing a very good job of hiding his trail.

When he'd skirted around the clearing, she'd been surprised. When Nat hadn't turned up at her family's cabin, she'd been convinced he would stash her in the ruins of his family's home, but he never went near it.

She clambered over a small rockfall in the middle of a long, narrow passageway. The cave had been dry enough when she'd entered it, but this area was damp. It was difficult to get a good grip to pull herself over it when she grasped her knife in the same hand. The pistol had ended up somewhere in the woods, knocked there when he struck her, and somewhere along the way, she'd lost her transmitter and with it contact with Hamilton and Perez. She hoped they'd followed her instructions. Not that it would help her much. It was down to her and Crimson. She was in no shape for a fight, but then, neither was he. If they couldn't help her, she was on her own to keep him from killing Nat.

For a moment, Jak teetered at the top of the pile, her feet sliding on wet rock. The small light clipped to the front of her fatigues bounced, sending shadows skewing across the walls. It had quickly become too dark for her night vision without some help. She caught her balance, but only barely, and wrenched her injured shoulder in the process. Her vision narrowed for a moment, and she breathed deeply to keep from passing out. Or at least she tried to. Something in there was definitely not right. With gritted teeth, she pressed on. Crimson was somewhere in this system of caves, but she didn't know where.

Idly, she wondered if these caves were the way the Orthodoxans had been infiltrating the area when she was younger. It was close enough to Crimson's home, practically on top of it really. If a family member had discovered the entrance, it might explain why the entire family had been wiped out.

Her mind was wandering and she dragged it back on task. Any sign of Crimson's passing would be helpful. This was the last passage and she hadn't seen any sign of him down the other two. She'd wasted too much time down wrong passages already. The longer she spent looking for him, the more time he had to do what he wanted to Nat. The threat to Torrin's sister sharpened her focus, and she forced herself on through the pain and exhaustion that threatened to cloak her mind.

Ahead, the narrow passage, little more than a crack, opened into a large gallery. Jak heard a voice raised in anger, and she slowed, hiding right inside the passage, checking out the large cave. She turned off her light. The last thing she needed was alert to him to her presence. She couldn't see him, but she could definitely hear him. Crimson chanted, his voice kicking up eerie echoes as it bounced around the cave.

"You might as well come out." His voice was a strange combination of anger and entreaty. "Come out, come out, little girl, little girl." He paused, waiting for an answer that didn't come. "You can't keep what's mine from me. If you come out now, it'll be soooo much easier for you. So, so much easier. Otherwise, when I find you, your death will be long. Long and lingering. Come out now, and I promise to kill you quickly."

It was strange, but Nat didn't take him up on his offer. *Good girl, Nat.* Jak wondered where she could be hiding. She turned on her light at its lowest setting. The light it emitted was barely visible to the naked eye, but when she engaged her eyes' night-vision capabilities, she could hardly make out the cavern's rock formations. Hopefully there wasn't enough light for Crimson to notice. There was no sign of a light from him and presumably he'd adopted the same strategy. She knew he was out there, but a little light could be easily blocked by the piled rocks and columns that filled the chamber.

She slipped into the cave and concealed herself behind the base of a large stalagmite. The chamber was large and lined with many pillars and spikes. It reminded her of the cave series she'd navigated with Smythe and Alston, except here she didn't see any signs of artificial excavation.

Taking a chance, Jak crept away from the pillar toward higher ground. Pausing for a moment, she carefully shed the ghillie suit, taking care not to make any noise. It wasn't going to do her any good in her current environment. The opposite in fact. A bush slithering around an underground cavern would be more than a little out of place. At the moment, she needed every advantage she could get, and freeing herself up for maximum movement definitely qualified.

Somewhere in the cavern, Crimson still chanted away in his singsong voice. It was hard to pinpoint where he was calling from; echoes bounced crazily through the rock formations.

Jak crept forward again, heading toward the far corner where his voice seemed loudest. She slunk along the base of a ledge, making her way slowly closer. Half the rocks were covered with algae and slime, slowing her progress considerably. Water dripped around her as it likely had for millennia, each drop marking her forward progress like a halting metronome. And over it, Crimson's continued entreaties rang out.

Finally, she sheathed the knife in her thigh holster. With her good arm freed up, she was able to make better progress, though it was still much slower than she would have liked. Jak chafed at her slowness but forced herself to move deliberately. One wrong move and she would betray her presence to the Orthodoxan.

By the time she made her way over to the far corner, she was drenched in sweat. It ran down her face and collected at the end of her nose and dripped into her eyes. She blinked rapidly to clear the stinging liquid as it accumulated and her vision swam.

The corner was empty. She could see no sign of anyone. Crimson's voice was softer now, moving away from her. The acoustics were impossible and she despaired at being able to track him down by sound. She'd already quartered the cavern one way. The best way to search the place would be to continue the process. If she couldn't find where he was, her next best bet was to find where he wasn't.

Jak gritted her teeth and moved on, working her way across the cavern at an angle to her original course. She kept her eyes open and her ears peeled.

"Come on out." Crimson's voice rang out loud, and she froze, her heart in her throat. She scrabbled for her knife, her hands slick with sweat and stood there, trying to control her panting. "You know I'll find you sooner or later. Sooner than later. Soon, soon. Any moment now…" His voice trailed off and Jak relaxed. It was only some trick of acoustics that had made it sound like he was on top of her, yelling in her ear.

To her left, Jak heard the unmistakable scrape of stone on stone. She swiveled and peered into the shadows, trying to determine what had made the noise. Quickly, she realized that she was still standing, frozen, out in the open. She scuttled to the nearest pile of rocks, taking care to keep it between her and the scraping she'd heard.

Try as she might, Jak was unable to make out what might have caused the noise. Was it Nat? Or was it Crimson? It was equally likely to have been pebbles falling from the ceiling, shaken loose from where they'd sat for an eternity, waiting passively for gravity to pull them from their perches. With all the possibilities that it might not be, even the slimmest chance that Nat had made the noise forced Jak to investigate.

A hulking slope was split through by a narrow channel. If Jak was right, the sound had come from in there. It looked like a good hiding spot. Crimson's voice had faded again. He sounded almost like he'd left the cavern, like he was calling out from an adjacent gallery.

Jak eased her way cautiously toward the large crack. She glanced at the slope, gauging how easy it was to climb. If she'd had two good arms, she wouldn't have stopped to question herself, but with one arm completely useless, she decided not to chance it. Fat lot of good she would be to Nat if she fell and broke open her skull. With a final glance around, her eyes aching as she tried to pierce the gloom, she slipped into the crack.

The walls quickly closed around her. She hadn't thought it possible, but she was sweating even more now. Her eyes stung from the sweat that ran into them almost without cease. Jak ran a tongue around lips gone suddenly dry and came back with salt. Her heart hammered in her chest, and she fought the almost overwhelming urge to go back the way she had come. The walls were closing in around her, tightening on her body; they would trap her in place. She stopped and extended her arm, touching the side of the crevice, trying to prove to herself that the walls weren't actually moving. The feel of solid rock under her palm steadied her a bit and she took a deep breath. Before she could make the decision to go back, she pushed on, shuffling her feet. The ground was wet. A couple of centimeters of water covered the bottom of the crevice and her purchase was tenuous at best.

Her claustrophobia wasn't helped by the fact that the walls came in closer the further she went. Jak estimated that she hadn't gone more than ten meters, but she felt like she'd run a marathon. Her breath rasped from her mouth. Ahead of her, the walls narrowed even further. It was going to be a tight fit, but she was fairly certain that she could slide through if she turned herself sideways. Maybe. But what if she couldn't? Her mounting anxiety slowed her to a crawl.

What if I get stuck? She would be a sitting duck for Crimson, with no way to defend herself or to escape. Precious seconds trickled by as she contemplated the narrow slit. With a convulsive swallow, she forced herself to keep moving. Nat was depending on her.

She was right. There was barely enough room for her to get through. The stone scraped against her shoulder and the barest touch sent agony raging through her. Once again, she chewed at her lip, trying to keep from crying out. Her breathing was ragged, the heaving of her rib cage adding to the pain in her shoulder. The only solace she could find from the situation was that the noise she was tracking down couldn't have been made by Crimson. There was no way he could have fit through this crack. If the noise wasn't falling stones, then it might be Nat. The thought was all that pushed her on.

The crevice widened and she moaned quietly at the relief from the pain in her shoulder and back. She stumbled into a round bowl. Water from the ceiling had carved out an almost perfectly round depression in the large rocks. The top of the bowl narrowed over her head. It was a good hiding place; it would be hard to see from the top, but was so dark that she would barely have been able to make anything out had it not been for the small light she'd clipped to her jacket.

A whisper of fabric on stone was the only warning she had. She turned as an object came hurtling at her head, threw herself to the side and cried out when her left arm hit the wall, wrenching it back. Pain speared through her back and shoulder.

"Stay back!" The hissed order filtered out of the shadows on the opposite side of the bowl. Terror quivered on the edge of her voice.

"Nat, it's me." She whispered back, trying to keep her voice down, probably unnecessarily. It was likely she'd already compromised their position. "It's Jak."

"Jak?" Nat's voice broke. "It's really you? I'm not dreaming?" There was more rustling on the bowl's far side and Nat moved forward, out of the shadows and into the pale beam of light from her jacket. Jak drew back in shock, unable to process what she saw. Torrin's sister was scrawny and filthy. Her clothing was torn in multiple places and covered in grime. Jak could see her collarbone through a rent in the fabric. It jutted out against her skin in sharp relief.

"It really is." She sidled forward, trying to get closer. Her light was so dim, she knew Nat likely wouldn't be able to see. Nat squinted at her and Jak reached out to grab her outstretched hand. Tears threatened as she watched Nat's face go slack with relief, some of the terrible load of the past month finally lifting. Nat brought her other hand around and grasped Jak's hand between them. A tear traced a pale furrow through the grime encrusted on her face.

"How did you…Where did…How did this happen?"

"No time for that now. We need to get you out of here before Crimson finds us."

A whisper from above and a heavy thud behind her sent a chill through Jak's veins.

"Too late." His voice was heavy with malice. Gone was the playful singsong quality.

Shoving Nat behind her, Jak turned to face him. He loomed over her in the dark. A vise locked itself around her neck, and she struggled, trying to draw breath.

"I thought putting a bullet through your neck from a thousand meters away was a fitting way to end you. I like this way better." He squeezed her neck even harder.

CHAPTER TWENTY-NINE

Crimson's fingers dug into her throat and Jak's legs twitched as she lost her purchase on his arm. Vainly, she kicked her legs, trying to reach the ground. Her vision narrowed, the edges folding in on her.

"I waited for you." His voice rang dimly in her ears, as though it was coming across a great distance. "How could you do this to me? After everything I did?"

Jak tried to bring her arms up, to pry at the hand that was crushing the life out of her. Her left arm refused once again to respond. She scrabbled at her thigh for the knife sheathed there and managed to drag it out. With her final burst of energy, she brought her hand up, aiming to drive the blade into his forearm.

Her efforts hadn't gone unnoticed and he shook her savagely. Her body swung back and forth, the strength leaching from her limbs. With everything she had, she tried to keep her grip on the knife, but before she could so much as scratch him with it, it slipped from her fingers. The edges of her vision closed in completely. The knife hit the ground with a tinny clank, like someone had dropped it down a deep well.

Air filled her straining lungs and she gasped, drawing as much sweet oxygen into her chest as she could manage. She looked around to find Crimson's eyes boring into hers.

"Why?" Tears actually swam in his eyes, threatening to spill over the edge of his lids.

"Why what?" Her voice sounded tortured, even to her own ears.

"Why. Didn't. You. Wait?" Crimson punctuated each word with a shake, his voice rising with each word.

Desperately, Jak brought her hand up to grip his wrist, to try to stabilize herself. "They told us you were all dead. That the Orthodoxans snuck up on you and killed you all in your beds."

The tears overflowed, flowing down his face. "They kept me alive. I don't know why. They said they were going by the house and saw it was on fire, that I was the only one they could rescue." He blinked rapidly, clearing his vision. The brown eyes hardened again. "Thinking of you kept me going. When I got older I went back to check on you. I saw what they were doing to you."

"I didn't know that was you. Why didn't you let me know?" How was she going to get out of this? Jak's mind raced, trying to find a way out. She still hung from his grip, and breathing was difficult but, for the moment, possible.

"With your father gone, I thought you'd go back to the way you were meant to be. What he did was an abomination and not to be suffered."

"He loved me. He was trying to help." Jak rolled her eyes to the side, trying to find Nat in the shadows. She couldn't see her. With her hand clamped around his wrist, she tried to pull herself up, to relieve some of the pressure on her neck. She barely moved.

"An abomination." Crimson sneered, lips pulling away from his teeth. "Like what you're doing with that whore of an offworlder. Neither of you knows your place. Since you refuse to learn..." His voice trailed off and he looked away from her for a moment before staring determinedly at her once again. "Since there's no hope for us, you have to die." The anger had leached from his voice, to be replaced by dreadful resignation.

Jak clawed at his hand as he tightened his grip again. She wouldn't last long. From the way his arm trembled, he couldn't keep it up much longer either. This was it, she was going to die. Her eyes prickled as she struggled. She was going to join the rest of her family and without fulfilling her promise. Crimson still lived. She would never see Torrin again and Nat would die after she was gone. All in all, she'd failed as spectacularly as it was possible to do.

Her vision grayed out again and all sound around her faded, to be replaced with the panicked thumping of her pulse in her ears. One final attempt to claw open Crimson's arm yielded no results and she felt her fingers slip from his wrist, her nails broken and slick with blood. She was so tired; fighting was so much effort.

Why am I fighting so hard? The darkness beckoned and beyond it waited her parents and Bron. *I'm coming Mom, Da. I'll be home soon, Bron.* She gave in to the darkness and let it roll over her. It didn't hold the welcome she'd anticipated for the past two years. It was cold, and instead of the respite she'd hoped for, all she felt was regret. Torrin's face swam in front of her eyes, smiling as she teased Jak about something. Probably about being too serious. Her face was replaced by Nat's, then Olesya and Axe and on and on. The faces flipped by faster, each one replaced by someone else who had somehow made their way into her heart, even Callahan and Smythe. She would have wept, if she'd had the ability. As hard as she'd tried to hold on, she couldn't any longer. With painful resignation, Jak let go.

She hit the ground with a grunt then an agonized shriek as her battered shoulder bounced off the unyielding stone. *Is heaven really this painful?* Jak opened her eyes in time to see Crimson kick Nat in the face with enough force to throw her back. She landed in a crumpled heap.

"You misbegotten, whorish cunts!" His bellow echoed back at them, his rage overlapping and feeding on itself. He reached for his thigh, where Nat had just embedded Jak's knife. This was it, her last chance. If she didn't move now, there would be no magical reprieve. She thanked Nat in her head for having the strength to keep fighting as she lunged forward, beating him to the hilt. He howled again when she hauled back on it. At first it wouldn't budge; the tip must have been stuck in the bone.

It was her turn to scream when Crimson got a firm grip on her bad arm and the muscles in it were forced in directions they really didn't want to go. Blinking away tears of pain, she reached out again with her good hand, closed it on the hilt and jammed it further into the wound. Crimson's grip slackened and she yanked the knife from his leg. Dark blood flowed from the wound, but she couldn't allow herself to be distracted.

First thing was to bring him down to her level. She drew the knife along the back of his knee, rolling out of the way as the leg collapsed and Crimson came down in an uncontrolled tumble of limbs. His cries of pain were little more than muffled sobs now. As she scrambled toward him, he flailed out at her, catching the side of her arm and sending the knife spinning off into the dark shadows at the bowl's edge.

Jak could feel her lips pulling back into a rictus snarl. She tasted salt and iron as her teeth pierced her bottom lip. It didn't mean anything. There was only one thing that mattered. She kept going.

Crimson lashed out again, trying to get her off him. Jak's response was to give him a knee in the gut. He coughed and swore or tried to. She hooked her good hand under his jaw and pressed down as hard as she could; soon he had no breath with which to curse her.

His eyes bulged disbelievingly from his head as she put all her weight behind the effort and pushed harder. His face was almost purple, his tongue stuck out of his mouth and he wheezed desperately for breath. His fingers scratched at the back of her hands, digging long furrows with his nails. The pain was nothing, though, compared to what he'd inflicted upon her, upon her family, over the years. The tears in his eyes should have moved her, but she felt nothing for him, only the grim determination to do what must be done.

Does choking someone really take this long? It felt like they'd been at this for hours. When he'd had his hands upon her neck, she'd gone into that long dark tunnel almost immediately, or so it had felt.

Crimson hooked one hand under hers, and succeeded in pushing it far enough away from his neck to pull in a half-breath. His face lightened considerably. He was going to get away! Jak breathed heavily, the air rushing from her nostrils as she tried desperately to find a way to use her other arm on him. She powered through the pain, but it flopped weakly toward his neck, to little effect. If she could only shift it over his windpipe.

His other hand reached over, grabbed the tip of one of her fingers and began to pry it up. She wasn't going to be able to hold on much longer.

Miraculously, another pair of hands appeared around his neck. Jak looked up into Nat's determined face. The side of her face was already swelling, but her eyes were fixed on the source of her misery. He'd broken the blood vessels in one of her eyes, which stared balefully down at him.

There was no way they could lose now, and Crimson knew it. He tried to dislodge her, his whole body thrashing, feet scraping the stone beneath them. Jak rode him easily and kept his hands away from Nat's.

He was losing strength rapidly. His grip around her hand slackened, then let go completely. He lay still beneath her, but Jak shifted her grip to keep hold of one of his hands, pinning the other with her knee. If he was faking, he wasn't going to catch them out. Her heart pounded in her chest. *Is this it? Are we done?*

Finally, it wasn't Lucian beneath her. It wasn't even Crimson. It was only a body. A thing. Her friend and her enemy were dead.

"It's over," Jak whispered.

Nat didn't move, her hands remained clamped around his neck.

"It's done, Nat. He's gone."

Nat's shoulders relaxed, and she looked up at Jak.

"Really?" Her voice was less than a whisper.

Jak nodded, then wished she hadn't. The movement sent her head to pounding and the bowl spun around them. She tried to watch Nat, who seemed to be listing to one side. She *was* listing to the side. Nat collapsed next to Crimson's head.

Try as she might, Jak couldn't slow the tide of darkness that was breaking over her as well.

Their pace was glacial and Torrin found herself running up the back of Petra's heels for the third time. To her credit, Petra didn't say anything, but instead glanced back and gestured her to back up. Unfortunately, Petra wasn't getting the hint that they had to move faster.

The other Banshee team had cleared one of the side passages and was headed down the other. The passage Petra and Torrin had picked was longer than the other two and it twisted and turned past side chambers. The floor dipped and rose and Torrin had to duck to clear the low-hanging ceilings. Clearing each chamber had slowed them down considerably.

Their night-vision visors had helped at first, but the further they got from the entrance, the less ambient light there was for the equipment to collect. They'd turned on small personal light sources to navigate by. Torrin fretted about that also. Trying to sneak up on someone in a dark cave while sporting lights was a quick way to tip off their quarry to their presence.

The passage widened slightly before opening into a large cavern. With their light sources, Torrin still couldn't make out the far end of the cave. Stalactites and stalagmites jutted from the ground and ceiling like teeth from the maw of a sandworm. At least they weren't rotating, she thought incongruously.

Torrin leaned forward and whispered into Petra's ear. "They could be anywhere in here." The Banshee held up her hand, cutting Torrin off. She froze, listening. A male voice filtered through to them. The words were too indistinct to make out, blurred together by echoes that overlapped them together. "He's here," she breathed, light-headed with sudden relief, followed immediately by her stomach seizing with an anxiety that was as powerful as her relief had been.

"And he's not alone," Petra said quietly. "Otherwise, why the talking?" She cocked her head to one side then the other. "That way, I think."

"How can you tell?"

"I can't, not really. But that's as good a direction as any." The Banshee led her forward, toward the center of the cave.

The fantastic rock formations gave the cavern an eerie beauty. Like everything else on the planet, beauty masked the danger below the surface. Behind every rock pillar, from beneath each ledge, Torrin imagined that Crimson had a bead on them. Her shoulders tensed as they moved forward. Petra kept them behind cover as much as possible, but every time they had to break into the open, the skin between Torrin's shoulder blades itched abominably.

They weren't far from the center when the flow of words stopped. Torrin stopped in her tracks and glanced over at Petra. The Banshee cocked her head, listening for any sound. They both jumped when a loud yell shook the cavern. It was followed by another. It didn't sound like Jak, but she had to remember to breathe. Torrin took a step toward the shouts, then stopped. As soon as she moved, it sounded like it was coming from somewhere else.

Another scream rent the air. That one was unmistakable. She started forward again, pulled by the agony in the voice.

"Jak!" Fear strangled her answering cry and it came out as barely more than a harsh whisper. She was wrenched half around by the iron grip around her arm. Petra shook her head and let her go with a hard stare. She pressed her hand to the back of her ear.

"Banshees, we have confirmation of Major Stowell's location at these coordinates."

"Understood. We are moving to your location." Shao's voice crackled through their transmitters, full of static.

Torrin nodded. The cavalry would be good to back them up, but she needed to get to Jak. She peered into the gloom, trying to make out which way the cries had come from. The acoustics in the cavern still messed with her sense of direction, but she was fairly certain the sound had emanated from close to the northeast corner.

"We should wait for backup," Petra said. "We have no idea who all is down here. It could be Crimson by himself, or there could be half an army."

"Wait if you want to." Torrin flexed the fingers of her right hand around the stock of her plasma rifle. "But don't try to stop me. Something's going down. Do you hear that?"

"I do, but we can't go rushing around down here. You don't even know where it's coming from. We need to wait for backup, then search this place on a grid. They could be anywhere and with anybody."

"You wait if you want to. I'm not going to let the woman I love get taken out while I stand around waiting."

Indecision warred across Petra's face. Her head shifted between Torrin and the corner from which Jak's cry had come. She firmed her jaw and nodded sharply.

"I'm coming with you."

"Good." Torrin moved to get started, but Petra grabbed her arm again.

"Follow me. I'm going to lay a trail for the rest of the Banshees to follow." She pushed past Torrin, leaving her to follow in the Banshee's wake.

This time, they moved at a decent clip. The urge to move even faster gripped her, but she tried to push it down. They checked every nook and cranny with no sign of Jak or Nat. She pushed forward, but Petra cut her off and forced her to walk behind.

"If you don't stop that, I will drop your ass and leave you behind."

"But–"

"But, nothing. I won't have you risking the major or your sister. Come on, woman. You know better than this! Start acting less like a scared civilian and more like the Banshee you used to be."

The muscles in Torrin's jaw bulged as she ground her teeth. Every fiber of her being screamed for action. She couldn't get at whoever had hurt Jak, but Petra was close at hand. It took everything she had not to attack the Banshee.

Petra held Torrin's eyes with hers. "I mean it. You won't win this fight. Hell, even if you do take me down, you'll tip off whoever's out here."

"Fuck! Fine." Torrin turned away from Petra to face back toward where she imagined Jak to be. "Just get a move on already."

Petra picked up the pace, which should have relieved Torrin, but she was getting tenser and tenser. She finally figured out why.

"It's quiet."

Petra nodded and hurried along even faster. They were trotting as much as they could over the uneven ground. Torrin had to swing her free arm to catch her balance again. The stillness of the cavern spurred her on regardless.

They crossed the cavern, picking their way over large mounds and around immense pillars. They skirted an area where dozens of narrow stalagmites grew out of the ground like grass. The light from their lamps occasionally reflected off a crystal and painfully into Torrin's eyes. She would be blinded for a moment as the light-collecting properties of her night-vision headgear worked against her.

Petra kept them to the same ground-devouring pace. Mostly, they stuck to low ground. When trying to sneak up on a sniper, keeping their heads down seemed like a good idea to Torrin. Worryingly, it was still silent except for their boots on the stone ground and the rocks they disturbed. Whatever had happened was over. An oppressive silence hung over them. The entire cavern seemed to be holding its breath.

A mound of rock rose in front of them, taller than either of them. Ripples of stone, frozen in time, ran down the side of the mound. It was steep, but not so much that they couldn't climb it.

"Around?" Torrin asked quietly.

"It's damn big and we're almost at the edge of the cavern." Petra chewed her lip, working on their dilemma. The screams could have come from somewhere in front of them, but at this point it was impossible to tell. They were running out of real estate. Did they risk exposing themselves to be picked off by a sniper, or did they stay low and possibly be too late to help Jak?

"Screw this," Torrin said. "Let's head over. We haven't seen any sign of anyone. If half the Orthodoxan army were in this cave, we'd have seen something by now."

Petra nodded decisively. "I can't fault your logic. Let's go."

Slowly, the two of them scaled the mound. There were plenty of hand and footholds, but some of the rock was deceptively smooth, worn down by millennia of geologic forces. Torrin checked each hold twice before daring to commit her weight to it; Petra was equally as careful. Even at their cautious pace, they still made better time than they would have going around.

Torrin's fingers were screaming at her by the time they reached the top. Her calves cramped and her arms felt like they weighed a metric ton, each. The top of the mound was fairly flat. Torrin stood stooped at the top and unslung the rifle from her shoulder.

Petra waved her hand and motioned toward the center of the mound. There appeared to be a depression there, though it was hard to tell how deep. Dim light, barely visible even through their visors, emanated from the center. She pointed again. Torrin nodded.

Slowly, careful not to make any noise, they crept toward the depression. The texture of the mound was sandy in patches and Torrin winced every time her foot made a small crunch against the stone. There was no more sound and they slunk into place.

Torrin slung her rifle across her back and scooted forward when the scene below unfolded before her disbelieving eyes. Millennia of dripping water had carved a bowl into the mound. In the center of that depression, a man lay. Half on top of him was Jak. She didn't move. Nat was in a heap to one side.

She dropped into the bowl. Petra hit the ground right next to her and made a beeline for Nat. Torrin half-dove toward Jak, not caring when her knees cracked into the unyielding surface. With trembling fingers, she felt her way gently around Jak's neck, seeking the pulse that would tell her everything was all right, that Jak was still alive. A quick glance confirmed that Petra was doing the same thing with Nat. She looked up and met Torrin's panicked gaze.

"She has a pulse."

Torrin couldn't relax. All she felt was Jak's cool skin. There was no sign of life. No sign of Jak's life. No sign of her own life then. Something fluttered beneath her fingertips. She froze. Had she imagined it, or was it really there? There it was again. And another.

"She's alive." Torrin sighed and gently gathered Jak to her chest. Livid red marks stood out around her neck, but she was alive.

CHAPTER THIRTY

The Banshee medic swooped in when Torrin looked up, grateful backup had finally arrived.

"I need you to let her go," she said when Torrin refused to relinquish her hold.

"No way," Torrin said, insistent. "Not until I know she'll be all right." Her greatest fear was that she would let Jak go and she would die before Torrin could say goodbye. Torrin's arms tightened around Jak; she loosened her grip only when she realized she was crushing Jak to her chest.

Recognizing she wasn't going to get anywhere with Torrin, the Banshee gave Jak a quick but thorough once-over with a portable med-scanner. She tutted once at Jak's broken shoulder and paid special attention to the livid bruising that was already developing on the sniper's neck.

"She's in no immediate danger. She could stand to spend a few hours in the autodoc and to be seen by a real doctor, but at the moment she's relatively stable."

Relief flowed through Torrin, leaving her euphoric in its wake. "And my sister?" She looked over to the other side of the bowl to where Nat was being attended.

The medic's shoulders stiffened and she flexed her hands before answering. "She's been through a lot. She's weak and a little malnourished. There are also...other injuries."

Torrin clamped her eyes shut against the anguish the last statement brought her. If only they'd found her sooner. If only she hadn't sent Nat along on the trip in the first place...

"Nat needs to see a full doctor and definitely a shrink too." The medic looked over at Crimson's motionless form. "If he wasn't already dead, I'd happily kill him myself."

"Let's get them out of here," Torrin said. The medic looked up at the silent body armor-clad forms that watched the small group in the bowl. She gestured and more of them hopped down. The bowl was getting crowded.

"You need to let us take her, ma'am," Shao said, gently removing Torrin's hands. "We need to clear these two out of here."

Torrin backed up, letting the Banshees break out collapsible stretchers. With practiced motions, they lashed Jak to one stretcher and handed her out the top of the hole. Assured that Jak was in good hands, Torrin went over and checked on Nat. Her sister looked terrible. Bones were too evident under her skin. One cheek was grotesquely swollen; her face looked like half an overripe melon.

"How is she?"

"Medic said she sustained some serious damage to her face." The Banshee securing Nat's unconscious body to the stretcher didn't look up.

"But she made it. She's still here and that bastard isn't." The fierce pride Torrin felt at Nat's toughness mixed uncomfortably with the guilt that still gnawed at her.

The Banshee stood and, with her partner, lifted the stretcher Nat was lashed to. Ropes were passed down to them from the women waiting above. Within seconds, Nat was being hoisted out of the bowl too. Around her, Banshees were boosting each other up and out. Before long, Torrin was left on her own at the depression's bottom. Shao leaned down and offered her a hand up.

Torrin leaped up and grasped Shao's hand. Another hand appeared as if by magic, and she grabbed it. Together, the two Banshees hoisted Torrin out of the hole.

"Thanks," Torrin said, pounding Shao and Perez on the shoulders. Ahead, the Banshees moved slowly down the stone mound with their fragile cargoes. Torrin followed at their heels, keeping an anxious eye on the unconscious women.

The trip from the cave was uneventful, if slow. The terrain had been challenging when everyone involved had been able-bodied. With two injured women along, the pace slowed to a crawl. For once, Torrin didn't chafe at that. She was happy that the Banshees worked to avoid jostling Nat and Jak. For her, they were moving at the perfect speed; she could hover over each woman and fret while they were transported across stone floors and up rock falls.

Finally, they emerged into open air. Torrin had never been so pleased to see Haefen's enormous trees.

Shao caught Torrin's eye. "The *Nightshade* is waiting for us over the clearing with the burned-out cabin." She hesitated before continuing. "She's not alone. There's a longboat from the *Icarus* waiting in the clearing. They're going to shuttle us to our ship."

Torrin looked up from watching Nat. "The *Nightshade* couldn't land?"

"Apparently not. I guess there isn't a big enough space for them to touch down. It's probably just as well. We don't really need to subject these two to an antigrav jump back to the ship. The longboat will be a lot smoother."

"I guess." Torrin looked back over at Nat, then craned her neck to catch a glimpse of Jak. The Banshees carrying her stretcher were further ahead, moving carefully between the trees. The League was sticking its nose in again. She wished she could trust them, but as much respect as she'd gained for Captain Mori personally, Torrin couldn't trust the government she represented.

"Either way, those are Axe's orders." Shao's eyes shifted. She didn't seem any happier with the situation than Torrin was. Most of the Banshees had no love lost for the League. How many times had they broken up a sex trafficking ring only to find that it was bankrolled by a so-called, respectable merchant from the inner worlds?

They moved through the trees and down the hill, back toward the overgrown remnants of Crimson's childhood home. Two Banshees brought up the rear. They had the unenviable task of transporting Crimson's body. His corpse was held within a vacuum-sealed bag. The Devonites would be pleased to have the body. If nothing else, it would give them an excellent propaganda opportunity.

Torrin forced herself to watch the woods around them and not get too distracted watching Jak and Nat. They weren't completely out of danger; they wouldn't be until they were back on the *Nightshade*. Hell, she wouldn't count them completely safe until they were back on Nadierzda. The burned-out cabin they headed toward was mute evidence of the potential danger posed by the Orthodoxans, even on the Devonite side of the fence.

It was up to her, Shao and Perez to cover their group. Allowing herself to be distracted by the plight of her family wouldn't help any of them if an Orthodoxan raiding party happened upon their group. Even knowing that Jak and Nat were stable didn't diminish her need to get them back to the ship for medical treatment. *They're stable now, but how long will that last?* Shoving the thought from her mind, she surveyed the surrounding trees, peering occasionally through the sight on her rifle. Nothing moved, but she kept her eyes peeled.

After a while she was able to lose herself in the routine of watching for Orthodoxans. She was surprised when the trees fell away and they were in the partially overgrown clearing by Crimson's old home. True to Shao's word, the *Nightshade* hovered, all dangerous sleekness, above the cabin. Vegetation around it was flattened by downdraft from the ship's engines. In front of it, a League longboat waited. Where the *Nightshade* was elegant black, promising violence if crossed, the longboat was more innocuous. Torrin didn't doubt that it was armed, but it didn't have the same bristling armaments the Banshees' ship did. It was boxy and white, a purely functional craft. It was also large. It could have easily fit twice their number and probably even three times if they were willing to be crammed in.

League Marines coalesced out of the foliage as they approached. They formed a loose perimeter around the longboat.

Torrin nodded at the marine she recognized from her time on board the *Icarus*.

"Ma'am," the marine returned her nod respectfully. "We're to take you on board."

"Understood. We have wounded. I need to make sure they're treated as soon as possible."

"Yes ma'am. We've been briefed on your situation. We will render medical assistance as soon as we're able."

The Banshees stood, watching their exchange in wary silence. The few who weren't burdened by dead or wounded stood with a stillness that promised a swift and deadly explosion of movement if the need arose. The League marines held themselves as still. The last thing Torrin wanted was an accidental bloodbath.

She looked over at Shao. "Shall we get moving?"

"Move out, Banshees," the sergeant barked.

The Banshees moved forward. Even though they were burdened, the marines made no effort to help them. Instead, they split their attention between the women and the surrounding forest. Not wanting to be left behind, Torrin stuck close to them, making herself a place between Jak and Nat.

The interior proved to be even more capacious than Torrin had assumed from the outside. Nat and Jak were secured into berths and the Banshees given places to sit. Torrin found a seat from which she could watch both women. Fortunately, her seat also had a great view of the cabin interior.

They had barely gotten themselves secured before they were joined by the Leaguers. Their numbers were evenly matched, one marine per Banshee.

The engines powered up. With some envy, Torrin noted how quiet the engines were. She could feel them throbbing through her seat and the wall where she leaned against it, but she heard next to nothing. Talking in the cabin would have been easy, though no one ventured an attempt at conversation.

Through a small porthole, Torrin could see the tops of the trees as the longboat lifted off. They seemed to be making their way straight up. Surely they'd reached the level of the *Nightshade*. Why weren't they docking with her?

A chime rang in her ear. "Torrin, it's Axe. Don't freak out, but the longboat is taking you to the *Icarus*."

"What?" Marines' and Banshees' heads alike whipped around at the sudden sound.

"I said not to freak out. There's a bit of a situation. The Leaguers aren't happy with the way we've handled things and now that they have you, they're determined to speak with you. Don't worry, my women won't let anything happen to any of you."

Haefen fell away beneath them and Torrin watched helplessly through the window as the sky darkened to be replaced with the midnight black of deep space. She was well and truly trapped. There was no way they could take over the ship, not with Jak and Nat effectively being held as hostages against their best behavior. None of the marines had made any movement toward them, but Torrin harbored no illusions that they would find weapons at the temples of the two unconscious women if they attempted to divert the shuttle.

One of the marines, an officer by the stripes on her shoulder, watched her closely. She was undoubtedly aware of Torrin's animosity toward the League.

Strangely, the Banshees said nothing. They must have been briefed. She had been the last to find out. Anger wormed its way hot into Torrin's belly, and she struggled not to let it out on her face.

The *Icarus* hove to through the small viewport, growing quickly larger as they approached the League vessel. Torrin felt none of the envy that had gnawed at her the last time she saw the ship. Instead she bit at the inside of her lower lip in irritation. Determined not to show how annoyed she was, she released her lip as soon as she felt her teeth close on it.

The dark of space was replaced by the well-lit interior of the *Icarus's* shuttle bay. The League marines rose to their feet before the longboat touched down.

"Are you going to handle him?" the marine officer asked Shao.

"The wounded are our priority. Let's get them provided for first."

The officer nodded her head, a sharp, decisive jerk of assent. "We'll take them to our medical officer."

"Good. I'm sending along a couple of Banshees with you. I don't want them to wake up surrounded by strangers. They've been through enough."

Torrin had been watching the interplay with little comprehension. More had gone on than her being left out of a briefing. It sounded like a deal had been struck, one she had no knowledge of and for which she had had no input.

"I'm going with Nat and Jak," she said when she couldn't stand it any longer.

"Yes ma'am." Shao's face didn't change. She wasn't surprised by Torrin's assertion. "I'll wait here with the rest of the Banshees. When the *Nightshade's* shuttle gets here, we'll take the prisoner to the captain."

"Prisoner?"

"The Devonite traitor."

"I see." There was no need for them to keep the bargain now, not when they had Nat back. In fact, Torrin could think of all sorts of reasons why they should hold onto the mole, not least of which was that the League should be stymied in its efforts wherever possible, no matter what those efforts were. But mostly to make sure they didn't try anything with Nat or Jak. She stared at Shao, trying to will her to see the error of the decision, but the Banshee remained stoic in the face of her glare.

The longboat's rear entry hatch clunked and hissed as the clamps released and the door lowered. Marines moved into action, clustering around the berths where Torrin's sister and lover were secured. Torrin had no choice but to hurry along behind them after they released Nat and Jak, and trooped out of the longboat. She threw a final glance back over her shoulder. The Banshees were moving around the shuttle, making preparations of their own.

Hamilton and Perez separated from the milling Banshees and trotted after Torrin's strange group. Torrin approved of the choice. Jak knew both of them and their presence would soothe her when she regained consciousness. Having awoken to unfamiliar surroundings in the past, Torrin knew the terror that stroked through the system under those circumstances. It was the ultimate vulnerability. Neither of the unconscious women would do well with that.

The marines moved at a respectable clip, not quite running, but not taking their time either. The group in front cleared ship's personnel out of the way and the group taking up the rear behind the stretchers carefully didn't watch Torrin and the Banshees closely. For a moment, Torrin wondered what they would do if she took off. Her mind was wandering and she shook her head to focus. Now that the adrenaline of hunting down Crimson was leaving her system, she realized precisely how exhausted she was. When she had her family back home with her, she would sleep for a week.

The medical bay was huge. It was actually multiple rooms. Envy rekindled in Torrin as she eyed the shining equipment. There was no autodoc in sight and a meticulously uniformed officer met them at the door. His hair was gray at the temples and he observed them coming with hands clasped behind his back.

"Put them there and there," he said, unfolding to point at the two nearest beds. "Was this one the captive?" He stopped the marines as they moved past him with Nat's stretcher. One of them looked back at Torrin and she stepped forward.

"Yes, that's Nat Ivanov. She was held captive for weeks. She's been injured recently and we think there's older trauma as well."

"Very good to know." He moved along with the stretcher to the near bed. Waiting orderlies swarmed the stretcher, smoothly and efficiently transferring Nat to the bed. As soon as she touched the surface, two nurses swooped in, running diagnostic devices over her. One reached over to the wall and an opaque force field sprang into existence around the bed. Panicked, Torrin looked over to the other bed to see Jak disappearing behind a similar field.

The marines didn't blink at the sudden barriers. Two of them walked through the field, dismantling the stretchers and returning them to their collapsed state.

"Ma'am," the officer said. She inclined her head in Torrin's direction, then led her troops from the room.

Abruptly alone in the room, Torrin walked slowly up to the nearest force field, the one around Nat. She placed her palm against the opaque gray field and her hand sank in. It was a privacy screen, she realized. Or rather, privacy field. Emboldened, she stepped through it and found the doctor examining Nat.

Nat had been undressed and was now mostly covered by a blanket. Removing Nat's clothes hadn't done her sister any favors. She was thin and looked like she could have used a month's worth of overfeeding. Torrin doubted that she had many fat reserves left on her body. When she'd been a Banshee, she'd seen women in worse condition, but they weren't her sister. Bruises speckled both arms, looking suspiciously like hand prints. Tears prickled at the back of Torrin's eyes and she blinked, not wanting to worry anyone. She felt a presence by her elbow and turned her head. Hamilton smiled back at her faintly.

"Perez is in with Major Stowell."

"Good. I'll check on her soon myself."

Though she had no love lost for the League, Torrin found herself admiring the efficient and professional behavior of the medical staff. She didn't know if they had any idea of the general dislike their visitors had for the Leaguers, but if they did, they didn't let it color their treatment of Nat. Satisfied that Nat was in good hands, Torrin walked through the gray field to check on Jak.

She found Jak being offered the same treatment by a young female doctor who looked up briefly when Torrin stepped through the privacy field.

"Doctor, she appears to have some old damage to her lungs," said a nurse who was peering at the display on a piece of medical equipment Torrin didn't recognize.

"Make a note of it. We'll take care of that while we're at it."

"Doctor, how is she?" Torrin asked.

"And you are?" The doctor spared her another glance before returning to her patient.

"I'm her wife." Torrin kept her face smooth at the lie. It wasn't that much of a lie, not really. It would happen one day, of that she was certain. One day very soon, if she had anything to say about it.

"In that case..." Before she elaborated, the doctor leaned over and ran her hands over the console that jutted out of the side of the bed. "She has several cracked ribs, a broken shoulder, a cracked hyoid, as well as new and old damage to her lungs."

Torrin blinked. She knew Jak had been injured in the course of her struggle with Crimson, but the litany took her aback. "The old damage is the result of a virus."

"That makes sense." The doctor looked up at the nearest nurse, a young man with a serious disposition. "Make a note to introduce the standard rever-virals. If the virus is dormant, that will take care of it. Don't worry, ma'am. We'll take good care of your wife. She should regain consciousness soon and be ready to go home in a day or so."

"Good. And thanks." Torrin watched for a little longer as they tended to Jak. Frustrated that there wasn't anything she could do aside from stand around, Torrin stepped through the privacy field. A low murmur of voices came from the field around Nat's bed. Concerned, Torrin stepped back through.

Mori stood next to the bed, looking down at Nat while she grilled the doctor on her condition.

"What are you doing?" Torrin sidled around the bed and stood next to Mori. She pitched her voice low, not wanting to disturb her sister. It was silly and she was vaguely aware of that. Nat was unconscious, not sleeping, though she already looked better than she had. The bones of her face were still too prominent against her skin, but her cheeks were already returning to their natural color. The swelling had gone down and she didn't look nearly so grotesque.

"I thought I'd come take a look at the woman behind this... interesting partnership." Despite the lightness of her voice, there was a slight edge that belied her attempt at humor. She looked down at Nat. "We need to talk." Her lips tight, she managed a strained smile. The expression softened as she continued to watch Nat. "But not here. Come on."

"How is she coming, doctor?" Torrin refused to budge when Mori shifted away from the bedside. She wasn't going anywhere until she knew that Nat was still doing all right.

"She will be fine, Captain. Her condition is stable now. Her facial injury is being mended and we're taking care of the malnutrition and other issues."

"Other issues?" Torrin snapped her head around to stare at the doctor.

"Yes, other issues." He met her angry gaze impassively. "They're nothing you need to worry yourself about. When she regains consciousness, we will deal with them then."

"You need to tell me what you're talking about." Torrin moved around the bed toward him. "Now."

"I'm sorry, ma'am. The problem isn't life-threatening, and it isn't yours to deal with. League regulations prohibit me from discussing certain medical issues with anyone but the patient."

"Fuck that. This is my sister. You tell me what's going on, or so help me, I will break every finger on your hands until you tell me. After that, I'm going to stop being polite."

A steel vise closed around her upper arm. "That's enough," Mori said into her ear. "Are you going to come with me, or do you need me to get some backup?"

"Torrin?" Perez stood, knees bent and one hand hovering, fingers twitching over the holster of her pistol.

The willingness of the Banshee to resort to lethal violence snuffed out Torrin's anger. A firefight in the med bay was the last thing they needed, especially while Jak and Nat were being treated.

"It's fine," she said, her eyes on Perez. She held up her hands and looked at Mori. "It's fine."

"Good." Mori's other hand reappeared from behind her back. With mild shock, Torrin realized the League captain had been going for a weapon. She stepped through the field, her hand still wrapped around Torrin's upper arm.

Torrin considered digging in her heels on general principle, but quickly abandoned the impulse. Not only would it make her look like a small child, but it wouldn't help anything. Mori kept going through the main room and into a small side chamber. A man looked up from a wall console as they came in.

"Out." The man quickly vacated the premises and Mori let go of Torrin.

Her upper arm felt like it might have been bruised and Torrin suppressed the urge to rub it. "What did you want to talk to me about?"

"Just this." Mori smiled again, with no more humor than before. This time, instead of being tight, it was wide and reminded Torrin of a shark's grin. All tooth, no mercy. "Despite your attempts to sabotage our bargain, we have succeeded. Your Banshees were very helpful and they're the only reason you aren't being thrown in the brig and being transported to the nearest League planet for trial."

"What?" Torrin couldn't believe what she was hearing. Sure, she hadn't been precisely enthusiastic in her pursuit of the fulfillment of the bargain, but things had come up. The situation hadn't allowed her to be exactly forthcoming. "You got what you wanted, didn't you? You have your rulebreaker."

"We do, and he will be tried by a military tribunal. Based on his reaction when confronted and the evidence of payoffs, I have no doubt that he will be convicted." Mori held up her hand when Torrin opened her mouth to defend herself. "But very little of this is thanks to you. Because the letter of the bargain has been reached, you are being allowed to go free. But know this, I will be submitting a thorough report to my superiors."

Torrin's teeth clacked together as she shut her mouth with a snap. *This isn't good.*

Mori's smile widened as she went in for the kill. "I will be recommending that your activities be monitored. After they read my report, I'm certain they will concur with my recommendations."

A chill shot through Torrin and she sat down hard on a nearby chair. She was being grounded. Not immediately, certainly. Word would take a while to filter through to the Fringe worlds, but League worlds would be closed to her almost immediately. They wouldn't keep her from coming and going, but every move she made would be scrutinized and documented. When the Fringes learned the League was tracking her movements, they would do the same themselves. Heat surged through her veins and her pulse throbbed in her temple.

Mori watched her, arms crossed across her chest, that too-wide grin still pasted on her face.

"You know what this will do to me, to my business." With herculean effort, Torrin kept her voice from wavering. She gripped the edge of the chair. Jumping up and decking the smug Leaguer would definitely get her thrown in the brig.

"Oh yes." The grin slid from threatening to smug. "I do."

"I need to get back to my family." Only the fact that Jak and Nat were being treated in the next room kept her from slapping the smirk off Mori's mouth.

"By all means." Mori stepped out of her way.

It would have been satisfying to "accidentally" ram her shoulder into the captain's on her way by, but Torrin carefully gave her a wide berth. She would be having words with Axe as soon as she saw the Banshee captain again. With no other choice, Torrin went back to hovering over Jak and her sister until they regained consciousness.

CHAPTER THIRTY-ONE

"Not much longer now," Torrin said. Jak looked up at her. She'd been caught looking out the viewport in the medbay.

"Busted," Jak admitted with a rueful smile. "You know I don't do well being cooped up."

"Don't I! Actually, I'm a little surprised you and Nat haven't engineered an escape attempt." Torrin squeezed Jak's hand to let her know she was joking.

"It's not that it hasn't crossed my mind, but I don't think Nat's up to it quite yet." Jak pitched her voice loud enough that Torrin's sister looked over from the next bed. Nat simply shook her head at the sally and gave them a half smile before turning her head to gaze out the force field at the stars.

Jak was worried about Nat and she knew Torrin was too. Nat still refused to tell them much of what had gone on during her captivity. Deep shame gripped Jak. If only she'd been able to make the connection earlier, Nat wouldn't have spent so much time at Crimson's mercy. It was still hard for her to reconcile her memory of the happy, generous boy of her childhood with the crazy and deadly Orthodoxan sniper. When she'd found out that Nat had been kidnapped to draw her out, her guilt had only intensified. Torrin didn't blame her, or so she said, but that was all right, Jak was perfectly capable of blaming herself.

"So, really, why can't I leave yet?" The pain was gone and so was her shortness of breath. Unable to stop herself, Jak drew a deep breath. The only sign that she'd been injured was some fatigue.

"Are you in such a hurry to get back to the Devonites?" The question was teasing, but Jak could read the tension in Torrin's shoulders. Her lover was afraid of what her answer might be.

"Not at all." Jak shook her head emphatically. "The Devonites don't need me. I know where I'm needed. Did you really believe I'd stick around here when you go back home?"

Torrin sat up straight as the stiffness drained from her posture. "I hoped not, but I wasn't going to try telling you what you were going to do. I've learned my lesson on that one."

"We're a family now." Jak smiled as the truth of the statement flowered in her chest. Shortness of breath returned for a moment as true happiness filled her. "You have a right to know. You even have a right to an opinion."

"I'll remind you about saying that." Torrin leaned in and captured Jak's lips for a sweet kiss, aching in its tenderness. Jak savored the kiss for a moment before cupping her hand around the back of Torrin's neck. She ran her tongue along Torrin's bottom lip, asking to enter.

With a groan, Torrin opened her mouth and Jak slid her tongue inside, tasting and teasing. She captured Torrin's lower lip between her teeth and tugged, pulling another moan from her.

Breathing hard, they came up for air.

"Oh please." Nat's voice floated across the medbay to them. "I'm supposed to be recovering here, not getting sicker. Do you think you could take that somewhere else?"

The tone was right, but there was a slight bitterness the teasing couldn't quite camouflage. Torrin and Jak exchanged a concerned glance.

"If that's what you'd like."

"We can put up the privacy field." Torrin and Jak answered at the same time. Torrin's voice was all solicitousness, but Jak had no problem giving Nat crap. As far as she was concerned, Nat didn't need everyone treating her like she was broken; she needed to feel like things were going back to normal.

"Whatever." Nat turned over, presenting her back to them.

"She'll be okay," Jak said quietly, gripping Torrin's hand hard. The anguish in Torrin's eyes cut her deeply.

"I know. I just wish…"

"I know."

Torrin sat up and looked over at the medbay door. "Are you ready for a visitor?"

"What?" Jak was confused by the abrupt change of subject. "What are you talking–"

Her question was cut off when the doors shushed open. Captain Mori escorted a familiar man inside; Perez peered in past them from her post in the hall. Smythe smiled when he saw her and Jak couldn't help but smile back.

The gray privacy screen flashed into place around Nat's bed.

"The lieutenant was sent to check on both your conditions," Mori said. She glanced over at the gray force field. "I'll leave you to talk."

Jak was surprised to hear a sharp sniff from Torrin as Smythe approached the bed. When she looked over, Torrin smiled at her, then transferred the smile to the Devonite lieutenant.

"Lieutenant Smythe." Torrin kept her fingers entwined with Jak's.

"Miss Ivanov. Captain." The salute Smythe snapped her way was crisp. Though she was seated, Jak returned it with the same intensity.

"Lieutenant." His eyes crinkled at the corners as he smiled at her. He seemed genuinely happy to see her and for a moment. "What can I do for you?"

"The general sent me to make sure you're doing okay. Oh, and to check on the young Miss Ivanov."

Nat lurked on the other side of the privacy screen and Jak had no doubt that she could hear every word. Smythe followed her glance across the room.

"She's recovering well enough."

"I'm glad to hear it." Silence dropped over their little group. Jak had no desire to carry the conversation. He'd come to her, he could do the heavy lifting.

"They want to give you a medal," Smythe finally said.

"They want to what?" Jak sat straight up, aghast. "Why the hell would they do that?"

"You did take out Crimson, you know. For that alone, they'd be happy to throw you a parade. There are the PR angles too, of course."

"PR angles?" Brow furrowed in concern, Torrin inserted herself into the conversation. "What does that mean?"

With a quick jerk to smooth out the wrinkles on the left arm of his uniform jacket, Smythe avoided both their eyes. "The general has pushed through legislation allowing women to serve in the armed forces. You're the poster child for the importance of his legislation."

"Son of a bitch," Torrin said. "He actually did it. What else did the legislation entail?"

"A whole passel of things actually. Women can now legally own property and run their own businesses. Advanced educational opportunities are now available to them at the same rates as men."

"Wow. How are the Orthodoxans taking it?"

Smythe chuckled, a rich, warm sound. "You could practically hear the screams of rage when we broadcast the information. They've vowed to crush us in five years." He lifted a shoulder and dropped it in elegant disregard for the Orthodoxan threats. "They've been vowing that for thirty years."

"I don't want a medal." Jak couldn't sit still any longer. Torrin and Smythe's chortles of glee grated on her nerves. The thought of being in front of all those men from whom she'd hidden her identity for years had her breaking out in a cold sweat.

"Jak, honey, this is huge. You've moved forward women's rights on Haefen in leaps and bounds."

"She's right," Smythe said. "Of course, they pretty much had to. News of your identity has been spreading through the ranks like trench-plague." At her grimace, Smythe winced. "Bad comparison, sorry. The point is, if they hadn't passed those laws, they would have had to explain why they were arresting the person who killed Crimson. He was the Orthodoxans' most prolific sniper, so that would have looked more than a little strange."

"The last Devonites who found out about my gender attacked me." Their sneering faces swam in front of her mind's eye and their taunts rang in her ears again. "What makes you think I'll allow myself to be put through that again?"

"Don't worry, we can pr–"

"If you say that you can protect me, I'm going to kick you in the teeth." Jak let go of Torrin's hand before she could crush it and grabbed a double handful of the blanket instead. "Now that it's common knowledge that I'm a woman, I need your protection, is that it?"

Blood drained from Smythe's face and he stepped forward, both hands raised. "No, that's not it at all. I was going to say that you'd be provided with an honor guard."

Torrin placed her relinquished hand on Jak's knee. "I think you should reconsider. Think of all the women who are in the situation you were or the girls who've wanted to serve their country. Not to mention the Orthodoxan women. You have the chance to do a lot of good."

"Torrin, I'll be nothing but a figurehead."

"So? There's value in being a symbol. And really, it's not like you haven't earned the medal and the recognition."

Leaning back, Jak glanced from her lover to her aide. They both regarded her expectantly. Unable to take the hopeful looks, Jak closed her eyes. "Fine, but I have some conditions."

"What are they?" Smythe asked eagerly. "The way the brass is feeling right now, they'll hand you pretty much anything."

"Those are for me to discuss with General Callahan. We'll see if he's still willing to bestow the medal on me after I give him my conditions."

Jak put the finishing touches on her final report. Wilson had been much less insistent about receiving this one. He seemed rather in awe of her and uncomfortable dealing with her all at the same time. There was no hiding who she was, not anymore. Reflexively, Jak took a deep breath. Her rib cage moved easily, free of the breastbinder. It was the first time in years that she'd been seen in public without it on Devonite soil.

So far, the response to her true self had been mostly positive. Those who objected to a woman serving in the army had chosen to steer clear of her. Still, she had no illusions that things would have gone very differently if her secret had been found out before she became a hero to her people.

Most of the responses had been more akin to what Wilson had been displaying. Admiration, but a complete inability to interact normally. Aside from those who had known all along, only a few could treat her with anything resembling normalcy. Jak was glad she planned to leave on the *Calamity Jane* and soon. If she'd had to stay, she would have been even more isolated than before. There was no way she would go through that again. No way she *could* go through that again, not now that she knew how it felt to be connected to others.

Jak chuckled quietly as she recalled Callahan's annoyance over her conditions. He'd been more annoyed about her insistence that the ceremony be small than he had been about her request that when they won the war the most damaged of the Orthodoxan women would be evacuated for rehabilitation. That he hadn't wanted to know where they would be taken had been unsurprising, yet still disappointing. It was only when she'd agreed that the small ceremony could be broadcast that he had finally stopped pushing her. The smile fell off her face. It was that broadcast which had her dealing with the unlikely combination of hero worship and awkwardness.

The report was as polished as she could make it and she deposited it in Wilson's in-box. She rummaged around in her files for a last time, making sure that she transferred anything of interest to the small tablet in her hand. There wasn't much. She'd always been as judicious with her electronic files as she had been with her belongings. At the back of her mind, she'd always known she would probably have to leave. Belongings, files, friendships, all of those would have been something to hold her in place, something to anchor her if she'd had to flee. Anything that had to do with Bron was transferred to her tablet, but aside from that, there wasn't much she wanted to remember.

Satisfied, Jak unplugged from the net. Sounds rushed in on her, becoming overly crisp for a moment before receding to their normal sharpness. She wondered if she would miss the sensation of coming back to herself. It wasn't that different to coming out of the pleasant stupor following one of the mind-shattering orgasms that Torrin could wring out of her. A little quicker maybe. Her last download had been wiped the day before and the medical staff had run a thorough diagnostic to make sure no traces of older downloads remained. There was no chance of any more data corruption in her brain. That was a relief, both to her and to Torrin.

Someone had helpfully left her a couple of boxes so she could clean out her desk. There wasn't much that she wanted to hold on to. Her weapons were practically a part of her, and they would go with her, but she'd taken everything else she truly wanted when she and Torrin had left those many months ago. Whatever else she might have been interested in had gone up in smoke when Crimson severed her final tie to the past. The more she thought about it, the more she realized that Crimson had given her a gift in setting her childhood home ablaze.

The medal looked silly in its back velvet case, which was dwarfed by the emptiness of the rest of the box. Jak leaned forward and picked it up.

"Admiring your accomplishments?" Torrin's voice drifted across the room.

"She gets one medal, and all of a sudden she can't help but pull it out and stroke it every chance she gets." Olesya grinned at her from beside Torrin. The two women crossed the outer office. It wasn't until they were all the way in her office that she realized Smythe and General Callahan were with them. Nat brought up the rear, silently, as she did most things these days.

Suddenly in the presence of a couple of Devonite men, Jak was conscious of the lack of breastbinder. She felt naked but forced herself to stand up straight anyway, fighting the urge to slouch and disguise her breasts. She was supposed to feel empowered, Jak thought. *All I feel is exposed. Getting out of here really is what's best for me.*

"Don't worry," Torrin said. "I'll make sure her head doesn't get too big."

"I don't think that's going to be a problem," Jak said, her voice dry. She closed the lid on the glittering medal and slipped it into her pocket.

"Captain Stowell." General Callahan stepped forward and extended his hand.

"Major Stowell," Olesya said, pointedly.

"Major Stowell." Callahan nodded in acknowledgment of the correction. He grasped her hand and shook it firmly. "You earned that medal many times over. Your accomplishments are public and I don't think anyone can deny them or you. When we open up the ranks to women next year, your example will go a long way toward their acceptance."

"Sir," Jak said. "Please don't take this the wrong way, but that medal isn't properly mine alone. I share the honor of your War Cross with the group of women who supported me in the pursuit of Crimson." She held up her hand to forestall him when he took a breath to speak. "You could have opened this up years ago. You knew about those of us in the ranks, but it took women who were impossible to deny to allow the 'weaker sex' to help. You've been shortchanging not only your women, but yourselves."

"If you'd only stick around, you could do so much good in that area."

"If you think–" Torrin subsided quickly when Jak shook her head.

"I don't belong here. The Devonites have more issues than sexism. The longer I'm here, the more familiar I'll become. It's better for me to be an example from afar. Your people won't like what they find if they look too closely, and I'm through changing myself to make them happy. It's time I did something to make myself happy. I need to move on. It's time."

Torrin reached out and took her hand and pulled Jak into a hug. "You are amazing," she whispered into Jak's ear, sending shivers rippling down her skin. Torrin pressed her lips to Jak's, then pulled back.

"My turn," Nat said, throwing an arm around Jak. "It's true, you did good. Are you sure you don't want to stay?" She watched Jak with too-serious eyes. Inside, Jak mourned the loss of the old Nat, the irreverent joker. Occasional flashes of humor came through, but they were buried beneath a layer of introspection and suspicion.

"Nat." Torrin's voice held warning.

"It's okay, Torrin." Jak squeezed Nat tighter. "I'm not staying. There's nothing here for me anymore. I did what I needed to do. I know where I'm needed, where I'm wanted. It's past time for me to be with my family, completely and without reservation."

Bella Books, Inc.

Women. Books. Even Better Together.

P.O. Box 10543
Tallahassee, FL 32302

Phone: 800-729-4992
www.bellabooks.com